The Devil's Nemesis

Quentin Black

Copyright © 2024 Quentin Black All rights reserved

The characters and events portrayed in this book are fictitious. Any similarity to real persons, living or dead, is coincidental and not intended by the author.

No part of this book may be reproduced, stored in a retrieval system, or transmitted in any form or by any means, electronic, mechanical, photocopying, recording, or otherwise, without the express written permission of the publisher.

ISBN: 9798884554115

Cover design by: Golden Rivet

https://golden-rivet.com/

DEDICATION

To Colin Lewis

Thanks for everything, Grandad.

man."

Connor watched Luke move to the centre as the instructor aimed with the sinisterly glinting taser.

"OK. Defend yourself."

Luke's head snapped to one of the trainees standing behind the instructor and barked, "No! No videos of this!"

The instructor's head whipped toward the phantom video taker.

Luke leapt off his back foot, his right fist striking the point of the instructor's jaw like an English longbow arrow.

The instructor stiffened before toppling, giving Luke time to catch him.

He laid him down, and Connor rushed over to check his airway before putting him in the recovery position.

Luke looked down. "Should we go?"

"Can't now," hissed Connor. "If he wakes up and wants to press charges, fucking off will make you look guilty."

Eventually, the instructor came around.

After Luke had got the instructor's and the witnesses' declaration of the legality of what had just happened on video, the pair left.

Outside, the Lexus LC500 was waiting for them with their older cousin, Tom, in the front passenger seat.

As they approached, Connor berated Luke, "The only people who don't have to worry about the law are billionaires and politicians—the rest of us have to be careful."

Larry MacKenzie stood on the stage of the Le Palais

Montcalm in Québec City with only a hint of nerves. He resisted the urge to crinkle his nose—a habit from his pre-laser eye surgery days.

The ensemble of reporters and members of the public reminded him of the black-headed Canadian geese he used to feed as a boy at Beaver Lake in Montreal.

"In this age of political correctness and censure, the truth is attacked and vilified. And, the truth is, hard-working Canadians are losing their opportunity to own a home. From the early 2000s to a few years ago, house prices have risen three hundred and thirty-seven percent—three hundred and thirty-seven percent! No one was looking to the future, or out for your interests back then. And last year, the crash came."

The edges of his dark suit waved in the breeze. He had to fight the control freak in him to accept its downshift in quality; his political team insisted the media would zone in on his attire, costing many thousands of dollars while campaigning and in office.

And they had admonished him for scoffing when fielding reporters' questions.

He continued, "You'll remember the current administration accused me of xenophobia for suggesting more stringent protocols against the foreign purchase of Canadian soil. They labelled my party as paranoid for suggesting Chinese involvement in the last election. This same administration is now making noise to enact policies against both. Noise is all it'll ever be. Look up their financial donors and see if you can find out why."

He looked up and watched the juxtaposition

of stony-faced media and nodding public. He knew most of the media to be gleefully left-wing. However, he knew his words would resonate with the Canadian people. At forty-nine, he remained in the age bracket to 'be in touch' without being unreliably youthful.

"Now, I have never used my sexuality as a tool to curry favour with the Left. But nor have I hidden it. And believe it or not, I was an effeminate child…before I succeeded the wolverine as the epitome of Canadian brutish masculinity."

His smile elicited a laugh from the crowd, and he raised his voice, "And I dread to think what would have happened to that child if I had been born today. What I might have been convinced of. What hormones I might have been pumped full of and, ultimately, what surgery I might have endured."

The approving nods scattered like flower heads in the wind.

"The conservatives in this country have lost their spine, and it has led to your children being led astray, hardworking Canadians unable to afford a house, and our injured veterans not being provided the equipment for assisted living. Did you know four people in Vancouver are randomly attacked every day? This government drains our economy of billions but pays a fraction of that towards our growing drug epidemic while Canada is suffering a now critical shortage of doctors. And if concerned Canadian citizens kick up too much of a fuss, they are not afraid to freeze your assets. But know this; it is our collective fault because, as my grandfather liked to say, *'You get what you tolerate'*."

Shouts of approval rippled on the agreeing murmurs.

"Now, I don't expect you to believe I'll carry out my pledges—people don't trust us politicians because we are untrustworthy!"

Laughter sang in the air, and he timed his next words on the first die down, "I am joking—kind of. Politicians can't always make everyone happy—but they need your vote. Need your vote but can't pull the trigger on the promises they make because they rely on the lobbying of others. I do not need that. Many of my detractors pointed out that if I truly cared about the people, then why haven't I put my billions to better use? At this, I got defensive and listed all the charities and educational funds my businesses gave to. But then I realised—I can do more."

He paused for effect. "And there are people who can't do more. People who have been dealt such a bad hand they can't even get off the starting blocks in life. These are the people this government chooses to ignore—not only in Vancouver's Downtown Eastside but now, in every major Canadian city, there are addicts living in seas of tents. Opioid-related deaths are climbing. Do not take my word for it; look at our government statistics. This should be a humiliation for our nation—that vast swathes of our brothers and sisters are being forced into lives of crime."

He waited a moment. "This is my pledge, not as a politician but as a citizen of Canada. This year, over three thousand of my company's rental properties will be discounted to fifty percent of their market value to be sold to first-time buyers. Married couples with children will get special dispensation. People with Canadian grandparents will get dispensation. People who have been employed for over eighteen months will get dispensation."

The murmurings spread to the media, and he signed off with, "I will not put the modern obsession of political correctness and virtue signalling above what's right and fair for ordinary hard-working Canadians. We will make this a country we are proud of once more."

The applause rose to a roar.

3

Connor Reed drove along the M74 motorway with the thunderous virtuoso engine sound of the black Lexus LC500 in his ears and the 'new car smell' in his nose. Beside him sat his elder cousin, Tom Ryder—a mechanic by trade and a car enthusiast—and in the back, their younger cousin, Luke Ryder.

They formed the leadership of the Ryder criminal dynasty out of the northern England city of Leeds.

They distributed minimally cut, high-quality narcotics to the middle to upper classes in places like Cheshire and Harrogate.

He remembered his deceased Uncle Michael's words, *'There isn't such a thing as a 'functioning drug user', just those that can afford it and those that can't.'*

The beginning of the journey from Edinburgh had begun with Connor telling Tom what had happened at the knife defence course, then Tom berating Luke. Luke had attempted to defend himself before conceding he had been reckless and apologising.

Connor kept a smile off his face at their interaction.

Months back, Tom had been caught in the lower back by a round amid a shootout in Amsterdam. The inflammation from the emergency surgery had compressed the spinal column, temporarily paralysing him.

At the time, the doctors couldn't tell if it would be permanent. To everyone's gratitude, the feeling in his legs increased as the inflammation faded. After nine hard weeks of physio, he walked without any discomfort. Connor had noticed his older cousin would straighten himself a little more often if sat for prolonged periods, but no more than that.

Not long after Tom sustained his injury, their cousin Curtis had been shot dead by an unknown entity. The assumption had been Curtis was killed by the same Irish gangsters he had betrayed his family to. The Ryder clan's investigation into the matter had been lethargic—as seemed the Police's.

And after a period of silence, Tom now gave Connor a review of the car worthy of a lucrative YouTube channel.

"It's only when you get to four thousand revs you get a feel for its performance, but it's refined enough to enjoy around the city centre," announced Tom, the shortest but broadest of the trio. "And it's Japanese reliable."

"And it looks fucking mega," Luke added. "But I feel like am in a fuckin' mini submarine on a Titanic tour in the back 'ere. Why didn't they just design it as a two-seater."

Tom answered, "Cos it brings the insurance down if it's four-seater."

The statements highlighted the difference between the steadier Tom and the wilder-natured Luke. However, both seemed to have taken on some of the other's traits recently, maybe due to spending so much time together.

Despite his insisting that the title should be Connor's, Tom, the 'patriarch' of the Ryder criminal dynasty, had wanted to step back from it all even before he had been shot. And Luke had recently proved himself a worthy successor.

It hadn't been long since Tom had first announced his desire to go straight. He hadn't mentioned it again for a while, and neither Connor—nor he suspected Luke—wanted to press him.

Tom gestured to the road. "Give it some kick down here. There aren't any speed traps or cameras down this stretch for a bit."

Connor began to accelerate. The engine's purring gradually built to a quiet roar as their backs pressed into the seats. Despite having driven faster cars with more violent acceleration—indeed, he remembered when he first caned a Nissan GTR down the motorway, feeling the pull in his groin—power blended with the refinement better in the Lexus.

"Yeh," said Connor. "That's horny."

"You get this type of performance without feeling like you're holding back a pit bull every time you drive it."

"Not to be pedantic, but it has ten gears—you're already speeding by the time you get to third."

"You never know if you'll need all ten," said Tom.

Luke's voice came over. "You know, I was watching a YouTube reviewer talk about used supercars you can buy on the cheap. You can pick up a Ferrari 458 for less than ninety. Think he said, 'Depreciation is the magic word'."

Tom sniffed. "A YouTube reviewer might say 'Depreciation' is the magic word, but do you know what real life says the magic word is?"

"Go on."

"'Maintenance'—the garage bills on that Ferrari will be the same as a new one. And the insurance."

This was a test, and a few years ago, he would be confident of Luke flunking it.

"It is not Black people in general that are great at sprinting; it's those from West Africa—West Sahara Africa—cos the people who live there have less red blood cells cos the vampire mozzies have killed off the ones who have with malaria. Red blood cells feed slow-twitch muscle fibres. So, these West Sahara Africans have more space for fast-twitch muscle. And you mentioned some power gene and how they are built—short bods but long legs."

Connor nodded approvingly. But in truth, Luke had proven his evolution from an unconjurable rascal to a mature leader during the recent war with the Franklin Organised Crime Group, or the 'FOC' as it came to be known. He took himself and a Ryder family associate, O'Shain Reilly, to hit their enemy in their backyard. This proved pivotal to their eventual victory.

Still, Connor didn't detect Luke wanting to change the dynamics between the three of them despite Connor and Tom treating him more and more like an equal.

The next couple of hours literally and figuratively flew by.

They merged onto the M62 motorway, and when the signs for Leeds first appeared, Tom said, "I need to nip into 'The Buxton' to pick up some stuff for Aidan."

"How is it being a dad?" asked Luke. "You the good cop or bad cop?"

"Neither, mate, I am like a **PCSO**."

Connor and Luke burst into laughter at another example of a rare but well-timed display of their elder cousin's humour.

However, Connor felt a pull under his abdomen in the knowledge his cousin was the doting dad in contrast to him being an absentee one.

Connor had a young son named Jackson with Grace—a paediatric surgeon he had been seeing off and on for years.

To protect them both from the dangers of his work as a black operations agent, Connor had not formally acknowledged his son.

Grace had understood despite hating it; she had been held hostage in Ukraine a few years before and witnessed the type of true evil he fought against.

The Ryder family owned a pub named 'The Buxton Arms' that lay close to a roundabout, feeding the cities of Leeds and Bradford and the towns of Halifax and Dewsbury.

As Connor pulled into the car park and stopped, Tom turned to them and said, "You both might as well come in. I'll be a while, and I have something to show you both."

"Alright, but be quick," said Connor. "Meant to be going to Gran's, and she went off her fucking head the last time I was late."

Connor grinned at the new statue of a Yoda—beer mug in one hand and a light sabre in the other—perched above the entrance frame.

His senses only attuned to something out of the ordinary on approaching the door—the distinct lack of noise.

Then, he immediately guessed why and braced himself for an acting performance.

He told himself—*Could be worse; at least you're not walking into a death trap.*

Arturo Bianchi washed his jowls in the basin of the 'Staff Only' bathroom of the sports bar he silently owned.

He popped back in his 'invisible' teeth-aligning tray. The discomfort of wearing it had receded since having it fitted a week ago. And because of the protocol of removing it to eat or drink anything but water, he found he was losing weight off his sixteen-stone frame.

A serene energy currently infused the crime boss—he was waiting for a final confirmation that the murder of his brother Marco had been avenged.

With the afternoon melting into the evening in Sudbury, Canada, he knew that with the UK being five hours ahead, the deed might have been done already.

The closed door muted the hollering of the hockey-watching crowd in the bar.

Bianchi had felt the sport grow on him over the years but still held a passion for football—or soccer, as they said here and south of the border.

His dark hair, salted with grey, remained short, as did the goatee beard. He dried his face with the inside of his sleeve. He put his glasses back on; he liked how different glasses changed his face—these black browline-style edging a sternness to his features.

He left the bathroom and cut his way through the jangling kitchen, where the staff didn't dare meet his eyes—though he hoped it was as more for their concentration on the food preparation than fear of him.

He came out into the bar.

Despite his Italian heritage, he chose the

manager—amongst other reasons—due to his Scots-Irish ancestry. And Bianchi had allowed him the layout and décor of his choice.

A giant screen hung over the bar, magnetising a large section of punters, while its children's screens gathered much of the rest as they looked down from various spots around the mezzanine floor.

The men leant from the upper balustrade with one eye on the game and another on the girls below.

Unlike other mafia bosses, Bianchi did not care that people knew he owned the bar. For one, he felt it lessened trouble—and less trouble meant more and nicer clientele, which meant more money.

Bianchi had witnessed many a bar go under due to the management and door staff allowing troublemakers in for an easy life with the oft-repeated mantra, *'Well, they spend a lot of money in here'*. The thugs would then proceed to chase away the more civilised customers, then take liberties with the bar staff—demanding a tab that always grew and never got paid.

Eventually, the business went under, and the cockroaches went somewhere else—but not in his place.

Fabio appeared. One of Bianchi's primary enforcers, the second-generation Italian, seemed taller than his average height and appeared to consist of squares—square head, square neck, square torso.

He spoke with a local accent, with Italian occasionally bouncing off the vowels.

Bianchi nodded before asking, "Is there any word from London?"

Fabio's face split into a joker's grin. "I have good news, boss. The son of a bitch's sister is dead."

Satisfaction rested on his soul. The

'Ndrangheta assassin, who killed Bianchi's brother, would no doubt request to avenge his sister's death—and they would deny him.

Indeed, when negotiating his new partnership with the Calabria hierarchy, he had overcome their strong resistance to her assassination by threatening to take his deal to Naples.

The Calabrese then demanded an exorbitant payment, which he rejected before both parties settled on a deal neither was truly happy with.

The best part would be that the assassin would see a fraction of the money and be ordered to stand down.

"Very good," he said in his scratchy drawl. "But I need to see it."

"They are sending the evidence soon. At the same time, they are sending it to her brother."

"Good," smiled Arturo. "What about that other thing?"

Fabio grinned, "He's downstairs in the basement."

"Well, let's not keep the prince waiting, eh?"

Arturo followed Fabio, the crowd parting before them. Through the staff doorway, Fabio slid out a standalone cupboard, revealing a doorway—not something that would hold up to any thorough and professional search but it was better than being on display.

Fabio opened it and led them down the blue-painted steel steps.

Arturo smiled as he heard muffled screams when nearing the bottom door.

The door opened to reveal a naked, long-haired, tattooed man on all fours, retching in a puddle of blood-flecked vomit.

The proud, gregarious outlaw biker gang leader had dissolved into a pleading mess.

Three of Arturo's men surrounded him.

"You know, I read a lot of history, Anton. I was watching this show on Genghis Khan. He would put out a white tent when he first laid siege to a city. That would mean if they surrendered before the end of the day, all the motherfuckers in the city would be spared. The next day, a red tent meant only the women and children would be allowed to leave."

He knelt at eye level with his prey. "After that, a black tent, and that meant everyone and their fuckin' dog would die."

He smiled and continued, "Now, you were warned. Nice. Then not so nice. And now this."

Bianchi held out his hand, and Fabio handed him an iPad. The empty chair scraped itself in front of the outlaw biker, and the crime lord put the iPad on it for his victim's view.

"I must say, your wife is *bellissima*, Anton."

"I'll fucking kill you," Anton screamed, rising to attack.

Whether due to fatigue or the pool of vomit and blood, Bianchi couldn't be sure, but his would-be assailant slipped to the chortles of him and his men.

As he attempted to rise again, a baseball bat thudded into his thigh, collapsing him back into the pool.

"Now, you have two choices. Either you can watch the rape of your wife. Or," Bianchi paused for dramatic effect, "You can be raped."

Arturo clicked his fingers, and steps sounded from behind.

A huge, black-bearded man appeared with a lumberjack shirt, seemingly a size too small. Spider's legs sprouted from the deep etchings on the grapefruit forearms.

"Anton, meet Devon. He doesn't speak much, but he's well known around the gay scene here—not for his gentleness. So what's it going to be?"

Bianchi kept his face straight as the anguish contorted Anton's face and said, "I never say anything I don't mean, Anton. Now, if you pick your wife, her rape won't be filmed. The children will be locked in another room. But your rape will be filmed—for insurance purposes only. But in either case, you will walk out of here alive. So will she. She can see your choice. So, which will it be? And if you don't answer in the next twenty seconds, it'll be the both of you. And one of you will die."

Though the biker decided several seconds before he thought he would, Bianchi had won his bet with Fabio.

The man's shaky finger rose and pointed at the screen.

Arturo could see the eyes of his men light up as they gathered around Anton and the screen.

The mob boss watched the high-definition picture of the wife's face turn from shock to horror as the seizing hands dragged her children off.

A hand then snatched her hair, pulling her upright. Strangely, the sound of quiet chuckling came from both inside the room and from the screen, as did the sound of sobbing—at least before the screams began.

Once it was all over, Bianchi watched the

woman convulsing in the fetal position, her quiet sobs barely audible.

He looked down at the kneeling biker, whose lips shelved snot and tears. Despite this, Bianchi could see the glimmer of relief in his eyes.

Perhaps because his wife's rape was now over. Or maybe because he had been spared the ordeal she had endured.

"Devon," Bianchi barked, snapping him to attention. "Fuck him, anyway! Make sure it's filmed."

The biker's screams of "Please" and "No" echoed off Bianchi's back as he turned for the stairs with Fabio in tow.

His enforcer said, "I have received the pictures from London."

"Good, let's look at them in my office in the light." Bianchi said, "Just think, that bald cocksucker might be looking at a picture of his dead sister now. I wish I could see his face."

The mafioso boss marched to his back office, dismissing the greetings.

Once inside, he turned to Fabio and said, "Show me."

Fabio produced a phone, and an image appeared of the slain brunette.

Bianchi's eyes narrowed—she looked different. A smirk appeared on his face— *A bullet to the forehead would do that to you.*

Then, her left hand drew his eyes.

Carlo stomped the stony sand on the tiny island of Hven, Sweden. A dark green igloo jacket helped his Italian blood against the cold.

An adventure in Japan well over a year ago

had left him injured—his left arm, broken at the elbow, being the worst—and lucky to survive.

He had barely allowed the limb to heal before he had taken a couple of sharp-end assignments in his capacity as ***consigliere per la sicurezza*** for the 'Ndrangheta.

He finally conceded to the need for physical and mental respite.

As he looked out to sea, he knew he was no different from a drug addict; in the same way they were destroying their bodies and risking death, he was doing the same.

But his 'poison' was the compulsion to risk himself in combat, mostly armed as the stakes were higher. The seed had been his killing of a wolf bearing down on him as an eleven-year-old when out hunting with his father.

From there, Carlo gravitated towards entering the Calabrian Mafia—'Ndrangheta—at the street level as a mid-teen. After discovering the possibility of his life being horse-traded by his Capo, he left to join the Foreign Legion.

For him, it had always been the thrill of combat—the thrill of risking his own life—so the idea of killing by explosive devices or poison or other such methods did not appeal.

So when Connor Reed contacted him, asking for help with an absurdly dangerous mission in Japan, Carlo accepted.

It was true he owed the Englishman a favour, but in truth, he would have accepted anyway. And he hadn't regretted it, even with the injuries he sustained.

Now refreshed, he looked forward to returning to the fray.

But thinking about his sister's words, the Mafioso began to ponder how long he could keep on with this lifestyle. He knew of Mafia hitmen working deep into their sixties; though their age gave them an air of vulnerability, it provided a useful inconspicuousness.

However, these tended to be the 'handshake and shoot' types dressed in casual clothes—there was very little hardship, endurance, or physicality in those jobs, and thus, no appeal for him.

Carlo did not kid himself; he did not care for exercise or healthy eating. His alcohol consumption, though not excessive, was regular. And his body had sustained a lot of punishment over the years.

He felt his phone vibrate but decided not to let it distract him from his thoughts.

But it kept buzzing against his thigh.

Eventually, he gave in and took it out. A text message read.

Carlo Andaloro, check your e-mail.

He suspected spam but checked, anyway. It appeared in his inbox. He took a chance and opened it to find a row of thumbnail images with the subject line **We are even now.**

His heart jolted as, on first inspection, the woman with a bullet hole in her forehead had an uncanny resemblance to Arabella.

Then his heart beat faster as he took in the rest of the image.

In the background, he caught sight of the sofa cushion patterned in the tri-colours of the Italian flag—not only did it look out of place amongst the perfectly blended décor, but he recognised it as the cushion he had gifted to Arabella when she had first moved to an architectural practice in Paris as a reminder of her roots.

Cold darkness swirled until his eyes flicked to the corpse's left ring finger—no ring, no tattoo.

Arabella, as a late teen, had a simple line circling the finger and crossing on the top of it as a tribute to their parents. A simple silver band usually covered it.

Dread enveloped him as he realised whoever had this girl killed intended for his sister to be the target.

He unscrambled his mind to phone her—the service provider informed him she could not be reached.

The assassin keyed in another memorised number.

4

Connor entered the *Buxton Arms* to a chorus of "Happy Birthday!"

Family members and friends packed the place, beaming at him.

He feigned shock and broke into a smile. The neon blue and white of **The Buxton** lit the collection of shelved spirits from above.

To its left, a polished dance floor—just shy of nightclub size—surrounded by black circular tables and seats.

On the right, a labyrinth of pillars, alcoves, and games tables watched over by old paintings—the oldest being a copy of a three-hundred-year-old tavern scene of card-playing, beer-supping men—framed photographs of iconic sports moments focussing on Leeds United, Leeds Rhinos, boxers and mixed martial artists, along with satirical pictures of dogs playing pool and nineteen-fifties sex symbols.

It led out into a beer garden warmed by overhead fire lamps during winter or at night. On the far side stood the apparatus for a projector screen poised for rolling down on sporting occasions. A small play park to the right enabled parents to watch the screen while keeping an eye on their children.

His eyes caught those of blonde Rayella's in the throng. The sister of his best friend who died in Afghanistan, he had been a quasi-brother to her ever since. Now seventeen and in her first year of college, Connor felt an immense pride in how she had turned out.

He caught a few male glances in her direction.

She returned his grin with a smirk, though he knew this to be a smile through her stolid demeanour.

It surprised him that some of his Royal Marine colleagues also stood in the crowd, and he felt thankful for the port behind the bar.

One of these was a hulking Fijian named Viliame—Vili for short—who had helped save his life in Ukraine a few years ago. As had former Para, John Foley, also present, a nutcase of average build with a shorn down 'Chuck Liddell' style haircut.

Connor felt uneasy—alcohol blended with men who liked to fight tended to cause combustions.

Still, the god-fearing Fijian now swore off alcohol, and Connor felt sure no matter how 'tapped in the head' John Foley could be, the Londoner knew how to behave at other people's family events.

The crowd quietened to hear him speak, and he said, "I take it the strippers come later?"

As the laughter blended and groans came back at him, a John Foley shout went up, "They might not come at all. Just like any woman who's taken their clothes off for ya."

Shockingly to him and presumably the rest of the gathering, Connor's gran broke the tension with an immediate laugh.

After a brief speech, Connor began to make the rounds of the attendees, starting with the ones least close to him. He saw Vili and Foley join his cousins at the bar, and Connor made a beeline for Rayella.

"How you doing, mate?" he asked.

"I am great," smirked Rayella. "You can stop calling me mate now."

He nodded in reply, and she said, "I am

smashing college and still keeping up with my training. Got a grappling competition coming up."

"How are you feeling about it?"

She shrugged. "I didn't think I'd get the same nerves as when I was doing Thai, but I do."

"It's just because you want to win so badly."

Connor had felt the opposite, having entered a few local grappling competitions. Besides reaching an exceptionally high level in boxing, he had competed in Thai, judo and, on one occasion, a bare-fisted **Vale Tudo** fight.

Though he considered a judo bout to be the closest grappling could get to being 'a fight', if the threat of being knocked unconscious by a blow was removed, he couldn't really get nervous about it.

Rayella turned a little, opening herself up to the approach of an angular girl of similar age with pony-tailed brunette hair and wearing a blue dress with white polka dots.

"Caz, this is my brother from another mother, Connor. Connor, this is my friend Caz."

"Nice to meet you, Caz," said Connor, holding out his hand.

She smiled shyly, shook it and said, "You too."

Both girls' eyes switched over his shoulder, and they straightened their postures. He saw Caz's pupils dilate, and Connor knew who was behind.

The mojito slid into his hand before Luke said, "You alright, Rayella?"

"I am great, thanks, Luke."

"You alright, Rayella's friend?"

Luke, at nearly six feet, with blond hair, sapphire eyes, and a physique resembling a wedge, had a physical attractiveness to women that outstripped all the males in the family.

Connor suppressed a smile as Caz blushed.

Luke said to him, "See you in a bit, cuz. Happy birthday!"

His younger cousin kissed him on the cheek and left.

Connor looked at the girls and said, "Bet you two are jealous of that kiss, eh?"

Rayella asked rhetorically, "Does he have sex with you, too?"

"Unfortunately for him, no," said Connor. "Keep out of trouble, Rayella."

"Who? Me?"

Connor walked off for the collective huddle of his cousins, uncles and friends at the bar.

"So, you threw the party a few weeks early, so I wouldn't suspect."

His boisterous Uncle Ryan said, "That's right, kidda—we knew you'd have some sort of 'trip' planned and couldn't let your Big 3-0 go without a party."

"I appreciate it," said Connor with sincerity. "Though I am not sure I appreciate you bringing these pair of mad bastards here."

He gestured to Vili and Foley.

"Hey," said Foley, feigning hurt. "I am here to celebrate your thirty years on this spinning planet. Vili is only here because he thinks there will be lap dancers."

Connor smirked; the Fijian would feel uncomfortable if a dancer draped herself on him, whereas Foley would be liable to dance for her.

The Fijian said, "Doesn't look like you need

to go to the Devil's Den. Is it usually like this, Connor?"

"Like what?"

Foley answered for him. "He means, is it usually crawling with more pussy than a paraplegic strip club?"

Connor said, "Must just be me."

Indeed, Connor saw the two bikers as an advert for how two people of different backgrounds, values and character traits could become such good friends. Vili, a former Royal Marine, and Foley, a former Para, had met each other through their membership in the same motorcycle club.

Ryan looked at his son and said, "Seriously though, Thomas, will there be strippers?"

"I think we're a bit past those shenanigans now," announced Tom.

Connor felt the collective disappointment before Ryan burst with, "You fuckin' what? You and your missus own two of West Yorkshire's most profitable topless bars, and you haven't put any girls on?"

Tom laughed, "Save your breath for cooling your salted porridge. We are going to *The Helena* later—Gran would throw a fit if I brought strippers down here. She looks down on any woman she doesn't see as 'classy'."

Arabella Andaloro's entire being hummed with a sense of elation as she touched the Snowdon summit cairn.

The cold air kissed her all over her face, combed through her dark curls and dove into her mouth to replenish her lungs.

She moved away from the cairn, slid out the metal cigarette case and lit a *Gitanes*, ignoring one of the female hiker's disapproving gaze.

She allowed herself a few moments to absorb the serenity of the view. The mountain ranges slid down into the glittering lake on the valley floor. The distant white line of the horizon supported the light, cold, blue sky.

The Hafod Eryri—the summit building—remained temporarily closed due to the work being done on the rail track, which provided the service train for its staff.

Arabella decided against eating her packed lunch on the summit as originally planned. She knew her body would seize if she sat for too long, hence the cigarette instead, the butt of which she deposited in a double plastic bag with a zip.

The Italian began her descent, knowing it would be more demanding on the knees, if easier on the heart and lungs.

A year ago, she had begun various hiking and climbing trips to recapture her 'mountain fitness' after a period of only gym work and running on the flat streets when initially taking over in London.

Her father often took her hiking through the various mountains of Calabria as a child.

He would take her over to her younger brother, as her father never missed an opportunity to remind Carlo that his gentle nature displayed the weakness of his character.

And this berating would have been worse if not for her protectiveness of Carlo and her father's favouritism towards her. Admonishing her father's teasing had lessened it, at least when she was around.

Not even their mother had that power over him.

Then, one day, almost by a flip of a switch, her father began to favour her younger brother.

This had been due to what had now become an Andaloro family legend. At just eleven, Carlo had been acting as an equipment carrier on their father's hunting expeditions in the Tuscan-Emilian Apennines.

It had been on one such excursion when he single-handedly killed a charging Italian grey wolf.

'Some hunters go a lifetime without shooting a wolf. My son did it at eleven years of age,' her father would boast in drink.

And Arabella had been glad at the time because their father's disparaging remarks towards the shy and quasi-effeminate Carlo almost ceased.

Her brother was neither of those things now. However, she sometimes thought he had gone too far the other way—as if he couldn't believe the shackles of meekness no longer constrained him.

At first, she had been so proud of him. She had been the only member of their family ever to see him in his Legionnaire's uniform and hat. When she went to place the hat on her head, she remembered him snatching it back and sternly telling her, *'This is a kepi, and no one will wear it who is not a Legionnaire.'*

That had been after watching him and his comrades perform elaborate and razor-sharp drills to commemorate Armistice Day in Paris.

As she trundled down the rocky path, smiling that awkward smile passing strangers give one another, she lamented that the Legionnaires would have been there and back, showered and changed by the time some of these hikers did Snowdon.

Despite her exertions, she absorbed the stress-free scenery, knowing how hectic the schedule would be when she returned. It had been her brother who had encouraged her to do this.

He had told her that after periods of stress, he would take himself off to a different country and, though he'd make the odd exception for her, would cease any contact that was not person to person. As her professional responsibilities increased, she warmed to the idea; this would be her fifth 'decompression' trip away this year.

And she had enjoyed her time on the Welsh island of Anglesey. Yesterday, she had visited a pub in Menai Bridge, a small town she had made her home these last few days and which had a 'lost in time' feel, and looked over a stretch of shallow tidal water.

A Rugby Union game between Wales and South Africa had resulted in a narrow win for the Welsh side, much to the raucous delight of the crowd packed into the pub. They soon engaged her in some good-natured ribbing upon discovering her being Italian and the close victory her country's rugby team had recently inflicted upon them.

More than one came on to her but took her gentle rebuffs good-naturedly.

As she trundled down the hill, the architect decided to wait until she had left Wales before turning on her phone; she did not want anything sullying the memory of her serene stay.

Connor sat in the warmth of being surrounded by his friends—friends he found interesting and entertaining.

They had moved as a collective to a larger

table adjacent the bar.

He felt lucky he existed in a universe where Tom and Luke were his relations, and John and Vili were his friends.

"How was he?" asked Vili of the recent show performed by a world-famous English mentalist and illusionist that Tom and his partner, Cara, attended.

Tom replied, "What a showman. I genuinely couldn't work out the things he was doing. Chooses members of the crowd by throwing a frisbee, so unless he's a frisbee world champion, I can't see how there are plants."

"Did you try to catch it?" asked Vili, not being familiar enough with Tom to know the last thing the Ryder family leader would want to do was to draw attention to himself.

"Nah, didn't fancy the old 'eating an onion being convinced it's an apple' routine."

"That's the least of your worries," piped up John Foley. "He's gay, isn't he?"

"So?" frowned Connor.

"It's not eating an apple, thinking it's an onion you must be worried about. It's him taking you backstage 'to train' you, and you think you're getting around a Solero ice cream, but it's his cock!"

The table broke into sniggers and smiles, except for Vili, who exclaimed, "He won't do that!"

Luke chimed in, "I don't know—it's not as if he can turn his powers off. I mean, would it be illegal? How would it be any different to a pick up artist using a chat up line?"

"Because," began Connor, despite knowing it not to be a serious question. "They are in a state of duress—they are hypnotised. Plus, even if it wasn't illegal, his career would be over if someone bubbled him."

"That's the thing. They would think it was a dream," countered Foley. "Or you wouldn't remember at all. He'd be like the human version of that 'Men In Black' bleeper forgetter-thing."

"A neuralyzer," said Connor. "Used to prevent hysteria to save lives."

Luke asked, "Connor, Bill told me he saved yours and Tom's lives without knowing it when you were teenagers. Up on the Moors, like."

"Oh fuck, aye," said Connor, remembering. "It was more Tom's fault, though."

"How do you work that out?" protested Tom.

"You getting agitated, sparking my concern for you."

Luke interjected. "Tell us the story so we can all decide."

"Tom?" asked Connor.

"Alright," began Tom, straightening in his seat. "We'd picked up debt from Halifax to drop it over to a businessman in Oldham. I was nineteen and driving the car over the tops on New Hey Road, where it's quiet."

"How come you didn't take the M62?"

"We didn't want to be picked up by the ANPRs," replied Tom, referring to the Automatic Number Plate Recognition cameras installed on most UK motorways.

"Old man Bill is up in the front, and our Connor is in the back. And we're on a high cos our cut of this thirty K debt is half. Anyway, the road is narrow, and this prick comes blaring up behind, flashing his lights, but there's not enough space to pass. The road opens, and he screams past gizzin' me the 'wanker sign'. We come up to these lights, and I bang the window down and say, 'What the fuck did you do that for?'."

Connor corrected him and imitated the man's nasally Manc accent, "No, you said, 'What did you call me a wanker for', and he said, 'Cos ya did a wanker thing din't ya'. But it was the way he said it, no anxiety in his voice. He was on his own. And when Tom had a bit of a go back, the lad said, 'You want to make something of it then?'."

"What happened then?" asked Luke excitedly.

"Connor attempts to get out of the car but forgets there is a child lock on it. When I try to get out, Bill puts his hand on my arm and says, 'We've had a good touch today. Let's go.' Bill has been there since our grandad's day, and our dads always said Bill's the boss when we were with him, so that was that."

The table retracted into a confused quiet, and Luke asked, "How's that you both nearly getting killed? Sounds like he had a lucky escape."

"Because the guy was Martin Boyles, the assassin who killed Paul Large and Jack Childs in Manchester—that very night—with a submachine gun. The reason he didn't give a fuck was cos he must have had it on the seat beside him."

Connor felt a chill at the memory. Tom left out that it had led to one of the extremely rare fallings-out between the pair, as Connor had insisted he should have been let out.

Months later, Connor caught the article regarding the assassinations and made the walk of shame to the garage Tom worked at to apologise.

Typical of his elder cousin, Tom had feigned ignorance as to why Connor was apologising, and Connor knew back then he wouldn't try to overrule Tom again.

As the table buzzed about the story, Connor announced his intention to get another drink and took their orders.

"Suppose the trampolines outside are just for the kids?" asked Foley.

"Fun fact, they used to be known as jumpolines back in the day."

Vili asked, "Wh..why did the name change?"

Connor answered, "Cos Foley's mum got caught on one."

He left the table before Foley could retort to a collective "Whooaa."

He leaned against the bar as the barmaid glided over to him, wavy golden hair bouncing off her shoulders—dark grey blazer draped over a white-collar shirt.

"Hey up, Eva," said Connor.

"You want a spacer, don't you?" she said, her blue eyes smiling through black-framed glasses.

"How did you know that?"

"Because you came up here by yourself. They think it's because you want to chat me up, but I know better."

"Can't it be both?"

"Of course," she said. "What do you want, a Coke or sparkling water with lime?"

"I'll have a coke this time, please," he replied, needing a sugar hit.

It came back with ice and a lemon.

"Good memory," he said.

"Let's hope it hasn't let me down with these exams."

"Confident, though?"

"Yeh, but cautiously so."

"Then you'll be a forensic scientist," murmured Connor, seemingly to himself. "I remember, when I was tiny, I think about six years old, one of my earliest memories was being there when my Uncle Ryan had 'The X-Files' on, and I just couldn't stop watching Gillian Anderson—remember being annoyed every time they cut to another scene."

"So you're saying all I need to do is dye my hair ginger for us to have a shot?"

Connor smiled at her light-hearted flirting. Her words lit a thought—*Maybe that was where my liking for redheads originated.*

Grace had red hair. He was looking forward to seeing her tonight.

"We'll see what happens when you start work as a forensic scientist and stop working here," said Connor. "Though I like to wait until the girls are in their late twenties before ruining them for other men."

She stared at him blankly for a few long moments. "I thought I'd let you marinate in that very eighties, very yuppie comment."

Connor nodded contritely, "Yeh, I deserved it."

She smiled, placed her hand over his in a 'there, there' gesture and said, "It's OK. I know you said it just to impress me."

The buzzing of his pocket cut away his retort, "Excuse me, I have to take this."

He answered, "Yeh."

"It's me," came the faintly Italian-accented reply. "I need your help."

Connor's heartbeat shifted up a gear. "Hang on. Let me go outside so I can hear you better."

He flashed his fingers at the table to indicate he would be two minutes.

The cold air—and his tipsiness—hit him outside.

"I am here," he said.

"I have a sister in London who is in danger."

"I am listening."

"Someone came to her apartment to murder her, but they killed the wrong girl."

"Where is your sister now?"

"I do not know."

"Kidnapped?"

"I do not know. When she goes on vacation, she switches her phone off—not even an emergency number. She says that anything in life can wait a few days. She does not use social media or check her phone. None of it."

"How can I help her if you don't know where she is?"

"When her phone comes on, I can track it. I do not know who will be watching. Maybe they discover they have murdered the wrong target—they have a picture—and decide to wait for her return?"

"Alright, I'll make some calls. I know people down there—"

"No! It must be you. These people are very dangerous."

Connor fought to peer through his inebriation. He cursed himself for breaking his rule of not becoming so alcohol induced that he couldn't operate effectively.

"Alright, send me the address and anything relevant, and I'll get myself down there."

"Thank you. Be aware, my friend," came the reply before the call ended.

Carlo referring to him as 'friend' piqued Connor—which he could not remember him doing before. Not in that tone.

He's scared—thought Connor.

He strode back in and beckoned Luke.

His younger cousin must have recognised Connor's 'work face' now because he asked, "What is it?"

"Grab Tom, Foley and Vili, and bring them outside. Them only," said Connor, not wishing for his now mostly straight-going uncles to be involved.

Within a minute, they came outside, and Connor began to brief them. "A friend of mine—well, his sister—is in trouble. I've got to shoot down to London, and I mean now."

"You can't drive now. You're half cut," exclaimed Tom. "And don't say you feel fine; every pisshead who gets in a car before crashing 'as said that to himself."

His elder cousin would always look out for everyone in the family like a cross between a gangster boss and a mother hen.

Vili—a teetotaller—immediately said, "I will take you."

"It'll have to be a car, mate. I want to take some equipment I can't carry on a bike," said Connor. "Do you have a licence?"

"Yes, gee, we have cars in Fiji."

"With engines?"

Vili smiled, though Connor knew he got his licence in the Defence School of Transport in Leconfield when in the Parachute Regiment.

Foley cut in. "You two aren't going anywhere without me."

When the group's attention flicked towards Foley, who'd drunk significantly more than any of them, he simply said, "I've been drink riding for years—in far worse states than this."

Connor knew it would be pointless to argue.

Luke asked, "Just how much trouble is she in?"

"I am not sure yet. Believe me; this isn't a guy that scares easily, but I could hear it in his voice."

Luke announced, "Then let's all go down."

"No," said Connor firmly. "I'll call you if I need you, but I'll be more manoeuvrable alone."

With that, he fished his keys out and threw them to Vili—as a test.

Skimming them with his first swiping hand, the Fijian caught them just underneath with the second.

"Good enough," Connor sighed.

Tom and Luke watched the trio roar off into the night under the gaze of the Yoda statue.

The blur of the talking, laughter, and music was barely muffled by the doors.

Luke murmured, "I'd rather fight three men armed with knuckle-dusters than have to explain to gran where he's gone."

"Let's not pretend that it's going to be you who has to break the news to her," said Tom. "Besides, she'll be fine with how I put it."

"I see," said Luke, guessing how Tom would put it. "If she's going to be fine, then why do you sound so unhappy?"

Tom sighed. "You know, one day, he won't come back."

"Connor?" exclaimed Luke, attempting to lift his elder cousin's spirits. "That cunt could come back from a holiday with the McCanns."

Tom rewarded him with the barest of a smile before he said, "Come on. Let's get back inside."

5

Connor kept his head immobile with his eyes scanning as he made his *clearance patrol* around the area of Arabella Andaloro's home.

It had taken just over three hours of constant speeding and slowing down for the speed cameras to make the two-hundred-and-ten-mile journey down the M1 to Eaton Mews West in London's Belgravia.

Her apartment lay on a cobbled street, the centre of a row of three-story houses painted white, cream, or beige. They reminded Connor of the hotels you saw in every British seaside town.

His awareness that subsequent reviews of surveillance video might reveal him prevented him from approaching the residence.

He wanted to see if any watchers lurked in the shadows. Maybe they had discovered they had murdered the wrong target and lay in wait for the real one. He had left Vili in his car a mile away to prevent any potential ANPR, highlighting it after the fact.

About fifteen minutes earlier, Connor caught sight of a black Mercedes AMG with the interior light on. He had made a mental note, and it was still there as he made around again.

Connor began to cycle through reasonable explanations.

Maybe he's waiting for a girlfriend or friend to finish a shift. But there are no commercial establishments still open nearby. Or perhaps it's a person involved in a meditative practice for a bit of levity between work and facing a spouse?

He decided on a plan and took out his phone.
"Vili, I have an idea."

Back on the Swedish mainland, in the Borstahusen hotel, Carlo flung his belongings into his case. He had booked a flight out of Malmö Airport, a drive of seventy-five kilometres.

He whipped his green, white and red striped mug off the bedside table. On it the text **Essere mio fratello è davvero l'unico dono di cui hai bisogno!**—*Being my brother is really the only gift you need!* He wrapped a sweater around it to prevent it from smashing inside the carriage.

He knew he shouldn't have it; a man like him might have enemies who would love to know he had a sister he was close to.

Carlo felt glad she left Italy years ago to find success in architectural design, first in Paris, now in London. And no longer in proximity to his criminal associates.

She had admonished him the last time they met, a few months ago—*'I love you, but you're sick, Carlo. This need for danger comes before everyone. You can't keep fighting as an old man. Sylvester Stallone lives in the movies.'*

His mother, still living in Calabria, welcomed his visits and never judged his nature. He did not feel overly concerned regarding his mother's safety as she was regularly checked in on and resided in a section of Reggio Calabria where the antennas of the locals would twitch with the presence of strangers.

Besides, the 'Ndrangheta held the sanctity of the family a little more closely than their cousins in Naples—even the severest internal wars did not physically visit civilian members of the bloodlines.

However, the same did not hold for

unmarried lovers—and so Carlo made sure not to involve himself with anyone on too regular a basis—hence his childless sister's reproach of, *'You will never make an honest aunt of me by gallivanting with your guns all the time'*.

Fortunately for him, his jet-setting lifestyle made not getting attached a little easier.

Carlo's phone began vibrating on the dressing table, and he scrambled for it.

"Yes," he said in English.

The voice replied in Italian, "Carlo, it is me."

He recognised it as belonging to Alessio Letta, a chief financial and unofficial consigliere to whom the Italian media referred as the Capo dei Capi—boss of bosses—Italo Mauro.

"Yes?" Carlo repeated, his blood already cooling.

"What's done is done. Go to London and bury your sister. Then you must come back to Calabria."

Carlo felt a plunge of differing emotions vying for his attention.

One, the burning, indignant rage that the organisation—the family—he had pledged his life and honour to had, at least, knowledge of the attempted murder of his sister.

The other, a glimmer of hope—they still thought his sister to be dead. He expected to see the condensation of his breath as he asked, "Why has this happened?"

"Not over the phone. You know this."

"Tell me now, or I will go dark."

He heard a sigh, and Alessio say, "It is the fallout from that thing over the big water."

Carlo knew he referred to a mission in Canada to disrupt a meeting between the Bianchi faction and the Romano crime family.

Marco Bianchi broke away from the Siderno crime family a few years previously. The Siderno held their stronghold in Greater Toronto.

In an attempt to consolidate power, they reached out to Montreal's Romanos.

Bianchi wanted to set up state-of-the-art meth laboratories in Northern Ontario; as manufacturing methamphetamine produces a very unpleasant smell likened to cat piss, Northern Ontario, with its sparse population, numerous lakes, and vast forests, was ideal.

The Siderno Group—named so because its founding members came from the Ionian coastal town of Siderno in Italy in the nineteen fifties—petitioned for Calabria to send **a *Consigliere per la Sicurezza*** to disrupt an initial sit-down between the Bianchis and the Romanos.

The assassin hissed, "On orders from you."

"You went off the reservation. We told you to attack the ones from Montreal so they would think the other group was behind it. You attacked both."

"So, what? The overall mission was to break that alliance. I achieved that."

"Montreal is now suspicious of our hand in this," said Alessio. "In killing the man, you brought the brother to the front. A man more capable and vengeful."

It had been well known that Marco and Arturo Bianchi had been estranged for several years.

"Why does the old man care about what the brother or Montreal thinks?"

"Since Montreal gave the brother their blessing to take over the new clan."

"So we're all back friends now."

"We have dissolved much of our differences."

Carlo deliberately injected a hue of sorrow into his tone. "And my sister's life was the price?"

"Yes," came the reply. "Now, the best thing for all of us is to put this behind us. And remember, you took an oath."

"My sister was innocent. Never involved in our life in any way."

"We can discuss it when you get back."

"Yes. We'll talk when this is all over," said Carlo, ending the call.

Aaron Edmonds smoothed his blond moustache, which looked a little out of place in contrast to his long, combed-back brown hair and cursed the cold. And he cursed the bad intelligence he had received.

Though born, bred, and living primarily in the UK, he had dual citizenship with Canada.

And he should have been on a plane to lie low in Montreal, where pussy, a *two-four* and a beavertail pastry dessert awaited him.

Not sat at the scene of the fuckin' crime.

He had done his first hit as a late teen, and it had always been drummed into him to leave immediately and get as far away as possible.

Some of his fellow hitmen liked to clean the weapon and leave it at the scene. Fortunately, he had not subscribed to this idea, which was just as well as he needed it to kill the actual target when she returned home.

He'd knocked her out first for the benefit of

shooting her behind a closed door, with her bagged head covered by a cushion to prevent blood from splattering on his clothes.

He took little pleasure from killing two women, apart from a slight sense of professional pride—but he felt no pain for them either.

He could never understand the abhorrence some held towards his profession—people were just people, some good, some bad, but all of them sucked up resources. And all were headed towards a more miserable death than the clean way he executed them.

And he never got the notion of seeing women and children as untouchably sacred. There were plenty of cunt women, and Hitler, Stalin, and Pol Pot had all been children once.

Not that he had been required to kill kids often, but his new boss had given the order that if they fell as collateral, then so be it. Aaron had no problem with it, though he always increased his fee.

He knew his reputation for taking on any task, no matter how dirty, as long as he was paid right, had found him in favour with his boss. But the downside was that he wouldn't be a stickler for the intelligence picture beforehand, and now he was paying the price.

He chafed in his seat and hunkered further into his Puffa jacket.

Bitch must be on a night out.

It was now half-past one in the morning, and he straightened to remain alert for her possible arrival.

A big, stocky man stumbled out of the darkness of a side street before bumping his way in Aaron's direction.

"Fuck"—he whispered, as he slid further into his seat.

He dared not catch the drunk's eye, who appeared to be of similar ethnicity to The Rock.

The man's eyes seemed to squint at him, and Aaron swore again, and the caramel face broke into a wide grin.

The gorilla began to amble over.

What would he do now? He couldn't drive off as he needed his eyes on the apartment.

And Aaron already knew he couldn't intimidate the apparent drunk; the guy was built like one of those rugby players who smashed into one another in a pack.

Just smile. Be friendly, and let him talk.

The man waved from about five meters away.

The smash of glass bounced off Aaron's eardrum as the shards showered his face.

A cold blade edged into his throat before the shock wore off.

A rough but clear northern English voice said, "Look straight ahead, and slowly put your hands on the steering wheel."

For a moment, he considered feigning not being able to understand but decided against it and complied.

When Aaron had done so, the voice then said, "I suspect you have a weapon in here, so if you make any sudden movements, I am going to slit your throat. Understand?"

Aaron nodded, remaining still as a hand removed the key fob.

His heart pulsed as the central locking clicked, and the back door on his side opened.

Someone sat behind him, and his heart rate rocketed as the rough hands came around. Absent of garrotting wire, however. Instead, they frisked him.

The hands disengaged, and Aaron could hear them rustling beneath his seat.

With the whisper of "Bingo," Aaron knew they'd found the gun.

The slide-stop sound of a chamber check was followed by a barrel pressing into the base of his neck and then the blade leaving his throat.

He noticed the original guy had lost his ambling stumble as he now stood sentry with his hands thrust into his jacket.

The passenger side door opened, and a dark-blond man with an athletic physique sat in.

"As much as I hate to be cliché, who sent you?"

"I don't kn—"

Aaron's head bounced off the door pillar before he had the chance to freeze his neck, rocketing pain through it.

"Fucking muppet! If you're going to lie, don't do it straight off the bat. Build trust first."

The voice behind him—which he recognised to be around London—chortled, "Just sitting in the dark with a silenced pistol, are you?"

The blond man beside him reached over and cuffed one of Aaron's wrists before ordering him to "Loop it around the steering wheel and handcuff your other tight. Think about how a cigarette put out on your eyeball will feel before attempting any tricks."

Believing the blond, he tightened the handcuff as if securing an enemy.

The blond asked, "Who do you work for?"

Aaron's mind revolved through his options.

The voice from behind said, "Let's burn the

cunt now."

The blond said, "Give him a moment to figure out it's best just to tell us. Because if we let him go unmarked, he can claim this never happened."

The hitman's mind latched onto the blond's words. So far, only the window had been smashed, easily explained away to the rental company. He could even say a group of drunks did it, and he had to leave.

It had been intimated to him he would be promoted as a permanent co-ordinator between his firm and the Bianchi crime faction after completing this job—the money and the perks would rise considerably.

But they'd never trust him again if they even suspected he had ratted them out. And if they knew for sure, he'd be dead.

Still, he might die right here.

"I work for a criminal organisation in London."

The hand snatched his ear into an agonising crunch before smacking his head off the door pillar three times, barely missing the shards of the smashed window. Without letting go, the blond said, "Stop being coy. Tell me everything. Bore me with the details because I won't hold back on you if you do."

A sense of futility enveloped him. Then, he had an idea, "I work as a liaison between a Mister Bianchi and the Norland-Greens."

The voice behind him asked, "You know the names?"

The blond replied, "Marco Bianchi broke away from the Siderno Group a while back and took a few soldiers with him. He got himself killed, and his brother took over. Not the nicest of men, apparently."

Aaron felt himself nod involuntarily.

"Why did he send you here?"

"For a hit."

The ash blond smacked him with the back of his fingers like he was a child who had just sworn.

"We know you fucking div. I asked why?"

"Not sure. I heard him sounding off about his brother getting killed in some sanctioned but not sanctioned hit. I heard this will smooth things out with the Siderno Group."

A few moments passed before the blond asked, "You accepted the assignment to kill a civilian woman?"

"What difference does that make?"

"It makes a difference to the man whose sister you tried to kill. And because I owe him, it makes a difference to me."

"So, what now?"

"We can't just leave you here or simply watch you drive off. You might feel compelled to come back and finish the mission. You see our point."

Aaron could only shrug, and the blond continued, "So we are going to go take a drive and hold you for a bit until the coppers cordon off the scene and have your original target in their custody. Then you're going to leave the United Kingdom and never come back. Got it?"

Aaron nodded numbly, and the blond said, "We're going to have to rearrange the formation."

Under the blond's instructions, which always kept a weapon system on Aaron, the hitman found himself sitting in the back with the guy he now guessed to be Fijian or Samoan. Handcuffs secured his wrists beneath his right thigh.

The big guy sat next to him. The guy originally behind him now sat in the driver's seat—rough beard, light brown hair cut into a wide Mohican, muscular frame.

The blond said, "Take him to the address."

"You not coming?" asked the driver.

"Can't discount that this Arturo character hasn't got other assets in place in case this yokel fucks it up."

The Mohican lowered his voice. "It's not him you want to be worried about, it's…I'll tell you later."

"Alright. Meanwhile, I'll locate the girl. Make sure she's alright."

The driver exclaimed, "So we get to hold this *vadge* while you get to hero an Italian worldie?"

"Not sure she's a worldie, but believe me, you wouldn't touch her if you knew who her brother was. As the vadge might find out," said the blond before speaking to him, "Look at me."

As Aaron turned his head to do so, a four-knuckled mallet whipped a thudding impact of pain into his cheek.

"Thanks for cutting short a great party," said the blond.

6

Connor felt a flutter in his chest as the car's Bluetooth rang—he had never called her while 'working' before.

Grace answered with a curt, "Yes."

"It's me."

"What happened?" she asked, a hint of concern softening her north-east lilted accent.

"I got 'called away'," he said.

"You never normally call me when that happens."

"I know," he said. "How is he?"

"He's fine. He's at my gran's."

"How come?"

"Because it wasn't appropriate to have him here for the surprise I had in store for you."

Connors' mind raced. "Holy fuck, what was it?"

"It can be postponed," she said. "It's worth staying alive for, Connor Reed."

She ended the call.

Carlo sat in the reception area, willing their valet to check the Vauxhall Crossland faster.

He remembered having to clean Rocco's—his old Capo's—silver Maserati 3200GT when he was a young teen.

The same Capo to whom the young Carlo used to kick up almost his entire earnings—because it had been impressed upon him that the ability to send money up the chain would protect him more than a fearsome reputation would.

However, though Rocco never really asked where the money was coming from when the Apulian Mafia discovered Carlo's series of high-line armed robberies in their territory, they demanded retribution or compensation.

Rocco—the snake that he was—caved and sent two of his men to punish the seventeen-year-old. Carlo sent them back disarmed and severely beaten before escaping to the French Foreign Legion to avoid reprisals.

Years later, the threat removed, Carlo returned home.

Ordinarily, military service would have hindered, if not prohibited, his entering the Calabrese Mafia. Though they did not share quite the same abhorrence for the government their Sicilian cousins did—indeed, preferring to pay them than to revert to street wars—they remained highly suspicious of anyone in, or formerly of, government employ.

However, because Carlo's had been for the French government—though many Legionnaires saw the Legion and France being almost separate entities—his had slowly got to be seen as an asset. He was one of very few who could plan and conduct paramilitary-style operations, as well as assassinate targets out of urban environments.

As a result, he had quickly become a 'made-man' within the 'Ndrangheta—perhaps their best asset outside of their financial guys.

However, he began to doubt his professional decision this time. He had sacrificed security for speed to take a commercial flight to Heathrow. On arrival, he'd taken an Uber to Ealing, having him stop nearly half a kilometre shy of this car rental.

He couldn't remember it taking this long before but thought perhaps his anxiety might be playing a time illusion on him.

Wide, yellow plastic trimmed the crease where the cream wall met the beige ceiling. An inoffensive radio played low as framed posters depicting the joyous occasion of renting a car looked down on him.

He used the reflective plastic covering on one of the posters to observe the reception desk behind him. His insides stirred as a congregation formed behind it.

The receptionist gave the phone to the manager, and their eyes flicked nervously in his direction.

Carlo knew he had been compromised. He briefly considered visiting the bathroom but thought it highly unlikely it would have a window, let alone one big enough to climb through.

The assassin stood and started for the door. He guessed it might be his Mafia colleagues impersonating the police; to involve the actual police would be a violation of the code. And it would not be pragmatic to volunteer a made-man into the judicial system.

He inwardly grimaced as he caught the manager's reflection coming from behind the counter. "Excuse me, sir."

Carlo feigned not to hear as he went through the door.

His eyes scanned the assortment of vehicles curving behind the Round-Top temporarily galvanised fencing to his right.

To his left, a minor road cut through two

rows of commercial high-rise buildings.

He cursed as the manager followed him out. "Sir."

Carlo wheeled with a blank expression, and the man asked, "Is something wrong?"

Not wanting to give the collar a hook, he replied, "I have changed my mind."

"I am sure we could change it back," smiled the man, reaching to put a coercive arm around the Italian's shoulder.

Carlo snatched the manager's wrist, forcing the hand inwards towards the forearm, causing his knees to buckle.

"If you try to touch me again, you will have to learn to pleasure your cock with your left hand," Carlo hissed.

The manager nodded his immediate understanding, and Carlo let him go with a shove.

The assassin began a brisk walk as the manager stepped back, nursing his sprained but unbroken wrist.

Whoever asked the manager to keep him in place would be here soon enough.

As much as the thought of ambushing whoever got sent, he knew his best course of action would be to put as much space between him and them as possible.

He knew how deep and far-reaching the 'Ndrangheta's connections stood, which included paid informants at most international airports.

But he didn't know how they had tracked him here. He no longer trusted his phone and knew he had to destroy it.

But that meant his sister could not contact

him.

Arabella felt a wave of sensory overload upon opening her phone.

She felt the train rumbling through her on seeing dozens of missed calls and messages.

The Italian connected her Bluetooth earpiece.

She wasn't sure she'd ever heard such agitation in her brother's voice before—so much so that she doubted it was him at first. She listened to him, exhorting her not to return home or contact the police without contacting him first.

Her concern grew when, upon trying to call him, the female automated voice informed her the number was out of service.

She knew she did not possess a nervous disposition—indeed, she'd heard the rumour of her Ice Queen moniker at work—but suddenly, the blue cloth of the train seat felt scratchy.

Though highly strung when it came to the trivial, her brother had always presented a calm demeanour in the few situations she had seen that would have unnerved 'normal' men.

She remembered, when first moving to Paris, she had a well-kept blue Peugeot 208, that required the ***contrôle technique***—France's compulsory test for roadworthiness. She had taken it in on a Wednesday and was told it would be completed on Friday. She called on Friday afternoon to be told a part had been ordered and would arrive on Monday.

A derivative of this repeated itself for a further two weeks.

During this, she had video-called her brother and remembered how shocked she had been to see an androgynous-looking figure sprawled out on the bed, drug-taking paraphernalia on the bedside table.

Refusing to judge his private life, she instead off-loaded to him, expecting him to tell her that this was the way of the world.

Instead, Carlo arrived on her doorstep less than twenty-four hours later and quietly demanded she direct him to the garage.

She did so and watched him enter the garage and witnessed the shutter doors roll down.

After twenty minutes, she received her pass certificate. When she enquired about the money, Carlo had stated, *"They didn't feel it would be right to charge you after the delay."*

But when she returned a few months later to have a cracked coolant reservoir replaced, feeling she owed them her business due to not charging her previously, they not only carried out the work that same morning but again refused to take her money.

She tried calling him again—dead.

Lifting her head to think, she knew paranoia had gripped her when she spotted two men looking right at her before snatching their attention away after making eye contact with her.

The younger one, maybe mid-twenties, could have either been mixed race or Middle Eastern in ethnicity, with his hair in 'cornrows'. The man opposite seemed about twenty years older, his cropped red hair simmering into white at the sideboards, framing a rugged, craggy face.

She forced herself to relax; though she did not consider herself pretty in a conventional sense—her mouth being somewhat wide, her hooked nose being a touch too big, in her opinion—she was no stranger to male attention.

Taller than average, with bright eyes and dark curly hair bouncing, just shy of the beginnings of a figure some described as 'man-killer'.

To her mind, it was a euphemism for 'big tits, tight waist and wide hips'. Though her full figure precluded her from catwalks, she knew how to dress.

As the train slowed towards her stop, she clutched her woollen beige jacket to her throat and stood. Her heart flicked against her chest as the two men stood. She briefly considered sitting again but convinced herself she was being paranoid.

She felt a slight relief when, on alighting from the train at the Crewe station, the two gentlemen remained.

Her next train would be eleven minutes and take her the rest of the way to London. Where in London?

Watching the two policemen approach her, she guessed the decision would be taken out of her hands.

It took her a moment to figure out what looked out of place.

It dawned she had seen the Cheshire police wearing baseball-style caps on her journey up at this same train station, and when she had asked a fellow passenger, she had been educated that even the most senior police in Cheshire wore them. The tall helmets these two men wore were now used for ceremonial events only.

They stopped in front of her, right in her personal space.

"Miss Arabella Andaloro?" asked the taller of the two, with the skin of match-striking roughness.

"Yes?"

"We need you to come with us, madam?"

"I am not going anywhere without you telling me what this is about."

The shorter of the pair answered, "You may need to sit, Miss Andaloro."

"I am sure you'd have enough time to catch me if I faint."

They straightened, and the taller of the two said, "Miss Andaloro, Claudia Lowndes was murdered inside your apartment two nights ago."

Arabella felt her insides vacuum out.

All she could say was, "Who did it?"

"We can't say currently. You need to come with us to answer questions."

"Am I under arrest?"

Though sliding into a daze, she could see the question briefly flummox the pair before the taller answered, "No, Miss Andaloro. But we believe whoever did this might have been targeting you."

"OK," she replied, gesturing her willingness to go with them.

Her mind flicked between her anguish for Claudia, the confusion of why this had happened and how the two men stood on either side of her like guards leading her to the gallows.

As they walked her out of the small station and down the street, she asked, "Why did you not park in the station's car park?"

She thought they flicked a look at one another before one answered, "We rarely stretch our legs."

"You saw fit to parade me to onlookers for exercise?"

"Not all, ma'am."

They rounded her into a small, isolated car park occupied only by a black BMW M4 and a dark blue Lexus LC500. She thought she could see someone in the Lexus's driver seat.

"Where is the police car?" she demanded.

"It is an unmarked vehicle."

She barely registered the click of the Lexus door opening. Her heartbeat and breathing accelerated as they walked her to within a few feet of the vehicle.

The officer beside her raised his voice. "Sir, please stay back."

The ash-blond, stocky man said in non-native Italian, "Questi uomini non sono poliziotti. Ti stanno rapendo."—*These are not policemen. They are kidnapping you.*

She instantly knew this to be true.

Her captors, seemingly believing the leather jacket-wearing man not to know English, and they not being able to speak Italian, stood in front of her, making their gestures larger while blaring, "Stand back!"

The scene ignited in a frenzy of punches, head butts, foot sweeps, and finally, head stamps.

Though she backed away in adrenalised shock, she did not run.

The ash-blond man stood over his fallen prey and said, "Carlo Andaloro is a friend of mine."

She sucked in the air to say, "Then phone him. I haven't been able to."

"Neither can I."

"Then why should I believe you?"

"Check their pockets. You won't find handcuffs. And where are their radios? Take the keys, check that Beemer, and tell me if you think it's a police car. But for fucksake, get a move on because someone is bound to be along soon."

She remained rooted but said, "Just because they are fraudsters doesn't mean you are not."

His face broke into annoyance. "I can't force you to come with me. If you're going to be fucking silly, then at least take either my car or this car and drive as far as you can. Hand yourself into the real police for all I care, but I wouldn't return to Italy. If you have a better idea of how best to protect yourself, fine. I can rest easy that I tried."

"Tell me something about my brother that only I would know."

"I can't—not really. All I know is he's a crazy Italian fuck, who gets off on embroiling himself and then walking out of situations that should kill him. But he's scared this time."

She nodded, "Good enough. I will come with you."

Arturo Bianchi gripped the phone in fury as he listened to the disappointment streaming into his ear.

He ground his toecaps into the carpet of his sports bar office.

Pictures of himself with Canadian sports stars adorned the walls. Two TVs hung at the front; the left one spliced into rectangles, showing various security images of the club, the right one for entertainment.

He spoke venomously down the phone. "You think I am fucking stupid. You've taken my money, and you can't even kill one bitch architect?"

The British voice on the phone protested, "Some prick came out of nowhere and ambushed my men."

"You expect me to believe that?"

"If I was gonna fack you over, I'd have taken your knicker and not called. But if you think you would be more successful with another organisation, you say the word, and you'll receive your deposit back. Minus expenses."

Arturo forcibly relaxed. He knew the man on the other end of the line belonged to an organisation that had as much chance as any on the British Isles of carrying out his wishes.

"Do what you have to do. The longer this goes on, the worse it is for everyone, eh."

"I get it. I didn't think she'd have some ultraviolent ghost watching over," said the Londoner, and then in a parody of Arturo's Canadianism, continued with, "But he'll be dead along with her…eh."

7

Aaron Edmonds almost forgot his being held captive as he watched the Netflix show 'The Crown' from the sofa. Only the rattle of handcuffs as he drank his tea reminded him.

The current scene showed the Princess Diana character giving an exposé interview to a British-Asian interviewer.

The room smelled of marshmallow and Irish cream from the air freshener perched on the mantlepiece and the lemon 'Shake-n-vac' from the dark green carpet.

The big Fijian sat in the chair to his left, half facing him and the television. He called to the man opposite him, the one with the wide Mohican and rough beard, "Can you remember this happening?"

They had been careful so far not to use one another's names.

"Vaguely remember her doing that interview. That actress's got her mannerisms, the way she tilts her head and looks out of her eyelashes."

"Was everyone in England talking about this at the time?"

"I was only young, can't really remember. No one I knew gave a fuck."

"Why did she go on there, telling everyone about Charles's girlfriend? I thought she was also **_bagging off out of watch_**?"

"I think it was to get back at him. He cheated with one woman, but she was under more bedsheets than the Klu Klux Klan."

"Was that the reason, though?"

The Mohican, seemingly irritated, answered, "How the fuck do I know? Princess Diana wasn't exactly my babysitter. Any other questions?"

"Yeh. What does 'no pun intended' mean?"

Edmonds frowned, wondering how he would answer the question. The Mohican began with, "It's like…like a pun is a play on words, ain't it?"

"Like what?"

"Like, I dunno, a duck walks into a bar and asks for a pint. He necks it in front of the barman, and when asked to pay, he says, 'Put it on my bill'. That's a pun, get it?"

"Yeh, his bill, like his beak. Not bill, like the cheque," said the Fijian. "But what does no pun intended mean?"

The Mohican sounded a little exasperated to Edmonds as he said, "I dunno, like maybe the barman says, 'Get out. You're barred for foul play. No pun intended'. Get it, the duck might have thought he meant 'fowl' play, as in F.O.W.L and thought he was being racist against ducks, so the barman says 'no pun intended'. Get it?"

"Sort of, yeh."

After a few minutes of quiet, the Mohican looked at his phone and announced, "That's him. Watch this one."

The Fijian nodded.

Aaron put his wrists in his lap to stop the handcuff chain from making a noise as he heard the Mohican converse with another man in the kitchen.

His heart rate rocketed when the visitor appeared with the Mohican shadowing him.

Though a touch shorter than average, the bald man with dark eyes had a compact frame that seemed magnified in Edmond's eyes.

He took a step forward and held out his hand. Edmonds almost involuntarily clasped it. The man held it without squeezing and said, "My name is Carlo Andaloro, the brother of Arabella Andaloro. The lady you came to murder."

Edmonds opened his mouth, but no words came out.

Carlo then said, "It's OK. Enjoy your cup of tea."

These might have been the most menacing words Edmonds had ever heard.

Edmonds spluttered, "I am part of the Norland-Green family."

The man smiled. "I do not care if you belong to Satan's hordes."

The Mohican reached out an edged hand to, but not touching, Carlo's navel and murmured, "We might have to talk about that."

Carlo switched his gaze to the Mohican.

The Mohican held it, even when Carlo said, "There is no way; unless I die, I do not get from this man what I want. Then you do not have to worry because I am going to fucking murder everyone involved in trying to kill my sister."

Aaron looked at the two men who, despite their proximity to one another, seemed like gunslingers contemplating their next move.

"I appreciate that, Tony Montoya, but do me a favour, and let's talk in the kitchen. He isn't going anywhere."

Connor listened to the ring and the immediate answer of "Yes" from the woman's voice.

He stood just off a coffee and cakes van stall outside a motorway services entrance. He had a view of the restroom Arabella had entered from his position.

"It's me."

"Are you alright?"—*Are you under duress?*

"I am fine," answered Connor—*I am not under duress.*

Connor had worked as a black operations agent for over half a decade. Bruce McQuillan, a mercurial Scotsman, had recruited him, seeing Connor's potential despite the criminality of his family and background.

However, Bruce, a former SAS soldier, had now taken an official position within the UK security services.

Connor now reported to Ciara Robson, a woman he partnered with on several missions. McQuillan then moved her into a role, shadowing him, giving her more and more responsibility before ultimately handing her the reins.

And Connor had approved, despite her admitting his ability on the street far exceeded hers because she had been a quick-thinking, courageous and aggressive agent.

And despite them previously having sex on several occasions, neither had unduly struggled with the transition of her becoming his superior.

"What's up?"

"If you have anything for me in the immediate, I am going to have to request you clear it, please."

"Can I ask why?"

"Remember the baldy fellah who helped me

in the Far East?"

Despite the security of the line they spoke on, using outwardly vague phrases had become habitual to both. He referred to Carlo aiding him—them—in a mission to salvage a renewable technology in Japan.

If Carlo hadn't helped him, the technology might have been destroyed at the behest of those who relied on oil for their riches, and Connor would have died.

"Do what you have to do," said Ciara. "I'll wait for your call, stating you can return to duty."

"Thank you," said Connor before ending the call.

Arabella exited the restroom, and he watched for watchers as she approached. He couldn't see any.

Once back in the Lexus, she asked, "Are you going to tell me what is happening?"

"Hang on," said Connor, dialling another number.

"Yeah," answered John Foley.

"I've got her," said Connor. "I can't get hold of her brother."

"He's here," said Foley. "Listen, we have to talk about something."

"Hang on," said Connor, disengaging the Bluetooth.

"Go on."

"I didn't get a chance to tell you before, but that Norland-Green crew are branching out and moving up in the world. If I were you, I'd either give the kid back unharmed or make sure he never came back to tell this story—cos it'll be a full-scale street war, and you can only survive so many of them. It's been as much as Vili and I could do to stop your friend from fucking him up 'til you got a chance to speak to 'im."

This news hadn't been new to Connor. Indeed, he'd been thinking along the same lines.

The Norland-Green Syndicate had been an amalgamation via several marriages between the Norlands of Essex and the Greens of Hornchurch.

To Connor's knowledge, the Norlands, reputed to be the brains of the union, controlled a few of the inlets along the Thames and had silent stakes in a couple of the shipping companies. The Greens enforced the distribution of the product. The partnership had proved successful, and Connor admired how the marriages almost feudally guarded against criminal greed imploding the alliance.

Indeed, Connor, Luke and Thomas had floated the idea of reaching out for a distribution deal. They had been reticent as they'd heard reports of the family ripping off outsiders. Connor had known since very young that it was standard practice amongst criminal entities working together that anything from 'holding back' on shares right through to ripping one another off was the norm. If it ever existed, the old 'honour amongst thieves' died out in the 1950s.

Still, obtaining a deal with Norland-Green was seen as a lucrative ticket, and Norland-Green would exploit this by getting prospective partners to do their dirty work.

Connor spoke, "Do you know anyone who could engineer a meeting between me and 'the stretched man'?"

The moniker belonged to Alexander Norland due to his height and wiry physique.

"I might know a guy who knows a guy," said

Foley. "You sure?"

"He's a businessman."

"He's also fuckin' dangerous, is what he is."

Connor knew this. But he also knew it would be more unnerving for the crime lord if Connor turned up alone.

"He's the more reasonable and powerful of their hierarchy. Can you set it up for me, John?"

What Connor was asking was, would he? Following a pregnant pause, Foley answered, "It'll have to be me. Not who I represent."

That meant John would enquire himself, not through his MC—Motorcycle Club. And Connor knew that would be against the rules.

"Nah, mate, don't do that. Take it to your guys. If they knock you back, I'll find another way."

"Alright."

"Put our fiery friend on the phone."

Connor handed the mobile over and said, "Tell him I want a word with him after."

She looked at him hawkishly.

As predicted, she spoke in Italian once her brother answered. Connor had only a light to fair grasp of the language. He knew enough, along with watching her expressions and listening to her tone, to get the gist.

First, she asked if she could trust Connor. Then demanded to know what was going on.

Finally, he saw her sag when her brother confirmed her friend had been murdered.

He guessed she hadn't quite allowed herself to believe it from the faux policeman he had saved her from.

Connor beckoned for the phone when she

didn't speak, which slid into his hand.

"Listen to me," he said. "Don't touch that man."

"I need information. Then I need him to suffer. No women, no kids, everyone knows that."

"They'll just send someone else. Someone better this time. They won't take a chance. You need to cut this off at the source."

"How? *Ravoli e una bottiglia di vino?*"

"I'll go and see these people. I'll bring your sister up to you. Take her somewhere safe and stand on me. You owe me that."

Alexander Norland watched the white ball bounce off the cushion of the snooker table to glide into position for the black.

He ran a hand through his wavy dark blond hair, striped with white, with a side parting and curled at the nape of the neck.

"Nice, Alex," said the stout, white-collared Jimmy, a friend since their seventies childhood and one of his primary estate agents.

The need to place the white ball in an appropriate position after a pot was one of the reasons he enjoyed snooker so much. It punished you for being too focused on tasks without thinking of repercussions. Through too much thought regarding the white's positioning, you might not even pot the ball.

Only on the second frame, the tall, angular Norland hadn't even removed his immaculately tailored grey suit jacket. Generally, it would come off later, then the waistcoat, before the tie and top button, towards the night's end.

As he wandered around the other end of the table, his towering, broad driver-slash-minder for the night entered and said, "They are here, Mister Norland."

"Send them in, Harry," the crime lord answered. "I'd make yourself scarce for a while, Jimmy."

His friend nodded before making a box by touching his forefingers to his thumbs and pretending to take a snapshot of the balls' position.

"Fack off!" exclaimed Norland before they laughed, and Jimmy wandered off.

The two Green associates appeared behind his driver, the shorter, darker-haired one looking at him in the face in what Norland knew to be an attempt not to show fear. The other seemed unashamed in his inability to make eye contact.

"Come closer, lads," invited Norland.

When they had both stepped forward into conversation range, Norland leant against the snooker table and looked down on them like a father asking his two young sons about an incident at school.

"What's your names?"

The shorter one replied, "James."

The taller murmured, "Stephen."

Though Alex had heard him fine, he still said, "Speak up, son."

"Stephen," he replied without looking up.

"Tell me what happened, then."

James said, "We did as we were told. And it was going well. No scenes or anything. She followed us to the car park, the small one out the way. There was another car there, though. Wasn't there when we left ours. And out gets this bloke. Blindsides us. Must have been tooled up. We woke up, and they were both gone."

"This man. Describe him to me."

"He was—" began James.

"Not you. I want to hear from Stephen."

"He…he…was about six foot two. About sixteen stone. Built."

Alex nodded slowly before asking James, "Does that sound about right?"

James's eyes flickered before he said, "He wasn't that big. I don't even reckon he was six foot and more like thirteen stone."

"Alright," soothed Alex. "People's memories get hazy when it comes to violent attacks."

Both nodded their agreement, and Alex said, "Stephen, go to the bar and ask for my cigars. Get yourself a drink while you're at it. You look like you need one."

Once Stephen had wandered out of earshot, Alex reached into the inside of his suit jacket and removed a needle knife. The brass handle and the carbon steel blade glinted in the overhead lights.

When the fear swirled in James's eyes, Alex said, "Stab this through his brainstem. I don't want blood everywhere. My driver will help you get rid of the body."

"But…but…I've known him for years."

"What did Mister Green say to you before you came over?"

James met his eyes. "To do whatever you tell me to do."

"Correct. So I don't give a fuck how long you've known him for. He's weak, making him a liability and a fuckin' liar. Now, you can go and clamp his forehead with your hand and shiv the cunt where his skull meets his spine, or the pair of ya can die. Your choice."

After a moment, the trembling hand hovered over his and took the knife.

Alex felt excited by the power enveloping him as James stalked away. To rule over the life and death of a man was a great privilege and responsibility.

He felt himself slowly nodding as he watched the young man approach his colleague.

His eyes narrowed as he saw James stand still within a few feet of Stephen, and he watched his shoulders and upper back rise and fall in tandem with his breathing.

Then, like a young, clumsy leopard, he darted forward, smacking his hand onto his friend's forehead and driving the cylindrical blade into the base of the skull.

Alex—despite James partially obscuring his view—could see the rigidity of brain death fired into the victim. James kept holding his prey long after his death.

The crime lord looked over at his driver and gave him a nod. His minder approached James and gently prised him off the corpse. The dead body fell with a thud on the deck.

As his driver led James toward Alex, like a nurse guiding a mental patient, the Norland-Green crime lord began to clap.

"Come 'ere geezer. Come 'ere."

When his driver planted the wide-eyed James in front of him, he slapped his hands on his shoulders and said, "Now we have a killer. You are more useful now than you ever were."

"I…I…," stammered James.

Alex's hands slid from his shoulders to his face. "Don't you worry about it. It's always like this the first time. But you did it. You are now a murderer."

Alex smiled on the inside as he watched his words sink into the shorter man's face, and then he continued, "But I am an accomplice to that murder. We are in this together. And don't worry, everyone makes mistakes, but you cleaned up after yourself."

James nodded slowly, and Alex said, "You work for me now. I've spoken to Mister Green, and he's happy. Before you help Daniel with the body, I want you to go through the back and fetch my snooker partner. I have a game to win."

8

Connor stood in a kitchen with John Foley and Vili, drinking black coffee from a ceramic mug—dark grey outside with orange innards.

The Yorkshireman had left Arabella with Carlo to give them some privacy.

He'd been expecting something a little more run-down and rustic. Instead, it looked highly upmarket, clean, and tidy, but lived in. Red stone walls contrasted with the dark wood tiles.

Modern and shiny appliances sat on the kitchen countertops, and the sunlight percolated through flower-patterned windows.

"It's a bit posh and well-kept for a safe house, isn't it?"

"It belongs to my auntie and uncle," announced Foley. "They are skiing in Switzerland at the moment."

Connor and Vili crowed in unison, "Ooooohhhhh."

"Couldn't give a fuck. I am proud my family has done well."

Vili asked, seemingly genuinely confused, "Why are you such a naughty boy then, John?"

"You have to be poor to be a non-conformist? Look at Prince Harry. Went to *Ganners*, dressed up as a Nazi, married a mix-race girl, and he's royalty."

"Good point, well presented," smiled Connor, who had read in one book that *'naughty men are born, not made'*. Indeed, Connor knew the average law-abiding citizen might be surprised by how many criminals came from middle-class backgrounds.

Connor changed the subject with, "Did our Italian friend play well with the captive?"

"Sort of," said Foley. "He was hurting him in a way that didn't leave many marks. He showed us how to waterboard using a plastic bag wrapped around the mouth and a shower head. Vili and I had to hold the geezer's head over the bath. Lord Voldemort wasn't even asking him questions after a while—think I'd be the same if I had a sister and someone tried to murder her."

"Who is he, Connor?" asked Vili. "That tiny man was ready to go with the both of us earlier."

"Everyone is tiny to you, Vili," said Foley.

Connor fought his reluctance to divulge the Italian's background, but his friends deserved to know.

"He's one of the 'Ndrangheta's top assassins. Not just a button-man or a John Wick type, but someone who can conduct paramilitary operations."

"What's the 'Ndrangheta again?" asked Vili. "An Italian Mafia, isn't it?"

"Yeh," replied Connor. "Has its roots in the south of Italy in Calabria. They aren't as burnt into the public consciousness as the Sicilian Mafia, but a lot of experts say they are more dangerous."

Foley nodded. "The first I heard about them was when I watched a series called *'Bad Blood'* a few years back. Some of our chapters do business with their proxies."

"What's his military background, then?" asked Vili, sipping his coffee.

"Two REP French Foreign Legion. And don't ask me how I know this, but the French Government used to select him for missions when they couldn't risk a Frenchman being caught."

"So he's an Italian Rambo then?" asked Foley.

"Pretty much."

Vili asked, "If he's so high up in this bad boy Mafia, why does he need our help?"

"I am not sure what's gone on," answered Connor.

They heard footsteps, and Carlo appeared. He gave a half-nod-half-bow to Connor.

"She told me what you did. Thank you."

"Don't worry about it. Where is she now?"

"Taking a shower and resting," replied Carlo before gesturing to Foley and Vili. "They said I couldn't….damage the hostage until you say—and you had a plan."

Connor looked at Foley, who said, "The MC can arrange a meet, Connor, but they can't guarantee your security unless you have something to offer them. Otherwise, I can arrange a meeting, but you'll have no protection."

Connor nodded. "We might do business down the line, but for now, all I need is the meet arranging."

"Why are you going in alone?" Vili exclaimed. "He's a shark of a man."

"Like I said, he's also a businessman."

"Exactly! What's saying you have anything to offer him over what this geezer in Canada can offer? Unless…" trailed off Foley.

"Go on," said Connor.

"Unless this street rumour that you have access to a drug that has the high without the low."

Connor simply stared at Foley, who

exclaimed, "Fuck me, I thought that was an urban myth. That's why I didn't even mention it to you."

Carlo asked, "What is this?"

"It's none of your beeswax," said Connor.

"Beeswax?"

"It means I am keeping it to myself for now," answered Connor, knowing he'd have to tell Carlo eventually.

The Yorkshireman had been close to a former Dutch crime lord named Raymond Van Der Saar before he died in a shootout orchestrated by Irish gangsters.

Van Der Saar's chemists had developed a drug that gave a high similar to cocaine but vastly mitigated the emotional 'come-down'.

Connor had tried the drug named NoLo. Though he found the myths were exaggerated—he had had better highs—indeed, the come-down had been mild.

And the Italian had loyalty to the Calabrian Mafia, and when they found out, they would put pressure on the Van Der Saar group for distribution.

Raymond Van Der Saar had been all about the experience his drugs could provide, and thus, one of his stipulations had been his product was not to be cut up at the supplier level. Many omitted this criterion because the missed profits were huge. The Ryder family kept to the rule and only dealt with the affluent in York, north of Leeds, Harrogate and other cities. Connor had a strong working relationship with Van Der Saar's successor and former head of security, Rayen Hauer, who thus far had kept to his predecessor's rule.

However, Connor doubted many men could

hold true to a dead man's wishes in the face of the billions to be made.

Carlo answered, "As you wish."

Alessio stood in a room of smoke-grey walls—not a dissimilar colour to the fifty-year-old's hair, though it frosted white at the temples.

The black leather seats gazed back at him, as did the floor-to-ceiling portraits—though the depictions of Augustus and Caligula also stared at one another.

To his front sat a grand, handcrafted elm wood table. On it lay a solid gold ashtray still smouldering with the end of a cigarette.

Behind the table sat Italo Mauro, the nearest the 'Ndrangheta had to a Capo dei Capi—*Boss of bosses*.

Italo, now in his mid-seventies, had a full head of hair—albeit white. However, the eyebrows remained dark, as did the irises.

Alessio admired how the old man wore his dark suit like he had a symbiotic relationship with it.

Italo leant back and asked in his Calabrese Italian, without any apparent malice, "Where is he, Alessio?"

"He is in England," came the reply in the same language.

"And his sister?"

"Still alive, presumably. The wrong girl has been killed. It seems she was house-sitting while the sister was away."

Alessio felt a little strange referring to Arabella as 'the sister'; he had known her for years.

"Do they know they have fucked this?"

"Yes."

"Then you are certain?"

"I haven't seen a body, sir," said Alessio.

The older man did not now leave Calabria. The last time he did, he barely survived an assassination attempt by dissenting members of the Camorra during a sit-down in the picnicking area of The Appennino Lucano - Val d'Agri - Lagonegrese National Park.

"If they have failed, this is a problem. 'It being less difficult to obtain forgiveness for it after it was done, than permission for doing it'. You have heard this quote, yes?"

"Yes."

"Then tell me."

"Asking Carlo not to take revenge for his sister's murder is easier than asking him to let it happen."

"Almost all men would accept the former, no matter what they say in bars or parties. And Carlo would have been the exception if not for his oath. But no man would, or should, be expected to hand over his blood—no matter what he's part of."

"But he can't hide forever."

"He won't be hiding."

Alessio frowned. "He'll offer his own life for hers?"

"Carlo knows if he is gone, no one will protect his sister. His mother lives here and comes under our wing," said Italo. "Besides, what does he love more than anything else?"

Alessio's eyes widened with the realisation. "Combat against the odds—he's going to Canada."

"That is right, my advisor."

"Then we have to alert them?"

Italo smiled, "No. We have fulfilled our part of the agreement. We did not interfere. Their assassin's incompetence led to this."

"But they might renege on our deal?"

"They will not. You will meet Mister Bianchi in Lisbon."

"He has accepted that?"

"Not yet. You must feign fury at this turn of events. You will tell Bianchi that we no longer have confidence in his organisation's ability due to his clumsiness."

"You want to terminate the deal?" asked Alessio, alarmed.

"No. I want you to make him believe we do. He does not have many options—some, but we are his best bet. Make him convince you of his worth. Make a display of being unconvinced, and allow him to talk you into proving himself."

For a moment, Alessio wondered if this had been the old man's idea all along.

"Yes, Don Italo," answered Alessio as he turned to make for the door.

Before he reached it, Italo called out, "Alessio."

"Yes, Don Italo," he answered, turning back.

"Missus Andaloro is a friend of ours. Put a discreet security ring around her. And make Bianchi aware that if he attempts to assassinate an old woman in Calabria, then everyone he holds dear will die."

Alessio nodded, "Yes, Don Italo."

9

Connor imagined the plume of his breath despite the summer edging into autumn.

In 'The Swan' pub car park, he sat in a ten-year-old silver Honda Accord with the windows down, over a hundred metres from the tailors across the road.

The black operations agent had arrived a couple of hours before to observe, having completed a couple of drive-bys. John Foley had done the same but had taken up position at the rear of the building, in the car park of a flooring store.

The words 'Norland Tailors' had been elegantly carved into the two-tone wooden upper skirting of the shop.

With the time for the meet approaching, Connor hit call, and the Bluetooth linked to Foley, who answered, "I haven't seen anyone go in through the back."

"Same out the front. Everyone who has gone in has come back out. He must have his muscle inside with him."

"Seen. I'll come in with ya."

"Nah, don't. Let's stick with the plan. There's no reason I should be in longer than half an hour. That's when you can storm in like a *Sass bloke* into an Iranian Embassy."

"Well, you don't want a Para coming in to rescue a Bootneck…again….so keep your guard up. I know you're a bit of an Achilles, but he's a fuckin' naughty geezer."

"So you've seen *Troy*, then?" asked Connor,

baiting his friend.

"I'll have you know I've read *The Iliad*."

"What will your mates back in **the Reg** say when they find out you read for pleasure?"

"Shame literacy doesn't equate to kit awareness, eh **Sea Hat**?" replied the former Para, referring to a media story of a rifle lost on a Royal Marine training exercise.

Connor ignored the jibe and said, "I never got the fascination with Achilles. Hector's the true hero—Achilles was the best scrapper the Greeks had, and a fucking Demi-god who's fuming cos Big H has killed his best oppo. Hector knows all this and fights him anyway—"

"Nah, mate, he runs away when Achilles actually rocks up. He's forced to fight him in the end. I mean, Tyson might have frightened the shit out of Bruno, but Big Frank didn't jump out of the ring, did he?"

Connor smiled, "Suppose not."

"Do you know who the real hero of that story is?"

"Go on," said Connor, despite guessing.

"Paris. Loses the only proper straightener with swords he 'as to Menelaus—the only reason he isn't killed is because a goddess thinks he's cute and rescues him. For the rest of the war, he hides behind his 'bow 'n' arrow' like a pussy. While all this is going on, he's shagging a bird who's as gorgeous as Ana de Armas with Kate Upton's tits!"

Connor smirked before ending the call with, "Right, I've got to get into character. Out."

He got out and walked to the tailor's shop, swilling saliva around his gums.

With a cursory glance through the window, he opened the door and stepped inside.

Leather sparkling under a chandelier. Diamond flooring and beautiful suits hung on both sides.

Connor inhaled the pine and blackberry air.

Despite his alertness to danger, he couldn't help but admire the place.

The clicking of footsteps turned Connor's head towards the opening of a corridor in the corner.

A three-piece navy suit with a white collar appeared with Alexander Norland inside it.

Connor judged him to be just over six foot one and thought he had the look of a lighter-haired Colin Firth.

"Mister Reed. I almost did not believe you to be real," said a voice full of London character.

"Shorter than you expected, am I?"

"Nah, I asked around. I heard you weren't exactly Geoff Capes."

"I appreciate you calling me Mister Reed, Mister Norland. The Reed part, I mean. Most assume my surname to be Ryder."

His father had once explained to him that Connor would keep his mother's name so as not to be tarnished by the nefarious activities on his father's side of the family.

"Like I said, I do my research," said the Essex crime boss. "You can call me Alex if you like."

"Then you can call me Connor."

Norland nodded, "You fancy a cuppa? Just put the kettle on?"

"Please, black, no sugar," replied Connor without hesitating.

"Biscuit?"

"Not unless you have one of those McVitie's Gold bars."

Norland began chuckling. "As a matter of fact, I fackin' 'ave."

"The most underrated biscuit ever," said Connor with a smile. "In that case, I'll have my coffee white. Something about dipping a biscuit into black coffee seems wrong to me."

"I know exactly what you mean. Be right back."

Connor began to peruse and admire the quality of the suits. When Norland returned with his Chelsea mug and biscuit, he asked, "You ever had a bespoke suit made?"

"I haven't," replied Connor, dipping the Gold bar and snapping a bite.

"Why not?"

"Because I'll get fucked off when I inevitably rip it or spill something on it," he replied, holding the mug and bar up for emphasis.

Norland smiled, "You see, having it cleaned or repaired adds character."

"I'd like to see you have that conversation with my cousin."

"He wouldn't agree?"

"His motto is that if someone is selling something at ten thousand, then someone else is selling it at seven and a half."

Connor thought he saw a flash of irritation before Norland said, "Do you know how long my apprenticeship took to learn the trade of making bespoke suits?"

"Several years?"

Norland raised his eyebrows. "I am impressed. Nine, to be exact. Nowadays, a guy who has been cleaning windows a couple of fackin' years puts a tape measure around his neck and calls himself a tailor."

"I imagine that would be annoying. A bit like a first aider putting a stethoscope around his neck and calling himself a doctor."

Norland smiled with a nod. "Fack me! That comment just made my bollocks tingle. Come on, I'll show you around."

"Where's your muscle?"

"You saying I need some?" asked Norland with a raised eyebrow.

"You're too shrewd to meet me without it."

"And I would say the same about you, which is why mine are probably where yours is."

Connor hid his nerves with a sniff. "Let's hope they don't bump into one another."

Norland wandered over to one of the racks, and Connor followed him.

The London crime boss asked, "Do you know what goes into making one of these?"

"An initial consultation. Choosing the colours, fabric and style. Measuring. Baste fitting. I heard that a proper bespoke suit requires three fittings."

Norland nodded. "You're only partly right. Most people think putting a canvas through the suit makes it bespoke."

Norland touched his suit in tandem to saying, "There is so much more to it. Can they draft from a blank piece of paper? Do they farm out, or is it done by people they pay in their workshop? Stretching the garment with an iron, manipulating it, shrinking it, getting it to fit perfectly through the chest and all the hand finishing and sewing. The lapels hand padded."

"I understand, or am at least starting to," answered Connor sincerely.

"Do you know how much one of these costs?"

"I believe they start from two and a half thousand to seven and a half," answered Connor, briefly thinking of Tom again.

"They can go higher than that. Do you know why they cost that? Because it takes eighty hours to make one of these. But when you wear one, you feel like a sartorial god."

"Maybe we can do business on one, Alex," said Connor.

"Speaking of which, should we get down to it?"

"If you like. I'll have a Bushmills whisky if you have any?"

His answer caused a flick of Norland's eyebrows. "Ahh, so you know I like to mix business talk with liquor?"

"I also do my research."

"Which is why you know full well I have a twenty-five-year-old Port Finish Bushmills."

"I've been told you have everything."

The older man tilted his head with a smirk. He collected Connor's half-empty mug and wrapper before disappearing through the carved arches. Connor didn't discount a couple of Norland's goons appearing and slid his lighter-disguised Kubotan so that it peeked out of his pocket.

Not much of a defence against a gun, but something told him that Alexander Norland wouldn't risk putting bullet holes in suits.

The London crime boss appeared with two glasses and handed Connor one with the words, "Here you are."

"Thanks," nodded Connor, taking it.

Norland gestured to the two-seaters facing one another and said, "Let's sit. Been on my feet all fackin' day."

He mirrored Norland in sitting in one of the turquoise leather seats and sipping the smooth liquid with a hint of tart apple and butter.

"Thanks, Alex, that is superb."

"Glad you like it," Norland answered. "What got you onto Bushmills?"

"I used to read my dad's old Jack Higgins novels. The protagonist in those, Sean Dillon, used to drink Bushmills. I tried and liked it."

"Good taste. You'd make a fine tailor."

"I must say, it's unusual for men in our line of work to not only have such a complex 'day job' but to speak about it with such verve."

"Well, this had always been my passion. I fell into the other line of work."

"Yeh, I heard the story."

Norland asked, "What story is that, then?"

"Local gangsters tried to rip your old man off. He refused to back down, so they beat the fuck out of him. Young Alexander thinks, *'I ain't fackin' having this',* and turns into a vicious cunt to protect what's his. Gains a reputation and maybe likes it. Some…influential members of your community take notice. Take you under their wing, and you rise within our sphere."

Norland swirled his glass and sipped before

asking, "And what sphere is that?"

"The business we share. The side of you I want to appeal to."

"Then I'll tell you what you already know. When a customer asks me for a bespoke suit, we sit, agree on the suit and the price, and I always uphold my side of the deal. That is how reputations are made."

Connor nodded his agreement and said, "What if the customer died, and a new customer made a vastly more profitable deal, where he would go to you for all his suits?"

"I think now would be when we stop talking in code."

"I agree."

"What could you offer me that I couldn't get anywhere else?"

"I think you know, or you would have had your heavies in here, and I would have been carted off to the basement of this place for a 'Q&A'…well, at least, attempted to."

Norland smirked, "OK. There is a rumour that a Dutch organisation has developed a drug that gives you all the high of top quality cocaine with none of the comedown?"

"A little hyperbole, but essentially true."

"I am intrigued."

"The high is more subtle and serene than high-quality coke. There is always a bit of a comedown, if from nothing more than the contrast, but yes, it doesn't cement you into your bed the next morning."

"And your proposal is?"

"We need to diversify our transport routes.

You have ports down here."

"Interesting."

"There is one rule, though. It isn't to be cut."

Norland frowned. "I can't control that once it hits the street, even if I wanted to."

"Don't sell it to the street. Sell to the rich pricks on the dark blue areas of the Monopoly board."

Norland sipped his whisky. "Let me tell you something you might not know. Our friend in Canada must have a very powerful backer over there."

"What makes you say that?"

"I know the proxy he uses for investments here—it's not just casinos and petrol stations now. It's developments into the billions. And he doesn't have that kind of money, but whoever he's working for does."

"Give me two weeks. You'll get to keep the deposit he gave you, and you'll live long and prosper."

"Awfully confident geezer, ain't ya, given what you're up against. Pretty fuckin' heroic if you managed it."

"If I asked you to make me a bespoke suit that made me feel like a 'sartorial god', you'd be confident, wouldn't you?"

"Of course."

"Competence leads to confidence. It isn't the final action that is heroic. It's the hours and hours of physically sickening and mentally draining graft that go into getting good. The constant overcoming of your fear to push yourself out of your comfort zone. That's what's heroic."

Norland took a few moments to stare at Connor before saying, "I give you your two weeks."

Norland's next words doused the Yorkshireman's relief.

"But if you fail, then you personally deliver that girl. Cos if you don't, our families will go to war—and I am thinking you don't want another one of 'em anytime soon."

"War can keep you strong and focused. You know that."

"That depends on the outcome," said Norland. "A couple of high-temperature chill-pills turned the Japs from kamikaze demons to Pokémon-adoring and weird game show-loving, sleep-on-the-train corporate slaves."

"We'll have this discussion another time, Alex," said Connor, extending his palm.

They shook hands, and Connor left.

Arabella sat in the farmhouse living room, nursing the hexagonal blue mug of instant coffee.

Though the television emitted a game show, her ears tuned into the muffled voices from the kitchen. She knew the discussion centred on where they would place her for her protection.

Her annoyance began to steam into anger. She knew this had been partially triggered by the fact she had been used to being treated as a superior, or at least equal, for the last few years.

And now, she sat like a naughty child while the headmaster and her parents thrashed out the consequences of her bad behaviour. Except, this situation had been brought on by Carlo's bad behaviour. And it had been he who told her to stay where she was.

Finally, her anger burned into a rage, bursting

her out of her seat and into the kitchen.

The one who had rescued her, the one they called 'Connor', bolted towards her before the others reacted. He stopped short upon seeing it was her.

Carlo snapped, "Arabella, go into the other room and wait."

She slapped the air backhanded, "Questa non è la Mafia. Questa è la mia vita."—*This is not the Mafia. This is my life.*

"Arabella, go—" started her brother.

But Connor interjected. "Lei ha ragione."—*She is right.*

She watched Carlo's eyes flick between her and Connor before nodding his consent.

"OK," she said, "Bring me to date."

"Up to date," corrected Connor. "We are arguing about where to keep you."

"Why can't I stay here?"

The one she knew as John said, "Because the owners are due back. Plus, I don't want to put them at risk with you here."

Connor said, "Your brother and I agree you shouldn't hand yourself in. The people behind this might still reach you."

Arabella felt a coolness around the back of her neck. She asked, "Then why are you arguing?"

Again, she caught her brother glancing at Connor, who answered, "Your brother's chances of killing the man who ordered your assassination rise sharply if I am with him. Which leaves us with the question of what to do with you."

She frowned. "And?"

"I've told Carlo that we should leave you here under the protection of people I kn—"

"From this moment, my sister will not leave my side until the heart of that *bastardo grasso* no longer beats, and his lungs no longer take in the air."

"Just say 'Until he's dead', we're not in a Greek play," said Connor. "And all this might have been avoided if you hadn't **Pearl Haboured** his brother."

"Was you there?"

Connor conceded, "No, I wasn't."

"My sister stays where I can see her."

"Then stay in Leeds with her. Use my house. And I will sort this out," said Connor.

Carlo guffawed. "You think I would dishonour myself by sending you to hunt my bear?"

"Then what do you suggest?"

Carlo took a moment to speak. "My sister will come with us."

Foley broke the room's silence with a laugh. "So your idea of protecting your sister is to take her into enemy territory? Sounds like an episode of 'Bodyguarding for Retards'."

Arabella's stomach clenched, but before Carlo could retort, Vili asked with incredulousness steeped in his voice, "There's a programme called Bodyguarding for Retards?!"

The Mohican and Connor burst into laughter, and she watched her brother's face mercifully soften.

She smiled, too, but more out of relief.

Connor said, "If you don't trust anyone else, that might work."

The Mohican exclaimed, "Connor you're **having a fucking bubble**. A chick without any training whatsoever? I know you're good, but you're making life harder. Just leave her 'ere."

Connor quickly spoke before Carlo could speak. "I have plenty of friends I trust, but you're all criminals and could potentially be under police surveillance. I don't want to rope you into aiding a fugitive. Besides, she might be useful."

Arabella felt a burning indignation.

"And I have no say in this?"

"Do you have a better idea?" asked Connor, turning his blue eyes on her.

After a moment, she said, "No."

She looked at her brother. "E la mamma?" she asked—*What about Mum?*

"Nessuna donna civile viene toccata in Calabria."—*No civilian woman is touched in Calabria.*

"If you say so," she said.

Carlo whirled on her and growled, "You do whatever I or *Signor* Reed tell you, Arabella! I do not tell you about designing buildings, so you have no opinion on this mission. *Comprendere?*"

She narrowed her eyes and answered, "Certamente."—*Of course.*

Arturo Bianchi tried to fight through the fog of his anger to reach a clarity of thought; the problem should have been handled by now.

And he felt like he was being summoned.

Still, the sea air dived into his nostrils and opened his lungs.

He had expected to be summoned to one of the 'Ndrangheta strongholds of Switzerland or Germany.

Instead, he stood on the pier of Lisbon port looking at the angular ferry boat with the blue underbelly. He hadn't known what to expect; he had heard a massive superyacht would not fit in with the 'Ndrangheta's quieter persona compared to the other Italian Mafias. And he didn't think a small yacht or fishing boat would be appropriate either. So, hiring a ferry boat seemed perfect.

Alessio stood at the top of the stairs and beckoned Arturo over—who seethed at the perceived insult.

He jerked his head at his bodyguard, and they both walked over.

The nearer they got to the bottom of the stairs, the surer he was that the 'Ndrangheta Mafioso had orchestrated it for the effect of superiority.

"Welcome, Arturo. How was your trip?" asked Alessio in Italian.

Again, Arturo burned, knowing that Alessio knew his command of the language to be a little rusted.

Still, he replied in the same tongue. "It was good. A nice flight."

"Good to have a break away from it all, Arturo."

Only just catching the gist of the sentence, Bianchi switched to English.

"I am a very busy man. Why could this not have been done over the phone?"

"Some meetings need a personal touch," replied Alessio in English. "Besides, I think technology is making us all robots, no?"

"If you say so."

"Come on board," said the Italian with a smile.

Alessio gestured to his bodyguard to go first.

The Italian-Canadian crime lord's feet felt like cement, but he forced himself to ascend the chrome bars after him.

Once on board, he felt akin to being somewhere haunted.

"Follow me," said Alessio, walking into the darkening vessel.

Bianchi wanted to protest, but his ego prevented him—he didn't want to sound scared or weak.

Instead, he followed, but behind his bodyguard. The quietness of the ferry felt eerie, with the rows of grey leather seats facing one another. Out of the polished wood-framed windows to the left, he could see the muted civilisation and, to his right, the deep sea.

They followed Alessio up a spiral flight of stairs onto the second deck of the three-tier waterbus.

There stood three men, two taller and broader than his bodyguard and the other not far off.

"What is this?" he sneered, despite his intestines cooling. "A setup?"

"You know if that were the case, you would not see it coming, Arturo," announced Alessio. "Please sit."

Two curved red leather seats faced one another, and Arturo reluctantly sat when Alessio did.

The 'Ndrangheta man said flatly, "I am afraid our deal will have to come to an end."

This felt like a blow to the stomach with an iced fist to Arturo, who asked, "Why?"

"Why do you think, Arturo? We agreed to your terms of vengeance. Against one of our own, and you have failed to eliminate a civilian woman.

Your failure is due to incompetence and affects our business relationship."

"It is not a failure. It is a delay," said Bianchi, trying not to let his desperation show.

"What is the problem?" asked Alessio, severity in his voice.

"The girl must have been tipped off. My man over there got the wrong girl. We will find the right girl. It is inevitable."

Arturo's mind began to whirr. He knew this deal would still be attractive to the 'Ndrangheta. The quality of the pharmaceuticals he could supply meant he could always go elsewhere.

However, partnering with the 'Ndrangheta meant global distribution of his products, handy for when the heat domestically got too much. Though there were other global organisations, none had the foothold in Canada like the Calabrese had.

And he needed them if he was ever truly to become the boss of Canada.

He knew they knew how much he needed them, but he knew how attractive a business proposition he was to them.

Alessio straightened. "You have two weeks from now. Not a day more."

"I understand," answered Arturo. "Where is her brother? If I know where he is, I know where she is."

"We gave you an allowance for an eye for an eye. Knowing you intend to harm him, we will not tell you the whereabouts of one of our trusted brothers."

Arturo prevented a smirk from appearing on his face—*They don't know where he is.*

"But you have told him to stay out of the

way?"

"We told him not to retaliate. That was when we thought you had been successful. However, we cannot ask him not to protect his sister."

"Then you cannot ask me not to kill him if he gets in my way," said Arturo before slyly adding. "Besides, you and I know how good he is at following orders."

Alessio, seemingly not to hear the last part, said, "We would prefer one or the other, not both."

"If he is there, he is in the way. I will not take the risk."

"You mean you will not allow your men to take the risk?"

"I won't take the risk with my men."

Alessio nodded. "OK."

The two men stood and hugged lightly, tapping one another's back.

Once off the ferry and within the safety of the black Mercedes, Arturo immediately dialled a number into his phone.

When the London-accented voice answered, the Canadian said, "If you kill the woman within ten days, I will triple your rate."

10

Ciara Robson strolled through the sun splotches on the tarmacked path in Hyde Park. The trees stood protectively on either side, with their canopies shining like dim bulbs.

Approaching thirty, with dark tweed encasing the physique of a powerful gymnast, she barely registered the sly glances in her direction anymore.

London smelled the cleanest here, and the quiet chatter did not disturb the peace.

The bob-haired silver-blonde pondered whether to aid Connor Reed in his forthcoming Canadian adventure.

The two had long understood Ciara could only support Connor as an agent for the black operations group known only to a handful of people as 'The Chameleon Project'. However, this support would not extend to the former Royal Marine's taskings involving his place within his family's criminal enterprises.

This agreement had been passed down from her predecessor, Bruce McQuillan, who now worked in a more official capacity for the Government despite his activities remaining largely classified.

Still, Ciara wondered if she could use Connor's situation for political manoeuvring within her field. This is why she had asked to meet her former boss, something that had become rarer now.

Ciara spied McQuillan at a distance, sitting on a bench. She lamented it almost seemed out of place to see a man just sitting in public, seemingly taking in his surroundings without staring at a screen.

The Glaswegian, about twenty-five years her senior, still retained an aura of danger despite his appearance softening over the last few years.

He wore a grey suit with a light blue shirt beneath, the top two buttons unfastened.

Though she had felt increasingly more confident in her new role as time passed, she knew not to go against any advice Bruce might give her.

She didn't see him as a father figure exactly, just a man she had an immense sense of respect and gratitude for.

He stood as she neared before offering her his hand.

"Good to see you again, Ciara."

"You too," she said with a firm shake.

"Let's take a walk, and you can tell me what's on your mind."

She fell in step with him and said, "Connor is going to Canada to give his Italian friend a hand."

"Do you know the specifics?"

"Carlo Andaloro killed the brother of Arturo Bianchi, a —"

"A Marco Bianchi, former member of the Siderno crime family who decided to create his own family?"

"Yes. It seems Marco and his elder brother Arturo were estranged years before Marco broke away from the Siderno Group in which Arturo remained."

"Why?"

"Nothing concrete. However, the head of the Siderno Group in Greater Toronto, Giuseppe Zito—out of respect for his capo Arturo—requested Calabria to send someone to disrupt a meeting between members of the Bianchi and the Romano factions over there. He could have simply ordered Marco's assassination."

"And Andaloro disregarded the order?"

"Connor says Carlo Andaloro's orders were indeed to attack the Romanos to lead them to believe the Bianchi cartel had set them up to destroy any alliance. But he states it wasn't specified Marco or any of the Bianchi faction were off-limits."

"He believed the overall objective of collapsing the breakaway group could be just as easily achieved by killing Marco Bianchi and his deputies?"

"Correct. Except, Marco Bianchi only brought one of his leadership; the rest were bodyguards."

"Which makes Andaloro's successful ambush all the more impressive," said Bruce. "But being that he's been a soldier in both the military and mafia sense, he must have had his reasons to deviate from the mission brief."

Ciara knew that Bruce knew one of the explanations would likely have been the Mafioso's thirst for danger.

She said, "In the aftermath, it was arranged that Arturo would take over the Bianchi clan—thus ending the war with Sidernos—and be afforded the right to assassinate Arabella Andaloro as restorative justice, despite her civilian status."

"Instead, Claudia Lowndes was murdered in a case of mistaken identity."

Her surprise at his seeming all-knowingness had receded over the years.

"It seems Arabella Andaloro was away in Wales at the time. Miss Lowndes was house-sitting."

"Kathryn's people are searching high and low for Miss Andaloro. Why hasn't she turned herself in?"

He referred to Kathryn Bainbridge, the head of Scotland Yard.

"Her brother does not believe she'll be safe under protective custody. Believes it will just fix her location."

"Kathryn is one of the few I trust regarding protective custody. Give her the location of Miss Andaloro, and she'll do the rest."

"Connor said he won't go against Mister Andaloro's wishes on this. They have decided to take her with them."

Bruce slowed and looked at her. "They are going to take her to Canada?"

"Yes."

"He owes him for Japan."

"Yes."

Bruce referred to a mission to protect valuable renewable energy technologies in the Far East. Connor had called on Carlo to aid him, and the former French Foreign Legionnaire answered that call.

"Why are we having this conversation? It's up to you what you do with your personnel."

"Because I remember Marco and Arturo Bianchi's name coming up at one of the security briefs you took me on over a year ago."

She caught his face displaying a rare smile, before he answered. "I have a contact within the CSIS. Maybe this could be turned into an advantageous situation for all."

Ciara had hoped for this but didn't want to let it show.

"What would be their interest in Arturo Bianchi? As a rule, the Canadian Security Intelligence

Service wouldn't deal with organised crime. And surely Bianchi's group isn't large enough to appear on their radar yet?"

"Tell me what you know of Arturo Bianchi."

"Unlike his younger brother, he was born and raised until the age of seven in Siderno. By all accounts, a very traditional, loyal, and brutal Mafioso—a consistent earner. And seemed to have a close relationship with his brother until just before Marco broke away."

"Before? Not because of?"

"Reports suggest before."

She glanced at Bruce when he took a moment to say, "That Marco Bianchi, still a few years off being even forty, had the confidence to break away and take a number of soldiers with him seems strange to me."

"I agree. Even Gotti was in his mid-forties before he officially took over his crew."

"What else do you know about how Arturo has been running his new 'family'?"

"There is not much that's concrete—even for Jaime to find. Rumours of a partnership with a motorcycle gang of former special forces for distribution and enforcement. I don't have names for the club, let alone any individuals. Maybe just an urban myth or, at least, an exaggeration. The mafia using local MCs for distribution and head banging is common."

The Scotsman stopped to look at her. "The Red Hauser membership is made up exclusively of former tier one special forces from either side of the US-Canadian border. At least one major US MC tangled with them and decided never to do so again. If The Red Hauser and Bianchi plan on expanding, the CSIS won't want that."

"How…how do you know this, but Jaime doesn't?"

"Never rely on just one source of intelligence, Ciara, no matter how talented they may be. You need to continually develop your relationships. And no one needs to know everything you know."

"I understand," she said before asking, "Can the CSIS not shut them down?"

"That might involve an open warfare, which that country has not seen within its borders. The Canadians would be ill-equipped. And their relations with the US are currently frosty."

"So, a pair of highly trained assassins, coming in from overseas to cause…an inconvenience, might not be entirely unwelcome?"

"Maybe. I'll need to make a call. If it goes well, I'll patch you in."

"Thank you; I appreciate it."

"How are you besides all this?"

"Getting more and more to grips with it. Prioritising and organising," she said before glancing at him. "If I asked you what I needed to focus on, what would you say?"

He took a few steps before answering. "A good black operations chief needs three things—it helps to be proficient in more, but you need three: organising; political game—aka fostering the right relationships, as I said—and capable of ordering ruthless acts of violence. It helps if your people know you're capable of committing violence yourself, which is a given in your case."

"A bit like a Mafia boss."

With a glance, she caught him smirking as he

said, "Exactly."

Connor and Carlo stood outside Lambert Transport LTD, a quasi-front company owned by Connor's family.

Though out of sight, Connor could hear the muffled shouts of drivers and depot workers in the mid-distance, the clanking of containers being loaded or unloaded, and engines starting up on the other side of the depot.

The M621 motorway hummed in the distance.

The inert surveillance cameras lacked the red eyes of consciousness—they would be awakened once the trio had left the site.

He did not want to involve his family in any way, but it was the only place he could be sure of the security in which to administrate himself, Carlo, and Arabella.

He had called Tom, who had arranged a clean vehicle and had items he'd asked for and one of Connor's tactical 'grab-bags' picked up from his house.

His elder cousin had also provided Carlo and Arabella with a suitcase each after Connor had relayed their needs and clothes sizes.

Having slung the cases into the grey Suzuki Swift—which Tom had made a point of telling him had a 99.5% reliability rating—Carlo requested a word with Connor away from the car.

Once out of earshot, Carlo turned to him and said, "I know that Arabella and I might seem to fire in our conversations, but even if she was not my sister, I would still want to protect her. She is… she is a very good person."

"OK."

"She helps people, even when she does not have to. Even when they do not know she helps them, do you understand?"

Connor briefly thought of Grace. "Yes."

"So..I…err—"

Sensing what he might be getting at and the difficulty he had in expressing it, Connor cut him short with, "If you die, I will protect her like she is my sister."

Again, Connor thought of Grace and his son, Jackson, and felt a lurch in his stomach. He had just made a promise to someone whom he highly respected as a man and professional, but he didn't know all that well. Not only that, but the vow was also to protect—with his life, if necessary—a near-stranger when he already had a 'dependent'.

Connor banished the thought from his head—he refused to allow having a son to soften him or make him turn away from using his skills and position to help a good person.

"Thank you."

"I want you to remember that my family—the naughty ones, at least—have helped me to help you."

Carlo nodded and answered Connor's telepathic question. "If you die, I will make my skills available to them whenever they call upon me."

With that, the Mafioso extended his hand.

"Thank fuck for that," said Connor. "I thought you were going to suggest pricking our thumbs and mingling blood."

As the Englishman gripped the Italian's hand, Carlo said, "Her pussy is off-limits."

Before Connor could reply, his phone

vibrated against his leg. He'd had it calibrated to shake with a different pressure and cadence depending on who it was.

"OK, Tony Montoya," replied Connor.

He released Carlo's hand, answering his phone as he walked away.

"Yes."

"It's me," said the voice he recognised to be Ciara's.

They went through the security checks, and he said, "What can I do for you?"

"It seems that your target is of mutual interest to us. You'll be supported. I'll have any relevant information sent to you through the usual means."

The call ended, and Connor thanked the God he wasn't sure he believed in.

Arabella watched the two men's body language intently from inside the ugly car.

Her index finger and thumb rotated the ring on her right hand that covered her tattoo.

She could not remember the adult version of her brother displaying such regard for another man outside of his 'family'.

Even their father had to work for Carlo's respect once her brother reached his late teens.

And yet, Carlo had never spoken of this Connor Reed before.

She thought he might have been a former comrade from the French Foreign Legion, but that was not the case. Not to say that this Englishman had shown her brother anything less than respect in his words and mannerisms.

She watched them as they began to wander

back in conversation, Connor having put his phone back in his pocket.

They reached the Suzuki, and Connor Reed entered the driver's seat beside her brother.

Connor turned to her and said, "A national BOLO has been placed on you with the police, with powers to apprehend on sight."

She felt her heart hammer the air from her lungs, but she steadied her voice to ask, "What now?"

"The BOLO doesn't apply to your brother or me, thankfully. And we can't risk a fake passport—even if I knew someone who could forge the embedded microchip on a biometric passport, it would still take more time than we have."

"So, what are we going to do?"

"We had thought about slinging you in the back of a delivery truck and getting you over the border that way. But decided against it as it is, one—risky, and two—if you're caught, then we are."

"So, you're leaving me here."

She caught the look exchanged by the two men, and Connor answered, "Your brother, point blank, refuses that option. So, here is what we are going to do. We will get the ferry from Liverpool to the Republic of Ireland. You will stand separate from us. You will be stopped before the check-in gate, and two security guards will take you into the back office. They will release you to us when we get through customs."

She refrained from asking how Connor could guarantee this would happen or if it was necessary and instead replied, "OK."

He answered as if reading her thoughts, "We can't risk your name being flagged there. The Guardia might not have a BOLO on you yet, but that could change, and we don't need the UK police to know you've been in Ireland."

"What about when we get on a flight from Ireland to Canada? What then?"

"If the UK police have no reason to believe you're in Ireland, they won't request your name flagged at Irish airports. Since BREXIT, it's harder for the UK to apply for European Arrest Warrants. If they don't know you've been in Ireland, they won't guess you're off to Canada."

"And you know these security men personally?"

"No," said Connor. "A guy who knows them."

"And you want me to trust these people?"

"No, I am asking you to trust your brother, who trusts me. If you don't, then you can figure this out between yourselves."

Her eyes flicked to her younger brother, and she asked, "È questo l'unico modo?"—*Is this the only way?*

He answered, "È il modo migliore."—*It is the best way.*

When she gave him a barely perceptible nod, Carlo said in English, "Listen, sister, that animal does not have the type of soldiers to defeat us."

11

Michael Rose felt the wind buffet his leathers as his Kawasaki ZX-10R zipped by the Hyundai Kona on the Trans-Canada Highway heading towards a deciduous forest outside Greater Sudbury.

Traditional MC members derisively referred to the bikes like the one he now rode as 'Rice Burners' and their Italian counterparts as 'Pasta Rockets'.

However, Michael Rose did not care for tradition for tradition's sake; it made him smile that the MC members would remain stuck to their Harley-Davidsons even if other cruiser-type bike makes and models were superior.

And he felt an air of superiority that his MC could ride sports bikes in tandem—a harder prospect than with the cruisers.

That said, he had to admit that it would have been nice to sit on a cruiser with a view like this: lakes, forests and mountains on either side. Miles and miles unspoilt by civilisation—lack of humans meant lack of witnesses, making it an ideal location for drug factories.

He slowed the ZX-10R to take in the scenery before sliding off the freeway onto a smaller road and speeding up again.

Rose had been one of The Red Hauser's founding members and the éminence grise behind it. Rose had used political manoeuvring to install a puppet president to allow himself freedom of movement.

Rose knew if he wasn't the best soldier in The

Red Hauser, he certainly was not far off, and everyone else knew it. And in addition, he could organise and strategise.

Although, when civilians asked which was the best unit in the US SF community, he would always reply, *"At what?"*

The various units had different remits.

Rose had been part of the US Army's Special Forces, whose primary mission was to train and lead unconventional or clandestine guerrilla forces against a force occupying their nation.

Therefore, his training emphasised language and cultural sensitivity skills.

However, the need to know the political, economic and cultural complexities of regions in which they are deployed had helped Rose in his current position.

The Green Beret had been a member of the 5th Special Forces Group oriented towards the Middle East, Persian Gulf, Central Asia and the Horn of Africa and thus had been on almost continuous deployment.

Almost all the men in the Red Hauser stood as good warriors, but some were no more than *doorkickers*.

Riding alone did not bother him. His ability and the bike's performance meant he could outrun almost anything with wheels.

He pulled onto a street road and slowed down; he didn't want to be that criminal who got away with murder and dealing drugs only to get caught for speeding.

Finally, he hit a rural track, and after ten minutes of pothole avoidance, he made it to the overhead hanger.

Rose had always admired how the synthetic drugs lab lay beneath a properly functioning barn. The smell of cow shit and hay masked any chemicals cooking deep beneath it.

Cocaine and heroin, in addition to incurring exorbitant transportation costs, also required an inordinate amount of other chemicals to process.

However, meth, fentanyl and isotonitazene required much less and hadn't the costs of paying off Afghan or South American farmers and drug lords.

And the US had put pressure on China to ban fentanyl. So, domestically produced products could now be sold for more.

The outlaw biker couldn't be sure how many, but he knew there to be at least a handful of such facilities. When he pointed out that more facilities meant more potential security risks, Bianchi had mentioned eggs and baskets.

Michael cut the bike's engine, parked it on its rest and walked to a steel casing with a diagram of a telephone on it.

Opening the box, he lifted the receiver, punched in the ten-digit code and watched the barn door to his right open.

He always hated this part—to prevent the smell of chemicals from escaping, the door closed behind him with the steel door in front remaining closed for a few moments, temporarily locking him in a two-metre square space.

He took his helmet off and ran his fingers through his black hair that had, despite his thirty-three years—acquired some grey flecks—his father had referred to them as 'stars' when the same happened to him when Mike was a child. A week's facial growth showed more of these 'stars'.

He had kept his helmet on until now for the slight chance of digital or human law enforcement surveillance outside.

The door in front of him opened and belched a whiff of chemicals.

Down spiral metallic stairs, he reached the floor and looked through the perspex window at the scene; silver chemical caldrons reminded him of nineteen-sixties television robots.

The blue floor with white speckles looked out of place amongst the silvers, lights, and glass.

Walking along the corridor, he came to an entrance made up of two steel doors with black glass for windows that reminded him of a sinister medieval knight's helmet.

Beside it lay a panel of numbered and lettered buttons; he punched in the code, and the doors steamed open.

Arturo Bianchi lay on the couch in a room that looked a cross between youth social, bar, and surveillance suite.

A wall of screens stood to the left, showing not only views of the meth compound and the barn above but also images of routes in and out for miles.

Rose had once warned Bianchi these would be moot in the face of an air assault, and this was when the quasi-Mafia boss took him on a tour of an extensive and ongoing tunnelling network.

The Italian-Canadian had hired an Ecuadorian team to work on the project for a hefty pay packet. That way, he had been able to send them home happy and worried less about them opening their mouths in a local bar and attracting the wrong kind of attention.

Mike knew that on the outside looking in, one might struggle to see how Bianchi managed to fund this. A few years ago, the Bianchi family was a struggling off-shoot crew, pumping dope, counterfeit scams, robbing warehouses and thieving cars.

Now, they stood as a mighty narcotics outfit.

"Michael. Forever early, I see," said Bianchi, struggling to his feet. "How was your trip?"

"Quick and scenic."

Bianchi ambled over. He stood a few inches taller than the shade under-average Mike and shook his hand.

"I like the idea of it until I think of how cramped I'd be and how I like to relax when I travel. I don't want a car or a truck flattening me."

Rose could have told him about the sensation of riding—the sound of engine and wind, the changing temperatures, accelerations whirling around the ear and how the danger heightened awareness.

Instead, he replied, "It's not for everyone."

Bianchi clapped his hands together gently. "So, what brings you here, Michael?"

"You wanted to discuss a business proposal with me. I like a face-to-face for things like that."

The Mafioso nodded with unbelieving eyes but gestured to the bar behind him. "Would you like a drink?"

"Yeh," replied the outlaw biker. "A bourbon. Michter's if you still have it."

Bianchi did, and in a couple of minutes, both faced one another, drinks in hand.

"So, what changes do you want to make?"

Bianchi sipped and said, "The US

Government pressured the Chinks to ban fentanyl. So, there are lots of fiends on both sides of the border clucking. We are here to provide for them."

"I thought that's what we were doing?"

"Yes, us and every Canadian *hoser* and American *redneck*."

"And you have a way of getting ahead of the competition?"

"There won't be any competitors soon. The US and Canadian governments signed a policy of co-operation last week to target illegal synthetic opioid manufacturers."

Though Rose remained impressed by Bianchi's intelligence gathering, it always seemed like the phrases he used were regurgitated after being given to him by someone with authoritative intelligence.

But Mike found the crime boss's boasting about his government and law enforcement contacts grating.

Rose's forehead creased. "Talking about quitting?"

"You know better than that," said Bianchi before laughing. He always seemed to laugh at things that weren't funny.

"Tell me your plan," said Mike.

"It would be better if one of the lab jackets told you. But I know your mantra 'Need to know', so I memorised it. We cut it with xylazine; the effects last longer."

"That's what the dealers do already. It's called Traq Dope."

"Not like ours. Other chemical compounds make it more addictive. But because we do it in bulk, we can sell it cheaper."

"Sounds great," said Rose, raising his glass. "So, what is the problem?"

"It kills people. I mean, very quickly kills them."

Rose felt a whoosh in his stomach.

"A dead customer is a source of repeat business gone, so why would—" Rose stopped talking once he realised Bianchi wanted to make a killing in both aspects of the word.

"You're wanting to cash in and cash out."

"Exactly."

"Seems short-sighted," said Rose, his heart rate flicking.

"I have my reasons."

"How many of the users who'll take it will die?"

Bianchi shrugged, "Maybe half."

"And by the time the investigation ramps up, you'll have hit pause on distributing in North America, and you want my crew to tie up any loose ends."

"Cops don't care about drug dealers being murdered. You'll be doing them a service."

"Politicians don't like a sudden rise in body count."

"But I have just said—"

"Prison in the US is far scarier than here," said Rose. "It better be worth my boys' while."

Bianchi grinned. "You will all be multi-millionaires after this. And no one will stop us."

Connor scanned for 'shadows' as he stood in the glass-domed terminal queue for the Liverpool to

Dublin ferry.

So far, he hadn't spotted any; a young woman leant down, alternately pleading and whispering venomously at the tantrum of a boy she had gripped by the sleeve while most other passengers had their heads craned towards the screen, pretending not to notice.

Carlo and Arabella stood several places ahead in the queue, and Connor could sense the tension between the Andaloro siblings.

Observing the dynamic between them, they seemed more amicable than he would have thought for two Italians given the situation; he got the sense this might have been down to an underlying respect between them.

And the black operations agent, through his training and experience, had picked up on Carlo's fear regarding her well-being. Connor had an idea of how he felt; he had a quasi-sister himself in Rayella, the sister of his friend who died in Afghanistan. She had once become ensnared in the dangers of his profession. Going to Amsterdam to support her, he remembered how much he had to fight through a cloud of fear for clarity of thought.

Though he hadn't known Carlo long, the combat-thirsty Italian remained his favoured battle partner. However, Connor could not be sure how the former French Foreign Legionnaire's concern for his sister would affect him operationally.

And the Englishman resisted the urge to sexualise Arabella in his mind's eye. Though he wouldn't exactly have described her as stunningly pretty—her hooked nose and her mouth were a touch too large for her face.

However, her face and gestures were expressive, and she carried herself with charisma and confidence.

The Italian ribbon through her English soothed him, too.

And he forced himself to stop looking at a figure that seemed equal parts curvy and robust—her big tits, despite her hiding them, were noticeable to any red-blooded man. Connor could sense how strong she might be in the ass and legs.

He glanced at her and could see the nerves she competently masked.

And Connor knew one reason she would be particularly nervous was he hadn't elaborated on why he was confident she would make it clear of security this side of the water.

In the encrypted package sent to his secured e-mail, Ciara informed him that though his mission would now be classified as a Chameleon Project operation, his companions would still be on a need-to-know.

And so Connor had stone-faced them with the words, "Trust me."

The queue jostled forward as the check-in swallowed the passengers towards the ferry.

The Englishman relaxed his shoulders upon reminding himself that he couldn't remember when Jaime, the Chameleon Project tech guru, had let him down where things like this were concerned.

Still, he felt mild relief as he watched them both pass through without incident.

Connor sailed through the check-in and spotted the shadows when boarding the ferry.

It was not due to his competency of spotting

shadows; he recognised two men as enforcers for the 'Norland-Green' alliance, albeit from the Greens' side.

Back when Foley had told him who he was dealing with, Connor had begun a thorough study of them, including asking his cousin Tom, a veritable encyclopaedia of British grafters, as well as large numbers of Europeans.

Connor doubted Alexander Norland had gone back on his word because the pair were not looking at him.

The two Green associates were Martin 'M&M' Meenie and James McLeod.

Though he had white skin, the thick, black curls on Meenie's head led Connor to believe he might have a black grandparent—*'A bit of ink in 'im,'* as the Yorkshireman's uncles would say. Though powerfully built, Meenie had a double chin that reminded Connor of a Dagestani MMA fighter style of beard.

McLeod, more unassuming in build but sharper in the eyes, had his blond hair swept back like a nineties boy band member.

Both wore dark hoodies, a size too large, with better-fitting tracksuit bottoms.

How they had anticipated Carlo and Arabella taking the ferry over to Ireland, Connor did not know.

The more he observed them, the more he became convinced their presence might be down to chance.

He stepped away and took out his phone. He messaged Carlo about the situation.

Professional as ever, Carlo nodded while

looking at his phone and not at Connor or the shadows.

Nothing could be done while on the Ferry. They would have to deal with it afterwards.

Martin 'M&M' Meenie couldn't believe his luck.

M&M had been doing DDs—Dublin Drops—for the past few months. They had been as regular as clockwork—the 21st of each month. However, now his boss sent him up a week early and told him it was to mix up the patterns.

But now, M&M wasn't so sure— There sat the woman the big man had been tearing his hair out over.

And there were two of them; all she had was some little bald man sitting with her.

He cursed to himself, knowing they couldn't make a move on a crowded ferry.

And he knew he'd have to kill them both.

It crossed his mind to call his one-up for authorisation, but he knew kudos came with initiative.

He had been planning for nearly an hour now.

Meenie nudged McLeod and said, "You rush off and get the rental, and I'll follow 'em on foot."

"What if they get into a car and fuck off?"

"I'll jump in a taxi and follow 'em."

"Yeh, but if we are gonna shank 'em, then that might come back on us. Fuckin' taxi drivers have memories like elephants."

Martin felt a shot of cold as he thought about the opportunity slipping through his fingers.

"I'll take the risk."

James said, "Why don't you make the call? Then they can send word to our contacts in Ireland,

and they can send more men to track 'em."

Martin sighed, knowing James to be right.

He took out his phone and dialled.

Connor watched the pair converse in quiet animation.

He silently cursed as he watched M&M take out his phone to make a call while continuously glancing at Carlo and Arabella.

He knew there would be a high probability of enemy reinforcements over the water now. And they might be armed.

Indeed, not long ago, Connor had allied with Eddie O'Neil, a former IRA member and armed robber whose exploits were legendary on both sides of the Irish border.

He didn't owe Connor any favours and was of an advanced age.

However, Connor was confident the old man hated those who would directly hurt women and those who dealt drugs to the local community. The only reason the Ryder clan got any semblance of a 'pass' in that regard was they primarily dealt with the upper classes of Harrogate, York, and Cheshire and had distributors in and around some of the affluent southern areas like Sussex.

Eddie had once told him those profiting off the desperation of those born into a life that lacked prospects and guidance had no honour.

The Yorkshireman took out his phone and dialled.

Charlotte Daniels ran her fingers through her dyed-red shoulder-length hair to release some of the tugs.

She had spent the previous day hiking and only managed a quick shower before arriving here.

The natural beauty of the Vancouver trails could rival anywhere in Canada. And because of this, she felt a vague sense of guilt as she looked out onto the sea of multi-coloured tents, realising very few of these people would ever experience it.

The addicts began to hover.

While fitting the galvanised poles together to make the tent frame, 'Big' Jim Crowther exclaimed, "Jesus, Char, it gets bigger every month. I don't think we have enough needles."

Charlotte had taken a sabbatical from her doctor's post almost a year ago.

"I have brought some more. They are in the car."

"You think of everything."

In their small group of volunteers, Charlotte and Jim stood as the only non-addicts; Polly, Max, and Jason had been heavy users of opioids for a long time.

And she had never met nicer people.

She wondered how much selfless discipline it took for them to help administer the opioids to the other addicts with the clean needles they provided. To get through the entire throng could take many hours; a long and hard enough shift for anyone, but especially if feening for a fix.

Despite the beach she and her brother played on as children now resembling a refugee camp, she had never felt such a sense of community.

Andy 'Crocodile' Sampson wandered over in an 'old man' crouch despite being only forty. He'd got his moniker by wearing an outback-style hat with hanging corks.

"Need a hand?" he croaked, fidgeting like most of the addicts.

Charlotte knew his offer to be two-fold; he genuinely had a kind heart and wanted to help. But he also wanted to be at the start of the queue to get his fix.

"It's OK, Mister Sampson," she answered, not wishing to set a precedent for any onlookers.

"Okey-doke. See you later, Alligator."

She smiled, "In a while, Crocodile."

Charlotte admired the seeming lack of drop in his enthusiasm at the sign-off.

He wandered off, and Jim said, "Your brother would be proud of you, Char."

The compliment wrenched, as they always did.

Her last conversation with her only sibling, Paul, ended with her exasperated cry of, *'Why can't you stop making these mistakes?'*

And he replied tearfully, *'I made one mistake. And now it has hold of me.'*

The next day, her beautiful brother lay dead from a fentanyl overdose.

Though many had told her that, unlike even heroin, fentanyl could kill a person the first time they took it, even the most experienced users.

However, she knew her brother took his own life.

Their parents divorced when they were young. Strangely, despite their mum's coldness towards them, Paul had chosen to live with her.

She remembered watching a therapist on a

talk show say, *'Emotional pain alerts us to the danger of separation that we rely on.'*

Though physically present, she could see how her emotional distance severely affected Paul.

A couple of months after his death, she took a sabbatical and began walking Eastside with a backpack of naloxone nasal spray, reviving overdosed addicts.

They began to call her 'The Angel', which made her feel more guilty initially.

The more she helped, the less guilty she felt. What had meant to be a six-month break of helping the best way she could had turned into a quest.

If she could stop them dying, she could buy time for the government to get their act together.

She recalled the words of a comedian she had watched years ago: *'The money is in the treatment, not the cure.'*

The statement had pissed her off. One of her friends was a very hard-working and dedicated pharmaceutical scientist.

Though she fully understood that there would be no 'cure' to societal drug addiction, she was convinced there could be a dramatic reduction.

However, with the stonewalling she had received from the Vancouver municipal governments and the research she had done in pharmaceutical companies, she wondered if, with drug addicts, it might not be true.

How many jobs would disappear if the demand for drugs were to even half?

She pushed the thought out as she nodded to Jim, who bellowed, "Pretend you are British and make an orderly queue. Anyone who causes mischief will go to the back."

12

Mike Rose sat to the right of the expansive club president, Miles Morris.

Unlike the rest of the clubhouse, the backroom meeting room—known to them as 'Church'—remained sparse of posters, artwork, or ornaments.

The big screen on the opposite wall to the room's main entrance remained switched off. They could switch it on if they received a warning knock on the door.

Though The Red Hauser almost prided themselves on non-conformity, it had been decided that the format for club meetings—shared by the major traditional MCs—was perfectly fine.

The Robert's Rules of Order—or Robert's Rules—were laws on the parliamentary procedure of mass meetings. They had been around since the late nineteenth century, formulated by U.S. Army officer Henry Martyn Robert.

The rest of the members sat around the round table—something Rose had engineered so as not to antagonise anyone's ego.

And in the special operations community, healthy egos roamed.

Order had been called, all members were present, and a motion had been brought to distribute Arturo Bianchi's souped-up product.

Morris announced, "I can't see the problem. They are fuckin' junkies, they are going to die, anyway. May as well be now than years down the line. We'd be doing the world a favour."

Rose knew Morris's lack of intelligence compared to his own to be a double-edged sword; on the one hand, he was easier to control, but on the other, he seemed unable to grasp the big picture sometimes.

Rose said, "There are two issues—one is the people we distribute to will be happy to make hay while the sun shines but not when we stop supplying them, and most of their customers are dead."

"The day America's cities run out of addicts is the day the world ends," Avery announced. "And we can put a move on some other gangs, get the cops' noses in their direction. That's the whole point of us going under the radar."

The Red Hauser had shunned many of the tropes of an outlaw biker gang. They did not wear patches or any epaulettes signifying criminal endeavour. They had agreed to this so as not to antagonise either law enforcement and other gangs unnecessarily.

Kyle Avery had been an operative in Joint Task Force 2, seen by the consensus as Canada's premier Special Forces unit.

He came out, did eighteen months of lucrative private security and decided to bike around the US for a year before returning to private security.

Rose had met him on the circuit and remained close. However, he counselled Avery on the pretence of seemingly going against Rose in some of the non-critical decisions.

That way, Avery's opinion would be given more weight in backing any motions put forward by Rose.

Rose formed this play, setting out his

metaphorical chess pieces on the board. If there were any major disagreements regarding an upcoming decision, dissenters would more likely approach Avery and attempt to get him on their side. Then, Avery would identify them and their plays.

Morris nodded, "Exactly. With our combined skill, we should make a killing and our enemies can take the blame."

Rose did not mind the former Navy Seal, Morris, but he had done his due diligence on the fifty-year-old and had discovered most of his war stories were outrageously embellished if not outright lies.

What Rose knew was Morris was part of the Navy Seal team conducting beach and port hydrographic and reconnaissance survey operations in the landing beach, airport, and harbour areas in Somalia back in ninety-two to ninety-three.

However, Morris had also inferred several times that he had been a Naval Special Warfare Development Group member—more commonly known as 'Seal Team Six'.

He'd often start a story with, *'Back in my time with Six…'* before describing some Ramboesque escapade.

Rose had it on good and multiple authorities that Morris had merely supported their logistics in a handful of training serials and even fewer missions.

And Rose knew the rest of the members suspected Morris to be full of shit but tolerated the stories because of Morris's entertainingly boisterous delivery.

Indeed, after it had been discovered his full name was Miles Oliver Morris, the members often called him 'MOM'. The chairman would laugh it off, but Rose sensed it was behind gritted teeth.

One of the other men asked, "If our main supplier is shutting shop, who will we distribute for?"

As they both agreed, Avery said, "Maybe with the money, we could invest and leave this behind?"

Silence descended on the room for a few moments. Most of the men present secretly liked the thrill of the action—that was their juice.

A scattering of non-committal musings followed.

"Or maybe we could invest in this business—cash laundering while it's still here, cryptocurrencies, anti-surveillance gear, maybe an armoury."

More enthusiastic murmurs resounded.

Morris announced, "Are we ready to vote?"

The ensemble nodded, and the 'Ayes' were unanimous.

The arrivals terminal at the Dublin port reminded Connor of a wet airport. From the back of the line, he slowed his heart rate as he watched the security men quietly take away both Carlo and Arabella.

M&M and McLeod, situated between him and the siblings, faced one another in what appeared to be an agitated conversation.

M&M tore out his phone before stepping away from the line to talk urgently.

And Connor had been unable to reach Eddie O'Neil by call as it switched to answerphone several times.

The near-seventy-old did not use social media, so Connor had to make do with sending a text message.

A text in which Connor had eschewed

security protocols to go into detail—in as much code as possible—the situation he now found himself in.

It wasn't only that they would likely be outnumbered, and their enemy would be armed. It was how he would deal with them in a place crawling with cameras.

He felt a coldness as his mind drifted back to an answer—to let them be taken and follow them.

Connor had already studied the port schematics on his phone through Google Maps. The access roads divided the port into rough rectangles containing training centres, terminals, warehouses, and other establishments.

Connor scrutinised the girl at the checking desk; there existed the possibility he might be stopped.

She glanced at him, smiled, and he was through.

Connor speed walked towards the rental service not far away. It somehow reminded him of a fairground games stall.

He did not know precisely how long Carlo and Arabella would be held.

He took a physiological sigh as he saw the queue to the counter five deep. He had learnt—generally speaking—that if you lengthen your exhale in relation to your inhale, it calms your central nervous system.

He took a pair of short inhalations through the nose and blew out without pursing his lips.

After briefly considering his options, he knew he'd have to wait.

He slid out his phone—no messages.

On reaching the counter, he tried not to rush

the lady as he realised it wouldn't shift her faster.

He had chosen a Honda Civic because where operational cars were concerned, reliability was King, discretion the Queen, acceleration the Prince, and aesthetics the dirty thief.

Right after the keys fell into his hand, he spotted him in a sign's reflection before feeling the tap on his shoulder.

"Young man?"

Eddie O'Neil, now touching seventy but still spritely, looked at him through black eyebrows contrasting with his snow-white hair.

"Young man?" said Connor. "You ever check your phone?"

"I am here."

"Nice outfit," said Connor, referring to O'Neil's green hoodie with a white leaf on the front, which the Englishman thought looked strangely cool on him.

"Why, thank you."

As they walked outside, Connor quietly asked, "Got an update?"

"Local crew. Spahtted about six of o'dem."

"Trigger happy?"

"Yeh, but I doubt they'll chucker anything within the port."

"How many men have you brought?"

"None."

Connor stared at him for a moment. "What the fuck are you playing at, you old bastard? I rang you for help."

"Stop yer ***giving out***. I am not risking any of my lads. We're even, remember. Besides, it'll be more fun with just the two of us yer dryshite."

"Is this you trying to relive your glory years? Because I never had you down as someone who takes unnecessary risks."

"I especially don't take them with other people's lives."

Connor, realising he had wasted too much time already, said, "Any ideas?"

"Your friends are still being detained, but'll have to be released in 'alf an 'our."

"And so."

"And so, I'll pick them up. You folly on. And we'll see what a surprise we can give them."

The reply rendered Connor momentarily speechless. Eddie O'Neil had been renowned within the underworld, law enforcement, security services, and the media for being a tactical genius.

Then again, Connor supposed he hadn't given the Irishman much time to plan. He held back his snippy reply and instead said, "Alright."

M&M stood in a state of agitation as he watched his exit.

He had been taken aback by the Irish lads letting him glimpse the Škorpion machine pistols.

When he identified them as Uzis, one had led the others in mocking him with a *'Muppet doesn't know a Škorpion from an Uzi, never mind 'is arse from his elbow.'*

Another had said, *'M&M? Giz a rap.'*

When they met his laugh with a stone face and a subtle, but not too subtle, pointing of the barrels towards him, M&M began with his face burning, *'Ama London G, ain't nobody messing wiv me. Ama—'*

Their uproarious laughter cut it short. He tried to smile it off as it descended into chuckling, but it shot up again when he asked if he could have a weapon.

Eventually, they gave him a folding knife and banished him to watch the back.

Not only had the blatant disrespect scorched him from the inside out, as they had done it in front of McLeod to rub salt in the wound, but they had also taken McLeod with them and had given him a gun.

The Londoner checked his phone even though he knew it was on vibrate.

He knew what he was going to do if they appeared; he'd walk up and stab the pair of them. There were no cameras around this part as far as he could see.

Besides, they weren't even British or Irish; he had heard if a case hadn't been solved within a few weeks, then the police dropped it, especially if they were immigrants.

The Irish lads might piss and moan, but they'd get him away from the area and back to Blighty.

Back there, he'd gain respect. He'd have solved a problem. And he'd be known as a killer.

He jumped at the voice.

"You lost, pal?"

He turned his head before the fist smashed through his jaw, collapsing him into an unconscious heap.

Connor fished M&M's phone from his pocket as he dialled his own.

When the call connected, he said, "Clear."

The reply came back, "Acknowledged."

The Leeds outlaw made a more thorough search of M&M's person and found a blade.

He briefly thought back to his conversation with Tom and remembered his cousin describing Meenie as *'a bullying cunt, mate. Got charged with beating up a fourteen-year-old girl who was muleing for him.'*

Connor flicked the blade out, pulled the saggy jeans and boxers down and flipped Meanie onto his front.

He scored a slash on each buttock about half an inch deep before pulling the underwear and jeans back up.

Gangsters used this technique in the mid-last century; the recovery process was highly inconvenient as sitting displaced the stitches.

It surprised him the Londoner hadn't woken with the pain.

The door opened to reveal Carlo and Arabella exiting alone.

Connor jogged to them and said, "We have little time. Let's go."

He led them to the Civic.

They bundled their luggage in and set off.

"What is happening?" asked Carlo.

"You'll see."

Connor turned the corner and drove slow enough to catch the attention of their would-be pursuers.

The black BMW M3 with tinted windows and the dark Ranger Rover were parked like a panther and a bear ready to jointly ambush prey.

When they moved, Connor accelerated. The vehicles morphed into pursuers.

Connor had attended several courses in defensive and offensive driving techniques in recent years. He had become well-versed in the pit manoeuvre, J-turns, breaking roadblocks and other techniques.

Though the tight roads aided him, it was difficult for the two pursuers to box him in, so he couldn't perform any manoeuvres to escape them.

And he had to ditch them quickly, as he would soon be heading into the open part of the port, and the cameras would highlight the registration.

Carlo barked, "Man to the right!"

Connor said, "He's one of us."

The green hoodie fired a 'stinger' spike trap behind the Civic.

Though he could see that the puncturing of the tyres had been successful, he also knew they would still pursue him for a while.

He slowed the Civic in time with the BMW and felt the bumper-on-bumper contact.

He snatched the handbrake and pumped the brakes. The vehicles screeched in their embrace.

Smoke went up with the metallic screams.

Connor's heart dilated as he could see what looked like a Škorpion machine pistol being pointed by the occupant of the M3's passenger seat.

The Englishman briefly accelerated before barking, "Brace!" and ramming on the brakes.

The driver behind managed to avoid shunting the Civic, but Connor could see the force of the braking had smashed the pistol-wielder's head into the windscreen.

The following Range Rover crashed into the back of the BMW, and Connor's acceleration narrowly avoided the BWM touching the Civic.

He sharpened his eyes and could see the BMW's airbags deployed.

Carlo looked at him as they sped away and asked, "Who was that?"

"Eddie O'Neil. He's what you'd be if you lived to seventy."

Carlo turned to his sister, "Stai bene?"—*Are you OK?*

"Si."

Carlo turned to him. "What now?"

"We go to the airport. Pray the police aren't aware of what's just happened. My friend will take care of the rental ."

"And what happens if the police have been notified?"

"Then we have to roll the dice and hope we are on the flight to Canada before being arrested. And that we are not arrested when we get there."

13

Charlotte, alone in her warm apartment, woke up with her saliva smeared on her cheek. And she still could not find any life force in her body to get up.

I'll rest on the sofa for a few minutes before showering and putting my nightclothes on—she had told herself two hours ago, knowing it was a lie.

The number of deaths in the past few days had risen at a terrifying rate: three today alone, two yesterday and two the day before.

She'd asked Polly about her theory, and the straggly-haired twenty-year-old addict had answered, *'This new shit. The 'Green Dream'—hits different.'*

'You tried it?'

'Oh, yeh. That's why you didn't see me on Monday.'

'We need to start warning everyone that it's killing people.'

Polly had chuckled, *'You do that, then more of us will want it. They figure if the shit can kill 'em, then it must be good.'*

The comment had hit Charlotte like a slap in the face, and anger flushed her cheeks. All this work and sacrifice for people seemingly intent on killing themselves anyway.

She had calmed herself—*You're helping sick people.*

Another overdosed girl had been taken by ambulance, and Charlotte did not know if she'd make it. After it had left, Charlotte had driven to the police station to lodge a report stating her concerns about a new variant of fentanyl. The desk sergeant nodded, had her fill out a form and ensured it would be investigated.

She didn't doubt it would be—eventually. But by then, the number of deaths might be in the hundreds.

She had reached out to a friend in the medical arena to prepare a pharmacological report on a sample.

Her fatigue skewered her thinking because when her phone went, she answered it hoping it might be the report—despite knowing it took a day or two for the results to come in.

"Yes?" she answered hopefully.

Jim Crowther replied, "She didn't make it, Char. I am so sorry."

"OK, Jim," she sighed. "Someone is at the door; I have to go."

"OK, Char, I am here if you need me for anything at all."

"Thank you."

She ended the call before he could extend it—no one was at the door. Though she knew his concern to be genuine, she also knew he had romantic designs on her.

He would constantly complain about his loveless marriage and enquire if she was seeing anyone.

Truth was, she did not see him like that, but because he had not asked her outrightly, she didn't want to go through the embarrassment of the conversation.

The news of the girl's death fired the energy into Charlotte; that young lady would never have the option of fighting another day now.

She remembered something her brother had

said, *Just before I wake up from my dreams, I realise they are just dreams, and I am about to be brought out of them. That's why I wake up crying, not because they are nightmares.*

She wrestled herself off the couch and headed for the laundry basket.

Mike Rose watched with a touch of admiration as Arturo Bianchi blatantly fed MOM's ego.

Purple velvet couches encased them as beautifully coloured, hypnotic fish swam in the blue-lit aquariums to their right.

The glass apparitions simmered the club's thumping music to a low hum.

Mike was used to the ten-minute preamble Arturo usually went through before talking business.

After the initial runs of the new product, the swarm had grown, and the money had come in.

MOM had wanted to meet Arturo, and Mike couldn't put it off anymore.

And the Italian-Canadian had pulled out all the stops to impress the former SEAL.

The two club dancers, Caucasian but with dyed black hair and thick eyeliner suggesting Arabian, sat on either side of MOM, feigning rapt attention to his words.

Mike had a blonde sitting beside him in a black leather crop top and bottoms, with a loose white shirt over the top. Her fingers lightly rested on his forearm.

Despite knowing her mannerisms as part of the act, he still enjoyed her company.

"The way you run those boys is outstanding, Miles," announced Arturo. "But then, you'll be used to that during your time. I don't have to tell you how difficult it is to find the professionalism."

Rose almost admired the MC Chairman's lack of modesty when he said, "I've always been a natural leader, but the military sharpens it in an individual."

"You would have thought dealing with it after all these years would have made me better. Sometimes I wonder, though," said Arturo.

"You shouldn't doubt yourself," announced MOM. "There is a reason you are where you are."

Arturo smiled. "Anyway, my friend. How can I help you?"

"We were looking for a cheaper rate to take more product faster."

"A cheaper rate?" repeated Arturo. "I already sell to you cheaper than anyone else."

"But that's for our professionalism, remember?"

Arturo let out a laugh. "Yes, I remember. But now we are talking money. You say you can take more of my stock like it's good for me. But if I am releasing more of it for cheaper, how is that doing me a favour?"

It still felt strange to Rose to listen to the Mafioso refer to the killer drugs as 'stock' and 'products'.

Mike answered, "Because the Canadian hospital beds are full of dying addicts. The Government will then instruct their law enforcement agencies to drop everything to stop it. And if it leads back to you, they'll bury you under the prison to make a statement."

"You too," said Arturo.

"Yes," answered MOM. "Which is why we've come here. To our mutual benefit."

Rose had coached MOM about what to say.

But he hadn't told his outlaw 'brother' he'd told Arturo he had coached him. Rose and the Mafioso had already worked out the deal between themselves.

Rose thought he could see Bianchi concealing a smile.

"OK," announced Bianchi. "What is your price?"

They haggled before arriving at the number Rose and Bianchi had already negotiated.

On cue, the girls on either side of MOM began to paw at him.

Arturo grinned, "There is a backroom, especially for you, Miles, if you would welcome it?"

MOM made a show of appraising both girls before turning to Rose and saying, "Can you handle the particulars?"

"Sure," said Rose, mockingly saluting as he squeezed the blonde's hand and tilted his head to dismiss her.

MOM grasped the girls' hands, more to steady himself, and they took him away.

Once out of sight, Arturo grinned, "Fuckin' got him on the strings, haven't you?"

When Mike smiled, Arturo sat back and said, "I heard a rumour."

"What rumour is that?"

"That you started 'The Red Hauser' after you took on a bunch of scary-ass Harley-ridin' bad motherfuckers by yourself?"

Mike smiled, "Did you get told it left me in hospital for six weeks with a hairline fracture to my skull, broken ribs and internal bleeding? Worse, my bike was smashed, too. In fuckin' Nebraska of all places."

Bianchi laughed. "I didn't want to mention it."

Mike smiled. "Thank you for your sensitivity."

Mike, a fan of the Jack Reacher novel series, had taken off being single, having money and time to follow the fictional hero's lead to tour the US.

He had already received the busty barmaid's invite for coffee when the said group of bikers had walked in.

Mike had noticed more than one having the tattoo 'OFFO' displayed on their forearms, which he knew stood for 'Outlaws Forever, Forever Outlaws'.

His relative inebriation, post-contract tension and male ego overcame his good sense when they began to disrespect the barmaid and then his choice of transport.

After a recovery in the hospital, several of his former colleagues came to visit. Not just from the Green Berets but from men in other units with whom he had formed friendships during contracting.

It had been around his hospital bed that retribution had been planned—an ambush of this chapter's clubhouse using stun grenades, assault rifles firing plastic bullets, telescopic batons, Kevlar vests and knives.

Mike had insisted they wait until he had recovered.

And revenge had been exacted—to their standard, and nine of the enemy ended up in hospital.

However, one had died.

Despite a police hunt, Rose and his crew were never fingered for the assault. Such had been the planning and sophistication of execution.

High on their victory, in the post celebrations, one of the men commented that he had not felt a high like it since Iraq. And seemingly, everyone agreed—and 'The Red Hauser' had been born.

And naturally, given their skillset and thirst for the juice of dangerous missions, their means of supporting themselves turned to illegal activities.

It had not been long before other MCs had been made aware of their presence, thus sparking the war they were currently involved in.

And The Red Hauser needed allies like the one sitting across from him.

"I've got to ask, how the fuck have you got the rest of 'em to follow Miles as their leader when you founded the whole fucking thing?"

Mike decided not to bluff a rattlesnake like Bianchi. "They don't follow him. If he has the official title as our organisation's leader, then he's the one other MCs and the authorities will be more interested in."

Mike allowed Bianchi to read between the lines.

The Mafioso nodded, "That's what I thought. You're a cagey bastard, Mike. I almost can't believe he thinks he leads you all—then again, having met him, I can."

Mike changed the subject. "Tell me about your new distributors."

"Toronto, Vancouver, Ottawa, and Edmonton are good to go. Problems in Quebec and Montreal."

"Problems?"

"Trouble with people I broke away from."

"Anything we can do?"

Arturo shrugged. "Maybe down the line, but I have another problem."

"What is it?"

"An Italian assassin killed my brother in an unprovoked attack. I took steps, but I have it on good authority he is going to Canada."

"Maybe he just wants a chat?"

"He doesn't."

Mike nodded slowly. "How many?"

"I don't know exactly."

Rose frowned. "A bump in your security should do the trick."

Arturo's chest expanded, and he blew out. "He's the best they have."

"I thought this was not allowed in your world without, how do you say? A sit-down?"

"They tell me he's gone into business for himself."

"You'll have to excuse my ignorance, but I thought that was a death sentence in your world?"

"It's complicated."

"You're asking for protection?" asked Mike, knowing the question would pique Bianchi's ego.

"Not protection. But if I can get a location on this man, I—"

"You would like for us to make him disappear."

"I would like him strung up and brought to me."

"Taking him out would have cost you. Taking him in alive will cost you more."

"I thought it would."

"So, he's the best assassin in the Mafia and

threatening your life. On top of that, we will be risking a twenty-year stretch," said Rose, almost to himself. "I think a mill and a half will cover that."

"A million and a half to kidnap some foreigner? You used to do things like that for, say, what? Fifty thousand a year?"

"I'll let you work out the differences between the two scenarios."

"I am not paying a million and a half. Seven-hundred and—"

"You will pay a million and a half. If it's a choice of risking being dead and money that you'll make up fast being alive, only an insane person would choose the first option."

Arturo's face took a few moments to break into a grin. He reached his hand over. When Rose took it, the Mafioso said, "I would have paid two."

Rose couldn't help but laugh. "I thought that would be the number. But I once heard the definition of a good deal is when neither side is fully happy with it."

"Not my motto, but I'll take your word for it."

"If he's alone, it shouldn't be a problem."

Connor kept his head still but eyes scanning as he walked through the bright white curvature of Toronto Pearson International Airport.

The checking-in monitor screens hung over people like robots from a seventies television show.

Other, larger digital screens unashamedly showed obscene delays.

Carlo and Arabella walked ahead, about twenty and seventeen paces, respectively.

Jaime had once informed him that some facial recognition systems could be foiled simply with a strip across the nose. Though he supposed he could explain it away as a left-on nasal strip to prevent flight-nap snores, he didn't want to draw attention to himself.

In his mission brief, Ciara had told him a contact, high within the Canadian Security Intelligence Service, could not only run interference but provide intelligence too—but it would be through her.

Though Connor trusted Ciara, he failed to see how a single contact could block communications between international law enforcement agencies.

Connor and Carlo agreed during their time on operations, they would separate as much as possible. It made ambushing or arresting them more difficult.

The black operations agent had been on numerous perilous missions now, but having to protect a civilian while on an operation threatened to unsettle him.

He had been impressed with Arabella's stoicism throughout and briefly thought of how his gran would approve.

However, he knew it would get harder, and her resolve would be tested.

That said, he wondered if he worried more about Carlo, with the distraction of protecting his sister while conducting an offensive operation in enemy territory.

A mild relief plumed as all three made it out of the airport without incident.

He took out his phone, and within minutes, an Uber driver pulled up in a black three-year-old

Mercedes-Benz S-Class.

Connor got in, and seeing the driver's name as Murad Singh, greeted him with, "Sat Shri Akaal."

The driver smiled widely. "You know Punjabi?"

Connor, despite having a strong grasp of the language, closed his index finger close to his thumb and said, "Thōṛā jihā."—*A little.*

"Very good, my friend."

Connor cursed his lack of professionalism—revealing he knew even a smidgen would make him memorable to the driver.

Connor's knowledge of the language began when his father came out of prison, knowing the language when Connor was young. Greg Ryder taught his son what he knew over time, and Connor had augmented this knowledge by conversing with the Asians at the boxing gym. It was there he was told *Sat Shri Akaal* was a phrase he should only use with Indians, specifically Sikhs and not Muslims.

This had proved extremely useful when dealing with the Asian elements that controlled much of the organised crime in and around West Yorkshire and the North of England.

The radio filled the quiet between them, informing them of the news headline that the debris of the imploded Titan submersible had been found.

Murad turned the radio down and exclaimed, "What is it with you rich white people having to explore every single thing?"

"Don't look at me, mate. I am not that rich," said Connor. "Besides, I don't think I could hold a fart in that long."

Murad burst into laughter before asking, "You

on vacation?"

"Yeh," said Connor.

"Bet you think this is the capital, don't ya?"

"I am aware it is Ottawa."

"Not a complete 'Brit abroad' then?"

"I'll take that as a compliment, Murad," answered Connor. "But you're disproving the notion that Canadians are super-friendly people? Is that not true?"

Murad looked ahead with a half-smile. "Kinda true. A bit less these last few years, though."

"Why's that?"

"I am a third-generation Indian, and my family and I haven't experienced much racism. Some, but not much, eh? But now, the government let loads in—not just migrant workers like my *Paṛadādā-dādī* were, but these millionaires and billionaires, buying all the land and property. People can't afford a house, however much they save now."

"Even your people?" asked Connor. "I heard thirty Indians died in Montreal the other week—a roof collapsed on a family home."

Connor dug his toes into his shoes in anticipation of Murad having a bad reaction to the joke, but the Sikh laughed, "You whites are the silly ones—splitting your families up and having to buy a house for every two people. And you wonder why we can afford nicer cars."

Connor smiled as Murad patted the dashboard and just said, "I presumed you all sold drugs."

The Sikh side-eyed him, laughed and continued, "People here are getting tired of the government constantly being in our lives, trying to divide us. The education system pushing sick ideas onto our children. And the drugs... you see more addicts than ever."

Connor made a show of looking out the window. "Seems alright to me."

"I am telling you, I could take you *out for a rip* downtown in ten minutes, and you'd think it was Los Angeles."

"That bad?"

"Maybe not yet, but I'll tell ya I have voted New Democratic Party all my life, but this time, I will for Larry MacKenzie."

"Really?"

"Yeh, really. He's the only one talking sense."

When Connor said nothing, Murad said, "I lived in England for a few years, about ten years ago."

"Oh, yeh? where?"

"Birmingham."

"Tell me some of the slang and things you have over here that we don't."

"OK, ahem," started Murad before rattling off quick-fire, "Canadian bacon is just ham. Milk comes in bags. A two-four is a twenty-four pack of beer. A mickey is a small bottle of liquor. Freezies are frozen tubes of flavoured sugar or fruit juice blended with water. Ketchup-flavoured chips are a real thing, and it can get freezing as shit."

"Thanks for that cultural lesson, Murad."

"My pleasure," said the driver cheerfully. "Why are you heading to a garage, anyway?"

"To buy a car for the duration."

"Why don't you rent one?"

"Because I am a secret agent who doesn't want to be tracked."

Murad chuckled, "Then I know a better place."

"Will they give me furry dice hanging off the interior mirror?"

"What?"

"Nothing. Yeah, take me to the place you know."

Murad drove him to a used car garage on the city limits. The red, white and blue of the French flag made up the signage of 'Finch Auto Showrooms'.

To Connor's surprise, Murad got out and greeted the squat, olive-skinned salesman stuffed into a shirt and tie.

They spoke in French, and Connor grasped enough of the rapid conversation to know that Murad was asking for Connor to be 'looked after'.

Once Murad had informed Connor that his 'main man' would look after him and took his suitcase out of the Mercedes, Connor extended his hand with the red fifty-dollar bill enclosed in it.

Figuring that Murad was unlikely to forget him now, anyway, the Englishman said the Sikh blessing of "Rabb Charhdi Kala Bakshe."

Murad broke into a joker's grin. "May your God keep you in high spirits as well."

As the Mercedes pulled away, Connor turned to the thinning salesman, who asked him, "What can I do for you, sir?"

Connor resented buying vehicles when on operations, but he'd ensure Ciara would reimburse him. He knew it to be better than renting because, generally, rental companies had better security camera systems installed and vehicles with trackers.

And he didn't want the pressure of returning

the vehicle undamaged.

"I've heard some good things about these Dodge RAMs," said Connor, gesturing to the black truck.

"Ahh yes, well, the one you're looking at was made after two thousand and nine, so it's called a RAM—Chrysler made them standalone after that time. But you're right; handling is great, and you'll love the interior—it is the most comfortable and best driving out of all the pickups. This one's a 300-horsepower, 3.6-litre engine with a V-6. Twelve-inch infotainment screen inside."

Connor smiled at him. "Alright, what's the downside?"

The salesman matched his smile. "You get what you pay for, and you pay for what you get. I can give you a few *Loonies and Toonies* off because of our friend."

Connor feigned wincing when told of the price. Haggling, he settled on a minor discount.

As he signed the paperwork, the salesman asked, "What brings you to Canada?"

"The sights."

"Not to emigrate?"

"You never know."

"Chance will be a fine thing. Major housing crisis."

Connor knew this from his prior research; for Canada to meet the G7 average for homes per person, they would need to build 1.8 million houses.

"Well, I'll be exploring most of the cities. I hear Vancouver is nice."

The salesman gave him a wry look. "The parts of Vancouver they let you see."

"Christ, just had this speech from Murad. Are there no Canadians left who like Canada?"

The salesman laughed, "No, of course we do. We just don't want to see it decline. What did Murad say?"

"Homelessness, drugs, lack of housing and all that. Threatened to take me to one of the ghettos here. It's like he don't want me to stay."

The salesman laughed. "You keep buying cars off me like you have today, I'll be begging you to stay. We are still a friendly country!"

They shook hands, and Connor drove away.

14

Ciara walked down the foot-scraped path of Primrose Hill, admiring the view of distant London as the afternoon light sank into evening.

Her fawn, wool-wrap jacket covered her from throat to knee against the cool breeze.

She had not been told anything about the CSIS contact due to meet her. Because she—via Bruce—had reached out for the favour, she didn't have the leverage to ask for the contact's details, even a description.

Her previous profession as a freelance journalist had aided her when she had been a field agent, as it meant she had a plausible in-built legend to travel to dangerous places.

However, now that she had been moved into a logistics role, she wondered if her journalistic background would spook would-be alliances.

She decided not to worry about things out of her control and enjoy the walk.

A pair of dogs, looking like Maltese with a little sheepdog in them, came bounding up to her, yapping.

Their owner, an elderly lady with short silvery hair, wearing a dark blue tweed coat to the knees, called out, "Jasper. Rose. Settle yourselves."

Ciara bent down to pet them. She would normally ask if they would bite but doubted the harm the pair could do.

The woman arrived, slightly out of breath.

After a moment, Ciara asked, "What are they?"

"Little bastards are what they are."

Ciara laughed at the contrast between the educated tone and the actual words. The lady continued, "But as to their breed, they are The Havanese."

"You wouldn't be without them, though," said Ciara, petting them.

"Well, I will be one day, unfortunately. Such is life. Unless they succeed in giving me a heart attack. You might find that to be the case running agents."

Ciara fleetingly stiffened; she should have recognised the woman.

She attempted to hide being caught off-guard with, "I didn't think they would send someone of your reputation, Martha."

The older woman smiled. "I look a little different since I've retired, as you will in twenty years."

"You look younger than your age," said Ciara, continuing with a grin. "Teach me."

"There is a saying that when a storm rages around you, don't let it encompass you. Now, that is OK for posters in a yoga studio, but life is life. However, make sure you meditate and make it a habit. Borrow a neighbour's dog and go for a walk. Hike. Do anything you have to do to avoid being chronically stressed. Because a few months will go by, and one day, you won't have a choice to rest. Your body will make you."

Martha Whyte had been the chief of Foreign Intelligence in the nineties when the CSIS was not meant to have an intelligence service. Ciara could only imagine the pressure she must have been under then.

"I'll try."

"Don't 'try'. I hate that word. Either do it or don't do it. If you do, then make it habitual. Even if you go through a stress-free period."

Ciara nodded, glad of the advice and unbothered by the mild rebuke.

She then asked, "I am surprised you have met me so openly."

Martha answered, "If our mutual Scottish friend says you're trustworthy, you're trustworthy."

Though it shouldn't have surprised her, it always did when discovering how far her boss's influence reached.

Martha's apparent clairvoyance raised its head when she said, "It's like any business. If you gain a good reputation over time, you'll make friends. You've already had your experiences with this, I am sure."

With that, she offered her hand and clasped her other hand over when Ciara took it, feeling the small plastic box in her palm.

"Contacts. Safe deposits. A safe house for your man only—not his associates. False IDs. Weapons caches."

"Thank you."

"But it stands to reason that—"

"If my man is caught, the CSIS will deny all knowledge."

"Exactly," Martha replied. "I, for one, hope the man you're sending is a good one. These people are not just against Canada's interests; they are not nice people."

"I gathered."

"There is something extremely distasteful about people who profit from the pain and death of the vulnerable."

"If they are not nice people, then the man I have sent will be the perfect man."

Connor enjoyed the drive on the Canadian highways. He found it shockingly smooth to drive. Indeed, he'd heard the older Dodge RAMs served a more visceral experience.

With his counter-surveillance duties so ingrained, Connor found he could admire the scenery.

Ordinarily, Connor would listen to an audiobook of some description, but to familiarise himself with the country, he whacked on CBC Radio One.

He listened to a female journalist give her take on the latest and most devastating HAMAS assault on Israel and her ponderings of why Mossad and the IDF had failed to anticipate it.

After a while, he switched to the audiobook 'Molly's Game' while taking in the view.

He remembered watching the film with Tom, who was convalescing from a lower back injury sustained in the shoot-out in Amsterdam.

He remembered Tom mentioned how the red-headed Jessica Chastain had a look of *'...the granddaughter of gran's friend, Rene. That Grace. The one with the nipper named Jackson.'*

When Connor agreed that she did, Tom ambiguously remarked while looking at Connor—*'I bet she's great in bed.'*

Tom rarely spoke about women in anything less than gentlemanly terms, and that's when Connor knew his elder cousin knew that Jackson was Connor's son.

Connor hadn't wanted the heavy conversation concerning why he wasn't publicly acknowledging his fatherhood. Instead, he replied, *'I should imagine Rene has picked up a few tricks in her seventy-odd years.'*

Tom smiled, seeming to understand as he didn't broach the subject again.

Connor looked out on the scenery as the RAM began leaving Toronto's suburbs.

Though short of man-made architectural attractions, this two-hundred-and-fifty-mile drive to Sudbury thus far had serene, pretty, natural views.

Due to how he'd found himself on this mission, he had not had his usual time to study—this concerned him more than the enemy he readied himself to confront.

On previous missions for The Chameleon Project—if it was even referred to as that anymore—he had been given a thorough briefing and, at least, some time to absorb any information he needed to.

He had only managed to snatch glances at the information Jaime had sent him.

Connor had never particularly liked relying on a foreign agency, especially when he had never met an agency member, but Jaime and Ciara had not let him down yet.

He could see why the Canadians might want the problem handled.

The public might have a degree of apathy towards the well-being of addicts, but that would clear up if influxes took up hospital beds.

The irony that Connor, a member of a family that distributed drugs, had been sent to stop the distribution of drugs in another country was not lost on him.

However, his family always sold high purity to the crowd that could afford rehab.

This had been the policy since Tom took over as chief of the family's operation, as it had been the policy of their old supplier, the now-deceased Raymond Van Der Saar.

Connor smiled, thinking of the old man. Connor had described the Dutch crime lord as *'part hippy, part Arsene Wenger, and part Don Corleone',* and the Englishman had some of his most entertaining times with him.

He had been a mentor to both Connor and Tom and had encouraged their practice of donating to rehabilitation clinics—anonymously—but ensuring that the right people knew they did.

The vehicle's internal Bluetooth rang, and he answered, "How are you?"

"I am fine," answered Carlo. Meaning *I am not under duress.* "We are mobile."

"Any problems?"

"No, but…but I think Arabella should stay with you."

Connor knew how hard it would have been for Carlo to arrive at that decision.

"It's up to you. It's your sister."

"Yes," said Carlo. "She is my sister."

Connor sensed the tone and managed to latch his tongue from making jokes in a way he would not have been able to a few years ago.

"I'll treat her like she's my sister," said Connor.

On the surface, it stated his intent to protect her at all costs. But also an assurance he would not attempt to fuck her. Not that he had detected any signs that Arabella was attracted to him, anyway.

"OK. Good."

"I will pull in when I can and send you the coordinates."

"OK. Out."

The exact wording of the message from Jaime concerning the safe house had been that it would remain off-limits to Carlo. Connor knew it was highly likely the tech guru, and therefore, Ciara meant it was for him to use only. However, he would plead ignorance.

Connor pulled into a gas station, the roof of which resembled a giant, luminous surfboard.

He filled up, unsurprised at how long it took, and bought a can of coke with his fuel—or gas, as they said here.

He kept aware as he made a meal of topping up the tyres and filling the screen wash and coolant.

Finally, Carlo pulled in, driving a dark blue Toyota Rav 4x4 and also filled up. The pair instinctively knew not to make the exchange under the gaze of the gas station's security cameras, so Connor drove the RAM just out of the gas station entrance. Carlo slowed, and Arabella jumped out with a holdall, which she threw into the back of the RAM before getting in.

Connor saluted Carlo with three fingers.

15

Larry MacKenzie leaned back in a red leather chair, smiling at the screen.

This silent Toronto corner office had one of the highest views of the city. Due to the cleanliness and lack of seams in the glass, the office initially appeared to be outside. Once he had decided to run for office, MacKenzie had a highly expensive technological upgrade in the glass where he could look out, but no one could look in.

The white wood floor shone around the stuffed Amur tiger.

Models of planets and stars housed the room's lighting, and they interacted with the light coming through the windows, automatically adjusting to set his ideal level of illumination.

The first payment from the Italian had arrived, laundered through one of his offshore accounts.

In truth, Larry knew that had Bianchi been a better businessman, he might have been the one paying him.

The alliance continued to prove mutually beneficial; Larry threw a cloak of protection over the quasi-Mafia boss through his contacts in law enforcement and purchased the commercial land rights and property for his drug factories.

In return, not only did he take a piece of Arturo Bianchi's now highly lucrative businesses, he also had the reach to order missions in intimidation, sabotage, counterintelligence and assassination, apparently through a gang of former Special Forces bikers.

Not that he'd ever met the mob boss; that would not do.

His intermediary, Richèl Vergeer, handled all that. She had initially been brought in as a translator to help international business deals and with indigenous groups comprising the First Nations, Inuit, and Métis peoples.

Larry pressed a button on the intercom, and shortly after, Richèl appeared.

"Yes, sir?"

Larry had long ago given up on getting her to call him by his name.

If he wasn't gay, he knew he'd be liable to attempt to bed her. MacKenzie had slept with many women in his youth, but all had been no more than a heightened sense of masturbation for him. However, he still appreciated a beautiful woman like Richèl.

Her large, square glasses—too big for her face, really—highlighted the tan stars of her eyes. The black hair hung in a near-perfect curve to her shoulders.

"It seems the first payment from our Italian friend has landed. Could you see to it that it is further cleaned?"

"Of course," she answered in an accent that he had heard described as 'mid-Atlantic' despite her hailing from Holland.

He thought for a moment. "Take a seat."

She did so, and he asked, "What is the progress we are making in the land purchasing in Northern Ontario?"

"Slow but progressing. Currently brainstorming some ideas on how to bypass objections by the indigenous and environmental groups. One of—"

"Indigenous people scream about the sacristy of their lands and gods, but tell them they will manage your casino, and suddenly, they worship dollars and dice. I've business partners in Australia. I know."

"The environmental groups are a little more difficult to dissuade. That's why I suggest we meet with the leaders of a selection of these groups. We'll present a cohesive strategy regarding energy conservation and our ideas on environmental funding. If we can tie the commercial and housing initiatives to the indigenous peoples, then we might convince them—or else force them to back off."

"Exactly," he said. "Do-gooders want to be seen to be doing good. Throw them a bone they can put on social media, and they will eat it up."

On observing her, he asked, "What?"

She gave an almost imperceptible shrug. "Isn't that what we are doing? Being seen to be doing good?"

He smiled. "We are in politics. We are seen as doing good, so the electorate allows us to do good."

Richèl gave him an unconvincing nod and said, "I will speak to our cyber teams about influencing the public towards the policies you have outlined."

"OK. Thank you, Richèl. You may go."

He admired her as she left.

As the RAM broke out of the forest, Connor fleetingly wished he had visited the country for leisure purposes.

The track cut through the meadow towards a

log cabin, reminding Connor of the television programmes depicting the old West of America over a hundred and fifty years ago.

He could just make out the vast lake beyond it. His eyes began to pick out likely approach routes for a kill team.

"Remind you of back home?" he asked.

"Have you been to Calabria?"

"Yes," he said. "Very beautiful country."

"The landscape is."

"Every country has its ugliness."

She snorted her derision. "Easy to say when you're from the idyllic Yorkshire."

Connor smiled but did not reply.

The RAM prowled up to the cabin. Connor lowered the windows an inch, and a pleasant, earthy smell smoothed in.

He said, "We are going to wait and listen for a couple of minutes."

It pleased him she did not ask why. Finally, he said, "Can you shoot a pistol?"

"Yes, but I am out of practice."

Connor reached beneath the seat.

"This is a Beretta M9. Carlo said this is the one you used to practise with."

"Why did you ask if I could shoot if you already know?"

"I wanted to hear how much confidence you had."

"I will shoot anyone who threatens my life."

Connor nodded. "We'll have to clear the cabin—it's an unknown. Stay on my shoulder, keep the Beretta pointed down at a forty-five-degree angle, and do exactly as I say."

"OK."

"We'll walk up to the entrance. I'll enter as you wait outside. When I shout 'clear', you'll come in. I'll do that with each space—I'll clear it and shout, you occupy the cleared space, and we'll continue like that. Understand?"

"You clear, you shout 'clear', I stand in the cleared space and repeat."

Connor nodded with a hint of approval. He didn't bother to ask if she knew any hand signals.

They crept to the entrance, and Connor dismissed his feelings of self-consciousness about having an untrained person covering him.

After making a cursory scan of the hinges, he entered the cabin with his FN Five-seven out to his front.

The aroma of woodchips and peach floated in the silence.

The stone flooring provided a respite from the blend of white and black wood riveting the inside.

A painting of a herd of elks in front of a mountain backdrop hung over a log fire.

"Clear."

Arabella walked in, and he said, "Back-heel the door shut, and aim your Beretta towards the stairs."

Connor cleared the rest of the cabin, with Arabella efficiently following his instructions.

Once done, they brought their things in, and Connor said, "I have security apparatus I have to put out. Put your strong boots and a jacket on, and we'll get it cracked. Keep your Beretta on you."

As they stepped outside back, Connor—after a scan—admired the view.

Red-bellied, blue-lipped clouds breathed from the snow-capped mountains like steam from a kettle. The high forest framed a huge lake, which, surprisingly to Connor, had more of an aqua-green tint than blue.

"Bellissimo," Arabella murmured.

"Thank you," said Connor. "I try."

Her eyebrow crinkled, but her mouth didn't twitch.

Connor knew Canada had more than half the world's natural lakes—that if it wasn't for its lakes, the country might have a similar population and industrial might of the US.

They began to cut a perimeter through the wood, with Connor stopping periodically to place miniature cameras.

They resembled dark marbles and fired a prong into the tree when he twisted and squeezed them.

Suddenly, she asked, "Why have you helped my brother?"

"I owe him."

"No, you do not. He said you are equal—I mean even."

Connor paused for a moment before answering. "It's worth me keeping Carlo as a friend."

"You mean it is worth keeping him in debt to you?"

Connor walked fifteen yards, picked out another tree to place a camera and replied, "If you want to word it like that, then fine."

"How would you word it?"

"That every relationship is a game of give and take."

"Do you know what he takes from you?"

"Protection for his sister?"

"I meant before that. Why do you think he would help you?"

Connor gave a sniff-laugh. "Because he's a 'head the ball' who loves the feeling of death stroking him through combat."

"*Esattamente,* it took me a time to understand that about my brother. The thrill of combat."

"Has he always been like that?"

She exhaled from her nose. "No. He was what you English would say 'a nerd', 'a geek', and my father did not like it at all. I was always my father's daughter. Then, one day, my father took Carlo hunting with him. I was so afraid."

Connor turned to her and frowned. "Why?"

He watched her open a silver pocket case, and he exclaimed, "Fuck me, I didn't even know you smoked."

"I rarely do," she replied, lighting up in a way that reminded Connor of a nineteen fifties actress.

As the familiar smell floated, she said, "I did not think I would see my brother again. I thought my father would come back and claim he had got lost—that he caught hypothermia or had been eaten by wolves."

"But he came back."

"He didn't just come back. He came back, with my father proclaiming him a hero. Carlo had been ambushed by a wolf… and he shot that wolf dead."

"And you were not a daddy's girl anymore?"

He caught her sad smile. "I guess both Carlo and I had to grow up that day."

After a few moments, Connor asked, "Are you telling me if it was a choice between your safety and his love of combat, you don't know which one he would choose?"

"My brother loves me, I know. But I know all about men and their compulsions."

The statement clicked in Connor's brain.

Surrounded by dark trees, Carlo knelt and watched the lively customers file into a sports bar resembling three stacked illuminated flying saucers.

Ice hockey was Canada's national sport, and Carlo had discovered tonight was Montreal Canadiens vs Ottawa Senators—a big rivalry.

The former Legionnaire felt a dark pull to walk into the bar and let the chips fall where they may.

However, he knew it would be unprofessional in the least, and likely, suicidal.

He'd hoped to see Arturo Bianchi enter but knew it was a fool's hope as Arturo would go through the back.

The assassin had attempted access to the rear only to discover a high-rise, spiked fence covered by multiple security cameras.

A group of sports bikers roared into the parking lot. Though Carlo could ride, he had never been avid. But he knew enough to know that one of the reasons biker gangs tended to use cruisers was that they were easier to ride in formation than sports bikes.

And Carlo felt uneasy watching the way they moved with relaxed alertness. He guessed them not being only ex-military but at least former elite, if not Special Forces.

He couldn't tell if he wanted these guys to be allied with Arturo.

He decided not—his adventures could wait until the threat on his sister had been removed.

Carlo made his decision—he'd seen more than one customer enter with a baseball cap and couldn't see a camera directly over the door.

The Italian placed his own red Canadien Montreal trucker cap on to cover his distinctive bald head. He had purchased it at a nearby gas station and thought it looked like a 'MAGA' cap worn during the Trump US presidency.

Five years in the Legion made him fluent in French to the point of sounding native. Sudbury had a large Francophile population, so a French Canadian would not be memorable here.

He turned back and walked a wide circumference into the parking lot and towards the door.

He cursed on seeing the two bouncers set back into the doorway.

Carlo had never seen doormen stand that far back into the door but surmised this pair's dislike of the cold had overcome their professionalism of keeping a wider and further view.

He dispelled the idea of turning back under their glare and instead walked normally.

One of them spoke in a tone more polite than Carlo had been expecting. "Good evening, sir."

The 'Ndrangheta assassin accented his voice. "Are the Canadiens vs Senators on tonight?"

"Certainly are. Top floor."

"Great."

He felt a breeze of relief when they did not pat him down, but then again, it was a sports bar.

Customers' voices and the sound of three screens displaying different sporting events blurred into a welcoming hum.

A monster screen hung over the bar, bulging out like one side of a giant fishbowl, hypnotising customers with the Mixed Martial Arts heavyweight clash.

The eyes of the men on the second floor flicked between the lower floor and the college American football game.

In a reversal to what he expected, the roars from the upper floor indicated the management had put the most popular sports on there.

He began to make his way up the chrome stairs, his eyes scanning.

The bikers crowded the second floor, and Carlo made a brief snapshot of their configuration. He couldn't pick out a leader.

And he couldn't risk loitering.

With no sign of Bianchi yet, Carlo went to the bar and ordered himself a beer.

He didn't want to conduct a reconnaissance of the bar immediately, as it might look suspicious. Instead, he sat back to take in a game he had developed an interest in over the years.

Originally, it had been on the discovery that opposing members were 'allowed' to fight. He remembered watching a game on a visit a few years back and being shocked when two of the players threw down their gloves, circled one another and began punching with ferocity—and the referees simply monitored the action to the roars of the crowd until a player fell.

Since then, he had spent a drink with a Canadian who had explained the rules and the intricacies of the game.

The former Legionnaire positioned himself in the most optimal position to view his surroundings using the bar mirrors and other reflective surfaces.

Carlo caught himself getting too entranced in the game and looked around.

The first twenty-minute period ended, and Carlo took advantage of the melee to walk downstairs.

His heart jumped upon seeing Bianchi. The bespectacled crime lord looked to be conversing at the bar with whom Carlo assumed to be the manager—and he looked slimmer in comparison to the picture Carlo had seen.

Spying his prey in the open, the assassin felt a mild expansion of his being.

He'd wait until Bianchi disappeared before making his way out.

If he stayed on the third floor, not only would his view of the ground floor be limited, but it would be too risky to make it down and out before Bianchi's potential reappearance.

He decided to stay on the second floor.

He stood a little off the balustrade and surmised he might just look like a man perusing the women below. He became aware of the bikers flicking glances at him but feigned a lack of awareness.

Carlo heard the game restart upstairs, and after considering his options, he opted to stay where he was.

Finally, as he felt the glances become stares, he watched the Mafia boss disappear.

The former Legionnaire galloped down the stairs, slowed, then looked up and behind. He caught a biker stride to one of the more massive security team members in the far corner. The biker spoke with apparent urgency.

The bouncer snapped his eyes on Carlo, touched his ear and talked into his sleeve.

Then, the Italian felt an invisible net closing in on him.

His eyes scanned while keeping his head still— the downstairs door staff began looking at him, then left their positions.

Hotly pursued, he burst back towards the second floor, rounded the corner and wrenched a fire extinguisher from the wall, the hulk within seconds of reaching him.

Screaming, "Fire," he blasted the doorman's features with the spray before smashing it into his nose, felling him.

The bikers stood but did not move towards him.

He rushed down the stairs and threw the empty extinguisher into the bouncers running towards him.

Shouts, gasps, and a scream cut through the swirl of sports commentary.

He vaulted the rail, powering for the fire exit.

The security team swarmed him like a gang of bear-sized rats.

Carlo knew he was in big trouble. Though well-versed in hand-to-hand combat, with a squat, hard physique and excellent fitness, one man dispatching multiple capable opponents was the premise of bar talk fantasies and Bruce Lee films.

When the first arrived, the Italian took a step back, smacked the reaching hand away and fired a smashing head butt into his attacker's face.

The doorman jerked back, and Carlo's punches felled him.

A strong arm snatched his throat like a whipping python. A hammer-like fist would have punched the air from his diaphragm had he not tightened his stomach.

He shunted back against his strangler, grasping at the choking arm, but other steel hands clamped his limbs, straight-jacketing him into relative stillness.

He braced himself for a procession of blows. Instead, his feet left the floor.

In addition to fear, he felt almost childlike in the face of his ineffectual struggle.

He ceased trying to save both his energy and dignity.

Knowing Bianchi's reputation, Carlo expected to be 'interrogated' before being killed.

Don't let him see you scared.

Hope billowed in time with the smoke and flashing bangs.

16

Hurricanes of shouts and screams whipped around.

Then, the fingers of smoke began to choke Carlo. He barely felt the hands releasing him like the tubes from *The Matrix's* Neo. The floor hit his arse, and he began to get up.

From the chaos, a hand smacked onto his neck, and an elastic strap ripped over his scalp.

Oxygen sang into his lungs.

His sight came back to reveal a masked man throwing a thumb up at him. Carlo realised this to be his rescuer and returned the hand signal.

The figure seized him, forced him upright, caught his wrist and barged him through the spluttering throng.

As they burst out of the fire exit, gunshots sounded from behind. His masked rescuer stumbled forward as if punched in the back by Goliath's fist.

However, he seemed to spring up unharmed.

Carlo reached for his mask, thinking removing it would make him less conspicuous to the patrons streaming out.

"Keep it on," rasped the mask, and Carlo recognised Connor's voice through the Vader-like distortion. "Follow me."

The two men shot through the forest. A few seconds in, Connor took his mask off, and Carlo did the same.

The Englishman glanced back every few seconds before eventually slowing.

Carlo rasped, "I need to go back for the sniper rifle."

"You fucking idiot," he heard Connor seethe. "Where?"

"I can lead us."

"Fuckin' go on then."

Carlo burned under the obvious anger of one of the very few men whose ability he respected in their dark profession.

In truth, respect was too mild a word.

Carlo had a sharp sense of distance and direction and led them through the trees.

It took just under six minutes to reach his weapons cache.

His eyes caught the blue flashes, and the barking cut through the woodland.

Connor growled, "Fucksake! Let's go!"

They careered off again, Connor snatching the rifle off him.

Carlo's lungs clawed for oxygen, and the lactic acid burned his thighs, trying to keep up.

The distant barking sliced closer and raised his heartbeat.

Connor turned to him. "If we have to shoot a dog, we'll be fucked."

The howls got louder until he could hear the snarls.

Carlo's brain fired signals to his defiant legs to speed up. He snatched a look behind to see a trio of German shepherds hurtling towards him—he gave himself less than fifteen seconds.

As he watched Connor, still seemingly in a sprint, he remembered a joke—two hunters being confronted by a grizzly bear; one says to the other, 'I am going to run', and the other exclaims, 'You can't outrun a bear!', to which the first guy says, 'No, but I can outrun you.'

Connor disappeared to the right, and Carlo could almost smell the dogs now. The sound of an engine changed his decision to turn and knife them.

Following the Englishman's path, he turned and leapt for the open door.

The pain shot through his ass and up his spine as the fangs sank in. He smashed the door against the raging canine's head and felt the release.

The RAM sped off. He grimaced through the pain as he turned to see his sister in the back.

The RAM jolted along, needling the ache in his backside.

When the vehicle swung onto a smoother, tarmacked road, his physical pain gave way to humiliation.

The Englishman shifted in his seat to remove his belt webbing. He threw it in the back seat and barked at Arabella, "Something in that saved me from becoming Professor Xavier. Can you tell me what it was?"

Carlo's shame deepened, realising Connor's stumbling onto his face out of the club had been as a result of at least one bullet.

Arabella's hand appeared with a black steel tube, flattened and holed in the centre.

"My suppressor. Luckily, I have a spare," Connor said. "Hey, Carlo."

Carlo turned to face him.

The Englishman's fist collided with his cheekbone, bouncing his head off the window.

Arturo Bianchi paced his backroom and seethed, "How the fuck did he get here so fast? I should have had him kidnapped and *then* killed his sister."

"You tried to have his sister killed?" asked Rose, who sat opposite the desk. "Is she involved in this life?"

"He killed my brother. It's an eye for an eye."

When Rose said nothing, Bianchi looked at him. "How did you know to alert my security team?"

"I was taught to notice things," said Rose. "Maybe you should lie low until we handle this."

"I can't be seen to be hiding. *Il ratto* is not going to make me cower in my own town."

Rose thought for a moment. "It's the second guy, the masked one, who we want to be worried about. He came in like the Dam Busters, and he's an unknown."

"You think there is more?" said Bianchi, and Rose detected a hint of trepidation in his voice, and he didn't like it. Weakness in men caused hurt in others, especially outlaw business partners.

"I am not sure," said Rose truthfully. "But why would they send just one man to the rescue if they had a team?"

Bianchi pushed the bridge of the glasses up. "If it is just two men, they shouldn't be hard to find."

"We'll see. I am more concerned about what we'll do when we find them. They aren't two-bit hitmen, however many there are."

"I know what Carlo Andaloro is. Everyone in the fuckin' Mafia has heard of him, even if they don't know his name."

"Relax," said Mike. "We aren't choirboys, and they are only two men."

The former Green Beret said this more to assuage any fears Bianchi might have. He knew he could not underestimate this new enemy.

Bianchi's expression hinted that he had been mollified somewhat.

Rose continued, "There must be some business engagements you could attend for the next week or so? Maybe across the country?"

A grimace appeared on the Italian-Canadian's face before a smile crept into its place.

"I believe there might be."

Arabella pressed herself back into her seat as the Englishman's fist connected with her brother's face.

To her great surprise, not only did Carlo take it without retaliating, but he also took the venomous tirade that followed.

"Don't you ever fuck off on your own again! You're lucky I came prepared. I couldn't fuckin' believe it, watching you just bimble in."

"I almost had him. There were other players."

"Fuckin' A. It's a Mafia bar."

"It wasn't one of the bar's security. It was one of the bikers—or Special Forces soldiers who ride motorcycles. They are different."

Connor continued as if he hadn't heard her brother. "You promised me you would keep your professionalism. What good are you going to be dead?"

When Carlo didn't answer, Connor asked, "Where did you park your vehicle?"

"I will direct you."

"That's another thing we are going to have to risk."

Under Carlo's precise directions, they reached the area of his vehicle within five minutes, Arabella being a little surprised at how far he had parked from the bar.

Connor said to Carlo, "Give me the keys, and I'll go."

"The keys are buried under a rock, five paces at forty-five degrees from the front right corner."

The Englishman said, "That's one thing at least."

"I'll come with you."

"You'll get into the driver's seat and wait. If you hear gunshots, drive off or else all this will have been for nothing."

When Connor alighted from the RAM, Carlos shuffled into the driver's seat.

A silence hung between Arabella and her brother.

He broke it in Italian, saying, "I am sorry. I thought I saw an opportunity."

"Really?"

"Yes. Why would you ask?"

"Because sometimes I think you have a death wish. But then I remember you have a wish to beat death."

Her brother remained silent for a few moments before asking, "How did you know I would be going to the bar?"

"I did not. Connor tried to contact you. Somehow, he guessed where you would have gone," she answered. "Who is he to you, Carlo?"

"He is…he is a professional acquaintance."

"Nice to have a professional acquaintance like that."

After a few minutes, Connor returned and opened the driver's cab. He tossed the keys to her brother and said, "I've cleared the immediate area and the vehicle. I'll contact you tomorrow, and we'll come up with a plan."

17

Mike Rose felt a sense of déjà vu as he sat at the MC's 'Church' table. That MOM remained full of bluster seemed almost amazing to him.

When the bald man had gone on the offensive, MOM had spluttered before shrieking, *'Let the nightclub staff handle it.'*

It wasn't the command itself that betrayed his cowardice but its delivery.

"This is personal now. Whoever that was attacked us also."

Mike did not like the way the conversation was going. As soon as the word 'personal' entered the fray, it had a deleterious effect on professionalism. And with MOM's ego being seared, he didn't know how far down that rabbit hole they could go.

"We were not the target. It wasn't a direct attack on us."

"Whether or not they knew, it needs avenging. He's our business partner."

When Rose heard the murmurs of agreement, he said, "I'll go back and check the footage. See what I can find. The assassins are probably still up there in the area. You're welcome to come up if you like, Miles."

Rose asked with an expression of, *'Let's do this together, boss'*. However, MOM didn't disappoint with his reply, "I think I am best co-ordinating from here."

"You're right. Napoleon didn't fight up front."

"That's right," said MOM proudly, his apparent gullibility only now failing to surprise Rose.

"But I'd like you to take Kyle with you."

Rose feigned an expression of discomfort before saying, "No problem."

Though it gladdened Rose that MOM was not aware of Kyle's loyalty to him, he felt a little disconcerted that MOM might not trust him.

However, then MOM announced, "Avery, Rose will be the commander for this. You'll follow his lead."

Rose smiled inside, watching the former **MARSOC** marine feigning the same expression he had before replying, "OK."

MOM said, "You two investigate, recon and track 'em. If you see the opportunity to achieve the objective, take it."

Rose knew this to be code for, *'Please handle it so I don't have to put myself at risk.'*

"Yeh, OK," said Rose, grateful not to have to attempt micromanaging him.

Over the past year or so, Richèl became aware of the truth of the phrase, 'slave to your salary'.

Though MacKenzie had practically given her a blank cheque to decorate her office, she had resisted putting up anything too personal.

Still, it resembled the office of the CEO of a smaller company. Indeed, it sat on the same floor as the company's CEO, though hers was about a third of the size.

Larry MacKenzie's original industry had been mining, first domestically, specifically in the Yukon, and then abroad. He had since diversified into several others before his Trump-esque run at a political career.

And he paid her the sort of money that could have extinguished any plans to pursue her ambitions for the time being.

She saved part of her salary diligently, knowing one day—good or bad—this would end.

The Dutch national had learnt a great deal managing the affairs of the demanding billionaire.

The marble-like bulb on her desk lit up, and she made her way to his office.

His eyes gave her the flickering appraisal as they had always done, which had surprised her in the beginning. Even if Larry had been straight, she would not have found him lecherous. However, she knew with authoritative men, their advances could be more about power and control than sex.

"You seen the news?" he asked. His skin shone the way many rich people did, from regular exfoliating and moisturising.

"Yes."

"Luckily, the bar isn't in our friend's name, but we want to make sure a talented reporter doesn't discover his involvement in it."

"OK, I'll speak to our advisors."

Larry nodded. "Apparently, the assassin would have succeeded, but the big man's Special Forces friends just happened to be present. One of them managed to distract the hitman before he took the shot."

"That was fortuitous."

"Well, he's decided to go on a tour of Canada until all this settles down. He wants you to meet him on the road."

Which means he wants to try to fuck me—she thought.

"You mean he wants to meet me on his own?"

As if reading her thoughts, he replied, "I have informed him that due to the present threat he is under, I will send you with your security."

"And what did he say to that?"

"He reckoned it unnecessary, but I insisted. He insisted on only one coming with you, though."

"Of course."

"Nothing will happen unless you want it to."

She felt her stomach convulse but hid her disgust.

"What did he say he wanted to discuss?"

"I am not sure, but it'll involve him wanting more money," he said. "It's thrown a spanner in the works for everyone."

Ciara kept an expression of contriteness off her face under the lambasting.

She had to quickly get over her distaste of taking work calls in her apartment, realising she wasn't yet—if she would ever be with this unit—in a position to delegate. Bruce had impressed upon her the importance of protecting her 'leisure time' but admitted there were no set work hours.

Behind her stood a pure white vinyl backdrop, which she had purchased for meetings like these. She didn't want anyone, ally or not, able to glean more information than necessary.

For this reason, she had also worn a collared shirt despite being in jogging pants.

The candle in the corner of the room flickered out the smell of lime and mandarin.

The nearing-middle-aged, bull-necked man on screen held the title of CSIS foreign relations officer. However, Ciara knew Philip Marr ran a clandestine unit not dissimilar to The Chameleon Project.

His dark hair had the same length throughout, including his beard, giving it the look of a furry helmet on a ruddy but handsome face.

"Our world is a clandestine one. Not a 'attempt to shoot a Mafia boss inside a crowded sports bar and then smoke grenade the place to escape' world. I thought that would be understood without having to be expressed."

Ciara held her reasoning and instead said, "Mister Marr, please accept my profuse apologies for this. It is an anomaly with these agents."

She watched his expression soften a little and his tone ease. "Look, he has plenty of enemies. We can pass the attempt off onto one of them. But he'll be on high alert. Your chances of success, our chances of success, will have narrowed."

"Please, give us the chance to handle this for you. If worse comes to worst, I can assure you your organisation will not be so much as mentioned, let alone implicated."

His eyebrows raised. "It's your call. I will understand if you want to call it off."

She sincerely told him, "I believe we can still get this done."

"I hope you're right, Miss Robson. This goes higher than a simple drug-pushing Mafioso. If we don't find the evidence of his higher contacts, there is a good chance Canada becomes a police-state."

Ciara kept a neutral expression. She did not know why she felt uneasy, but she did.

18

Michael Rose and Avery arrived at the bar just as the police wrapped the cordon away. With it being daylight and outside of the bar's business hours, the establishment reminded Mike of a winter tree.

They watched briefly before Mike said, "I don't want to turn this into a recon. We'll come back in thirty minutes."

"Had enough of watching *Ali Babas* in *the sand* to last us both a lifetime," said Kyle, a year the younger.

The two men had first crossed paths ten years ago under the umbrella of Combined Joint Task Force—Operation Inherent Resolve, a multi-military formation aiming to 'degrade and destroy' ISIS. Though Avery had been sent under the Canadian sub-mission of Operation Impact to train Iraqi personnel, he spent much of his time carrying out recon and sniper missions on ISIS targets.

"I am sure you have," said Mike, swinging his leg over his bike.

"Come to think of it, our relationship hasn't changed. You tell me what to do, and I do it."

Mike smiled as they rode away. He had first met Kyle when issuing a brief to the Joint Task Force 2 sniper team of which Kyle had been part. JTF 2, Canada's premier Special Forces unit, had fielded their best guys to the operation.

Mike had been a twenty-six-year-old corporal at the time and given the responsibility of a brief, usually given by an officer or at least a staff sergeant.

It had surprised Mike, though gladdened him,

to meet Kyle again whilst on the circuit a few years later.

The outlaw bikers returned after half an hour to a scene now clear of the police. They rode down from the upper car park, alighting from the bikes just outside the bar.

The phantom-like smell of the previous night's gas danced in Mike's brain.

Kyle said, "They are fucking late already."

"What were you expecting after seeing their performance the other night? Professionalism?"

Kyle smirked, "Guess not."

Mike asked, "I never asked you how Vienna was."

"It was OK."

"One of the most culturally rich places in the world. Or so I've heard."

"When you've seen one massive beige and white building with a statue on it, you've seen them all."

"What about the women?"

"Nice ladies there. A lot of them have arm tattoos, but guess what the best thing about Vienna was?"

"What?"

"They have these electric scooter racks all around the city that you hire through your phone, and off you go, eh?"

Mike tilted his chin. "Here they come."

The trio of the bar's security staff ambled down from the upper car park on top of a gentle hill.

On the left walked a very tall man with curly, rustic red hair tufting out either side of his head. This, and his light-caramel complexion, suggested a mixed-race parent.

On the right, a man with cropped hair, shorter than average but with a width, making him nearly square in shape.

Mike watched the man in the centre. Almost as tall as the man on his right but in the same shape as the man on his left.

He sported a balcony-like belly over his belt and had been the one who had initially attempted to apprehend Carlo Andaloro.

The black eyes denoted a badly broken nose.

A fire extinguisher to the beak would do that, thought Mike.

Rose could sense the hulk still smarting from it.

A seared ego would not help them in this situation, so Rose refrained from reprimanding them for being late.

Instead, he said to the black eyes, "The dirty fuckin' rat. I watched him blindside you."

Rose didn't mean it. He admired how the compact, bald Italian had managed to fight his way past security.

And Rose had put out feelers to some of his former comrades regarding Carlo's background.

Mike had read his share of military files to know that what appeared—an operational career with the 2nd Foreign Parachute Regiment of the Foreign Legion—though impressive, would pale in comparison to the redacted content. Mike could tell Carlo had been 'sheep dipped' several times during his career to do god knows what for the French.

"Tell me about it," grunted the big man. "The boss always said we should be gentle with the customers. This is what listening to him gets me."

It was your underestimating him and being out of shape that got you that, you fat fuck, thought Rose.

And the fact he would speak about Bianchi in a derogatory way, no matter how mild, sent an uneasy feeling through Mike.

"I am Mike, and this is Kyle."

"Am Sid, this is Patrick," said Sid, gesturing to the tall man with the rustic side-head afro before pointing to the muscle ball. "And this is John."

"We are going to need to see the security footage," said Rose.

"We had to scrub that from the storage to stop the police from getting hold of it. Mister Bianchi didn't want them getting to these two before we did."

"We are aware, like we are aware you keep off-site digital recordings, which is what we want to see."

"Nah, we've been over them. There is nothing for you to see. We work on a need-to-know basis, and you two don't need to know. Or see, or whatever."

Rose knew the man's embarrassment was causing the stall—that and a power play to regain his standing amongst his colleagues.

Rose needed full transparency and immediate obedience to increase his chances of hunting this man.

He also knew Bianchi did not use 'made guys' for door security.

Within a fraction of a second, the Beretta M9 transferred from his waistband to his hand. The bang exploded, toppling the ogre with a scream.

The colour seemed to drain out of his bulging eyes as he struggled into a sit-up. His hands hovered over his bullet-shattered knee.

Rose said, "We, as in all of us, haven't got the time to be tiptoeing around this fucking yokel's ego. I want that footage, and I want it now. Or else what good are you?"

After quiet moments, save for the whimpering, Patrick said, "There is a laptop in the car. I can get it."

"Kyle here will go with you. Give him the key fob."

The tall man nodded and did so.

The big man hissed through gritted teeth, "You shot me in the fuckin' leg."

Rose swung the Beretta to his face and said, "I could always put you out of your misery."

Sid's meaty hands flew to his face.

Rose always thought it strange that people's instinct would be to use their hands to shield a bullet.

Avery walked to the black Ford Explorer behind the security staff member.

He had spent a lot of time mastering drawing pistols, in this case, a SIG Sauer P320, which he had become familiar with during his JTF2 days.

He remembered the burning embarrassment of the first time he had been put through a range serial in plain clothes. Whilst attempting to unholster the SIG, he had failed to pull up his sweater, which caught the pistol, leading to an embarrassing fumble and his shots mockingly sounding off a second or two after his contemporaries on the point.

Since then, he had become swift, not needing the full extension of his arms to get off an accurate shot, instead barely needing it out of the holster to hit a torso at ten paces.

Usually, he'd have reservations regarding leaving a colleague outnumbered by men capable of violence.

However, he knew he needn't worry; Kyle had seen Rose in enough action to know he'd be fine.

At first, Avery couldn't fully understand why Rose hadn't taken the top position despite having everyone's support.

Rose had told him, *'MOM wears his ego on his sleeve. He's easy to manipulate and the one that any law enforcement will want the most.'*

He understood the principle but didn't bank on it in practice. However, watching Rose play MOM gave him a greater appreciation of the asymmetric warfare mindset Rose had.

He hadn't yet asked what turned Rose to the 'dark side'.

Avery felt the warmth of the Canadian sun on his face. One thing he hated about Canada was the constant cold.

His tours of the Middle East had shown him his body could stand the heat more than the cold.

He meandered up to the grassy knoll, shifting his eyes back and forth for lone fighting-aged males.

There did not seem to be any—just a few dog walkers and a couple in their thirties.

The duo began to walk in his direction, but on observing them, he ignored them.

They passed him, sharing a kiss, and Avery's thoughts drifted to Nikki, a dancer from back home he was considering making his old lady.

I even think like an outlaw biker now, he thought.

Pressing the key fob, the central locking

unlatched.

The English voice made Patrick jump.

"You want to get that door mirror fixed."

Avery frowned. The door mirror was intact. Before he could turn, a silent bullet smashed it.

The voice said, "Don't make any movements unless your name is Neo."

"OK," replied Avery.

The English voice said, "Did you hear that, *Sideshow Bob*?"

Despite his predicament, Avery couldn't help but smirk at the accuracy of the nickname.

Patrick's voice betrayed a tremor. "Yeh, I got it."

"Throw the key fob behind you."

Kyle did so.

The Englishman said, "You can alert the dog walkers if you want, but the sniper will shoot the pair of you. In the following melee, we'll run away shouting there is a shooter. People will run, too. And there are no security cameras up here, which is why these div doormen parked here."

Avery admired the logic. By using a sniper, the Englishman didn't have to hold a gun himself.

The forest in which the sniper must be hiding was about 300 yards away; to hit the wing mirror must have taken a degree of skill, depending on the rifle and scope. Enough skill that Avery decided against an immediate attempt to escape. Besides, the timing of the shot indicated communication between the Englishman and the sniper.

The voice said, "We will do a little dance where you turn a hundred-and-eighty degrees to your left, and we match you to the right. This way, you don't get to see our faces. Then you will both wait here as we drive away with this Explorer. You'll wait here until your friends standing outside the bar come and see where you have gone. If you move before then, you die. If you even glance back, you die. Understand?"

"Yes," replied Kyle and Patrick in unison.

"Then tell me. So that I don't have to feel guilty when you die for deviating."

When Avery repeated the plan, the Englishman asked, "You get that, Sideshow?"

"Yes."

"Good," said the Englishman. "Move."

They began to rotate in time, and Kyle and Patrick stood in place.

The former Canadian Special Forces soldier wasn't sure what concerned him more: the sniper rifle's crosshairs hovering over him or having to face Rose.

Connor sped away from the scene once Arabella secured herself next to him.

It had meant to be a simple recon of the bar. Though a risk, Connor had agreed for Carlo to bring his sniper rifle on the off-chance Bianchi might turn up.

The former Legionnaire had his arcs on the outside of the bar, but given the sniper rifle range, he could also shoot accurately on targets in the upper car park.

Connor and Arabella only had an initial view of the upper car park. When the bikers showed up, they briefly kept their helmets on, frustrating Connor's chance for a clear photo of their faces.

Because there was only one entrance route to the bar, Connor didn't think to obtain a second camera—another oversight he cursed himself for.

Instead, Carlo had observed the meeting between the bar's security team and two bikers who had almost a military bearing about them. The former Legionnaire had been confident he had seen them the other night.

An altercation had developed, and the leader of the pair had revealed himself by shooting one of the men in the leg and dispatching another, along with his fellow biker, to the vehicle.

Initially, Connor thought the pair might be driving off somewhere but dismissed it when Carlo radioed that the one with the gun was holding the other two in place. Then Connor realised they must have been getting something from the vehicle—potentially significant, seeing as one of the bikers went with one of Bianchi's men to retrieve it.

For an action so opportunistic, he felt it had gone as well as could be expected.

Connor stopped the Explorer at the rocky outcrop. Carlo appeared, slung his kit and rifle bag in the trunk and got into the back.

"What now?" asked Carlo.

"I'll drive you to the RAM. You'll follow us to somewhere remote. We'll search this properly before torching it to lose the DNA. There's that laptop beside you, at least, that we'll look to break into."

They eventually dropped Carlo off.

Connor drove fast, mindful not only of speed cameras and unmarked police vehicles, but that the Explorer might have a tracker on it.

Arabella cut through his thoughts with, "Do

you have siblings?"

"No," said Connor. "I have cousins I am unusually close to and am…no."

Connor prevented himself from going into his relationship with Rayella.

He saw her smile, and she said, "I like that. A bit of mystery."

"I wasn't trying to be mysterious."

"I know. That's why I liked it."

Connor refrained from any flirtatious comeback, and she continued, "But if a man holds it all inside, it can consume him."

"I am set without your attempt to convert me to Catholicism, thanks."

"You don't believe in God?"

Connor surprised himself with having to think about the question. But after a moment, he gave his stock answer to the question.

"Yes. I believe God is simply the concept of cause and effect to levels beyond our comprehension. It's like an ant trying to comprehend why there are three 'world' titles in boxing."

"So you don't believe a man should have a practice of centring himself?"

"Is that what you heard by what I just said?"

"No. I asked a related but separate question. Or, are you sensitive like a woman?" she asked without irony.

"If I didn't have a practice of centring myself, then I might have risen to your 'sensitive' barb."

"Then you do, then? Reflect, I mean."

"I am attempting to be a man of mystery, remember?"

"I thought you were not trying to be

mysterious?"

Fuck, she got me there.

"I've tried to acquire the habit of meditating. I let the sediment of my mind settle and then ask questions."

"So you ask God questions?"

Connor answered, "I ask. I am not sure who or what answers."

Eventually, they reached a small rocky outcrop deep within a wood. Under the Englishman's instruction, they built a fire break around it using the stones.

Once satisfied, he set the Explorer ablaze.

They walked far enough away to avoid harm should the fuel tank explode but short enough to be able to dash forward to extinguish the flames if they went beyond the firebreak.

After a time, Connor lifted the laptop. "Let's go and see what's on this bad boy."

When Kyle and Patrick hadn't returned after ten minutes, Mike marched John up to the car park by concealed gunpoint, deciding to leave Sid clutching his knee outside the bar.

The surreal scene of Kyle and Patrick standing in place soon confronted him.

Kyle had explained to him what had happened.

Mike decided it would be unlikely that the sniper would still be in place but cursed the possibility that he might be being observed.

"What exactly was on the laptop?" demanded Mike of Patrick.

"Just the security footage of that night."

Mike didn't like the micro-expressions, as the bouncer answered.

"It'll be easier if you told me now than we find out later."

"Just the security footage—it's encrypted, anyway. Nothing else to do with work. Just a few of my social media accounts, and I don't talk work on there. YouTube, too."

"Is there a tracker on the vehicle?" asked Mike.

Patrick shrugged, "I don't know."

Knowing that he couldn't trust any of these guys' professionalism or honesty, Mike began to think.

19

Richèl's stomach tightened as her black Audi Q8 approached the log cabin complex. Under another circumstance, she might have just admired such architecture set against the majestic backdrop.

The sun lit the faces of the enormous log cabins, whose roofs reminded her of Little Red Riding Hood head coverings.

A contrail streaked across the blue sky behind them but in front of the white-capped mountains.

The gaggle of sunglasses, standing outside smoking, snapped their attention to the Q8 as it rumbled up the hill.

Her minder drove. With him being of average height and build, she felt vulnerable despite her boss assuring her that Pierre was former Canadian Special Forces.

She felt glad her oversized sunglasses hid her eyes. She knew enough about masculine psychology to know showing a feminine vulnerability could bring out a protective instinct. However, she knew enough about criminal psychology to know that weakness attracted *handsy* men like sharks to blood.

As the vehicle slowed to a halt, she reminded herself to stand tall, speak confidently and not show any sign of intimidation.

Her pant-suited legs swung out, and she approached the men who openly admired her.

She spoke, "My driver can take his luggage. Please take mine from the trunk and lead me to my room."

Upon hearing a guffaw, she asked, "What's so

funny?"

One said, "You thinking you're Cleopatra, and we're your slaves."

She inhaled through her nose to prevent her nerves from strangling her voice.

"An Egyptian Queen would not have to ask and certainly would not have said 'please'. No matter; pleeasssee, tell Mister Bianchi to rearrange our meeting. Pierre, let's depart."

As she began to walk back to the car, another called after her, "Sorry for our friend, Miss. We will grab your bags and take you to your room."

She turned and removed her glasses. "No. He will."

The man fidgeted for a moment. His look of defiance melted under her stare, and he made his way to the trunk and grasped her two cases.

She made no effort to assist him.

"What's your name?" she asked.

He seemed to hesitate. "Dom. I mean Dominic."

"So, Dominic, lead the way."

He did so through the wooden doors of the giant Wendy house.

She frowned on seeing mattresses strewn over the floor.

"Why are they here?"

He stood straight. "We are here to protect you, Miss Vigar."

"Vergeer. And why would I need your protection when I have my own?"

"These people are no joke. And you have only brought a single man."

Her mind whirled through her retorts. If their

orders were indeed to protect her, she couldn't ask them to stay outside or in the next cabin.

"I thought you were here to protect your boss?"

"We do. There are two teams. We are yours."

"I am flattered, but shouldn't the protection be further out in the forest? I am not a military expert, but maybe attacks should be dealt with as far away as possible from their targets?"

The man seemed almost to sag. "There are teams out there."

She nodded. "Lead on."

Dominic trundled up the stairs, elbows flared so as not to let the cases hit his legs.

He set them down by a door and opened it to reveal her room.

Bianchi had not skimped on her accommodation. The smooth stone walls almost shone, framed by rustic, stained wood.

Richèl felt relief upon spying the en suite bathroom—she had feared sharing with her 'protective team'.

She wondered if one could ever tire of the blue mountain view.

"When is Mister Bianchi arriving?"

"This evening. You have a business meeting in his cabin tonight."

She caught something in his tone she didn't like but simply asked, "When do I eat?"

"You eat at the meeting."

She began to feel uneasy. The Mafia boss play lacked any subtlety.

"What time?"

"Eight o'clock."

"Why so late?"

"Boss wants you to have an appetite."

She turned to him and said, "Thank you. You can leave now. Send my bodyguard up."

Connor sat alone at the desk in his room at the cabin. He had swept the place for bugs, surprised not to find any.

He thought the CSIS would have wanted to keep tabs on a foreign agent.

First, he fired up his laptop and sipped his black coffee, the aroma of which blended with the pine of the walls and awaited connection.

Ciara's emerald eyes appeared within seconds.

They went through their initial pre-determined questions and replies protocol. They would sound like simple greetings to the uninitiated but were duress countermeasures.

Recently, Ciara had also used codes at the beginning of any rare video instructions to distinguish between her and potentially false AI creations.

She then asked, "What happened?"

Despite her directness, the question lacked an accusatory tone.

Their professional relationship began when Bruce McQuillan brought Ciara in as a field agent. Connor, more experienced and talented on the street, had acted as a quasi-mentor to her.

They had fallen into bed and continued a sporadic sexual relationship until recently. He had made the more robust attempt to curtail that aspect of their relationship despite failing the few occasions she had initiated.

However, since Bruce McQuillan had

promoted her to be in charge of 'The Chameleon Project', her days of coming on to him ceased—to his relief and disappointment.

"Our friend went off the reservation."

"Is he likely to again?"

"I don't think so, but I can't make guarantees regarding other people's natures."

"I know you can't guarantee any more incidents in the open, but none of this can lead back to the CSIS."

Connor knew she had to say it, even though they both knew it to be redundant.

He said, "I've retrieved a laptop from Bianchi's security team. Not sure what's on it, but I could use some help in cracking into it safely."

The 'help' Connor referred to was Jaime, the tech genius of 'The Chameleon Project'.

"He's ready to be patched in after our call," she said.

"How did you know?"

"I am learning," she said.

Connor raised his eyebrows approvingly.

She continued, "You need anything else?"

"No, thank you."

The screen pixelated her image into Jaime's. This was a first; usually, Jaime only conversed with him via audio-only calls after the passing of certain security protocols and with his voice distorted.

Connor didn't ask why.

"Hello, Connor," said Jaime stiffly.

"Alright, Jaime?"

"Yes," the Peruvian replied. "How can I help you?"

"I've taken possession of a laptop. There is a

fair chance that the encryption is beyond my capabilities."

"Select the blue lead with the initial HCC on it."

Connor, used to Jaime's abrupt method of communication, snatched the said lead and showed it to him.

For the next three minutes, Jaime talked Connor through the procedure of connecting the two laptops, booting up and bypassing encryption—which Connor correctly anticipated to be more than a mere password.

"I will organise the data," said Jaime.

The Englishman watched the folder appearing on his screen.

Connor sat in silence, knowing his efforts were futile compared to Jaime's.

He smiled inside, knowing the Peruvian's brain likely wouldn't acknowledge Connor might be uncomfortable just sitting in wait.

"It seems he has had communication over the past few months with someone working from the Canadian Parliament Buildings. Difficult to tell who or where exactly."

This surprised Connor; Jaime's superlative skill usually pinpointed the exact person.

Jaime said, as if reading his mind, "I'll need more time to narrow the user without risk of detection. The communication is not part of the official servers, but the encryption is a level above."

Connor frowned. "You're saying whoever this is has comms that surpass the Canadian Government?"

"Seems so."

"A foreign intelligence agency? Didn't the former leader of the opposition complain that Chinese interference might have led to him being ousted?"

"I do not have enough data for assumptions yet."

"Alright."

"But I think… Bianchi might be in Lake Muskoka, between Port Carling and Gravenhurst, Ontario."

"I'll be on my way."

"Connor. Our… organisation relies on its friends."

"I understand, Jaime. You want me to kidnap him so I can find out who his connection is in the Canadian Parliament Buildings?"

Jaime gifted a smile. "Yes. Can you do this?"

"We shall see, won't we?"

20

Larry MacKenzie relaxed his shoulders and breathed clean, grass-scented air.

The golf course reminded him of something out of the *World's Most Scenic River Journeys* but without the river.

When MacKenzie first came to the course a few years ago, it took him a moment to take in the expanse and range of the mountain forestry down the fairway. And he had wondered if a particularly determined photographer could have taken pictures of some of the most influential individuals in Canada and the world in conversation.

A few months later, the golf course's security chief arranged for him to be taken for a flight by helicopter around the wider area. He soon realised the fictional photographer would need the stealth and fitness of a Special Forces soldier to navigate the dense mountainous terrain while avoiding all the security apparatus.

When MacKenzie had asked about drones, the pilot had laughed, *'We have counter-drone systems throughout the area, but the eagles attack most.'*

At first, Larry didn't like how long these games took when he could have dealt with more pressing matters—he always had more pressing matters.

But he had learned to enjoy golf as the most powerful men he knew preferred to discuss sensitive issues in places like this.

The open ground made listening devices redundant unless worn by the parties.

Over time, he had begun to see that the conversations on the golf range, depending on who he had them with, could be worth months of money.

Still, he had insisted on a nine-hole game rather than the standard eighteen, which his opponent quickly agreed to.

The Chinese man wore a khaki bucket hat and white polo shirt, with his caddie more resembling an Oriental stuntman than a golf expert. Larry's attendant had a similar look, albeit Caucasian.

The two caddies kept a further distance from the two billionaires and one another than was necessary.

Alfred Lau's face always reminded Larry of a burger in that the spaces between the eyes, nose and mouth seemed narrower than average.

Officially, Lau had the title of CEO of Moneyorg, a Canada-based financial service reputed to be accessible to the working man.

Larry admired Lau's restraint in waiting for the fourth hole before bringing up business.

"So, Larry, what do you want?"

The businessman-politician played it coy. "What do you mean?"

"What do you want in return for granting my family's businesses exemption to your proposed policy of not allowing foreign enterprises to buy real estate here in Canada?"

"The policy doesn't say you're never allowed. Only that—"

"Cut to the chase, Larry. We are both busy men."

Larry hid a smile. "I want exclusive mining rights in Guinea-Bissau and Chile."

"It isn't enough for you to own half the mining in the Yukon?"

MacKenzie smiled at him but said nothing.

Lau said, "You want to take advantage of the future demand for aluminium and lithium?"

"Of course."

Lau's smile didn't reach his eyes. "Those rights will be coming up for auction soon. You're as welcome as anyone to bid."

"Oh, I will. But you're not going to disclose the bids."

"Why would we do that?"

"Because I suspect my bid will not be the highest, and you do not want people asking why that is?"

Lau let out a low laugh. "You think my family is going to release those rights for quarters when multinationals and governments are prepared to pay obscene numbers?"

"As am I. I just don't want to pay the full amount if I am to grant you this concession. And we must devise a plan so I can explain it away should the media find out."

"Something tells me you already have the particulars worked out."

"Disguising it through a charity doesn't take much working out," replied Larry.

"Why do I get the feeling your play for Prime Minister is simply a way for you to make more money?"

"Because that is how you would think."

"That is true," laughed the Chinese billionaire. "I am thinking of entering politics myself."

MacKenzie knew Lau would be a lock to

become a member of the Chinese Parliament, which already had about 100 billionaires.

"A different game of business, but there are some cross-overs."

"I bet," said Lau as they trundled down the green. "But what happens after your tenure? Think they won't notice you will be one of the world's wealthiest men?"

"Money can buy everything, Alfred, even silence. You know that."

Connor stood in the kitchen of Carlo's single-storey safe house.

From the outside, it looked strange in that, though not much larger than a chalet, it had a lengthy driveway and vast open grassland—*Like a small areola on a big tit*, thought Connor.

The Yorkshireman knew, through Jaime, that Carlo had simply procured the place under an alias through 'Airbnb'.

According to Jaime, it had been an identity he used several times and was impressively layered.

Now he stood in the Tudor-styled kitchen, watching brother and sister argue in low, rapid Italian.

Connor hadn't been sure of the best course of action. If they left her, she would not be a distraction during the operation, except with Carlo not having the reassurance of sight on her.

She proved calm and effective when they took the laptop, but this would be entirely different.

One thing he had begun to suspect was that her level of fitness might be the equal of her brother's.

When their bickering reached a crescendo,

Connor said, "Alright. Have a bit of space. Carlo, let's have a chat."

Connor picked up his coffee and caught her lips pressing as he turned.

The men walked down the short hallway. Above the entrance to the back porch hung a large photo of a curly-haired, red and white-shirted hockey player holding a massive silver trophy on the ice. The inscription below read, **'Bobby Clarke. 1976 Canada Cup.'**

Connor said, "I notice there isn't a bath."

"So?"

"So, showers can be death traps when you're on operations. You can't hear properly or bring a weapon to bear quickly unless you shower with it."

Carlo narrowed his eyes at him as they stepped out into the crisp air. "You think I am to wash my face in the same water that I have cleaned my ass?"

"I would think that was secondary to—"

"People do not wipe their asses before bed. Who knows where your fingers go as you sleep? It is disgusting. But wiping your ass with toilet paper is not good."

Connor, despite himself, asked, "Why?"

Carlo again looked at him like he was a child. "Unless you have the arsehole of a woman, you will have hair. If I slapped your head with shit, do you think a wipe with dried tissue will clean it?"

Connor took a turn to squint. "Then why the 'arse-wiping-before-bed' routine? Surely, you've defeated own your argument?"

"I use baby wipes."

"Right, OK. Let's talk about the task at

hand."

"What do you think?"

Connor looked at Carlo over the top of his coffee. "She could prove useful."

"And she could die."

He shrugged. "And she could be kidnapped here. Then be at the mercy of Bianchi if she isn't lucky enough to be killed outright."

Though his combat partner feigned to be making up his mind, Connor knew he had already decided.

He didn't answer, just gestured that they go back in.

Carlo addressed his sister. "You do exactly as Connor says when he says it."

"Ovviamente,"—*Obviously*—she replied tersely.

Connor said, "We'll have to drill her in hand signals. It'll be quite an insertion going in."

"Insertion?" she frowned.

"A hike in."

"I can do that," she answered. Connor believed her.

"Let's take a look."

He sat on a high chair and slid out his laptop as the siblings crowded in.

He opened Google Maps.

"This is the general area. Several multi-millionaire holiday homes dotted around. I believe it's these."

He zoomed in on a cluster of five cabins.

"Why do you think that?" asked Arabella.

"Because the sophistication of security measures put in place to hide whoever owns them is excessive."

She asked, "Are you a computer expert?"
"Depends what game it is."
Her answer of "OK" impressed him.
He said, "The general layout makes its security tighter than a young Kevin Keegan's perm."
She frowned, "Kevin Keegan?"
"Never mind."
Carlo chipped in. "The larger cabin is where Bianchi will play the king. The others will be for guests and his security."
"Are you saying that he will have no security in his cabin with him?" she asked.
"That would be extremely brazen of him," said Connor. "But he's a brazen character, isn't he?"
"Maybe not so much after the other night," said Carlo. "We will still have to use stealth."
"There's an obstacle with that," said Connor. "The thread alignment on my spare suppressor has gone. I didn't tighten it properly when I was initially checking my kit. I can't get another in time."
He turned to Carlo. "What's that smirk for?"
"See, *mio amico,* we can all make mistakes."

Arturo Bianchi felt the swirl of anticipation as the black Cadillac CT6 V smoothly processioned him up the long road.
The first time he had seen Richèl Vergeer sparked an intense desire to have her.
Initially, she reminded him of the character Mia Wallace from 'Pulp Fiction'. Now, she seemed more like Cleopatra, and he had wondered if she had royal blood.
She will when she becomes my Queen, he thought.

He remembered being made to watch a programme on Napoleon Bonaparte as a kid in reform school. He became fascinated with the French emperor—how he came from nothing to be the most powerful man in the world.

The programme talked about how much his relationship with Joséphine de Beauharnais had helped him. Though it had been the woman who had helped smooth out the feathers Napoleon ruffled in their relationship, Bianchi knew he'd have the more popular personality between himself and Vergeer.

A good fuck would sort the stuck-up bitch out.

He was late after picking up his custom suits from the tailors. Most women wouldn't have appreciated such a thing, but he knew Vergeer would.

Other women would be impressed with the flash of a Rolex or the wing of a Lamborghini, but Miss Vergeer would appreciate subtlety.

For this reason, he hadn't brought the Huracan.

He knew he couldn't yet compete with the resources Larry could bring to bear, but he knew he had an air of danger that women like Vergeer were attracted to, even if they didn't admit it.

The luxury sedan floated along the road towards the log cabin complex.

He purposely had the driver—one of his foot soldiers—drive up this stretch of road; he wanted her to see so she could see he was making her wait.

He looked up at her window and felt a tinge of disappointment. She wasn't there watching.

She might be asleep, he thought.

His men stood like meerkats as his vehicle pulled up to his lair.

He had spoken to Mike Rose, who informed him of what happened at the bar. Bianchi had felt a sliver of fear, realising the risks the 'Ndrangheta assassin was prepared to take to reach him—and that his 'team' consisted of at least another man and a woman.

And he felt a ribbon of excitement when he sent Mike a picture of Arabella Andaloro—and was told that though Mike's colleague couldn't be sure, he would bet she was the same woman in the car park.

The crazy fuck might have brought his sister with him—hoped Bianchi.

Patrick had insisted the security footage on his laptop was encrypted—and even if Andaloro managed to access it, it was the only sensitive information on there.

His Capo stepped towards him.

"Good to see you, boss."

"Thanks," he said. "How was she?"

"Feisty," said Fabio. "Was gonna skedaddle, but we convinced her back."

"Why?"

"She started ordering the boys around like she was Mussolini. Said she wanted her bags taken up. One of the boys gave her a bit of chat, but we got her back when she made to drive back."

"Which one gave her the chat?" he growled, already knowing who it would likely be.

His guess proved correct when his Capo said, "Dom."

Bianchi nodded, flicked a look at the culprit and shouted, "Dominic, come here a minute."

He observed the 'soldier' straightening his back as he walked over.

Bianchi knew he mustn't show his desire for a woman to supersede his affection for his men.

Seeing the flash of petulance on the youth's face before it straightened into contriteness, he changed his mind.

Still, he said jovially, "Dominic, what was the last thing I told you all before I left?"

Dominic shrugged. "That she was a star and should be treated well."

"Oh, that's bad," said Bianchi.

"What do you mean?"

"I mean, you don't have an excuse."

Bianchi slapped him hard with his palm before whipping the back of his hand through his face.

Wanting to go further but not trusting his cardiovascular fitness, he gripped the lighter man by the throat.

An idea flashed before he lashed him verbally.

"Guys, I want this man in the hospital tonight."

He laced his heel around the back of Dominic's foot and threw him over it as he pushed his glasses back up his face.

With his prey now sat before him, Bianchi looked at his men and asked, "What the fuck are you waiting for?"

They began to crowd in on Dominic like tentative vultures before one braved a punt with his toecap. This acted as a trigger, and they all began to boot their victim viciously, like frenzied piranhas.

It took him a moment to realise his thrill. His smile deepened into his cheeks, and his eyes flicked to Vergeer's window.

Now she stood watching. He couldn't quite make out the details, but he guessed she was smiling, too.

21

Mike watched Bianchi's security team through the Trijicon TR24 AccuPoint scope of his Colt M4A1 SOPMOD Carbine rifle.

He had lain for over three hours, barely a hundred yards away without even a ghillie suit on, and no one spotted him.

He had thoroughly briefed Bianchi's auspiciously titled 'Head of Security' on the importance of shallow clearance patrols and binocular checks.

Though he had a burning disrespect for their unprofessionalism, he understood that adherence to **SOPs** to guard against scenarios that might never happen had to be ruthlessly drilled into individuals through hard training.

He had brought a small team with him to form an outer position, covering any approaches through the forest to the cabin complex.

The more he got to know Bianchi, the less surprised he was Larry MacKenzie had contacted him through an intermediary.

Bianchi was smart and cunning, but he had an insecurity and ego that bled into the lines. Whereas MacKenzie might have had the same, Mike suspected he'd have them tightly leashed.

Though MacKenzie, unlike Bianchi, would never get his hands dirty by physically dishing out violence, he frightened Mike more.

That Bianchi was a pawn in the billionaire's chessboard was obvious to Mike—and maybe Bianchi knew it, too.

And Mike knew he was also a pawn, but he didn't care. Everyone worked for someone.

Still, he knew there was the ever-present danger of becoming a loose end for a billionaire who saw having people disappear as part of business.

The best way to avoid his bad graces was to make himself useful.

And in this instance, it meant keeping this Bianchi alive.

Mike flicked the scope to the upper window of the next cabin.

And it definitely meant keeping her alive.

Richèl Vergeer's shining black, beautifully coiffured hair reminded him of how Cleopatra was depicted. She seemed delicately feline in her figure and movements.

Though Mike kept strictly professional while working, he could see her beauty was harshly striking—even without her glasses on.

She looked the type a rich man might keep around as eye candy, but he remembered MacKenzie's words: *'When I am not there but she is, then she is me.'*

He flicked his scope back to Bianchi's window. Placing his phone over his scope, he snapped a picture of him and then sent it to the Mafioso chief.

Mike waited for Bianchi to end his call and look at his phone before calling him.

"Yes?"

"That's how close I've managed to get with a rifle. I suggest you have a word with your security or else replace them."

He ended the call before Bianchi could retort

and patrolled back to the defensive position.

Being in the woods like this imbued him with vague nostalgia.

He remembered the Afghanistan green zone had a dangerously hypnotic effect during long spells of quiet.

And he didn't want to fall into that trap now.

He approached the small makeshift camp, holding his carbine by the stock in his left hand to indicate he wasn't under duress.

Due to the good visibility, the inward-facing sentry simply waved him in.

Mike asked, "Patrol back yet?"

"Not yet," answered Roger, a former MARSOC operator.

Mike frowned. "They go out late?"

"No," replied the marine. "But it's only been ten minutes, boss. No need to crash out the QRF just yet."

"Raise them," commanded Mike.

Roger's face flashed the barest hint of annoyance before touching the pressel of his radio.

"Kasper Four, this is Rico One. What is your ETA to base, over?"

Silence.

Roger repeated his transmission.

Mike barked, "Keep your eyes forward!" before zipping around his team to organise the QRF.

He didn't know how, but Mike knew something had happened to the patrol.

Each held a suppressed M4 CQBR (Close Quarters Battle Receiver); Mike had used them for CQB in Iraq and not in open-air settings like this but rated it for manoeuvrability.

He barked out orders concisely, and they moved off after checking their weapons and kit.

The thought occurred that, on this occasion, he had consciously decided to be the predator.

Connor kept his body angled so the tree hid him entirely. He remained statue-still as the two soldiers approached.

He banished the thoughts of gratitude they had seen the patrol first. And that there didn't appear to be any dogs.

Connor didn't want to assess his and Carlo's chances of pulling off what they were about to attempt. Failure for them didn't just extend to dying but allowing an unsuppressed rifle report to sound this far away from the cabin complex.

He heard Carlo's voice through his comms set. "Move around the tree to your left. Thirty degrees and no more."

Connor did so.

The former commando could hear the tread of boots crunching the undergrowth. He slowed his breath; his actions needed to be violent but precise.

Carlo's voice again, "Left-hand man will pass your position at two metres. Follow my count. Five, four, three, two, now."

Connor whipped around in a wide arc. He barely registered the blood mist pop off the soldier's head.

He simultaneously smacked a hand onto his victim's forehead and punched his Fairburn Sykes fighting knife into the base of the skull.

The severing of the medulla oblongata had the desired effect—the trigger finger didn't twitch.

He lowered the tremoring corpse to the ground and wiped his commando dagger on it before sheathing the blade away. He paced over to the second downed enemy to perform the 'dead check' of pressing his thumb into the eyelid before checking the pulse.

He opened the line to Carlo. "Tangos down. Commandeering the comms kit. Keep overwatch."

"Acknowledged," replied Carlo.

Connor began rifling through the corpse's kit. He decided against taking the Beretta M9 but took a couple of the fragmentation grenades and stuffed them in his webbing pouch with his own.

He rapidly donned the slain man's communication set, configuring it so he could use his own at the same time.

The Brit didn't recognise the radio; it resembled an AN/PRC-148 handheld tactical radio, except smaller and with a cordless earpiece.

He could see Carlo keeping his arcs behind a tree to his right, twenty metres away at a forty-five-degree angle.

And he could just make out Arabella crouching two trees behind.

Connor now regretted their decision to take her—the corpse at his feet was once a real soldier, and the others would be, too.

He surmised it must be a small group husbanding their resources.

Connor picked out a distant tree where his Garmin GPS watch directed.

He began to mentally plot his route through the forest.

He stopped. His mind whirred for decision;

they were still well over a hundred metres off the log cabin complex.

The element of stealth would be over soon as the dead soldier failed to check in.

Ordinarily, he would simply tell Carlo what they were going to do, but he decided to feel him out.

He signalled Carlo and pressed the pressel of his comms set.

"I think we should abort."

"Why?"

Connor explained his reason concisely.

It took a few moments for the reply to come through, which Connor expected.

He knew the Italian's thirst for combat would be wrestling with his will to protect his sister.

"OK. Let's abort."

Connor caught a flicker of movement in his peripheral.

He opened his mouth to shout a warning.

"Claymo—"

22

Arturo Bianchi stood at one end of the dining table and his butler at the other.

Woods of differing colours and finishes almost entirely made up the back dining room save for a coloured, stained glass-panelled ceiling.

This glass also made up the open-topped holders in which the vanilla-scented candles flickered on a wrought iron circular tray.

Clear frames replaced his browline glasses.

He smiled inwardly at the sight of Richèl Vergeer. Though he felt a pang of disappointment that she hadn't worn a dress, the European woman still looked smoothly elegant in the denim shirt over a black undershirt—though it seemed a size too big—and the flat, slipper-like shoes.

Bianchi watched her face for signs she was impressed—there were none. Reminding himself she had been working for a billionaire cooled his frustration.

It reminded him of 'Scarface', one of his favourite films—how Pfeiffer's character, Elvira, wouldn't give Tony Montoya the time of day until he ascended to the position of king. She would know how rich he was about to become but nothing of his true plans.

Her apparent lack of enthusiasm intrigued him more, not least because she remained effortlessly attractive.

She must have been wearing contacts, as the square glasses were gone.

Two of his men stood either side of her in the

doorway.

Richèl looked at him. "You didn't have to go to this much trouble."

"I didn't," he said. "This is standard for all my business meetings."

A blatant lie, but one that might assuage her feelings that she had been set up.

"OK," she said.

"Come and sit down."

After a moment, she started for the table. The butler pulled out her chair.

Arturo sat after she had and gestured to the menu. "Anything you want."

He watched her peruse the offerings, her noir hair falling below the sharp jaw.

He snatched away his eyes as she looked up and said, "I will have a bison steak with a side of poutine."

He nodded and said, "Bistecca alla Fiorentina. Al sangue."—*High cut of grilled veal. Rare.*

Again, she did not react to his fluency.

The waiter smiled, collected their menus and asked, "And to drink?"

She answered, "Coke with a slice of lemon."

"And a bottle of my family's red, Marcel."

"I don't drink at business meetings," she said.

"It's my family's wine. Just a taste," he said, pressing his palms together prayerfully.

She raised her eyes and said, "When I refuse another glass, please do not be offended."

"You will want more of it, but if you can resist, I will respect it."

"Getting this place was good thinking of my boss. Well, our boss."

Arturo bristled. "He's not my boss. I do him favours, and he does me favours."

"Then a partnership."

The waiter brought out the wine and mineral water.

Once he had poured both their drinks, Arturo held up his glass. "To friends and business partnerships."

She repeated his toast and took a mouthful.

Richèl tried to hide her unease.

The pig didn't seem to realise she knew how he usually conducted business meetings—strippers and free drugs were his MO, not wining and dining in a rustic room alone.

Still, her brief had been to avoid being churlish, so she relented to having a small glass after hearing it was from the family vineyard.

Though she doubted that to be true, she had done a deep dive into his background and not found even tenuous family links to the wine business.

She couldn't help but poke his ego with references to MacKenzie being his boss, though she sensed not to push too hard.

The wine tasted great, with a weird but welcome hint of cherry.

"Very good. Your family has my compliments."

"Thank you," he said. "Do you drink socially?"

"I haven't in a while," she said sincerely, already feeling the effects of the alcohol.

"I only drink while I eat. Seen what this stuff can do to an empty stomach."

As if on cue, their meals arrived. Despite the flavoursome sensation of the perfectly cooked bison steak, she ate quickly, hoping to line the stomach against her lowering blood pressure.

"You OK?" Bianchi asked.

"Yes. How strong is this wine?"

"Not that strong," he frowned. "Maybe eat the rest of your food before drinking again."

She briefly considered not drinking any more but did not want to give this oaf the satisfaction of not finishing a single small glass.

"So," she asked. "When do we discuss business?"

"We discuss it after our meal, of course."

She nodded and smiled. "Of course."

The steak and poutine slid down her throat with decadent ease.

"Where did you grow up?" he asked.

"Delft, a little town just outside of Rotterdam," she said. "Yourself?"

"Port Hope, a small town outside of Toronto."

She raised her glass. "We have that in common."

Christ, she thought, *I am flirting with this ogre.*

She finished her wine with a gulp to get it over with.

The waiter appeared and asked, "Dessert, Madame?"

She felt a girlish excitement. "Yes, please."

What's wrong with me?

"What would you like?"

"What would you suggest?"

"We could do a lovely blueberry grunt?"

She began to salivate. "Yes, please."

"I'll have the same."

She felt a warmth towards Bianchi.

How has this happened? She thought. Maybe it was the common ground they had.

Arturo couldn't believe it was working as well as it was. The chemist had said it would be subtle enough that the victim would not be aware they had been drugged.

Bianchi had had many women the average person would consider a piece of ass, but Richèl Vergeer was truly something else.

Larry MacKenzie's braying when Arturo had asked if she was seeing *'anyone important'* rang in his head.

'Anyone important' had been Bianchi's way of telling MacKenzie, *'I am going to fuck her'*.

Once Larry choked down his laughter, he said, *'As long as you don't force yourself on her, then you go for it, Arturo.'*

He said it like a father to his teenage son.

While he feigned offence at the notion he'd rape her, the truth was he would have engineered a situation where it was easier for her just to give up her pussy than say no.

But that seemed unnecessary now as she began to resemble a purring cat.

The Mafia lord had swallowed Viagra before her arrival and could now feel its effects in his sinuses. The mental images of the filthy acts he would make her do flashed.

Once she finished her dessert, Arturo suggested, "Ready to talk business?"

"Oh, yes, business. Let'sss do that."

The chemist had told him that the first inkling of slurred speech would be the time to pounce. If he left it much longer, she would begin to resemble someone who had overdosed on an opiate.

He wanted to see her expression as she handed herself to him. To watch her feel it.

The crime lord fought a smile as she rose unsteadily.

He walked over to steady her, and she giggled. The change in her demeanour almost put him off; he wanted to break an ice queen, not some college girl.

Her beauty would compensate.

Bianchi led her to the huge leather sofa unit, with a view of the mountains through bullet-proof windows.

He lowered her down and sat a foot away.

"Very unusual place for a business meeting."

"I am an unusual type of guy."

Her face became serious, and her slur receded when she said, "This is a business meeting. You do not need to sit so close."

Bianchi felt frustration singe.

"You don't have to be nervous around me," he said, painting on a smile.

"I am not nervous. I am just informing you of my boundaries of comfort."

Arturo steadied his breathing to control his anger.

Then he remembered, *Women do this so men don't think them sluts. She wants to be taken.*

He moved closer.

His ears picked up what he thought to be a dull explosion in the distance.

Her eyes widened. "What was that?"

"Relax, it'll have been a firework," he said. "If an attack was happening, it would be much closer."

She seemed to relax a little, and he said, "You know I am glad you're here with me."

He reached over and placed his hand on her knee.

She reached down, gripped his hand, and removed it.

Temper shot through his body. He snatched hold of her jaw.

"Listen to me. If you think you can come here and cock-tease, then you're fuckin' crazy."

He heard what sounded like several smaller fireworks popping off in the distance.

Grabbing her shoulders, he rag-dolled her into a pin.

The ferocity of her fight back startled him as her hands came up to claw his face. With his arms straight, her nails waved an inch from his lips.

He grinned.

Pain shot his grin into a grunting grimace as her teeth sank into his hairy forearm.

He snatched her throat with his other hand and squeezed.

The teeth slackened, and he removed his hand.

The sound of an American voice briefly remonstrating with his waiting staff caused Bianchi to let go and sit up.

One of The Red Hauser's soldiers glided in with Vergeer's security officer behind. Bianchi caught a brief frown on both men's faces as they surveyed the scene before the biker barked, "There is an armed attempt on this place. We must get you both to safety."

"Armed attack?" said Bianchi. "But why—"

"We don't have time. Let's go."

Bianchi's protest did not reach his vocal cords as the biker steered around and directed him.

23

Arabella's heart thundered in her ears as it seemed God hammered the ground. She saw bark ripping away from the surrounding trees.

Then came cracks she recognised as gunfire.

She had the awareness to stay put, knowing her movement would attract death.

Who appeared first determined her fate.

Watching *phunfts* of ground tear seconds before hearing the cracks looked surreal.

She gripped her Beretta but knew she lacked the training to help her brother or Connor—*If they were still alive.*

As if perfectly timed, the Claymore mine's blast caught the left side of Carlo's back as he made to extract to the nearest tree.

He caught the flashes of camouflage at fifty metres.

Connor, knowing he would expose his position, opened fire.

He caught a pair with headshots despite one of them moving.

The remaining members of the ambush team—the ones he could see at least—numbered around four.

Not trusting the exposure time to throw a grenade, he flicked the selector to auto and fired bursts.

He sprinted back on an angle to another tree as return fire hammered his previous position.

Connor knew from experience being shot at could give a human the legs of a hare, but if you run hard enough, for long enough, especially carrying weight, then no amount of adrenaline could make you run faster.

From his new position, he could see Carlo and was temporarily out of the enemy's field of fire. The Italian lay on his back, applying a tourniquet to his thigh.

Connor waited until he finished before raising communications. "OK, prepare to fire a long burst to cover me getting to you, and—"

"No. Listen to me. I am going to die here. If you try to get me, we all die. I need you to keep Arabella alive. Do not doom her to rescue me."

Connor opened his mouth to retort, but the comprehension of the reality killed the words.

Hoisting the Italian in his combat gear would mean slowing down his ground covering and removing their suppressing fire.

Connor's heart threatened to slide into his stomach with its increase in weight. "Alright."

The Italian heaved himself into a sit-up before clambering up against the tree. He flicked his eyes towards Connor, gave him a casual salute and began to fire automatic bursts.

Arabella decided to shoot whoever came for her. She knew now that her brother and Connor were dead. No one could survive the blast and the firestorm of bullets filling the entire area.

She felt a calmness descend on her.

A movement flashed to her right. She jerked her Beretta, which tore from her hand.

Connor stood with it in his hand. "Don't point this at anything or anyone you're not going to destroy."

She nodded numbly. "Where is my—"

His steel fingers gripped her upper arm and straightened her to standing.

With his face inches from hers, he said, "For you and me to get out of this alive, you'll do exactly what I say and when I say. Understand?"

"I understand."

"Your brother is going to cover our exit. Don't let him down."

The corner of her brain registered what he might mean.

"OK," she said as resolutely as she could muster.

"See that tree?" he said, pointing his clasped four fingers to a large tree ten metres away.

"Yes," she called over the cacophony of noise.

"When I start firing, you will run and get behind it. Then you're going to fire three rounds in this general direction," he said, thumbing to the left behind himself. "Don't stick your head out. Just stick your pistol out and fire three rounds. Tell me what you're doing."

"You will fire. I will run behind that tree. Put my gun out but not my head and fire in that direction."

"Good," said Connor. "You ready?"

She nodded as her heart thundered. Connor took a crouch behind the tree and began firing.

Her heart picked up her legs to spin her towards the tree that seemed half a mile away.

She reached it with what felt like a small animal attempting to escape her chest.

It took a second for her to remember, but she punched her hand out and fired three times.

She made herself small against the tree, and the firing intensified. The smell of expended bullet casings began to dance in her nasal passages.

Her peripheral vision caught a blur, and as she turned, Connor took a position behind a tree to her left.

He shouted out to her over the din, "Same again. That tree this time."

Once they had completed the bound, Connor shouted, "Now, when I fire, you're going to run behind me to that tree to my left. Don't fire your Beretta when you get there, OK?"

She nodded, her chest heaving.

"Ready?" he shouted.

Without waiting for acknowledgement, he began firing.

She forced her burning legs to reach their destination. Her adrenalin-induced brain warped the five seconds into five minutes.

The firing seemed a little less loud and more sporadic.

Connor came running past her to take up position to her left.

He called out, "Move."

Mirroring him, she ran past him. After a few more bounds, he closed in on her.

"We're going silent until I say otherwise. Now you're heading in that direction," he said, indicating a clearing about a hundred yards to their southwest. "Go."

She did.

Once through it, he directed her to the Dodge RAM they had arrived in.

Just before they got in, she asked, "What about my brother?"

"Get in, and I'll tell you."

Tears pressed on her lower lids as she climbed in. He gunned the motor and accelerated away.

"Carlo was hit in the legs, Arabella. I went to fetch him, but he said he would fight me if I came near him. He sacrificed himself for you."

24

Mike felt the flickering candle of admiration for the corpse of the bald enemy he now stood over.

It seemed this lone soldier had managed to pin down Mike's team long enough to allow whoever was with him to escape.

His men eventually appeared, led by Avery, who stopped short and said, "There isn't anyone else. Found *jackets*, and I reckon they bounded back before peeling—the basics but done well."

Rose nodded. "A lot of jackets?"

"Surprisingly not. I'd be surprised if there were over three or four of 'em."

Mike knew the area was absent of traffic cameras for miles around. Indeed, this had been one reason they chose the site.

"Alright, let's get the body in the truck and take it to see if Vito Corleone recognises him. There is nothing on him to ID him."

They carried the body before loading it onto the truck.

Mike had called ahead to quell the worry of the Mafia boss's supposed security party.

Indeed, when he arrived, he could see the nerves—despite attempts to veil them—in the body language of Arturo Bianchi and his men.

Mike jumped out as the MC soldiers formed a loose three-hundred-and-sixty-degree security circle.

He beckoned Arturo over, who, after a frown, stepped forward.

Before Bianchi could say anything more, Mike stripped back the canvas on the trailer and heard

Arturo Bianchi's sharp intake of breath.

"Holy fuck, that's him," exclaimed Bianchi before a grin split his face.

"He wasn't the only one."

Bianchi seemed not to hear him. "The fucking balls on this guy to try and kill me twice! Dumb motherfucker!"

Mike shrugged. "If we hadn't been here, he might have succeeded."

"I have my security team."

"Hate to tell you this, but this guy, and whoever was with him, would have torn through your guys."

"But they didn't," announced Bianchi before he lent down to his vanquished foe and said, "Now no one is going to stop me murdering your sister, you fucking ***mangiapatate***."

"He's dead. That's your eye for an eye. It's not as if killing her is going to hurt him now," said Mike, genuinely confused.

His words briefly hung hollow before Bianchi said, "His sister is still alive. My brother isn't."

The former Green Beret said, "You'll have to use someone else for that. We don't directly target civilians—waste of our skillset."

He kept the disdain out of his voice and didn't mention his distaste at the crime lord, still thinking a civilian woman was fair game.

"Don't you worry about that. I have people who can handle it."

When Rose didn't reply, Bianchi gestured to the body, "And now this piece of shit has seen his maker, we can get on with the important work of dumping my remaining product, so we can all get filthy rich."

"I hear you. We'll be in touch."

Mike noticed the stunning noirette stamping from Bianchi's lodge towards her own.

Bianchi's head turned before twisting back. "She's hot, eh?"

"An understatement."

Bianchi leaned over and whispered conspiratorially, "This close to fucking her before this bastard interrupted. Might be worth taking his sister alive if I can."

Mike's smile didn't reach his eyes.

The Mafiso chortled. "Wolves and lambs, my friend. Wolves and lambs."

Charlotte Daniels sprinted towards the convulsing vagrant.

A black, frizzy-haired woman cradled the ODing addict's head in her lap, wailing for help.

Jim Crowther grasped the woman gently by the shoulders and said soothingly, "We are here to help. Let us do our job."

The crowd on this Downtown Eastside street resembled a Halloween party kicked out of a club into the daylight.

An assortment of litter stuck to the tarmac like morning makeup.

He managed to pry the woman away. Charlotte inserted the naloxone spray into one nostril, closed the other and sprayed the life-saving mist into it.

The smell of piss hung in the air.

"Come on," she murmured when the man did not stir.

One of the street dwellers called out to the sobbing woman. "He'll be OK. She is the 'Eastside Angel'."

This had been Charlotte's moniker amongst the Vancouver addicts since not long after she began saving them.

Still no reaction.

Though naloxone could take two or three minutes to fully restore normal breathing, the recipients typically showed signs of responding to it well before then.

"What's wrong? Why isn't Jeff moving? Jef…Jeffery," anguished the woman, and Jim held her tightly.

"It just takes a while, that's all," soothed Jim.

The crowd's hum of quiet expectancy bled into murmurs.

A strand of hair fell, and for a split second, she grasped it in her mouth—a childhood habit of comfort from anxiety.

She flicked it out as her heart pounded in her ears. She couldn't administer another dose.

A furtive glance at her watch told her two minutes and thirteen seconds had elapsed.

Keeping a neutral expression, she ripped open the Velcro top of her first aid bag and whipped out the Bag-Valve mask.

The collective gasp of the crowd set off the woman, who cried, "Oh my gaadddd. Please gaaddd, please gaaddd."

Charlotte blew two rescue breaths and began thirty compressions.

The anxious cries went up like flares as she and Jim began to swap during the cycles to prevent exhaustion.

Eventually, the paramedics arrived, and after a brief interaction, Charlotte and Jim melted away.

She looked back to see kids no older than twelve looking on. Her stomach convulsed—street gangs employed these kids to peddle poison because they worked cheaply and couldn't be prosecuted by Canadian law under the age of thirteen.

Once in the white Toyota Sienna, the back of her head pressed hard into the passenger seat headrest. She could barely hold the tears back.

"Jesus Christ, Jim, what are they getting high on? It used to be so rare we couldn't bring someone back. And now it seems we can't resuscitate anyone?"

"You can't blame yourself, Charlotte. Remember what Polly told ya—they hear this new drug can kill them, and they seem to want more and more of it."

She knew what conservatives would say to that in private—*'If they want to kill themselves, let them.'*

Her frustration and sorrow morphed into anger.

As they hit a patch of traffic, she spotted a giant advertising poster displaying Larry MacKenzie rallying a crowd under the slogan,

When does support become everyone's crux?

She spat, "It's bastards like him that's vetoing the funds for these people."

Jim remained quiet, and she said, "Don't you agree?"

"I am not sure, Char," said Jim. "There have

been drug addicts for a long time."

"Not like this, Jim," she said, "And it's always those rich pricks. Who is worse? The street dealers the police love to arrest or those fucking bastards who mislead doctors and patients in claiming that oxy was less addictive than other opiate medications? Not one of the corporation executives saw a prison cell."

She consciously attempted to calm herself. Jim remained quiet, probably shocked to hear her swear, she thought.

"I am sorry, Jim. Just seems I am a stick against the tide."

Richèl stood in the cabin room, breathing deeply to calm herself.

She couldn't fathom how she had become embroiled in such a situation.

Her disbelief grew as she recalled her thoughts towards him a few minutes before the attempted rape, and she slowly sank to sit on her bed.

Mental images showing a rerun of the events began to revolve.

She had been her usual stand-offish self at first; she knew.

Richèl remembered her reluctance to accept his offer of red wine but accepted it because he insisted it came from his family's vineyard.

Though she had not drunk in a while, she was confident one glass with a meal would not have a discernible effect.

She began to pack—if her bodyguard hadn't insisted they leave, she would have anyway.

Her calmness surprised her, but then, she had already been through the massive trauma of being kidnapped and tortured for a prolonged period.

Two years later, she still could not fully remember how it had happened.

The hellish torment still seemed surreal—taken to an Adriatic island and brainwashed.

Despite her father being her idol, the ordeal had developed a more profound mistrust of men.

And her therapist had warned her of developing a need to control powerful men as a result. Maybe this was why she had not insisted on her bodyguard accompanying her to the meeting with Bianchi.

She should have insisted he be present but out of earshot.

Her guard now stood outside her room.

But she wouldn't trust him in it.

She still sometimes dreamt of the man with the dirty-blond hair who rescued her and exacted vengeance on the island compound's guards.

Her last one was one of the island morphing into a Venus fly trap closing, only for her rescuer to turn into a rat and gnaw his way out with her and the other prisoners following.

Other dreams included a jaguar and a black panther fighting with bears.

She looked at herself in the full-length mirror. She had had sex three times in the last two years. With people she knew and trusted but ultimately not attracted to.

And she had never been able to relax, making them anxious, awkward, and frustrated.

From nowhere, the realisation came—Bianchi had drugged her.

Course he had!

He had scientists making all kinds of chemical evil.

She would take a toxicology test. Then, she would take the results to MacKenzie and berate him for putting her in that situation.

And… he would feign rage on her behalf but would ultimately placate her; she knew, to a man like that, money would supersede everything.

And there was the possibility that Bianchi could prove the link between himself and MacKenzie.

What she was not sure about is what MacKenzie might do if she resigned, given what she knew. She could hide behind the *'I would be prosecutable too'* line, but they both would know she could skate across the ice rink of immunity if it meant a publicity-hungry Minister of Justice could have his scalp.

She could work this out—she had to.

25

Larry MacKenzie sat in his main office. He smiled as Mike Rose's digitalised voice relayed the events at the lodge complex.

"Maybe our friend will relax now," said Larry.

"Negative, sir. He still wants to go after his original target."

Larry frowned, "Why? If this mobster hitman is dead, then he won't feel the pain of the death of a loved one."

"Some sort of honour of an oath type thing."

MacKenzie snorted. "His petulance can be a nuisance. Has he asked for your help with this?"

"I told him it wasn't an option before he asked me," said Mike. "But this Italian had help. Whoever it was is probably on his way back to wherever he's come from—he can't have the motivation that the Italian had to kill our goatee-wearing friend."

Larry took a moment to answer. "But this mystery man is a loose end."

"Yes."

"Well, you better tie it up then."

Arabella did not speak for a long time—and beneath everything, she felt a mild sense of gratefulness that he let her float in the sea of silence.

Finally, Connor touched her arm gently. "What do you want to do?"

"What do you mean?" she asked numbly.

"I could get you out of Canada. Go anywhere

you like. But there is no guarantee this guy still won't want to kill you."

"Then what is our other option?"

Connor glanced at her. "I don't think anyone else would have any strong malicious feelings towards you other than this guy."

"He disappears, I am safe?"

"And your brother avenged," said Connor.

"You think vengeance interests me?"

"Why wouldn't it?"

She didn't speak for a few moments. "I love my brother. Loved. Fiercely. Even his crazy side. Mia madre used to say, *'You should accept the bad in people like thorns on a rose'*. But this was always the way it was going to end."

"Maybe," admitted Connor. "But he died because this scumbag thought targeting civilians is a done thing."

"And this offends your sensibilities?"

"It does."

She stared at him. "Why are you doing this?"

"What do you mean?"

"My brother is dead. You don't—"

"You think honour expires when the person you swore an oath to dies?"

"No," she said, taking a couple of breaths, "I want to know why you made that oath, and it isn't just because my brother would owe you."

He stared ahead. "You remind me of someone. You all do."

"We all do?"

"That's all you're getting," he said, and she could hear the finality.

She said, "And you need my help?"

"I need not to have to worry about you."
She repeated, "And you need my help?"
"Yes. I need your help."
"Then what's your plan?"
"All truly great thoughts are conceived by driving in silence," he said. "A bit of Nietzsche for you there."
"He really say that?"
"Well," said Connor. "A derivative of it."

After a while, a strange feeling rose within Connor as he drove. He had failed before and sometimes with disastrous consequences.

However, as the rippling postcard waters of Georgian Bay blurred by, he wondered how he could have fucked up so badly.

As self-doubt began gripping his throat, he remembered something Gabor Maté wrote: *'Your worst enemy cannot hurt you as much as your thoughts if you haven't mastered them. But once mastered, no one can help you as much—not even your parents.'*

He calmed himself; the soldiers they'd encountered in the forest had been just that—soldiers.

Everything Connor had been told, studied and observed led him to believe that mafia bosses used street enforcers and, on rare occasions, high-level assassins. Indeed, Carlo had been the only real soldier he had personally known of within an Italian Mafia.

He glanced at Arabella; there had been no tears yet.

As if catching him looking, she said, "You decided on a plan yet?"

"Whoever Bianchi has around him is very good and very experienced."

"Then how are you going to kill him?"

Connor looked ahead and said, "You don't know me that well, but you must know I wouldn't deliberately go out to directly harm an innocent civilian."

"OK?"

"But that doesn't mean I can't make him think I would."

A short silence.

"You want to kidnap someone in his family?"

"Yeh."

"And you don't think kidnapping someone is directly harming them?"

"If you treat them well enough, they might even get 'Stockholm syndrome'."

When she side-eyed, he said, "We might be able to lessen the psychological harm."

"Who is it?"

"He has a son he thinks no one knows about."

Another short pause as Connor manoeuvred onto the single-track road heading towards the lodge.

"And you would like me to do what? Be a femme fatal?"

"Be a bit weird considering he's seven."

"We are to kidnap a child?"

Connor thought of all the ways he could justify it now that it had been said aloud.

He wanted to use phrases like 'greater good' and 'lesser evil'.

Instead, he said, "Yes."

"OK," she said. "This isn't to save me—it is

to save everyone that animal will hurt if he lives."
"My thoughts exactly."
"For the greater good," she said.

26

Mike Rose sat in his clubhouse committee chair seat next to MOM.

They had taken a bit of a mauling in the woods outside the cabin complex.

Two of their men lay departed with two wounded to one enemy dead.

Despite them successfully protecting Bianchi, it had been seen—rightly in Rose's eyes—as an embarrassingly tragic failure.

"How could this have happened?" asked MOM, his tone almost gleefully accusing.

Though Rose maintained a demeanour of confidence, he knew he had to take ownership of what had occurred.

He had been in charge when the laptop was taken.

And it had been him in charge during the ambush.

"Our friend's security swore there was nothing on the laptop detailing the location. Fortunately, we ran a contingency that worked."

"Worked?" exclaimed MOM. "Two of our men are dead, and two more are in the hospital, and the enemy escaped."

"They didn't all escape," Rose said coldly, looking at him. "And injuries happen in war."

He held his stare challengingly—knowing MOM had barely touched a frontline.

"Of course. I am just angry, that's all."

Rose gave him a look of contrite apology and said, "I am angry, too."

Another asked, "Do we have any idea who they are?"

"No," said Rose. "But I have strings I can pull. Whoever this is, I will find them."

"How?"

"I can't say yet, not even amongst my brothers."

Mike steeled himself for the insistence he tell them.

But it never came.

"I would have to ask that Kyle assist you."

Mike knew this meant he wanted Kyle to report back to him.

"If you deem that necessary."

"It's for the best."

"Then I'll be happy to take him."

Giovanni Callari could smell chlorine lingering through the changing rooms down the corridor. He watched Louis through the glass partition swim in a circle, a result of cerebral palsy affecting the left side.

The Mafioso soldier had only feigned complaint when he had been assigned to bodyguard the seven-year-old.

Bianchi had told him the lad was the illegitimate son of one of his very important business associates and to apply for the position. When accepted, Bianchi had subsidised the pay packet to over triple the standard rate.

However, Bianchi's pointed finger had told him, *'Guard them both with your fucking life. And if you have to take a murder pinch, I'll make you a fucking millionaire. Also… touch her, and I'll chop off your fucking feet.'*

Also, Giovanni had been one of the originals to leave with his friend Marco Bianchi, who had told him about his having a secret nephew.

Though the money soothed most of Giovanni's misgivings about the assignment, he was becoming restless now.

Because he was working alone, he had to be on the boy almost twenty-four-seven. He had thought about reaching out to Bianchi for another man but had been reluctant to do so, as he would have to share the money.

He hadn't drunk, gambled, or even had a woman for three months.

And it was now obvious this was just a glorified babysitting job; no one had said a cross word to the pair, let alone tried to harm them.

He had warmed to Louis over the weeks. Despite his ailment, the boy always seemed to be smiling and laughing, his missing front teeth adding to the effect.

But it couldn't go on. He would tell his boss soon enough.

He heard the swim instructor blow the whistle, signalling the end of class.

The burly bodyguard watched Louis being told to stop running as he giddily made his way to the changing rooms, shooting him a wave as he did so.

Giovanni swirled the dregs of his coffee, binned the styrofoam cup and made his way to the toilets while he had time.

He entered the cubicle and found himself to be alone for a few moments.

Amid drying his hands, he glanced up to see

who had just entered.

The fist knocked a hollowness into his legs. He sagged against the wash basins as electricity seized him on the back of the neck.

He convulsed into unconsciousness.

Connor veered from the plan when he watched the bodyguard enter the toilets alone.

The plan had been to set off the building's fire alarm along with the sprinkler system, taser him, claim he'd had a heart attack and lead the boy away in the confusion.

Even in concocting the plan, he suspected too many working parts could go wrong.

Once he saw the man enter alone, Connor decided it was a gift horse whose mouth he should avoid looking in.

The punch had caught the hulking, bull-necked Mafioso sweet at the point of the jaw. However, even with a Kubotan disguised as a lighter in his fist, he failed to put his lights entirely out.

Luckily, he had planned for this contingency, and the taser did the rest.

Within twenty seconds, he had managed to heave the deadweight into one of the cubicles.

He walked out to see Arabella crouching down and speaking to the boy.

Connor stood off and didn't approach, not wanting to spook the boy but also not wanting to let Arabella out of his sight.

Finally, the boy clasped her hand, and she led him out.

Connor walked out to the Dodge RAM and watched Arabella cajole the boy into the blue Toyota

Camry.

As they pulled off, Connor followed behind.

His mind snapped to a thought of Myra Hindley and Ian Brady—a couple who sexually assaulted and murdered children in the north of England back in the sixties. He had read that Hindley would initiate the pickup of their victims due to her less threatening femininity.

The parallels sent a worm of unease into his stomach.

He followed them for well over an hour until he called Arabella. When she answered, he said, "Pull over at the next parking bay."

It took another twenty minutes, and he followed and parked behind her.

He took out a burner phone and dialled a number.

A voice answered, "Yes?"

"Put Bianchi on the phone," said Connor.

The SIM he had placed into it automatically distorted his voice.

"Who is this?"

"If he isn't on the phone in ten seconds, I'll be hanging up, and who knows how he'll find the boy."

A pause. Muffled voices.

"Who is this?"

"I am the one who has your boy."

Breathing. And then, "You're fucking dead."

"If you don't calm your son, that's what he'll be. Because if he's a nuisance, then he's a liability. And if he's a liability, he's not worth the trouble to me."

"When?"

"Stay by this phone. You answer it next time—not one of your secretaries pretending to be a man. It'll be on speaker, so no codes. You tell him we are his new bodyguards and to trust us. And if he means anything to you, then pray you succeed."

Connor hung up. He did not bother to warn against tracing the call, as he knew it wouldn't be possible.

The Englishman approached the Toyota before knocking on the window at the passenger's side.

Connor painted on an expression of friendliness, feeling faintly creepy as he did so.

The lack of fear on the boy's face stood as a testament to Arabella's acting skills.

The window came down, and Connor said, "Hi, Louis, nice to meet you."

Connor held out his hand. After glancing at Connor's hand and face, Louis reached out.

When he made contact, Connor did his old trick of feigning to be electrocuted.

Shock splashed onto the lad's face, followed by a giggle.

"Don't do that again," said Connor with mock outrage.

Louis tentatively touched his hand again, and Connor went into convulsions. The third time, he remained unaffected and said, "You've run out of charge."

Louis only seemed mildly disappointed and stared at his hand.

"What are your names?" asked Louis suddenly.

"My name is Luke, and that is Leila."

"Ahhhh, cooolll; we all begin with an L."

"That's right, Louis," said Connor. "Listen, I will call your dad so he can speak to you. For all you know, we could have been kidnappers!"

Louis grinned a gap-toothed smile.

Connor stepped back and dialled the number. Bianchi answered, "Yeah."

Connor told Louis, "Your dad wants to speak to you," and disengaged the voice distortion.

"Hi, Dad."

"Hi, Lazy Lou, you OK?"

"Yes, I am with your friends."

"That's good. Now be good for your mum's new helpers. Mum is visiting her friends, but you'll be back with her soon."

"How long?" asked Louis, anxiety tracing his voice.

"Shouldn't be too long."

"OK. Love you, Daddy."

"Love you too, Lazy."

Connor took the phone back, stepped away from the car, reengaged the voice distortion and said, "Just remember, you're the one who thought it was acceptable to target civilians. And a woman at that. So if you fuck around, don't pout when they find your son's head."

He ended the call.

A rattlesnake of unease had a fit in his stomach as an image of his son came to mind.

27

Arturo Bianchi slowly put his phone into his drawer. A moment passed before he leapt up, looking around wildly like a lion surrounded by hyenas.

Everything seemed far too expensive.

He settled on one of the ergonomic executive chairs he kept for guests—his red leather premium high back being far too expensive and heavy—and hoisted it onto his chest before smashing it over his desk.

After a few blows, the seat eventually broke from the back post.

The crime boss smashed it repeatedly, but it refused to break any further, and he exhausted himself.

He heard the door handle disengage the lock and bellowed, "Don't come in."

"You OK, boss?" called out one of his staff.

He screamed, "I said fuck off!"

He rested his hands on his barely marked solid oak desk.

Struggling to regain his breath, he forced his brain to fire.

He had held within a massive sense of guilt towards his brother's death.

After the old man, Giuseppe—seemingly soft in his older age—had decided to pass him over as his number two for his nephew Gerlando.

Though the younger Zito was sharp and capable, he'd only been earning at Arturo's two-decade-long level for the past few years and hadn't done anywhere near the shakedowns, tortures and hits that he had done for the old man.

And so Arturo had concocted a plan; Marco had followed it to the tee.

They had staged a fight at their aunt's wake, with both refusing to discuss it further.

To lessen any suspicion towards the plan, they had waited a couple of years until Marco 'deciding' to form a breakaway crew.

With Arturo directing and protecting him from the inside. It had been his idea to reach out to Calabria for a *Consigliere per la Sicurezza* to ambush the Romanos.

And that had led to his brother being killed by that ***Figlio di puttana***.

And righting that wrong had led to his son being taken.

It was obvious to Arturo that God had forsaken him.

Luckily, he knew who to call instead.

MacKenzie let the phone ring a few times after being informed that Bianchi was on the other end.

All Vergeer had said was that their business meeting had to be cut short due to an attack on the supposedly secret location.

However, the bodyguard he had sent with her had told him that the attack probably interrupted the greaseball's sexual assault on her.

MacKenzie had read that rape was more about dominance than being a sexual thing. He had his reservations, though; it seemed to him that rapists almost always went for young fertile women.

Usually, she would field calls from Bianchi—who always identified himself as Mister Copson—but when MacKenzie heard, he instructed his operator to put any calls from Mister Copson through to him personally.

And the billionaire had been considering his options—or lack thereof.

He needed the Italian. Needed him to do his dirty work. Needed him as a lightning rod.

Thankfully, Vergeer hadn't told him, so MacKenzie could feign ignorance and save face in front of her.

He answered, "Yes."

"It's me."

"I was told."

"I need your help."

"How can I be of service?"

A pause. A stutter. And, "They have my son."

"What son?" asked Larry with a contrived obliviousness; he'd known before starting their business relationship.

"I have a son. A dancer babe I used to fuck who worked for me. She got pregnant. I didn't want to marry a whore, but I haven't had any kids before."

"You know it's yours for sure?"

"Of course I fuckin' kno…sorry, I am just stressed."

"Calm yourself," said MacKenzie. "I will handle this."

He heard the hope edge Bianchi's voice. "Really?"

"Yes. Send me everything, and I mean everything you have on the boy, and I'll be in touch with people who handle this sort of thing."

"He said, if I didn't play ball, he'd cut off his head. Said that I chose to target civilians first."

MacKenzie didn't see the point in pointing out the statement's truth.

"Unlike you, my friend, the people who work for me can be quiet or loud."

Connor sat in front of the laptop in his room at the cabin. He had been planning how best to use the boy without putting him in harm's way.

The moral ambiguity of what he was doing continued to gnaw at him, and he wasn't looking forward to telling Ciara what he had done. He looked at the time—about seven minutes to their face-to-face.

Their relationship had the complex element of them being former lovers—for want of a better expression—from when she had been an agent like himself.

Connor had seen the reasoning behind her taking over The Chameleon Project even before Bruce McQuillan had stated to him that it was his decision.

Ciara had been an excellent agent, but her look, though less so now, had been too distinctive for long-term espionage.

And Connor knew his value to The Chameleon Project would always be on the street.

He knew one of his values to The Chameleon Project was his criminal background giving him an inbuilt legend for visiting the darker parts of the world.

And there was no expiry to that unless the entire criminal entity of his family went straight.

Connor thought back to the task at hand. Unsure whether Bianchi would risk his son's life, he knew he couldn't use him as any form of physical human shield.

Connor had to attempt to use Louis to bring his prey out into the open without the boy being present.

He began to open the encrypted Zoom app and watched the screen.

The white line expanded across the black before opening the image of Ciara to him.

They went through their security checks, and she asked, "What's the status?"

"My colleague is dead."

"The sister?"

"She's with me."

"I'll touch base with our counterparts and have her transported back."

"No," he said sharply. "I mean, no, please."

She frowned. "Surely she is a hindrance to you now?"

"Not necessarily."

Ciara took a moment to speak. "What have you done?"

"I've taken his boy."

"You've kidnapped his son?"

"Yes."

He watched her blink and say, "Why?"

"Leverage."

"You can always leave him somewhere safe. There is still time. You don't have to cross this line."

"Are you ordering me not to?"

He watched her take a breath and say, "I give you your objective. How you choose to proceed is up to you."

When he nodded, she said, "But Connor,

don't kid yourself. If he's with you, then you're putting him in danger."

"If I can't get to this man, Ciara, then I am putting a lot more people in danger."

"You should know how far men will go to justify their actions."

"I know."

28

Mike and Kyle zipped past the fume-belching cars.

The former Green Beret wondered if he would ever truly get desensitised to riding his bike; the changing sounds of the wind and the engine, the tactile vibrations on the inner thighs and the feet, the smells of tyre smoke, the fuel, urban congestion or countryside freshness.

And the constant need to be alert to the danger of other road users, the speed of the bike, and the awareness that when taking corners, only two small patches of tyre touch the tarmac at any time.

The discomfort curbed the romanticism only a little; the pressure on his wrists, his balls compressed against the tank, and the strain on his neck added to the visceral experience.

He found it difficult not to think of cars as moving cages sometimes.

The journey from Detroit to the South Mountain just outside of Newark spanned almost exactly six hundred miles, and they had hit the last twenty miles.

Larry MacKenzie had given him the instructions to meet with a former CIA cyber tech on his payroll.

Mike wondered why he had to meet him face to face but didn't question it on this occasion.

He caught sight of the Booton reservoir and knew the terminus to be a few more miles away.

Kyle had kept admirably tight to him for the duration.

Mike's Garmin satnav showed that he had

arrived at his destination, but he had purposely not set it to the exact location. He had memorised the rest of the way.

As they arrived, Mike stared incredulously at the redwood structure.

As Kyle dismounted and they removed their helmets, he said to Mike, "Holy fuck! Have you gotten lost?"

"No."

"This can't be it. It looks like a tool shed."

"Only one way to find out."

The two men instinctively parted and walked up to the sloping bi-door.

Mike knocked.

Nothing happened for thirty seconds, and he felt embarrassment creep in—maybe he had got the wrong place.

The partitions opened to reveal a tall, middle-aged man sporting a black beard with blond highlights.

"Welcome to the dragon's lair, gentlemen," he said in a scratchy voice, theatrically spreading his arms out wide. "Call me Cliff."

After a moment, the two Red Hauser members introduced themselves.

The former Green Beret perhaps expected that the outside would be a mask for a more hi-tech interior.

Yet, on looking in, though not untidy or unclean, the inside appeared very simple.

A steel kitchen unit lay at the back with a stove and a microwave. A pair of cupboards hung head high with the window looking into the forest.

A lamp of powder-painted, black galvanised

tubes shaped like a man, with the bulb coming out of the face.

A flat-screen hung on the wall, but Mike hadn't seen any aerials on the way in or cables leading from it.

A wooden sculpture of a life-size octopus stared at him from the corner.

"So," said Cliff. "Coffee?"

Both men nodded.

Within a few minutes, the bikers sat on the right side of the table with Cliff on the left.

"How can I help you?"

"There is an individual or team that we have to locate."

"Anything to go on?"

Mike handed him a disc. "Everything I can think of is on there, Cliff."

"A disc? I thought I was old-fashioned?"

"I thought it would be easier to destroy if I had to."

"I see your logic. Not sure if I would agree," said Cliff. "Well, if it's all on here, then I will get to work."

As if reading his mind, Cliff added, "Follow me."

He walked over to the octopus and whispered something in its ear.

It seemed to elevate an inch before swinging out to reveal a set of stainless steel tread plate stairs.

They followed him down to a room that reminded Mike of the control room of a nuclear submarine.

Screens of differing sizes permeated throughout under a low blue light. A panel of controls lay in the centre.

Cliff smoothed the disc into one of the thin boxes, and the information appeared immediately on screen but displayed in a startlingly concise way.

"Not much to go on," stated Cliff.

"Whoever they are, they are cagey."

Mike raised his eyebrows as traffic video surveillance of a Dodge RAM appeared on the larger screen.

Cliff murmured, "Look at how he shields his face when the cameras are coming up."

"Any more?"

"Looks like he keeps off the highways, but I should be able to find an image."

"How long could that take?"

"Not sure. A while, maybe. You should hightail it, and I'll be in touch."

"Roger that."

"In my experience, the people with the stealth skill are not good at the warry side—and vice versa. So when you find this scoundrel, he should be easy work."

"You're mistaken there," said Kyle.

Mike backed him up with, "Yeh, think of Batman crossed with Rambo."

"Well, a man with a skillset like that will be rare and thus not difficult to find."

Connor sat cross-legged on the floor of the cabin room.

He followed his breath, imagining the intake of mental energy on the inhalation and the lethargy of the mind on the exhalation.

He imagined the benefit on his focus of returning his attention to his breath.

After about fifteen minutes, he realised he couldn't keep the boy.

Ciara was right. As long as he had him in his possession, the lad was in danger.

Currently playing *Charades* with Arabella, Connor could hear Louis excitedly guessing, "Ice Hockey!"

After watching and listening to Arabella interact with him, he wondered if she'd considered having children.

He felt a plunge in his stomach at the thought of someone kidnapping his son.

He'd drop the boy off somewhere safe.

Connor got up, grabbed the iPad-like device and checked the images projected from the tiny cameras he had set up.

No sign of danger.

Then he took out his case and found the case containing two identical Casio standard digital watches; his uncle Michael had worn one for years, declaring, *'What do I need an expensive watch for? Does everything I need this.'*

Jaime had issued these tracker-fitted watches to Connor. The signal would be strong enough from hundreds of miles away to give a rough location; as the tracker got closer, the accuracy improved.

As he climbed down the stairs, he saw Louis taking his turn.

"Connor, what is this?" he asked excitedly, feigning the snapping of jaws with his arms and clawed hands.

"Aaaaa monkey?"

"Noooo!" he exclaimed, approaching Connor, snapping his arms wider.

"A giraffe?"

"Come ooonnnnnnnnnn."

"OK, OK. A crocodile."

"Nope!"

"An alligator?"

"Yesss."

"Do you know the difference between an alligator and a crocodile?"

To Connor's surprise, the lad answered confidently, "Alligators like salt water and crocodiles prefer no salt in their water."

"Ye. Also, crocodiles, you see in a while, but alligators, you see later."

Louis looked pensive for a moment, then burst into laughter. "See you later, alligator. In a while, crocodile."

Connor frowned. "Kinda ruins the joke when you explain it."

He smiled, unsure if Louis could pick up on dry humour.

Louis grinned back, but his face descended to neutral and asked, "When am I going back to my mum's?"

"Next couple of days, OK?"

Louis nodded. Connor braced himself for the question, 'Can I speak to my dad?', but it never came.

Connor took out a Monopoly game set from one of the cabinets and asked, "Louis, have you played this before?"

"Yesss."

"OK. Can you set it up?"

He passed it to Louis, who held it awkwardly

before setting the box on the floor and rifling through it.

"Say Louis. You don't have a watch?"

"Nope."

"Can you tell digital time?"

Louis narrowed his eyes. "Of course I can."

"Close your eyes, and hold your arms out."

The boy did so without hesitation. Connor slipped the Casio onto his left wrist.

"Open your eyes."

"Woah," exclaimed Louis, shaking his wrist.

Connor spent a few minutes showing Louis all the functions.

"This is so cool," said the boy.

"Listen to me, Louis," said Connor. "If you see your mum first, you tell her that your dad's friend gave it to you from your dad. Remember the man who took you swimming?"

"Of course, I remember Gio…duhhh."

The Englishman smiled. "But if you see your dad first and only if he asks, you tell him your mum gave it to you. I don't want your parents getting mad at me for giving you your first watch."

Louis squinted up at him. "What if someone else asks me?"

"If they know your mum, tell them it was from your dad. If they know your dad, you tell them it was from your mum. OK?"

"Yes, OK."

"Right. Set that Monopoly board up."

Connor found Arabella's eyes and jinked his head to the kitchen.

When she followed him in, he said, "Got to hand him back."

"Of course," she said, looking at him with incredulity.

"No, I mean, we'll have to find another way to get at our target."

She raised her eyebrows. "OK. I am a little surprised. My brother says you are one of the most ruthless men he knows…knew."

"Carlo and I went through some harsh times together, but we didn't really know one another."

"My brother told me that because of the harsh times, you knew one another well."

"He had a point," Connor conceded. "But as long as the boy is with us, he's in danger. When you start looking at innocent people as a means to an end, you're on a path that leads to the slaying of younglings at the behest of Senator Palpatine."

"Who is Senat….Where are we going to take him, then? Louis, I mean."

"I have an idea about that."

Charlotte Daniels watched the two addicts, long dead, being loaded into ambulances.

A tornado of exasperation and despair trapped her on this Eastside sidewalk.

The naloxone hadn't touched the pair, and now the eyes of the crowd focused on her.

When the ambulances screamed away, two police officers dispersed the accusing eyes.

Then they turned to her.

As they approached, Jim moved closer to her.

The taller one on the left raised his hand assuringly, but Jim still said, "She's a qualified doctor."

The shorter replied, "We know who you

are—we have for months. We are not here to bust you."

As she heard Jim inhale to speak, she placed a hand on his arm and addressed the officers, "What can I do for you?"

"This is Staff Sergeant Malone, and I am Detective Brown," the taller one said. "How long has the nax stopped having an effect?"

Charlotte said, "We started noticing about a month ago."

"Nothing before that?"

"It had a high nineties efficacy rate."

"Is this just here?" asked Jim.

The staff sergeant glanced at the detective, who replied, "No. The media will be all over this soon—not just the major cities but the towns and villages too."

"Seems like someone wanting to cull the streets of the homeless," Charlotte said.

The detective either didn't catch her insinuation of government foul play or chose to ignore it.

"Whoever they are, they seem to be targeting the immigrants and indigenous Canadians more."

"The socially displaced do tend towards drug use. That's sociology One-O-One," she said tersely.

"Not like this," he said. "We want this to calm down before a frenzy begins."

"You mean the Prime Minister doesn't want to be embarrassed by this before the election," declared Jim.

The detective looked at him sharply. "Some of us do have a sense of civic duty."

Charlotte thought she saw Jim lowering his

chin a little.

"Sorry," Charlotte said. "Our interactions with the police haven't been the most pleasant at times."

The detective said, "It's understandable when you're dealing with the negative aspects of our society all the time."

Charlotte wasn't sure if he was saying that to her or himself.

"Anything else you need from us, detective?"

"We are not asking you to do our job for us, Miss Daniels; it's just that you might hear things we don't for reasons you have outlined. We need a thread, on anything—a dealer, a transport guy, anything. Please do not put yourself in danger, but if you hear anything, please don't hesitate."

He handed her a card.

29

Larry remembered a few years ago when he would drive in a sub-standard vehicle just for the kicks.

He'd spoken to a few other billionaires, who seemed almost reluctant to buy the luxury cars and superyachts.

'Everyone knows I am a billionaire,' said one venture capitalist to him. *'So I don't have to prove it with fancy clothes, Lamborghinis or big boats I'd only use twice a year.'*

But that had never been him.

MacKenzie thought it to be a kind of reverse snobbery—why wouldn't he give his money to hard-working and talented people who produced and sold these art and engineering marvels?

Still, he couldn't remember the last time he had driven himself anywhere. Today, it was the Mercedes-Maybach S; though it had a massive V-12, it could only be heard once the revs approached their limit—like a stalking elephant breaking into a charge, except with the smoothness of a leopard.

One of his security members acted as his chauffeur while the others rode in inconspicuous vehicles around him.

Soon, he would be Prime Minister—he had thus far used his money to hush the media about the increase in drug-related deaths. He had told them derivatives of the following line, *'Give the Prime Minister and Law Enforcement time to deal with this. If I think he isn't doing enough, then by all means. But this country is already divided and down, so let's give him the chance.'*

He knew that in appearing magnanimous to

his political opponent, they would be more damning of the current administration when he let them off the leash.

And then he'd walk into the top office.

Not that the office would be quite as hi-tech as his current one.

That lay as a crown on top of the two hundred and thirty-metre tall Toronto skyscraper housing the nucleus of his various businesses.

He called out. "Pierre, take me around the back entrance."

"Yes, sir."

"When are you going to start calling me Larry?"

"When I am not working for you anymore," said the South African.

"Well, I think it'll be, sir, for a long time."

Pierre smiled with his eyes in the rear-view mirror.

As the ramp to the lower basement began to descend on sensing the vehicle's GPS tracker, Larry felt akin to driving into the Batcave.

When parked, Larry got out and checked his phone to find three missed calls from the reception desk.

He rang the number back. "What is it, Mary?"

"There is a little boy here—on his own—by the name of Louis, with a letter saying he's here to meet you. He said he's been told to ask for you, as you know his dad."

Frowning into the phone, he replied, "Ahem…OK, I'll be up soon."

He turned to Pierre and said, "Going up to the ground floor. A boy is waiting to meet me. Son of a friend of mine."

"Were you expecting this boy?"

"N..not this time."

Pierre looked at him for a moment. "Sir, let me go up and check him out."

Aware of how hesitant he had just sounded, MacKenzie said firmly, "I doubt a seven-year-old is going to attempt to assassinate me, Pierre."

"No, but he could—"

"You can stand between us if you like. If he sets off his suicide vest, then you can take most of the blast."

They made their way up to the foyer. As soon as the door opened, Larry's suspicions were confirmed as he saw it to be Bianchi's kid.

Mary sat with the boy.

Pierre walked slightly left and forward of Larry as they approached Louis.

"It's OK, Mary, I've got this."

She left with only a glance.

He sat beside the black-haired child and said, "I know your daddy, Arturo."

"Yes, the man said."

"What man?"

"A man and a princess," exclaimed Louis.

"What were their names?"

"Luke and Leila."

Cute—thought Larry.

Before looking at Louis, Larry said, "Do you want to see the view from the top?"

Louis gasped, "The top, top. Up in the ssskkyyyy?"

"Yes."

"Yesssss," he enthused.

"Then follow me," said the billionaire.

"Wait, I have to give you this," exclaimed the boy, thrusting his hand towards Larry.

Pierre instantly snatched the boy's wrist and growled, "Drop it."

Louis did so with a look of horror. A USB stick fell into Pierre's hand.

The bodyguard immediately let go, and Arturo could see Louis was about to cry.

Larry laughed. "See, Pierre, I told you he wouldn't cry. He can be trained in our superhero programme."

The billionaire pulled a joyous face, and Louis eyed him with what looked like suspicious optimism.

"Really?"

"I'll have to ask your dad."

A smile spread across Louis' face. "He'll say yes."

Larry turned to Pierre. "I want you to use the side office at the eastern corner to review the cameras; see who dropped him off."

"Sir, I—"

"I've got this, Pierre."

"Yes, sir."

He led Louis across the floor to the lobby elevators and asked, "Where are Luke and Leila now?"

"I don't know?" he said with an expressive shrug.

"But they must have taken you somewhere before here?" asked Larry.

"Oh yeh. To a cabin in the woods. Luke said it belonged to Red Riding Hood's grandma before she got eaten."

"He did, did he?"

"Yes, I said he did."

Larry looked at the brief confusion on Louis' face and realised the lad took the statement literally.

MacKenzie halted them in front of his black-doored private elevator—the odd one in a row of silver panels. He tapped in the code. A chime sounded, and the elevator door steamed open, and they stepped in.

"How did you get here?" Larry asked.

"Luke took me."

Larry nodded before gesturing to the chrome circular railing. "Hold on tight to that. We'll be going in fast mode to the top."

"Whoa, cool," said Louis.

Larry rotated the accelerator dial slowly, and Louis's eyes widened as the elevator began to gain speed.

Within a few seconds, it began to slow to a stop, and the doors opened into his office.

"Whoa," gasped Louis. "Is that a real tiger?"

"It was."

As they made their way to his blue marble corner desk, Louis skirted around the stuffed animal like it could still be alive.

Then he said, "How many people work here?"

Larry grinned. "Just me."

"Whoa," murmured the lad, staring up at the planets and star lights.

He had to admit he had got used to it, which he thought was impossible the first time he saw it.

Louis bolted towards the window, pressing his palms and nose against it. "It's like you're the king of the whole world up here."

"Well, maybe the king of Canada. The whole world is a little big," said Larry. "Go on, take a look around."

No sooner had he said this, his intercom chimed.

Pierre's voice came through. "Sir, I have had the security footage from outside sent to your system. You should have a look. I'll stay on the line."

He flicked on his screen. It showed the front entrance to the offices, guarded by two security staffers with concealed carry licenses. The timestamp showed it to be an hour ago.

A pair of what looked to be homeless people, wearing COVID-type face masks, approached the door waving placards, attempting to gain entry.

As his two security guards accosted them, a man, also wearing a face mask and a baseball cap, approached, holding Louis's hand.

He let go of it and gestured to Louis to run through the door. As soon as the seven-year-old did so, the 'protesters' seemed to immediately give up the cause and left.

"Can you run their faces through the recognition software?"

"I already have. The masks have scrambled it," said Pierre. "But I am guessing the first pair are addicts from downtown—wouldn't take a lot of money for them to do this."

"I doubt he'll have left his fingerprints on the USB he gave you, but it might be worth checking."

"I already called a contact regarding it, but be aware, the kid has had his fingers all over it, sir."

"Keep me updated."

He ended the call.

The boy had his palms and nose pressed against the far window.

MacKenzie made another call.

"Hello, sir."

"Hello, Kuresh. I am about to put an unknown USB stick into my laptop."

"Give me the access details."

"4,8,6,4. Access Foxtrot, X-Ray, Oscar, 2,4."

"OK. Put the USB in."

Larry did so.

A series of small screens appeared with rolling codes in green text.

"OK, sir, this is free of viruses."

"Thank you, Kuresh."

He tapped one of the files to reveal an audio recording.

The digitalised voice came through.

"We do not have any quarrel with you yet. Ask Arturo Bianchi if it is worth his son's life to go after the innocent sister of a dead man."

The recording ended.

Larry silently cursed—*How do they know my connection to him?*

He couldn't have loose ends, and he began to think of a plan.

Arabella turned to Connor and asked, "Why do you think the boy won't immediately be reunited with his *Madre?*"

They sat together in a ten-year-old Chevrolet Cruze bought from a private dealer for cash—he in the driver's seat. They were parked in an alcove overlooking the shimmering Lake Ontario and part of

Toronto.

"I am banking on his dad wanting to ask him questions first," said Connor, who finished tapping on his phone before putting it in his pocket. "We have to stay within half a kilometre or so of the tracking signal so we can be ready when he moves. If he or we move out of the half-a-click radius, my phone will let me know."

"What if they find the tracker and lead us into an ambush?"

"Then we'll be dead, won't we?"

"You seem very calm about it."

"Yeh, seem," said Connor, his fingertips sandpapering his stubble.

"What do you mean?"

"If I am afraid, what good is it to show it?"

"So, you are scared?" she asked, looking at him.

"Why wouldn't I be?"

"So, how are you so good at it?"

"Practice."

"From childhood?"

Realising she wasn't going to let go, he said, "I remember before my first boxing match being scared. But my dad said, *What's the point in showing that you're afraid? If you get beaten, then you're going to be seen as someone scared beforehand and then beaten, instead of just beaten*'."

She nodded and asked, "So he taught you how not to show fear?"

"Not really, other than to stand up straight and look my opponent in the eye. I read a lot; my family thinks of me as a bit of a geek—like a skint man's *Will Hunting*. I learnt some techniques that helped."

"I can't remember ever seeing my brother scared until…"

"His love of combat overrode his fear until it involved you."

"Do you think that is why he's dead?"

Connor snorted. "He's dead because standing in the open anywhere within fifty metres of seven hundred tiny steel balls being blasted out at one thousand two hundred metres per second isn't good for anyone's health."

She just looked ahead. After a while, Connor asked, "What are some examples of your favourite architecture?"

"Well, this will make you laugh from an Italian. But I like some of the brutalist structures. Do you know of this?"

"British reconstruction projects post World War Two."

She raised her eyebrows. "You know architecture?"

"I know some."

"Why?"

"To impress women in conversations like this."

"Hmmph, it worked," she said. "People think brutalism is a description of its looks but it—"

"But it derives from the French word for 'bare concrete'," interrupted Connor. "Because of this, you could build large structures on the cheap."

"Yes," she said, raising her eyebrows.

"Why do you like brutalism?"

"It was born out of the need to help the people. Not a man's dream of praise for the grandeur of his vision."

Connor smiled. "Maybe some men understand the importance of creating beauty for people to marvel at—to inspire."

"So, what are the examples of architecture that you have admired?"

"I enjoyed La Sagrada Familia. Antoni Gaudí must have known he would never live to see it finished. Well, at least at one point, but he cracked on. Besides, I thought a good Catholic girl like yourself would have appreciated the basilica."

"The Catholic girl might. The woman who has seen what affordable housing can do for devastated communities appreciates the idea of brutalism. And one has happier memories of the home of his *Nonna* than one building he might visit once or twice."

"Fair enough," said Connor. "I guess you take more after your mother?"

"Because I am different from my brother? And you think he was like our father?"

"I remember now. You said Carlo was a sweet boy until a hunting trip with your father."

"Yes. I am less emotional than my brother. But, when our father died and my brother left, my mother was not given the support they promised one another within that world. A code is only as strong as the people who hold it."

Connor stared ahead and said almost to himself, "In the beginning, when a group is more vulnerable, a code of honour is necessary….until it's not."

"Yes?"

He flicked her a glance. "If you ask a soldier if

he would lay down his life for a member of his section, say eight to twelve men, depending on which unit it is, he will say yes, and most would mean it. Maybe even up to a troop level, about a hundred and fifty men, but it dies off after that."

Connor started the engine and reversed out of the bay.

"Where are we going?"

"A hotel," he said. "I think they'll hold the kid here for a while. Same room but two single beds. Don't worry."

"I wasn't worried."

"I had to choose a place that wasn't littered with security cameras. Might not be to your exalted standards."

"I can bear it for one night."

He drove ten minutes before manoeuvring the vehicle into the car park of the 'Hazelnut Hotel', comprising a cylindrical red brick base supporting rectangular white stonework. Connor had researched the hotel to be upmarket enough not to have to worry about random thieves but not so much that he would feel obliged to remove his baseball cap.

He parked and said, "Lift your leg."

Arabella did so, and he slid a Beretta beneath it.

"If anyone attempts to force you out of the car when I've gone, then you at least have the option."

"OK," she said. "What happens now?"

"I'll go in first. Check it out. Then I text you the room number, and you follow on."

Connor donned his baseball cap and angled his face away from the camera overlooking the entrance.

The black operations agent knew tactical awareness to this degree bordered on paranoia, even if Larry MacKenzie couldn't have access to the feeds of every hotel in central Toronto. Nonetheless, if a balance between carelessness and paranoia couldn't be reached, he'd go with paranoia every time.

He took the keys from the receptionist with a painted-on smile and barely any interest behind the eyes—good.

He bounded up the stairs, entered the room, threw his bag on the bed and went to the window.

Connor surveyed the scene for a few moments before texting Arabella the room number.

He gripped his pistol tighter as he looked for any watchers. She got out of the Cruze with her bag and approached.

He admired her. She had kept it together, and he thanked his luck—if she'd fallen apart, it might've been impossible to protect her.

The Italian disappeared out of his vision into the entrance, and he couldn't see anything untoward.

After a minute, the door clicked open, and he heard her lock it.

He continued to watch before he was satisfied they hadn't been followed.

Before he could turn back, he felt Arabella press her tits into his back, reach around and grasp his crotch.

"Wow," she said.

Briefly stilled, he found the words, "Thanks for the compliment, but you know we can't do this."

Despite his words, he could already feel himself hardening under her massaging fingers.

"Why not?"

"I promised your brother I'd keep my hands to myself."

"My brother is dead, and we will probably be too," she whispered with her lips brushing the back of his ear. "Unless you do not find me attractive?"

Connor took a moment to answer. "So, you're saying if I turn you down, your self-esteem would be devastated, affecting your awareness?"

She laughed but kept her hand skilfully manipulating him. "Hmmm, maybe if I am not satisfied, I will lack the concentration to survive."

"It would kill you," he offered.

"I'd rather this was killing me," she said, squeezing him.

He reached back to grasp her ass before turning around. He brought her close, inhaling her perfume before her painted mouth collided with his.

Mike stood inside the reception area of Timpson Motorcycle Garage in Hamilton, gazing at the various bike pictures and magazine articles that adorned the burgundy and cream walls.

He could make out The Who's 'Behind Blue Eyes' emanating from the garage's radio and the comforting blended smell of oil, degreaser, solvent and a smidge of gasoline.

Ordinarily, there were only two shops he would take it to, and both were in Detroit.

However, the warning light had come on not long after they had passed the Canadian border, and he had decided to get it fixed.

The tech guru they knew as Cliff had contacted them to tell them to head to Toronto.

When Mike asked if he had a specific location on the individual, Cliff replied in the negative but said he would expand once they arrived.

Kyle had gone for a couple of meals from the McDonald's over a mile down the road.

The headlines of the newspaper articles of the garage and a squat, cropped-haired, goateed man caught his eye. He quickly ascertained the garage to be more than just a garage.

Just as he began to read one of the articles earnestly, the woman arrived with his coffee in a china mug.

"Here you go, Honey," she said, handing him the mug.

He guessed the smiling brunette to be about thirty. Lumberjack shirt with the sleeves rolled up. Tattooed forearms.

"Thanks," he replied before nodding at the photos. "Who is that?"

"That's Max; he's the owner, baby."

"He seems like an important man."

"Max is this community's slice of Jesus, though he'd never describe himself as special, and he ain't particularly religious."

"In what way?"

"Max takes on former criminals and addicts—the people no other employer will touch. And no matter how many times he gets burnt. No matter how many wash out. He's still here. Still a rock. He's never let tragedy turn his good heart away from people."

Her last words hollowed his diaphragm. She asked, "You OK, honey?"

"Where is he?"

"He's the one replacing your voltage regulator

on your pussy ZX10."

He smiled broadly at her good-natured jibe.

He asked, "Are there many that get clean, stay clean and go on to better things?"

She smiled and turned her palms to reveal the faded needle marks. "There are enough of us, sugar."

He nodded his understanding, and she said, "I best get my ass back to it."

As he watched her back, he felt a need for some air.

He spilled outside and inhaled. He calmed himself, sipped his coffee and watched a gaggle of teenagers walk down the street, vaping.

The former soldier felt a vague distaste watching them before remembering that he engaged in the decidedly less healthy and more odorous practice of smoking as a teen.

He had always been a rebellious kid, especially where his father had been concerned.

When his dad had been insistent that, *'When it comes to thrash metal, there is Metallica, and there is everyone else.'*

'That's not right, Pops,' countered a teenage Rose. *'Megadeth is the harder, faster and more true-to-genre band.'*

'You don't know what you're talking about, boy. Dave Mustaine would give it all back if it meant he could have stayed with Metallica.'

'Why? They would've held him back.'

And in truth, Mike loved both bands, as did his dad—but neither would concede arguments.

And he secretly loved the old man, but with both being strong characters, they clashed often and sometimes violently.

And the most rebellious thing Mike could think of doing was to join the military.

But after the initial loggerheads regarding his newly chosen profession, relations with the old man improved.

Improved to the point where Mike was devastated by his death a few years ago. He could see now how the authorities handled the case as a miscarriage of justice.

And this had trashed Mike's belief in law and order. He realised he would not have become a member of an outlaw gang otherwise.

Max, who Mike reckoned to be about fifty, appeared to be cleaning his hands with an oily rag. "That's it ready."

"That was fast."

"It was **hooped**—replacing is quicker than fixing—and you paid for it to be fast," said the old-timer. "I might not have taken the extra cash, but I am up to my neck in it."

Mike smiled. "I would have paid more."

"Ah, shoot," said the mechanic deadpan.

Mike took a breath. "I was speaking to the girl in there."

"Donna," smiled Max. "You like her, huh?"

"She's very nice."

"I could—"

"Why do you do it? Taking on the addicts?"

Max looked at him for a moment. "Son, I was an addict—coke to come up, heroin to come down. Just chipping at first—until it wasn't. Just bought what I could afford at first—until I didn't. Did terrible, terrible things to my fellow man. Some of those things will remain between God and me."

"Donna told me you weren't religious."

"There's a difference between believing in a higher power, a higher virtue, and being religious."

Mike nodded. "What made you stop?"

"Nearly twenty years ago, I got convicted and a suspended sentence for B and E. If I had been caught for some of the other shit, I'd still be there now."

"How hard was it to get clean?"

"Very. Sent me to rehab where I got physically clean, but the real challenge starts when you get out. I couldn't even do the 'one day at a time' method. I had a huge wall calendar; I would line off forty-eight boxes. Every half hour I didn't use, I took a permanent marker to colour one of the boxes in—seeing the black gave me confidence. Had to do that for six months. Had to wear a toque for a good few months, too."

"A toque?"

"A knitted cap Canadians who collect the *Pogey* usually wear."

"You learn something every day," said Mike. "Then what?"

"I went to the support group as mandated by the judge. Met a guy there who was never an addict. Years before his son was, before he choked to death on his vomit high on fentanyl—thankfully, not that popular when I was using. After his death, his father came to the meetings, never said why, and no one asked. He just listened. One night, he approached me and asked me what I was doing for work. I told him I was working nights in a steel factory—which I hated but was one of the few jobs I could get with my record. He gave me a job."

"He owned this place?"

"Sure did. Twelve years ago, he let me put down what small amount I'd saved and pay the rest over three years. He died a month after the final payment."

When Mike took another sip of his coffee, the mug hid the tremors in his lower jaw. He composed himself and asked, "So, this is your way of paying it forward?"

"That's all a man can do in the face of the world's cruelty. He can add to it or get busy becoming part of the solution," replied Max before glancing at Mike and saying. "Hand me your mug. I'll send Donna out in five to settle your payment."

Mike passed it to him, wooden, unable to look at him through shame. Kyle rode into the car park.

Arabella broke away from the kiss to allow Connor to unwrap her.

Her face felt hot with blood, and her pussy throbbed—she could not remember the last time she felt this turned on.

The grave danger of the situation acted to enhance her libido.

However, it was him, too.

Though quite good-looking, with a physique corded with dense muscle, he was not tall and seemed at least half a decade younger than her usual type. Still, the way he could handle dangerous situations had turned her on.

And the restraint he had shown—she had caught but a few glances in her direction—had inflamed her.

He spun her away from him as he unbuttoned

her shirt, unbelted and stripped down her trousers, unclipped her bra and finally slid down her French knickers.

"Turn around," he said.

Her breath hitched, and she did so.

She felt her heartbeat under his lustful gaze as he said, "A bit of a work of art, aren't you?"

"Yes."

He smiled at that.

She jutted her chin, and he frowned. "What? I have to undress myself?"

Smiling, she gripped the hem of his t-shirt and peeled it upwards off him.

Her fingertips stroked the Superman tattoo on his chest, and it felt like warm marble before her nails lightly drew on it.

She sank to her knees and opened his jeans.

Arabella sat back on her haunches in excitement before using the flat of her tongue to lick him from shaft to tip.

His fingers slid into her hair, gripping without pulling.

She raked her nails over his hard stomach and the back of his leg as he began to gently fuck her mouth and then her throat.

Arabella choked before standing under his easy pull. They kissed passionately as she ground his steel-hardness against her stomach.

Connor's hands grasped her waist, walking her back before effortlessly flinging her onto the bed.

His strong hands seized her by the back of her legs, spreading her wide as his mouth mashed against her pussy.

Her knuckles turned white as she gripped the

duvet in her tight fists.

She could feel his teeth as he ate her deeper.

Her fingers scrabbled for her clit as he climbed over her.

Arabella gasped at his entrance, her head flattening against the bed. His mouth fell over all her tits, throat and lips.

Her orgasm spasmed as he picked up the tempo.

"Stop, stop…fuck, fuck," he said, as she felt him pulse inside her.

He lay on her for a moment before she turned her head, and they began kissing.

When they broke, she asked, "Why did you say stop?"

"I didn't want to cum that quick."

She laughed. "I already came, so you are forgiven."

"I was thinking a bit more selfishly than that."

"Oh, you thought this might be the last time?"

He partially slid off her. "I didn't know whether you would need to visit a church between out-of-wedlock performances of the Devil's Tango."

She sniffed. "The confession, not the priest, gives us absolution."

"That statement would have hit harder had you not stolen it from Oscar Wilde," he said, voice partially muffled by duvet.

Cazzo—she thought.

"Shall we go out?" she said, sure he would say no.

"We can't go too far away from the kid's current position, remember," said Connor. "But yeh, let's find a bar close by."

Arturo Bianchi could almost see the relief in his exhalation.
 He sat in his office with Richèl Vergeer on speakerphone.
 "And he hasn't been touched or harmed in any way?" he asked.
 "He seems fine," answered the cold, professional voice.
 He thought about apologising to her but dismissed the idea in the same instant.
 "Great, great, great."
 "We'll arrange for him to be dropped off home to his mum."
 "No. Bring him here. Or else I'll have him brought here."
 "You want us to fly him—"
 "He won't fly."
 "You want him to road travel four thousand kilometres? I'll discuss it with Mister Mac—"
 "The fuck you won't! He's my son."
 "I am sure he'll be fine with it."
 "Listen, you fuckin' bitch. My son better be here by Sunday, or your boss and I will have a problem. A serious one."
 Bianchi hung up, glad to have that over her. He began to seethe that he had been interrupted in fucking her.
 She might be regretting it now, but she had wanted it—The drug in her wine had seen to that. She liked the rough stuff, too.
 But he knew he wouldn't get another chance.
 His mind switched to the people who had

taken his son.

It had meant to be a warning, but it just screamed that they didn't have the balls for a follow-through. And now, he would find out who it was and wipe their entire families out.

30

Mike and Kyle met in the hotel lobby bar.

The barman—dressed in a cream suit with burnt orange lapels that strangely matched the colouration of the drinks cabinet behind him—served them both a crisp beer.

"You're not normally one for drinking on the job, Mike?" said Kyle, studying his pint before taking a sip. "Fuck, that's good."

"Cliff has contacted me. Our Italian friend's son was delivered to Larry MacKenzie's main offices here in Toronto earlier this morning."

"A weird place to drop a child."

"It's not that weird."

"The fuck it is. I understand not wanting to drop him at the cop shop, but at MacKenzie's? Unless it's a political thing."

"Why do you think Bianchi has gone from a Capo in the Siderno Group to become such a powerful boss within the time he has?"

It took a moment before Kyle exclaimed in a low voice. "No fucking way! I mean... w..why?"

"I am not sure," Mike lied. "But a drug epidemic looks very bad for the current Canadian Government."

"Not as bad as it'll look for MacKenzie if anyone makes the link."

Mike sniffed. "When you've gone from having nothing to earning billions, it must be hard not to develop a God-complex. If you've been used to succeeding all your life, you never think it will end."

"That's deep, Mike," said Kyle with a smile.

"So, this is one for the road back to Detroit?"

Mike sipped his own, agreeing with Kyle's assessment of the beer. "No. Cliff thinks there is a fair to middling chance the kidnappers are still here."

"Ahh, it makes sense now," said Kyle. "I always thought it was weird that the Italian would know a guy like Cliff. It'll have been this Larry MacKenzie who put him on to him."

"Good guess," said Mike. "Anyway, we've been assigned protection duty to the boy when escorting him back in the morning. We're to set off at nine."

"Where are we escorting him?"

"Not sure yet, but must be a long way because Cliff has assigned a Nissan Titan to strap the bikes into. I am guessing we're going to have to switch driver duties for at least one night. With that in mind, I didn't want to be stuck in the room all evening."

"Why would they hand him back? But stay in the city?"

"Maybe they think Bianchi will come himself," said Mike with a shrug. "Anyway, I want you to keep this on you."

He handed Kyle a small 'dumb' phone with the capacity for calls and texts but not much else.

"What's this for?"

"I have one too. The number is saved. Wherever we are going, they might take our regular phones off us. I'd like for us to have options, and this phone gives off a lower signature than the smart versions."

Kyle slipped it into his pocket and said, "Well, if we have the night, we might as well explore the city."

"Last thing we need is a hangover," said Mike, trying to disguise his half-heartedness.

"Riding between bars is time we won't be drinking. The closer we are to the kid, the better."

They finished their drinks and left.

After a ten-minute ride, they came across the green-backed sign of 'The Charmed Clover' in gold lettering.

They entered the sports bar and decided not to bother going anywhere else after a swift assessment.

Mike did a quick reconnaissance of the bar on the pretence of going to the toilet.

A pair of long-haired men arm-wrestled in the corner. They looked like bikers despite their lack of 'cuts' and Mike not seeing any motorcycles outside—*maybe rockers.*

A couple within their little zone—her with short blonde hair and him with a mullet—sat in the opposite corner.

A few older men sat on a long table to the left playing dominoes while youths played pool in the backroom with a back exit in the corner.

The dents in the black and white diamond tiles gave credence to the bar's popularity despite gleaming with cleanliness.

Bulbs of light, hung from the ceiling and the glass drinks cabinet, shone an orangey-red behind the bar.

As Kyle shuffled to the table with two heavy-glassed beers, Mike said, "Remember, we are working tomorrow."

Kyle belched a mocking laugh. "I remember the days when I could drink all night and roll into a ten-mile ruck without sleep the next day."

"Could you solve a Sudoku puzzle hung over?"

"Probably not."

"Exactly. We need our wits about ourselves."

"Why are we doing this babysitting job again?"

"It seems the Italian only trusts us to bring his boy back safely. And…"

"What?"

"Why did they give him back?" asked Mike to himself as much as Kyle did.

"Maybe they didn't want to go that far with him? I mean, he is only a kid."

Mike sipped his pint. "Then why take the risk of taking him in the first place?"

"Lost their nerve when it came to the crunch?"

"Do you think whoever this man is, he's the type to lose his nerve?"

"Some men are brave, brave, brave, for years and suddenly, something topples 'em."

"Maybe."

Kyle took a sip. "I suppose that beating you took in Nebraska should have toppled you. But instead, it led you to form 'The Red Hauser', and Amen to that."

Kyle lifted his pint, and Mike chinked it before saying, "It wasn't just that."

He regretted saying it, as now it required him to expand. He continued under Kyle's gaze, "My grandad was one of the straightest, honest and accepting guys I know. Back in the early forties, he worked at the Packard plant and was one of the few who didn't join the protest against Blacks coming onto the workforce. Didn't join the Detroit race riot either. His friends ostracised him from the plant. I remember over ten years ago, my grandad—nearly ninety then, having a full-blown argument with my old man over why Detroit had to file for bankruptcy."

"What did your dad say?"

"My dad could argue in an empty room. Said that Blacks were lazy and had a genetic predisposition to crime—he's always said that. *'Why aren't there any great ancient buildings in Africa? And don't say the Pyramids—everyone knows Egyptians are Arabs.'* When Kwame Kilpatrick—the old Mayor—got convicted of federal felony counts involving mail fraud, wire fraud, and racketeering, my dad saw it as proof of his theory. Always said Detroit's automotive industry went down when they allowed Blacks on the workforce."

"What did your grandad say?"

Mike tilted his head back. "Told the old man that he didn't know what he was talking about. Said Detroit declined because the white bosses at the automakers were not prepared to take a wage cut to compete with Japanese car makers, who built a better quality car at a lower price. Said all the cars in the seventies and eighties—even the expensive ones—that came out of Detroit were junk."

Mike took another sip and continued, "My grandad used to read a lot in retirement. I remember him telling my old man that only seventeen percent of Egyptians were Arab. Most were North African, and he listed a lot of discoveries made by Africans in astronomy and math and said nobody was more criminal than a white banker."

"What's this got to do with you going from a

Merica, man-in-a-white-hat soldier to a crazy outlaw biker?"

"Because I found out they were both right—and both wrong. My dad got killed in a carjacking—bored, rich white boys from Corktown. A Black judge presided over the trial—he gave them a community order of two hundred hours. My grandpa died within a week of the verdict. You could say my views on law and order and America changed."

"Fuucckkk! That would do it."

"Tell me about it."

After a few moments, Kyle said, "I know what you said, but I still think you should be our leader. Can't be good having Miles heading it—officially, I mean. He's stupid and cowardly. If this was caveman times, he'd have had a swift club to the back of the head."

"The right people know, and hopefully, the right people don't. We hav—holy fuck!"

"What."

"Don't turn around," said Mike. "It's the girl. Which means that's the guy."

"What girl?"

"The one our Italian friend wants dead."

"How did they find us?"

"I am not sure they did."

"Course they have," said Kyle with urgent incredulity. "Of all the gin joints in the world, they choose to come in here."

Mike saw not an ounce of recognition in the man.

"Maybe this is a gift horse," he said. "If he recognises me, then he's an actor after Marlon Brando's heart."

"He'll recognise me if he catches sight of me—he walked within a few feet of me before he carjacked me."

Mike thought for a moment. "There's a back exit down the corridor. I'll meet you at the bar across the street."

"Aren't you coming?"

"I am going to try for a picture of this guy if I can. Go."

Kyle did so.

Connor scanned the other patrons, assessing for potential threats and exits.

He remembered the Jason Bourne quote, *'I can tell you the license plate numbers of all six cars outside. I can tell you that our waitress is left-handed, and the guy sitting up at the counter weighs two hundred and fifteen pounds and knows how to handle himself. I know the best place to look for a gun is the cab of the grey truck outside, and at this altitude, I can run flat out for a half mile before my hands start shaking.'*

Remembered it, and also remembered thinking—*Fuck off, nobody is that switched on.*

However, like any skill, it improved under focused practice, and he could now dissect a room into most dangerous threats, most likely threats, potentially developing situations, and, as a result, where best to sit.

He assessed that the two men sitting in the centre, opposite one another, were the most dangerous in the room.

However, despite one's furtive glance in their direction, no doubt towards Arabella, the men he deemed more of a threat were a long-haired duo in the corner who were in striking distance of middle-age but didn't quite know it yet.

Their voices carried around the room despite them sitting near one another.

They wore hoodies, so he supposed they could have been wearing patches beneath but didn't reckon it likely. Most outlaw bikers were proud to be so and not shy about displaying it.

And the pair were not shy about staring at Arabella, either.

Ordinarily, Connor would usually perform a recce of the bar on his way to the toilet before anything else. Yet, he didn't want to leave Arabella standing, so instead, he asked her what she wanted to drink and gestured to the high table in the corner.

The man, who had his back to Connor and Arabella, walked towards the back, presumably towards the toilets.

The long-haired twosome gave the walking man a blatantly threatening stare as he walked past.

The mid-twenties version of Connor would have engineered a scenario in which he could batter the pair. Since childhood, he had taken an almost perverse pleasure in hurting those who preyed on people more vulnerable. The more heinous he considered the culprits, the more hilarity he took in watching them in pain.

However, especially given the circumstances, he didn't want to antagonise the pair—but he didn't want to leave either.

He walked to the bar and ordered, diverting from his usual gin and tonic for a vodka and coke and an amaretto for Arabella.

Connor walked over to her and set the drinks

down.

"I am just going to the bathroom."

Connor resolutely ignored the staring pair as he noted the backroom occupants and the location of the back exit.

He went into the toilet and could see the cubicle was shut. Connor squeezed a piss out, washed and dried his hands and left.

The voices of the two men carried over as they argued about a recent rule change in ice hockey.

Connor reached Arabella and said, "Fuck me, they talk like they have the caps lock on."

"They might just be excited to be out. Good social relationships are the number one protector against depression."

"Beats pills."

She sipped her Amaretto. "You don't agree with medication for depression?"

"No. They unbalance your neurochemistry, making you reliant on them. I have friends who have been on them for years."

"You can come off them bit by bit with little side effects."

"In a perfect world, you can, but humans are humans. Besides, they don't address why a person is depressed in the first place."

"Exactly, you need to do the mind work. But doing that when you're depressed is so hard. It is like having a gremlin on your back while doing DIY. The medication gets rid of that gremlin."

Connor said, "I didn't think about it like that. Thank you for educating me."

One of the men in the corner went to the bar. After a few minutes, he was given a tray of eight beers.

"Come on," said Connor to Arabella. "We need to leave now."

"Why?"

"Because a situation is going to develop. One that your departed brother would love, but I will have to avoid."

The entrance banged open with the bellow of "Who the fuck do those rice-burning crotch rockets outside belong to?"

Mike's eyes leapt to the now open entrance in which members of a biker gang crowded.

As one turned to close the door, he caught sight of top and bottom **rockers**, alerting him that these belonged to the Toronto chapter of the Benetton MC.

Their name was a play on the fashion brand 'The United Colours of Benetton' in that they prided themselves on being a diverse and multicultural MC.

Being a relatively young MC meant they were burning with a desire to prove themselves. And proving themselves initially meant through acts of violence, not necessarily business savvy.

At the shout of "Who the fuck do those rice-burning crotch rockets outside belong to?" stress hormones bolted from Mike's adrenal gland like wild horses from a stable.

"Ours," Mike called out, trying to strike a balance between confidence without being over-aggressive.

The leader sported a black goatee beard and hair curtains falling past the ears. Mike judged him to be of Mexican heritage by his accent and complexion.

The former Green Beret thought he recognised him but then realised he bore an uncanny resemblance to the 'Sex Machine' from the film From Dusk Till Dawn.

The MC leader theatrically cupped his ear, "Whose?"

Mike stood as the group approached.

He made eye contact with the leader and said, "Listen, we are from out of town. We apologise if we've offended you by stepping in here. We'll leave."

Mike could hear and almost feel the two that had already been in the bar step up close behind him.

"Absolutely," said the leader cheerfully. "Just hand over your keys, and then you can."

With a grave sense of déjà vu, Mike knew there would be a fight. And he knew he would lose—the numbers were far too great, even if all the men were inept at fighting.

And he couldn't simply hand over the keys—how would he explain why he no longer had a bike to ride protection for the boy?

He threw down his last gambit.

"How about you and I, man on man? You beat me, you take the bikes."

"We are taking the fucking bikes, anyway. Now give me the fucking keys before—"

A chair smashed into the biker's face before he could complete the sentence—collapsing him with a bloodied mask. The sandy-haired man leapt into the momentarily stunned gang like a leopard attacking chimps.

Connor seethed at the scene—*These fuckin' pricks are going to take the lads' bikes. While one is on the shitter, too.*

He knew he should slide out the exit with Arabella, but they had a pair guarding the door.

His hand slid into his pocket to retrieve a heavy kubotan, doubling as a functioning lighter.

He leaned over to Arabella and whispered, "When the doorway clears, escape and head back to the hotel."

The Brit turned before she could ask questions. When he first arrived, he identified the chairs as light enough to swing but heavy enough to cause damage.

He snatched the one to his left and whipped it into the face of the gang's leader.

He hurtled the chair at them, taking advantage of their impersonations of statues. He threw the Kubotan into his weaker punching left hand and stormed in, firing short punches.

Looking out of his eyebrows, the first two fell, one to a straight right and the other to his 'steeled' left hook.

The return punches rained on him, and he went into 'Mike Tyson' mode, bobbing and weaving, reckoning it unlikely they could punch as venomous as he up close.

Mike spun around to knock out one with a left-right-crushing head-butt combination.

The rest of the gang attacked like hyenas.

Mike took a leaf out of the man's book to pick up the chair he had been sitting on.

One looked at him and flicked out a switchblade. The former Green Beret immediately jammed the feet of the chair into his face.

The bone-thunking impact on the back of his

skull sent Mike flying forward.

He stumbled and fell onto his face.

He scrambled onto his back to see he was about to die.

Letting go of the now protective chair with one hand to protect his face from the stamping boots, the chair tore from his grasp as his knife-wielding attacker raised the blade for a death plunge.

A knee collided with his would-be murderer's temple, sending him sprawling. Mike caught the view of the sandy-haired man knocking out the man attempting to dance on his head.

A hand came down with the question, "Are you OK, mate?"

It took a moment to realise the threats had been neutralised.

He reached up and clasped the hand.

Hauled to his feet, his head spun to see bloodied human puppets strewn on the floor.

The stranger said, "I don't fancy being here when the police arrive."

Mike cut through his surrealism to ask, "Why did you help me?"

"It's a sad state when one man has to ask another that. But then again, the word 'honour' is almost dead in the west...almost."

The words punched Mike in the gut, and he said, "Thank you."

"Maybe you should ask your pal hiding in the toilet about the word."

Before Mike could reply, the stranger shouted across to the barman, "I can't see any cameras. Why?"

"I...I...it's...no reason."

The stranger walked to the barman and asked

again in a voice rinsed with venom, "Why?"

"Because it's a drops bar for the guys you have just beaten up."

The stranger laughed and looked at Mike. "Beautiful irony. And, speaking of honour—"

The stranger walked up to the one who had taken out the knife, "There is no honour in using a knife when you already have numbers on your side."

With that, he crashed his knees onto the man's upper arms as he sat on his chest, scooping up the knife. The man screamed even before the blade punched its way through both cheeks and an agape mouth.

The man's head-shaking seemed to aid the knife's way out.

"I know that as a Glasgow Smile," the stranger laughed. "But I've heard it called the Chelsea Grin. Still, chicks dig scars."

31

Charlotte sat, forcing a smile through her tiredness.

Polly lay sprawled on the opposite soft green sofa of a Mercedes Sprinter that Jim had converted into a motorhome himself.

The faint smell of vinegar hung in the air.

After half an hour, Jim said to Charlotte, "I'll go and get her some cigarettes."

They both knew the heroin the twenty-four-year-old had just taken could last up to an hour.

They had picked Polly up from her counsellor's office and were now parked outside the addict's sister's home—but Patricia wasn't in or answering her phone.

Charlotte could see the mixed-race girl was once very pretty.

Now missing teeth, rake thin with bloodshot eyes, Charlotte wasn't sure if she'd survive the year.

Polly had always been one of her favourites. Most of the addicts were sweetness and light until she told them she'd run out of whatever substitute drugs she'd usually distribute.

However, Polly had never done that, usually saying, *'Even fairy godmothers run out of magic sometimes'.*

Charlotte would laugh at the compliment despite it tearing at her insides.

And they didn't have any methadone today.

This time, Charlotte and Jim had relented and provided Polly with a clean needle for her to shoot her drugs, knowing due to the young girl's agitation, the alternative would be for her to go shoot up god knows where with god knows who.

Charlotte almost felt jealous of a look of serenity that passed over Polly.

Finally, she asked, "How's the therapy going, Polly?"

"Fine an' dandy. I was talking to him about you, the angel of the streets," she answered lucidly.

"Oh, really?"

"Yeh. He's married…say, why don't you have a man?"

"How do you know I don't?"

"I just know these things," she sang.

Charlotte couldn't help but laugh and replied, "Guess I never felt those butterflies."

Polly blew a playfully derisive raspberry. "I had that feeling for my last two boyfriends. Those butterflies in my stomach soon left when they started kicking me in it. We girls are so stupid; can't see what's right in front of us sometimes. Especially you."

"Why especially me?"

"Be..because you have a man who lurrvvesses you and protects you, but you just want to brush him off, hoping for these butterflies of yours? Disney has spun your mind crazy sister."

Charlotte smiled. Maybe it was true. She tried to think of a couple that she knew personally that she wanted to emulate. Depressingly, she came up short.

She didn't mention that Jim was married, mainly because it wouldn't have made a difference if he wasn't.

Instead, Charlotte said, "Say, Polly, I wanted to ask you something. Now, you don't have to answer, and it won't affect you and me if you choose not to."

She raised her eyebrows and palms. "You can

always ask."

"Sometimes, I get talking to the other people who come and see me, and they tell me things."

"Like how they come to me for their drugs?"

Charlotte felt relieved she hadn't had to ask outright and said, "Yes."

"And you want to know where I get it from?"

"Kinda."

"I get it from the ex I told you about."

"Where does he get it from?"

Polly sighed, "From his cousin, he says. But—Well, yes, his cousin."

When she said 'but', Charlotte had caught something in Polly's eyes.

"Go on, Polly. I won't tell," said Charlotte, childishly throwing a finger to her lips.

Polly giggled, "OK. One time, I saw him with a biker. One where you sit forward, a sports bike. A white boy. Gerald is not scared of nada, but he seemed to be awfully nervous around this dude."

"Did you ask him?"

"Not unless I wanted a smack in the mouth."

"OK."

"I can show you where he meets him if you want?"

Charlotte felt a little nauseous. She knew anyway you cut it, she'd be putting Polly in danger. She took a breath and said, "Maybe just tell me."

"Not that it makes any difference."

"What do you mean?"

"For an educated sista, you ain't too smart sometimes," grinned Polly. "Slapping the supply chain just increases the dollar we have to pay. You have to reduce us addicts, not the dealers."

The expression on Kyle's face matched Mike's feelings.

A screen secured to one of the pillars playing Global News Toronto.

They looked at one another from the corner seats of their hotel bar.

"Could he have set that up?" asked Kyle.

Mike burst out with, "By paying a fucking incredible method actor to allow his mouth to be ripped out with a knife?"

"You're right, I am sorry."

Mike calmed himself. "It's alright. It is a fucking weird coincidence he was there."

His eyes flickered to the scenes of paramedics frantically attending to collapsed people in the street before flicking to a reporter.

"Not just that he was there, that he would dive in to help a stranger like that. A man like that must be one in a thousand."

"At least," murmured Mike.

"So, what now?"

"What do you mean?" asked Mike, despite knowing.

"We meant to duel this guy after he saved your life? Or, at least, our bikes."

"Look, our mission is to protect the boy until he gets to his father. He's an innocent boy."

"I mean, after that. We have been given the order to hunt and put this cat down. And not for nothing that means killing her, too."

Mike couldn't answer him. He stared at the screen, looking at a tearful girl of about twelve talking to the camera. Mike didn't have to have the sound on to know she had lost her mum to an overdose.

Maybe she's going into care now?

Kyle said softly, "How did we get to this? Killing women."

"We haven't killed any women."

"Yeah, well, I don't want to."

"Yeah," Mike finally admitted. "Neither do I. I don't want to do a lot of things anymore."

Connor's phone had alerted him that the tracker had begun to move.

The pair had been in the hotel dining room enjoying a coffee having eaten breakfast. Their travel bags had been at their feet so they could leave immediately.

Now, thirty minutes later, they had well cleared the Toronto city limits.

He admired the responsive handling of the Cruze with Arabella in the passenger seat next to him.

"It's pretty good, given it's nearly ten years old."

"You consider ten years too old?"

"I don't fancy emigrating to Thailand."

"What?"

"Nothing," said Connor. "Depends on the car. I quite like this—it's fun to drive."

"You like a fun ride?"

"I said drive."

"I know you did. I can make jokes, too."

"It's good to know," said Connor with a nod. "Humour in the face of adversity."

"An Oscar Wilde quote I do not know about?"

"No. It's one principle of the commando

spirit—well, it's actually 'Cheerfulness in the face of adversity'."

"What are the others? Unless it is ***omertà**?*"

"Courage, determination, unselfishness. And so to be called a shit-house was bad, to be known as a **Rap-hand** was worse, and to have a reputation for being ***Jack*** was horrendous."

"A Rap-hand?"

"Someone who gives in easily. Might derive from the way players of certain board games signal they can't continue by rapping their knuckles on the table. But a mate of mine thinks it's to do with wrapping yourself in a blanket and sleeping when the going gets tough."

"And Jack?"

"Someone who just looks out for themselves. A Jack-cunt puts in the minimum effort in team tasks, being content to let others take up the slack."

"So a good commando makes jokes in dangerous situations, never stops, and…"

"And what?"

"And still helps a woman you don't need to."

"I, err… I watched a woman… " Connor felt a whoosh in his chest but fought it down. "I was too small at the time."

"But you are—"

"Stop talking for a bit."

After a few minutes, he said, "You know, I didn't ever ask you if you had been to Canada before."

"I haven't. I have always wanted to. Maybe not like this."

"If we make it out alive, I'll treat you to a 'Timmies'."

"A 'Timmies'?"

"The doughnut and coffee culture is strong here—and Tim Horton's is popular. I heard a Canadian asked for a double-double in London once."

He had to explain that it meant two creams and two sugars.

Arabella pulled a face. "Western people want to destroy their sense of taste. I think our mother's cooking was the only reason Carlo would risk his life to return home in the early days."

"Why was he risking his life in the early days?"

"My brother transformed from a shy boy to the craziest man I know. And crazy men get themselves into trouble with the wrong people."

"I find it hard to believe anyone could scare your brother out of town."

"My brother was not the ***cazzuto*** he became. Besides, this boss was with the people who owned the town. My brother was just a teenager and doing crazy things—things that they liked when he brought in the money, but when threatened, this so-called 'man of honour' tried to give my brother up. Fuckin' ***fica*** sent weak men, and my brother escaped. My brother could always face death and…"

The suddenness of her guttural sob took Connor by surprise. His heart rate sped a few beats as her howls reverberated through him.

After a while, the energy in her cries spiralled into weeping before feathering into even but shallow breaths.

He waited a while before saying, "You ever heard that vengeance doesn't make you feel better?"

"Yes."
"It's a lie."

32

Arturo Bianchi watched the strange motorcade of a black Lexus RX and a blue Nissan Titan with a pair of sports bikes strapped in the back.

It had been a little over two days since he demanded his son be brought to him. The drivers of the vehicles must have switched and driven through the two nights.

And he had to reject air travel, as he knew from experience that Louis would have gone berserk at the sight of a plane or helicopter.

The bikes looked alien in this mountainous, snowy territory of Yukon, the inhospitality of which made it a natural fortress.

Arturo had meant to bring his son to this place for a long time. He told himself he had been waiting for his son to be old enough to appreciate it.

The truth had been that he didn't want to get too close to the boy until he had solidified his position.

And until now, for security reasons, he had kept this place a secret from even The Red Hauser.

This was his main hub, where eighty percent of his produce came from.

Larry MacKenzie had subsidised it through various proxies, shell companies and offshore accounts.

The Prime Minister-to-be also owned mines throughout the Yukon and hired some of the staff as 'rangers' to report anyone hiking within the vicinity.

Back channels had been painstakingly forged, Central American experts smuggled in, and private security companies protected the work.

And those same contractors were now protecting the site. Frank Johannes, the leader, had informed MacKenzie, who informed Bianchi that *'No one would be in a fit state to fight if they attempted to hike in.'*

There was only one real way in and out of this compound by vehicle, and high-tech sensors and cameras covered it.

It was the safest place for his son now.

The car door opened, and Louis got out tentatively.

Bianchi watched him squint at him and said, "Louis, come here."

His son's face seemed to scrutinise him, and Bianchi realised he might not recognise him.

"It's your father. Don't you recognise my voice, bub?"

His son's face lit with recognition, and he began to shuffle-jog towards him.

Bianchi wanted to scoop him into his arms but remained mindful of the eyes on him.

Instead, he rested his arm on his shoulder as Louis hooked his good arm around his leg.

Mike and the other Red Hauser biker alighted from the Titan and leant on its bonnet.

Richèl Vergeer also alighted from the Lexus, her fur-lined, hooded jacket matching her boots.

Bianchi felt unease in his stomach as the security leader approached to speak in her ear.

Louis distracted Bianchi by pulling on his trousers. "When is Mum getting here?"

"You've had a long trip. I thought we would have some father and son time."

He felt the boy tense and remembered an

episode where Louis had screamed the place down.

He remembered the beating he put on the boy, thinking the fear of it would assuage any repeat performance. However, a mere two weeks later, it had occurred again.

The boy's mother had thrown herself in front of the boy, spouting that he had a condition and couldn't control himself.

Bianchi wasn't sure at the time, but enough episodes had since occurred to convince him.

"But we can get her as soon as you want."

"Yes. Yes," said Louis, breathing hard. "Tomorrow?"

"I will speak to her. Hopefully, we can get her here."

"Please, please, please—"

"Calm down. She'll be here."

"OK. OK. OK."

"Do you want some ice cream?"

Louis nodded his head.

"OK, you go in with Johannes."

"No. No. No."

"Johannes is my friend?"

All he got as a reply was a shaking head. Then he remembered that his mum said, *'If there isn't a woman around, he doesn't feel calm.'*

Bianchi gestured to Richèl.

He watched her expression alternate from disgust to softening, in tandem with her eyes moving between him and his son.

"Seems Louis wishes you to stick around until his **mamma** gets here."

"I am afraid, I cannot, I have to—"

"No. Please. Please. Please," pleaded Louis.

Before Richèl could speak, Johannes said, "We're here. Your safety is our responsibility."

Bianchi went cold at that—It meant that MacKenzie did know about the rough stuff between him and Vergeer. And it was Johannes's way of telling Bianchi he didn't work for him.

"Luckily, I have some luggage packed," she said. "I'll see if I can reschedule."

Louis craned his head up at her. "Can I stay with you?"

"I don't think you would like that. I snore a lot," she said.

"I don't care."

"Your mum might get jealous."

"She won't. Can we call her?"

Bianchi said quickly, "I tried. No reception."

He widened his eyes at Vergeer as his son's body began to vibrate.

She seemed to get the hint because she said, "OK. As long as your mum is OK with it."

When she gave him a nod, Johannes called out, "Marcus. Show Miss Vergeer to her room. Callum, take the Lexus around to the compound."

The soldiers broke away to carry out their orders.

When Johannes left, Mike approached. "We're not staying."

Bianchi frowned with confusion. "Why not?"

"Let's just say I've had perception adjustment."

"Look, I am sorry I insisted you protect my boy across Canada. I know it was a bastard thing to do, but you're one of the few I fully trust, Mike."

"I appreciate that, but that's not the reason."

"Are you telling me you're definitely out?"

"I am telling you I am out. I am sure The Red Hauser will still be in."

Bianchi's mind whirred; MacKenzie, who saw everyone out as a loose end, might be glad of the heads up.

Might be glad to have the problem solved for him.

"Well, it's a long way to the nearest town. May as well stay the night and head off in the morning."

He watched Mike's eyes as he replied, "I thought that was a given."

"Of course."

"Some fortress you have here. More than a hundred kilometres over the most inhospitable terrain in Canada. Surprised you need this private army if the approaches are covered. I don't think anyone will be parachuting in soon. Maybe helicopters."

"We have answers for that," said Bianchi proudly. "Besides, my friend has friends in high places. If this place is discovered, he'd hear about it, let alone an assault with helicopters."

Connor felt the intimidating breeze across his face.

It had been over two days of non-stop driving.

Despite them switching the driver's role, the distance between them and the tracker had steadily grown as the signal had regularly fallen out, taking them off-course in several instances.

Eventually, for the first time since they left Toronto, the tracker had stopped for more than fifteen minutes. Connor guessed they had reached their designation.

The black operations agent saw the GPS

signal to be about fifty miles away from his current location as the crow flies.

He sat on a wooden bench just outside an equally wooden, peak-roofed general store. The simple sign proclaimed its name as 'Grizzly Joe's', complete with a silhouette of a bear.

The snow-capped peaks stared at him from a distance, threateningly reminding him of the mountain training he had done in the Scottish Highlands as a ***sprog*** marine. If anything, this terrain looked even more unwelcoming.

He took out his phone and dialled the secure number.

"I think I have found it."

"Are you sure?" replied Ciara.

"No."

"Explain."

"I'll forward you the kid's GPS position."

He watched Arabella sitting in the car, still uncertain as to what he was about to do.

"Northern British Columbia forest region. Just shy of the Columbia forest region," Ciara stated.

"It's at least forty miles from any highway or major metalled road."

"I can't see anything on the satellite maps," said Ciara. "Just a road that eventually peters into a smaller road before disappearing into an expanse of forest with mountains all around. There are just a few small openings in the treeline."

"And that's where I would place an illegal facility if money were no object."

"I can't go to our contacts over there based on a suspicion."

"I thought you might say that," said Connor.

"I can't risk coming from here in the south. The main road looks quiet enough for them to have eyes and ears along there. We'll head in from the west."

"We'll?" she exclaimed. "That's fifty miles of mountains covered in forests teeming with wolves and bears—"

"Yeah, I've seen 'The Revenant'."

"I am not joking, Connor."

"I know," he said. "Which is why they won't expect it."

"For good reason. And you can't take her, Connor."

"I made a promise, Ciara."

"To who? A dead man?"

"Yes. She'll remain with me until I've neutralised the target."

"Connor, you're officially there to take pictures and confirm the site. They won't sanction a hit."

"They might not sanction it, but I don't think they'll cry too much about it."

He could almost hear her sigh. "What do you need?"

"I can obtain the equipment needed for the hike myself, but I need a complement of weapons—for self-protection—that includes a C14 Timberwolf."

Mike felt a sense of unease as he stared at the ceiling.

He didn't like the look in Bianchi's eye when he told him he was out.

The former Green Beret could see the mistake and lamented how his normally cunning mind had let him down on this occasion.

He couldn't insist on Kyle staying in the same

room as him, or else the Mafia boss would get suspicious.

He had placed a chair in front of the door and had the Pit Viper pistol beside him.

And strange thoughts crept into his mind—of the addicts he had helped to kill.

It had been the pandering, liberal judicial system that had let him down for justice. He could see now that not only had his resentment made him lash out—but punch down on the wrong people.

The dark thoughts of the damage he was helping to cause began to invade his mind.

He looked at his phone—no signal. No internet.

This is bad.

33

Arabella watched Connor through the window, and it struck her how lucky she was that her brother turned to him and not one of his 'brothers' in the 'Ndrangheta.

She felt sure he would ditch her after Carlo's death, but here he was, still determined to remove the threat to her life.

He ended the phone call, approached and got in the car.

He turned to her and asked almost rhetorically, "So, Carlo told me you were an avid hiker and climber."

"Yes, I can climb good despite not having the physique for it."

"Can you hike and climb through eighty kilometres of mountainous forest within forty-eight hours? Don't say you can if you can't."

A butterfly with cold wings fluttered in her stomach. "I can."

"OK," he said, starting the vehicle. "We are going to drive to this town. Shop for equipment, and then make our way in."

"OK."

"I have, for want of a better expression, friends here. But they can't help us with this outside of getting me a few bits and bats. But, I am going to give you this."

He handed her a digital watch.

"I guess this isn't just a watch?"

"No. I understand you don't want to be taken into any custody, but if I die, you're fucked anyway."

"OK," she said cautiously.

"I'll show you how to access a distress signal. She will send one back, and this watch will automatically set a waypoint for you to follow—it has settings for 'tactical' to keep you away from pathways, bottlenecks and skylining yourself; 'easy', which takes you the least arduous route to 'straight', which is as the crow flies."

"She?"

"My boss," he said, turning to face her.

Arabella nodded and decided not to ask for elaboration. Instead, she said, "This is an emergency measure, is it not?"

"Yes, the likeliness of at least one of us dying isn't insignificant."

She didn't speak for a moment and then said, "But us not doing this increases that likelihood?"

"Exactly."

"We best get shopping then."

He nodded before asking, "You said your dad used to take you shooting as a kid."

"Yes."

"What sort of guns?"

"Different ones, but mostly, a .30-06 Springfield. I became a more accurate shot than my father."

"Women tend to be good shots—they don't snatch the trigger as much," said Connor.

Bianchi stood across from Johannes in a small office in one of the two control rooms.

The aqua-green walls reminded Bianchi of a hospital the first time he had seen it, and the desktop and screens were like a submarine's conning tower.

Noise insulation within the walls of the control rooms made hearing the outside world impossible unless the audio of the security cameras were switched on.

The almost automaton-like personnel manning the various vehicles remained oblivious to their conversation behind the soundproof glass.

The hawkish South African said, "I have passed on your concern regarding Mister Rose, and Mister MacKenzie does not wish him to be disappeared as yet."

"Strange. He's never liked loose ends before."

"And he doesn't like them now, so he's given you forty-eight hours to convince Mister Rose to stay."

"How?"

"You are instructed to reveal your affiliation with Mister MacKenzie to Mister Rose. And that Mister Rose's continuing business relationship with you will prove fruitful. And that a termination of it might not."

Bianchi's mouth opened before he nodded his understanding. "Could you send Rose here?"

"Of course," said Johannes before leaving.

Bianchi stood alone with his thoughts.

He resented the white-bread MacKenzie telling him what to do but knew how powerful an ally he was.

And it wasn't like the future Prime Minister made Bianchi eat shit; it was just the Mafioso resented anyone treating him like a subordinate.

Arturo Bianchi could see Mike Rose approaching the door on one of the monitor screens.

The crime lord went to the entrance, keyed in

the access code, and the steel doors steamed open.

"Mike, let's take a walk."

Part of him looked forward to showing The Red Hauser éminence grise the complex.

Larry MacKenzie might have helped to fund it, but it had been Bianchi's plan all the way down to the location.

Bianchi took him on a walk through the lower floors, showing him the labs and the manufacturing wings.

Eventually, he led Rose outside to show him the security systems.

They opened out into the crisp forest air.

"Why have I never seen this before?" asked Mike, looking out across the frost-layered open ground leading into the dark forest.

"We had to wait until The Red Hauser could be fully trusted."

"How has this all remained a secret?"

"You must know I have backers. One that is particularly powerful."

Mike guffawed, "No shit."

Bianchi leased his anger at the jab and asked, "Any ideas who?"

Mike looked at him with a frown. "No."

"Larry MacKenzie."

The biker raised his eyebrows. "Really?"

"Yes," said Bianchi, expecting more surprise in the biker's expression.

"Yes, and he wants you to know your continued support will be very profitable to your organisation."

"I see," said Mike. "Who are the security?"

"Private contractors from a company

called…forget the name…oh…SouthArch Services Group. You heard of them?"

"I'd have to have been living under a rock not to have," answered Mike. "And what about all the…chemists?"

"That was our friend again. He'd yell in Parliament about bringing in the 'right' type of immigrant. What's that bill he brought to allow skilled workers into the country?"

"The HSWP— The Highly Skilled Workers Programme."

"That's it. People thought the motherfucker used it to prove he wasn't racist. The other side had to cave to prove they weren't either or be destroyed by the wokeism wand. But it's our friend's people that oversee it. All these are from Asia, South America and Africa."

"Isn't he worried about them returning home and spilling their guts?"

"I think most of them think they are making top-secret experimental drugs for the military. Only a few know the truth. Besides, he's put so many layers between this and him that it would take ten Sherlocks to find a link."

"What about the woman who comes around? She's a direct link."

"Believe me, he'll have that handled."

Mike said, "Sounds like you've both got it figured out."

"That's the point. We wanted to show you what the future looks like."

"It looks very impressive."

"And we want you to be part of it."

Mike looked around and said, "Maybe I was a

little hasty yesterday."

They laughed in unison before Mike said, "Could my comments yesterday be kept amongst us?"

"Our secret."

As they continued to walk, Mike asked, "So what are the defences here?"

Bianchi shrugged. "About sixty contractors working in a rotation. But I'll show you something very special."

He led Mike up a spiral of chrome stairs.

Various miniature satellite dishes spun at intervals on top of missile silos, as well as huge panels.

Bianchi laughed. "Our friend had this site designated a 'sensitive zone' and got a dispensation for this place to be protected by anti-aircraft weapons."

"So there are people in the Government who know about this?"

"A few. Friends of his. So they are **Amici nostri**."

Mike smiled, "Friends of ours."

"I am impressed."

"So it is impregnable to attack?"

"Well, not unless they drop a nuke. And it is practically invisible from the air. Those massive panels are…a kinda lens that makes it invisible."

"Lubor Lenses?"

"That's it—high-tech shit," grinned Bianchi. "Besides, no one could get a lineup of men through without us knowing, which means we could escape. The soldiers, at least."

He watched Mike frown. "What about the rest?"

"Well, we couldn't risk them being questioned."

"How?"

"There are enough explosives to blow this place four times over," said Bianchi. "From either control room, I can lock any section I wish and detonate them individually. It would be the most humane way."

34

Connor and Arabella stood outside the Toyota under the ominous, cold gaze of the snow-scarred mountains.

Whomever Ciara's CSIS contact was proved extremely resourceful as almost all of Connor's wish list appeared in the back of a pickup, including not only a Garmin InReach comms set, neoprene socks and water shoes for river crossings but also the weapons he had requested.

The pair of body armour vests provided only stood at Level IIIA, offering protection against high-velocity 9mm and .44 Magnum ammunition but no more than that. Connor had decided to have them packed in the bergens, as he knew how fatiguing it could be to hike wearing one.

Their black base layers clung to their skin beneath olive and brown jackets, matching their hiking trousers.

He lay on the heavy bergen and threaded his arms through the straps. He made the awkward transition from laying to turtle to standing.

Arabella, lighter bergen already on her back, said, "I could have helped you up."

"My male pride got the better of me."

He kept the discomfort off his face as his body adapted to the weight. The straps of the heavy bergen bit into his shoulders as his heart rate began to thump its alarm.

He'd been here many times before and knew his body would accept its new state in five to ten minutes. It would then remain quiet for a long while until, like neighbouring dogs in the morning, his trapezius would begin barking, eventually setting off his lower back.

Both had applied vaseline to the inside of their upper legs before setting off to ward off chafing.

He knew he'd have to strike a balance between speed and arriving at the target fit to fight whilst accounting for Arabella's well-being.

He had taught her basic hand signals and how to use the watch.

Connor remembered his envy of some of the arduous 'yomps' he had done as a young marine towards the unburdened dog walkers strolling on the same terrain.

"Let's go," he said, and they stepped off.

Barely over two hours in, he was reminded why being a Royal Marine ML (Mountain Leader) held no practical appeal. He reckoned he got it on an intellectual level; the hardship, the scenery, the clean air, the being at one with nature.

But he couldn't see himself actively pursuing Scottish Munros or other expeditions.

But he knew now Arabella loved hiking, and he thanked ***Tyche*** for that.

At this stage, he could see other walkers at a distance through the trees, so he was happy not to go silent for a bit—there wouldn't be any wandering patrols this far out.

"Remind me never to become a coke addict," he said.

"Why is that? Aside from the next day depression and wasted money."

"Because this is what getting off it turns you into—a tell-everyone-you-know hill-walking, ice bath dunking, God botherer."

When she rewarded him with a rare laugh, Connor asked her, "You OK with the weight?"

"I was going to ask you the same thing."

"Of course—Commando, aren't I."

He heard her smile, and she asked, "Do you miss it?"

"Not really. They haven't been involved in war fighting for a while. Be a bit like you drawing architectural designs and never seeing them finished."

"You're saying they are not doing their job?"

"No, not at all. They are still doing some gnarly stuff in dangerous places. I think training for war-fighting is too mentally and physically taxing not to put into practice, at least sometimes. They provide security for the UK just by their professional presence, so I am not saying they aren't doing their job."

"I am surprised, though. I sensed my brother missed the Legion."

"Most military people miss the people they work with, the camaraderie. That is the military's stock answer—'I'll miss the lads'."

"You miss the clowns but not the circus."

Connor smiled, "That's a good one that, Arabella."

"Do you miss my brother?"

"We weren't that close, but I miss what type of man he was. Without being disrespectful, your brother was crazy," Connor smirked. "And I liked that about him."

"I did, too. Eventually," she said before removing the ring from her left hand and showing Connor the tattoo.

"How many hours did that take?"

"Very funny," she said, giving him a smile that didn't reach the eyes. "Carlo would always make me angry. But he would always watch out for me. There were just the two of us—rare in families in Calabria—so I got this when I was nineteen to remind myself not to forsake him. I am ashamed of telling him once that the tattoo was to remember my parents. You see, you might have liked him being ***Pazzo***—crazy—but my parents never did."

"I bet your dad secretly did."

"Why do you say that?"

"Because if it's a choice between having a son who's a pussy and a son who's a tearaway, then most would go for the latter," said Connor. "Apologies. When I say pussy, I mean a lethargic weakling. Not equating them to women."

"I think you're a pussy for trying to explain yourself to me."

When Connor smiled again, she continued, "Why would a father want a tearaway?"

"I didn't say he would want one. I said if it was a choice between the two, he'd choose to have a tearaway than a pussy. Learn to listen, woman."

"I will try, sir."

"Stop it. You'll give me a ***semi***, and I'll end up blacking out."

"A semi?"

"Never mind."

After a few moments, she said, "A semi-erection?"

"You're very smart, Arabella," he said sincerely as he pushed the pace.

Connor decided to attack the insertion in

intense legs followed by short breaks rather than long slogs. He would dictate the breaks when Arabella began to lag.

However, after another two hours, she kept right on his shoulder.

He looked at her and said, "You on PEDs?"

She smiled, "It has been a while since you were rough, tough marine."

"OARMAARM."

"What is that?"

"Once a Royal Marine, Always a Royal Marine."

"You made that up?"

"No, but I'll probably be an old man down the British Legion, spouting it off to the rest of the veterans."

"Will you?"

He took a few moments to answer. "I can't remember the last time I've pictured myself living to an old age."

"Does that make you sad?"

"Life is a series of trade-offs—everyone pays the man, eventually. And if it's a choice between doing this and dying young or not doing this and living to a peaceful old age, I'd choose this."

"Choose killing bad men."

"Choose killing evil men," he answered. "I am a bad man."

"You think you're a bad man."

"You can't kill as many people as I have and expect Logos to give you a pass. It doesn't matter who they are."

They began an ascent, skirting a ravine before cutting into the forest of red cedar trees that appeared to Connor to be about half a football pitch in height.

Finally, she began to lag a few steps, and he snatched the opportunity to say, "Let's take a break here. It'll get harder now."

They slid their loads off and sat on them.

"Can I smoke?"

He nodded, knowing how much morale 'a tab' could be on arduous hikes despite the smell being tactically unsound.

Connor said, "We'll give our feet a quick check. I'll go first. Remember, one boot at a time."

Once they had done so, he handed her a flask. On opening it, she said, "It better not be tea."

"It's black coffee."

She poured it into the lid cup he gave her. She said without a hint of irony as she lit a cigarette, "It'll stain your teeth if you drink too much of that."

"I usually use a straw."

"You do not."

She chuckled when he didn't answer, "It is a funny image in my brain, you, Mister Assassin Man, drinking coffee through a straw."

He smiled. "I'll probably fuck it off in a few weeks."

"Fuck it off?"

"Yeh, not do it anymore," he answered. "I try a lot of things. Some things stick, like cold showers, morning workouts and studying. And some things don't, like waiting ninety minutes after waking for a coffee, blue-light blocking glasses and taping my mouth before sleeping."

"You taped your mouth before sleeping?"

"It's to help you breathe through your nose, which is good for you."

"Interesting," she said. "You seem to know a lot."

"I try. Speaking of which, what are some things women notice about men that men don't notice about men?"

"Why?"

"In the interests of learning."

"Ahem," she said, seemingly in thought. "How loud you all are."

"How we talk?"

"Not necessarily. You cough, eat, vomit, and shit louder than we do, even though we have the same physiology in those areas."

"I suppose we do," admitted Connor before standing. "Come on. Let's get rambling."

Mike had been allowed to wander the perimeter of the complex as his breath billowed out. At first, he wondered why before realising he'd probably not make it out on foot, and he had no real means of communication, as his and Kyle's smartphones had been confiscated by the complex's security.

Though they still had their 'dumb' phones, the signal proved distinctively weak.

Looking around the snow-iced woods, he was reminded of the philosophical thought, *'If a tree falls in a forest and no one is around to hear it, does it make a sound?'*

MacKenzie, unable to communicate with him directly, had decided to go through the Mafioso crime lord.

It impressed Mike that MacKenzie had kept Bianchi clueless to the fact Rose secretly worked for the billionaire politician.

He whirled around at the sound of footsteps,

but his cardiovascular system settled upon seeing it was Kyle.

His comrade said, "Do you get the impression that we are being held hostage?"

"That's because we are."

"For how long?"

"Not sure," said Mike sincerely. "He took me for a walk around the compound and gave me his pitch for staying on the team."

"And?"

"And I acted like I bought it. It's either that or we can kiss goodbye to any hope of us getting out of here."

"Is that what you're doing, Mike? Acting?"

"That's exactly what I am doing."

"You sure your 'acting' didn't start when he started to talk money?"

Mike stepped towards Kyle. "Believe me, helping do whatever it is they are doing is the last thing I am doing. Not anymore. You'll have to trust me."

Kyle nodded. "If it were up to me, we'd burn this place to the ground."

Mike gave him a sad smile. "Considering they have a small army of highly trained killers, anti-aircraft and high-tech surveillance, I don't think there is a great chance of that."

The bearded, bulbous-nosed man's head snapped toward the distant sounds carried on the cold breeze.

He estimated them to be coming from over the treeline, nearer the river.

Delvin James had worked in the Yukon forest for over a decade, first as a miner and then as a log harvester. He hated to say lumberjack, as people would make jokes about being part of the seventies wrestling tag team named 'Yukon Lumberjacks'.

He remembered the day over a year ago when he had been told land developers were to swoop in to take control of the area.

The thirty-four-year-old lived alone deep in the forest and had raised all kinds of hell.

The college drop-out had hoped they might palm him off with a payout.

Their job offer had taken him aback.

The live-alone's remit was to patrol the area and keep out trespassers.

And after a few months, a big man with a strange accent and white collar deputised him as an agent and gave him a badge.

When he asked if he could now arrest people and carry a weapon, the man smiled. *'Who out there is going to challenge you about anything with that badge? But remember to always report trespassers to me immediately. I am your one up in this chain of command.'*

He loved it.

James had been part of the Canadian Army during the Afghanistan conflict. However, he had never been off the Kandahar Airfield (KAF) base, as he had hurt his ankle in a pick-up basketball game.

When he used to head into the city for the weekend, it had embarrassed him to remain vague when asked about his wartime exploits in the bars.

And he yearned for action.

He now regretted deliberately underperforming on his hearing test; had he kept pressing the button during his hearing test, he'd still be in. Yes, some of the sounds had been faint due to the Nickelback concert he had attended the night before, but he had heard them. He heard them because his hearing remained razor-sharp.

The promise of a medical pension had proved too tempting.

He crept down but decided to round back. If the voices' owners came towards him, he couldn't do or say anything to them, anyway. But if they were to press on into the no-go zone, then he could confront them.

The sensible option would have been to stop them before they entered the exclusion zone, but he didn't want to.

He'd track them deep and then take pleasure in knowing they would have to trek back. And if they got rowdy, he had other ways.

35

Connor had hiked them hard into the night.

An hour after midnight, he pitched the small tent, thankful for the clear sky, allowing his night vision to complete the task without fuss.

He allowed her to sleep several hours as he kept sentry for strangers and bears.

He woke her so she could keep watch while he snatched an hour. His first tour of Afghanistan had shown him how little sleep a human could get by on if necessary.

He emerged and said, "Now is as good a time as any to show you how this sniper rifle works. We'll zero it the best we can."

"But you'll be packing it away again?"

"At the range we're likely to be firing it, the rifle's disassembly won't significantly affect its accuracy. Nor will the Coriolis effect. Or that we're nearer the North Pole. Your shooting mechanics will be the biggest factor."

Connor unpacked and assembled the C14 Timberwolf, complete with the suppressor.

He had fired the C14 and rated it for accuracy and penetration for a medium-range sniper rifle.

"What's the scope?"

"A Schmidt and Bender. When you look through it, you can see as clearly as if it were just your eyeball."

Though uncomfortable leaving rounds embedded in the trees, with the distance to the target being thirty kilometres away, he felt the risk outweighed the reward.

Arabella shot within the natural pause of her exhalation, without a hint of rifle *cant*—tilt—nor did she snatch the trigger. And after observing her fall of shot, he murmured, "We should change your name to Lyudmila Pavlichenko."

"Who?"

"She was a Soviet sniper who *merced* hundreds of Nazis," he answered.

He took out the Heckler & Koch UMP 45 with suppressor.

It hadn't come with his preferred fitted accessories of rails, a hand stop and a tritium front sight.

Also, he usually liked to modify the trigger pressure on a UMP 45. down a lb but hadn't the time or tools.

The former commando liked it for several reasons; its mechanical simplicity equalled reliability. The calibre had more than enough stopping power for what he'd likely encounter, as would the twenty-five-round magazine, of which he had three. He preferred the ergonomics of it over the MP5.

The trigger group this one came with included semi-automatic burst mode—three rounds as opposed to two and full-automatic.

However, it had its drawbacks; the cyclical rate and recoil made groupings challenging to keep tight—for an average shooter, at least, the round was susceptible to the wind at range—not that he planned on firing it at a distance.

He quickly found his point of aim at a few near-distant ranges.

"Let's pack this away. We are still in the earshot of civilian adventurers. Last thing we need is for them to get excited about a submachine gun being carried."

Just as they completed the task, she said, "Hear that?"

He did, faintly. "Wolves?"

She nodded.

Connor knew between four and five thousand grey wolves inhabited the Yukon.

He asked, "How far?"

"Maybe two kilometres. They are more active at both dusk and dawn. You should keep your weapon to your side for a while."

"It's not being eaten by wolves that worries me. It's leaving a pack of dead wolves in our wake."

"My father used to walk in the river to throw them off the scent."

"That's fine for the next few miles, but rivers are a focal point for patrols," he said. "We'll have to risk it."

His head snapped around.

"What is it?" she asked.

"I am not sure," he said and thought for a moment. "This is your last chance for a cigarette."

Delvin James frowned as he watched the dark-haired woman sip her coffee and smoke while sitting on her backpack.

He thought he had lost the trail, but he had picked up what sounded like 'clacks'.

His eyes narrowed on her for a while, contemplating what to do—the singleton could have sworn he had heard a male voice not long ago.

He waited a while longer to leave enough time

for someone to return from having a shit—and for the bleed of dopamine he got from just watching her.

Eventually, James cut down, and when her head turned towards him, he barked, "This is private property."

Her eyebrows raised. "I didn't see any signs?"

The accent sounded pleasantly exotic.

He crept closer. "We can't be putting signs everywhere now, can we?"

"And you're the police?"

His temper bubbled. "I am the park's ranger."

"Can I see ID?"

He felt a swell of pride at being asked this. He delved into his jacket and produced his wallet ID.

She leaned forward and said, "OK. I'll turn back."

Something stirred within, and he said, "This is not the place for a woman on her own."

"Thank you. But I am capable of making my way back."

"Who knows that you're out here?"

The brunette squinted. "No one."

He couldn't help but grin. "You're going to come with me to my cabin, and we'll head out back in the morning."

It would be nice just to have some company, he thought.

"No, I think I'll head back on my own."

He sneered as her words plummeted to his stomach. "I am not asking you. I am telling you."

He lurched for her.

An impact to his mid-back threw him forward.

He got up, whipping out the twelve-inch

blade of a hunting knife.

The seared ego whirled around and attacked.

On reflex, Connor threw an oblique kick to the knee for the knife-wielding frenzy coming at him.

It only momentarily halted the slasher.

Connor's fear exploded in his torso; the blade resembled a short, curved sword with a serrated edge.

I should've fuckin' got the UMP out.

But more ominously, its owner seemed to have an adrenal deafness and a manic intent to kill him.

No chairs, pool cues or even sticks lay around to help him maintain the distance— *Cheers Bas Rutten.*

He also knew techniques like trapping and disarming would melt like a sugar hill in the rain; the adrenaline grip of the knife would be ridiculously hard, and the return of the blade after a stab would be as fast and violent as the thrust itself.

Watch the undersides of your wrists and your throat—he thought as the man lunged with a straight stab to the solar plexus.

Connor, turning his shoulder to protect his throat, parried downwards with his left while simultaneously punching with his right.

His shot cracked the nose, sending the man back, snorting like a seal.

Connor, mindful of the blade, leashed the instinct to finish him. The focus he had placed on the parry had skimmed the edge off the power and accuracy of his punch.

The murderous demon straightened, and the Englishman could see the contemplation in his eyes.

"Just back off, and we'll be on our way."

Instead, the knife wielder leapt forward with a series of spastic, jerky feints before the blade arched down at an angle towards Connor's head.

The black operations agent managed to block with the outside of his forearm—the slice to it barely hurting despite the blood creasing the blade.

His punch to his would-be killer's stomach gave him space.

A tiny part of his mind wanted to beg the man for a reprieve only to be drowned by the internal dark roar of —*Make sure you severely hurt this cunt*.

The cutting edge darted for his neck. Connor pivoted, using his shoulder to protect his throat. He didn't feel the cut but heard his clothing and flesh unzipping.

Though neither cut had severed an artery, he knew he couldn't take many more.

He watched the man's slack jaw suck for air. Connor knew the term 'being fit' was far too broad; he had seen a top-rated triathlete gas after his first five-minute grappling round and a nationally rated gymnast almost collapse after a five-mile run.

The ranger could probably hike through this terrain for days but was not 'fighting fit'.

Connor easily side-stepped and booted his assailant in the hip, sending him sprawling.

The Yorkshireman dived after him.

He snatched the wrist of the knife-gripping hand and pinned it and did the same to his enemy's other hand that careered around for the blade.

With the beard keeping an electric current grip, Connor slammed his head into the nose.

The effect reminded Connor of a wasp singed with a lighter.

Connor decided against throwing another.

Instead, he bent down and clamped his jaws around the nose.

The scream pounded his eardrums as his mouth filled with warm liquid iron.

He ragged his head like a pit bull until his head unexpectedly snapped back as the nose came away from the face.

The macabre image of the screaming face with a blood and bone hole seared into his eyes.

And Connor spewed out a belly laugh along with the lump of cartilage and flesh. He held his victim by the throat to prevent his giggling from unbalancing him.

Connor shunted up to press his shins into the crook of the screamer's elbows.

Then he took a double grip of the former knife wielder's left wrist, removed his shin off that arm and wrenched on a double wrist lock—a **_Kimura_**—and broke the shoulder joint and elbow.

The screaming did not intensify. Instead, wind-sucking sobs punctuated it.

He leapt off his prey and watched him spin onto his front to escape.

Connor seized the right ankle and hoisted it high. Trapping the leg between his and the heel beneath his armpit, he wrenched on an awkward but effective heel hook.

With the satisfaction of popping bubble wrap, Connor tore the anterior cruciate ligament before switching his grip and direction to tear the meniscus.

The screams fell into wails.

The Englishman gained control of his laughter as his opponent's howls simmered to crying.

"You thought forcing a woman back to your cabin was OK. To murder me, and probably her, because I stopped you with a boot to the back?" Connor asked rhetorically.

When further sobbing formed the reply, Connor continued, "And you're going to tell me about who you work for and your communications with them. And if you do, you'll get these."

Connor produced a green plastic coffin with a vial of morphine and the man's torn-off nose.

"A good surgeon will be able to reattach it and leave you with a cool-looking scar for the chicks."

The ranger's hand clawed out to signal his agreement to the terms.

"What's your name?" asked Connor.

"Dev…Devlin James," said the man, tilting his head so as not to choke on his blood.

"Devlin, who's your employer? And before you say 'the national park', remember you still have other appendages that I can remove."

"P. Hulme Pharmaceuticals."

"How did they approach you?"

"A suit. When I was in town collecting my mail."

"What were the terms?"

"Sixty a year," he rasped. "To keep my mouth shut and report back any suspicious activity."

"So you have no powers of arrest?"

The man shook his head wide-eyed in reply.

"Where's your gun?"

Connor watched as James sheepishly nodded to his pack. And then Connor began laughing. "I bet you wish you suffered the discomfort of carrying it on your hip now, don't you?"

"Please give me the morphine."

Connor nodded and threw him the auto-injector, which he also knew as a combi-pen from his time in the military.

He watched the relief wash over the horror mask.

Connor gave him a few moments of reprieve before asking, "Drones?"

He shook his head. "No. I don't think they want the attention."

Connor took out his unmarked map. "Show me on here what area they want you to patrol specifically."

Devlin peered at it like he was trying to focus his eyes, and Connor knew he might lose him to the opiate's embrace.

Connor pressed his thumb on the blood-stained cartilage where the nose used to be and barked, "Concentrate!"

Devlin blinked rapidly, squinted his eyes and began to trace a circumference with his finger.

The ranger did not question how Connor knew which grid squares of the map to display to him.

Connor got up and rifled through James's bag. He found a Beretta Px4 Storm.

The Chameleon Project agent pulled out a Sat Phone from it. He smiled on seeing all the codes and call signs taped to the back of it.

"Any specific way you make contact?"

Devlin simply grunted, and Connor knew he had lost him to the morphine.

As Connor stood, he turned to see Arabella slack-jawed before she asked, "Is he dead?"

Connor took the Px4 Storm, placed its barrel

over the ranger's nose and squeezed the trigger.

"Pretty much," said Connor, wiping the pistol down.

He placed it into the hand of the corpse with the pomegranate-smashed face. He then began arranging the scene the best he could to aid in the appearance of suicide.

"Not enough to fool an investigator, but maybe it'll buy time before the hounds are released," he said.

He glanced at her to ascertain her distaste for what he had just done—he couldn't see any.

Next, he studied the map before folding it away back in his pocket.

"Let's go," he said.

The architect said, "Your wounds? You'll leave a trail."

Of course. Fucking idiot—he admonished himself.

Connor sat on his bergen and began to remove his outer layers.

She said, "I can treat lacerations."

The Englishman looked at her momentarily and then handed her the first aid pack.

He pressed a dressing onto the cut on his forearm and raised it above his heart level.

As she began to clean the other wound, she asked, "Why did you bite his nose?"

"Because he wasn't a nice man."

"You wanted to punish him?"

"Yes."

"You don't believe it's only God's place to punish the wicked?"

When Connor smirked, Arabella asked,

"What?"

"I was watching a film named 'The Town' in which a guy recounts a conversation between an explorer and a priest. Have you seen it?"

"No."

"Superb film," he said. "Anyway, the explorer tells the priest, *'I happen to know there's no God.'* The priest says, *'How's that?'* The guy says, *'Once I was caught in a snowstorm at the North Pole. Freezing and unable to see, I prayed, if there is a God, save me now, but God didn't come.'* The priest says, *'How's that? You're alive. He must have saved you.'* The explorer said, *'God never showed up. An Eskimo came along. Took me back to his camp and saved me.'"*

She applied the antibiotic cream and covered it with the dressing. "So you see yourself as an agent of God's good work?"

"You're right, that did sound like Kevin Spacey's John Doe," said Connor. "Maybe I am just hoping he turns a blind eye for a while."

She began to treat his forearm cut and said, "When he pulled out the knife, I wanted to run because I knew when he killed you, he would kill me, too. Maybe not then, but eventually."

"Why did you stay? You could have just set a bearing and escaped."

"Because then I could feel that he was going to die and not you."

"We done?"

She smoothed the dressing and said, "Yes. We are done."

"Let's get going."

Then, the silent ghosts began to appear from the treeline.

36

Back in her apartment's 'briefing room', Ciara watched the hope in Philip Marr's face as she told him of the suspected location.

"When can you confirm?" he asked.

To a civilian, it would seem he remained impassive, but she could feel his anticipation piqued.

"In the next forty-eight hours. I was hoping you could arrange a team to secure the perimeter for extraction."

His lips briefly pressed. "I cannot risk that. MacKenzie has friends in very high places. If we are wrong, I'll be out of a job, and the only person whose commitment to bring him down I trust is my own."

Ciara believed him and found her attitude softening towards him.

I might be cantankerous if I were that isolated, she thought.

"How much evidence do you need? Surely not a sample?"

"Nothing that dramatic. I need something substantive. I will quietly check for any planning permission for a structure in the area. I remember legislation passed about two years ago for an ecological research facility in the Yukon area. If a team of commandos descends on a conservation base, MacKenzie will make sure the CSIS is thrown under a media circus, and we'll never get him."

"What's the options then?"

"I might be able to mobilise a small team, but it might take a few days."

"You said yourself, we haven't got a few days.

All it will take is a few more loads of those drugs hitting the streets. There'll be anarchy soon afterwards."

"I know," he said, with contriteness creasing his eyes. "Let's hope my intelligence is faulty, or—"

"Or that my man can send back the evidence in time."

"Yes."

Connor could not believe how soundlessly these men appeared.

To him, they looked like a blend of Native Indians and the Mongols.

He counted four and guessed a similar number behind him. They dressed in a mixture of native and western-style dress; two had black Puffa jackets on, while the rest had parkas made of what appeared to be moose hide. A different pair had hiking boots, while the rest sported brown ankle moccasins. They all had on grey-brown embroidered tunics.

And all held a weapon, half with bows and half with hunting rifles—Connor guessed the bows to be used for 'quiet' kills.

He didn't even attempt to go for any aggressive act.

Connor said to Arabella, "I don't suppose Google Translate has English-Tlingit."

"I think they would kill you before you took out your phone."

Connor raised his hands and said, "Hél dáanaa ax ḵee!"

The men glanced at one another before Connor then said, "Ax éet_aa hís'!"

Most of them burst into laughter with Connor's smile before a man whom Connor judged to be in his fifties shouted, "Ya-jaak̲", and they fell silent.

Rimless glasses perched on a gnarled nose, with the temples disappearing beneath thick, iron-grey hair that covered the entire scalp.

He turned to Connor, his hunting rifle pointing lazily toward him and said, "Where did you learn Tlingit?"

"I didn't—I learnt a handful of phrases, including that, to break the ice."

"You wish to break the ice after you have killed a man?"

"That was self-defence."

"I have seen men forced to kill, and I have seen men who enjoy it."

"I didn't say I didn't enjoy it. I said it was self-defence."

A pause.

"I know. I saw."

"So, what now?"

"Why are you here?"

"To stop a bad man doing bad things."

"What is your name?"

"Dances with Wolves."

"Dances wi—"

"Connor. My name is Connor."

The man stared at him for a while and then said, "You will both come with us and explain who this bad man is doing bad things."

Connor nodded, sensing the futility of doing anything else.

Am a fuckin' criminal from Leeds, and now I've been

captured by the indigenous people of Canada, he thought.

"And what about him?" asked Arabella, nodding to the corpse.

The elder barked in his native tongue at the men, and four of them peeled off, picked up the body and carried it away before the rest of the group had moved.

"Head start?" asked Connor.

"No, we are going in another direction. Search party dogs might come here. He will be buried where no one will find him."

"Why are you doing this?"

"Because that man believed he owned this land. But there are no owners of the natural world—he could not see that another white man owned him."

Larry MacKenzie stared for a moment at the screen.

The fifty-three-year-old, salt-and-pepper-haired Gérard Riel squinted through his glasses and said, "Larry, I am grateful for your support, but the more development there is in the Yukon, the greater the backlash. And they have a voice now."

Riel was perhaps the most powerful political lobbyist within the Canadian political sphere. Not only that, but he belonged to the 'other side of the house'.

Luckily for MacKenzie, not only did the Montréal-based politician advocate for French rights over all other cultural groups, but he also loved money.

"Gérard, with all due respect, all I ever hear is how the First Nations in Canada, not just the Yukon, have poorer health, housing is a massive issue, incarceration is higher, high unemployment and when

I—"

"Larry, those issu—"

"Don't interrupt me, Gérard. All those issues can be remedied if they accept progress. Do they not understand that rising tide lifts all boats?"

"Most do. But there are a few of the more…old-style tribes that do not suffer from the issues other First Nation people do—they live a traditional lifestyle deeper in the Boreal forests. They are self-sustaining and see the residential and commercial developments as encroachment and a threat to their way of life."

"What the fuck? This is real life, not Avatar, Gérard . How are these few managing to hold up our plans?"

The Liberal politician tilted his head to one side. "One of the tribal leaders is a very influential man. He's inferring that the recent drug epidemic amongst other indigenous peoples in Canada has something to do with the recent commercial and industrial developments. And it isn't only that —"

"Does he have anything to do with sabotaging my construction sites?"

"I can't say that, no. But he has spoken out against them."

Larry forced himself to relax and said, "One thing I know is whatever this group is, there will be people within it who disagree. Men who are sick of hunting caribou and wiping their asses with leaves. And for the right incentive, will tell you who these terrorists are."

Gérard didn't speak for a moment. "How much money?"

"I'll set them up with a new life, Gérard, them

and their families. And I don't bullshit, not with money, and you know that. It'll be through you the usual way."

"OK."

"And remember, if they are caught anywhere near the research facility, the security there has been given a federal disposition to kill in defence of property."

37

Though Connor had researched the Yukon as much as he could before setting off on the insertion, the modernity of the settlement mildly surprised him.

Because of its location deep in the forest, with a lack of through roads, he had been expecting something more primitive.

The structures reminded him of European holiday chalets, though some sported decorative paintings that looked almost Aztec.

As he and Arabella were led through, Connor found it strange that it seemed deserted.

The elder, who still had not told them his name, led them into one.

There lay a couple of mattresses separated by a partition.

Behind sat a loose semi-circle of beach-like chairs with a simple-looking kitchen at the rear.

"Where's the bathroom?"

"Bathroom?"

"Toilets?"

"Outside."

"I thought the First Nations people had embraced things like indoor plumbing and toilets."

"You don't know what this is, do you?"

Connor answered, "It looks like a makeshift barracks, but I am not sure what war you're meant to fight."

The Elder smiled, threw his hand out to the chairs and said, "Sit."

When both Connor and Arabella went to do so, the man said, "Not you. You wait outside."

"She doesn't leave my sight."

"She is not to sit with men when we discuss such things as we are about to discuss."

"She. Does. Not. Leave. My. Sight. Don't make me hurt you."

Instantly, the other three men took a combat stance against him, and the man said, "You think you could be victorious against four?"

"I didn't say that, did I—I asked you not to make me hurt you."

The two men stared at one another for a moment before the Elder said, "Do you believe in compromise?"

"Yes."

"She can stay in here. We will talk outside."

Connor said, "There are two entrances."

"Connor," said Arabella sharply. "I'll scream if anything happens. Now accept this man's compromise."

The two men still stared until Connor said, "Alright, let's talk outside."

Once on the other side of the door, the man said, "My name is Eric Schafer of the Nomadic First Nations tribe."

"So, you're the man who they call 'the most divisive indigenous political leader in Canada'," said Connor.

"I see you have done your research, Mister?"

"Reed."

"So, Mister Reed, why are you hiking in the most inhospitable of terrains carrying Rambo's arsenal?"

"I promised a man I respect that I wouldn't stop until his sister was safe."

"Safe from what? Surely, you have risked her life bringing her here."

"A mafia boss who happens to be a very sadistic man."

"Why isn't your friend helping his sister?"

"Because he is dead."

Eric nodded. "And you think Mafia bosses live in the forests of the Yukon?"

"I think he's here, yes. I am not sure why. I have to find this man. Once he is neutralised, then I'll be returning home."

Eric briefly spoke to his men in his native tongue. Though Connor couldn't tell what was being said, he heard concern in their voices. The conviction in Eric's voice turned the tone of their reply to one of acceptance.

"We believe we know the location. It is considered an ecological research place, but we do not think it is."

"Why do you think that?"

"I first suspected when we noticed the Helicopter Rescue Services making a frequent number of 'rescues' in a given area. We were naturally curious about what was causing all these hikers to get stranded."

"Especially as not many get this far in," said Connor.

Eric nodded. "We discovered what we thought was some plant or factory. I enquired through my political contacts and was eventually told it was a research facility."

"I sense you have your doubts?"

Eric commanded one of his men, who produced a packet of purple-tinged powder. Eric asked, "Do you know what that is?"

Connor shrugged. "Some kind of opioid powder dyed with monk fruit extract."

Eric looked at him inquiringly, "A fantastic guess for just a glance."

"It's not my first rodeo," said Connor. "But I don't know what it is, specifically."

"This, my friend, is fentanyl mixed with xylazine and etizolam, and you're correct, a monk fruit extract. There is also a compound in it that we haven't been able to identify."

"What? None of you could figure it out with a Bunsen burner and a Petri dish?"

Eric gave him a sardonic smile. "You'd be surprised what and who we know, Mister Reed."

"Fair enough."

"What is most concerning is that the doses in these packs can kill even the most experienced users. This is what has been killing certain addicted populations and the US."

"Where did you find this?"

"We found it after we watched it fall out of one of the helicopters."

"I see," said Connor. "What did the police say?"

"You think they would believe me saying it fell out of the sky?"

"Surely be better than you keeping it."

"Who do you think knows more about the political situation here? You or I?"

"You."

"I do not want anyone knowing our whereabouts."

"Because you don't know who to trust."

"Yes."

"Including me."

"Especially you," said Eric. "Yet, seeing you kill one of them makes me wonder if I should take a chance."

"You don't have to take a chance; just tell me the GPS coordinates to this place, and let me do the rest."

Eric smiled again, addressed the group in Tlingit, and they all laughed.

Connor managed to catch the word 'Rambo' and laughed with them. Then he said, "How often do you sharpen your knife?"

Eric's forehead creased. As he reached back through his tunic, Connor raised his hands.

The Englishman detected a hint of emotion as the Elder asked, "Where is it?"

Connor leisurely pulled his sweater up to reveal in the waistband of his trousers the dagger with the ivory eagle's head on the bottom of the handle.

"I might not be Rambo. But I am good enough to take your dagger from you without you or your men knowing."

The Englishman slowly pulled it out before offering it to Eric, handle first.

The First Nations man accepted it and said, "I apologise for the insult, but you will still need our help."

Arturo Bianchi sat nursing a glass of whisky as he watched his son draw pictures. Even to his eyes, Louis had a natural talent for it.

The underground suite looked almost Arabic in its décor.

The crime boss felt glad this had held his son's attention and stopped the incessant flow of questions, most of which had centred around when he was seeing his mum again.

It was a surprise that the boy agreed to accompany him without Richèl Vergeer with them. He knew that her powers of persuasion worked on Louis.

He answered the knock at the door with a "Come in."

Johannes walked in and said, "One of the rangers hasn't reported in. We've tried his other means of communication. He isn't answering."

"Couldn't he be just lying in the gutter somewhere?"

"Maybe, but we need to find out. I'll send a team."

"Won't we need all hands on deck here for a large shipment move?"

"We shouldn't be long," said the head of security as he exited.

It still jarred Bianchi how Johannes spoke to him. Though not impolite, if it had been one of his men, he would have broken his legs for insubordination. In addition to being paid directly by MacKenzie, Johannes's guys could easily overpower his men.

He knew he couldn't hope to take on MacKenzie; it would take him time he didn't have.

But maybe he didn't have to. He had enough evidence of the link between them that he could always manipulate MacKenzie if their relationship ever soured beyond repair.

Still, their ultimate goals aligned for now.

Bianchi wanted MacKenzie to hold the head position almost as much as he did.

There would be no stopping him with the Prime Minister in his pocket.

Within a week, addicts will have congested the hospital wards. Then, they will be strewn all over the streets in full glare of the media.

The current Prime Minister would be hounded out of office.

And Larry MacKenzie would ascend to the top position as Bianchi's puppet.

Connor kept his discomfort off his face.

He could accept the First Nation guys not showing signs of exertion, but the fact Arabella wasn't either was pissing him off.

One of the black Newfoundland dogs—Newfies—looked to be positively enjoying himself. It reminded Connor of the Old English Sheepdogs used on the UK television adverts to promote *Dulux* paint.

Though the former marine felt glad to be led in, his lungs began to claw for the cold, oxygen-thin air.

He would regularly insist on Eric giving him a navigation check. He remembered his old training sergeant warning his recruit troop of the perils of simply mindlessly following, or as he had said, *'yomping with your thumb up your arse'*.

Eric stopped them again and handed Connor a few strips of meat that reminded him of biltong.

"How you feeling?" asked Eric.

"I am alright."

"You have had a couple of days with little sleep," said the First Nation's leader. "You've been wounded and been involved in a fight to the death."

"Still…meant to be a commando, aren't I," said Connor. "I'll check flashes."

"What does this mean? *I'll check flashes*?"

"Tactical recognition flashes are a patch worn by military personnel denoting regiment. Checking flashes is just something we say to ourselves to remind ourselves who we are."

"Interesting," said Eric. "Why did you learn some of our language?"

"It's a habit. The British military has a doctrine named WHAM—to Win Hearts And Minds—and learning the local language, even a few phrases, can be part of that."

"The British would know about such things."

Connor steered the conversation. "Map check?"

"OK."

Connor took out his map, had a brief look around and, using a blade of grass, pointed to the position he thought they were at.

"Correct. Impressive."

"Without wishing to sound like a child in the back seat, can you tell me how far we have to go?"

"Over one day's hike. We cannot use any of the direct trails. As we get closer, we will have to move at night."

"Why did they post that ranger so far out?"

"They have numerous lookouts, which is why we are taking this route in."

"All armed?"

"Yes. Professionals. The only reason we have evaded them is because this is our home."

"Professional soldiers?"

"Yes."

"What are they armed with?"

"Too far away for us to identify the make and model, but definitely assault, not hunting, rifles."

"OK."

"What are your thoughts?"

"How did you know I had any?"

"I saw."

Connor, impressed, answered, "Maybe we don't want to avoid them."

"You want to draw the others out?"

"More away than out."

Connor caught the Newfies standing to attention before looking at their masters.

The First Nations leader turned to him. "Seems like that has already happened."

38

Mike Rose took a knee with the rest of the patrol as the leader of it scanned the dark horizon.

Back at the compound, the principal security officer, Johannes, had approached him with, *'I hear you're a former Green Beret?'*
'That's right.'
'How's your fitness?'
'I keep up to it.'
'Any injuries?'

When Mike answered, *'No'*, Johannes requested him to join the patrol.

This surprised Mike, as he knew tight units resented newcomers, especially without integration training.

However, Johannes told him he needed to reserve as much manpower as possible and that Mike would be doing them a favour.

'Your friend will have to stay,' said Johannes, and Mike instantly understood the inference.

And he didn't have the time to remind his MC comrade to switch on his phone—he just hoped Kyle did.

Petrus, the squat, thickly bearded patrol leader, welcomed him with a gruff mission brief lasting no more than ten minutes—a full set of orders typically took a couple of hours, but Mike surmised that time was of the essence.

However, Mike admired the crew's patrolling skills—the stealth, the hand signals, the correct drills and how they managed to cover all the arcs.

The cold night air billowed into his lungs.

He'd been told the patrol out would be about twenty clicks.

By his calculations, any excursion from civilisation to the compound would be over four times that.

And Mike didn't see how someone could be in a fit state to fight making that sort of trek. Not unless it was taken over several days.

He didn't know how, but he had been led to believe Bianchi enjoyed some air surveillance.

Mike had read that one of the reasons the British had defeated the Argentines over the Falkland Islands back in the eighties had been because the Argentine military chiefs had underestimated the **Paras** and Royal Marines ability to travel on foot under a full operational weight and had thus discounted the route taken to battle.

Suddenly, the point man snapped up a fist in the military signal for 'halt', and they took a knee as a collective to watch their arcs of fire.

Mike watched Petrus move up to the point man's position.

They both looked in the same direction through their rifle optics.

After a few minutes, the patrol leader slid into the group's centre and signalled for them to close in on him.

They did so while still facing outwards.
The patrol leader whispered, "An unknown group has encroached. Counted five so far, approximately a click away. We are going to split the group into Alpha and Bravo. One three-man team will stay in sight of them under Davis, and I will take the remainder right around to flank them. The **LRR** will stay in my team.

They'll have to cross the river, and that's when they'll be their most vulnerable."

"What is our ***ROE***?" asked one of the men.

"Shoot whoever is armed. We can clean the scene later. Roger that?"

They all sounded off in the affirmative, except for Mike, who whispered, "Won't that bring down the heat on the place?"

"That doesn't matter now, my friend. Wherever those boys come from, they will not be expected back for a few days at least, and this will all be over."

"Roger that," answered Mike, who didn't know if it was a good omen or not when he was selected for the 'killer group'.

Arabella inhaled the cold beauty around her as dusk threatened to fall.

The land had a true allure to it. From this vantage point, she could see the dense patches of differing shapes and colours of the trees covering parts of the blue and white mountains, the aqua-green water of the lakes and the rushing water of the far-side river.

Her happiness in the moment occurred to her, and she felt gratitude for that.

And she suspected it might partly be down to the high threat to her life, not despite it.

Then it dawned on her. This feeling might not be dissimilar to what drew her brother to danger, like a bad romance.

Connor stood beside her but didn't say anything.

Eventually, she gestured to a mountain range

that looked seemingly another world away and asked, "I wonder if that's Mount Logan? How tall is it again?"

"About six thousand metres," answered Connor. "That's not it, though. Right sort of direction, but it's a bit further on. That range is the Saint Elias Mountains."

She watched Connor walk off to converse with Eric. The suspicion the group had towards him had apparently dissipated.

Arabella realised a long time ago there was something inherently attractive about highly competent people.

He looked at her and walked over.

"Listen," he whispered. "We're getting close now. We don't know who's about and what their intentions are. As you're hiking, think to yourself, 'Where should I dive if we come under contact—if there is gunfire in our direction—that will cover me the best.' OK?"

She nodded. "I will keep looking for hiding places. Cover my eyes and ears until—"

"Don't do that. I will—"

"I know, Connor. I was making a joke."

"Nervous?"

"Yes, but…ahem…I was thinking how beautiful it is here."

He followed her eyes.

"Maybe you can stay. Renovate their homes."

"I don't think—"

"You can make a joke but not take one?"

"It must have…what do you English say…Gone over my head."

"Let's hope any potential rounds do too."

As the Yukon night rapidly extinguished the day, Mike felt a sphere of nauseating desperation as his team stalked up through the frosted, wooded slopes.

He lamented on the irony that in trying to extricate himself from the evil, he now found himself about to commit murder.

Something he had found strange about the mercenary team was that they came from different parts of the world. Though private armies were not beholden to the citizenship of a particular country, the better ones tended to recruit from a single country's military, specifically from the same regiment.

When in Iraq, Mike had come across members of The Olive Group and knew the majority to be former British SAS members.

Though these guys displayed slick individual skills, he began to sense a subtle lack of cohesion with their patrol movements and voice procedure over the net, which contrasted his initial assessment that they were a tight unit.

Still, he knew whatever group they were tracking had little hope against them.

All had assault rifles, some form of body armour and both smoke and explosive grenades.

The only thing this 'enemy' might have over them is knowledge of the land, but Mike had been told that the nearest First Nation settlements were many miles away, so they might not even have that.

He couldn't object; he'd be killed and buried out here, too.

And there were too many for him to take down on his own; Kyle was still at the compound.

He could hear chatter between the leader and the point man, and Mike felt they might be close.

His heartbeat rose, pushing pimples out of his skin.

The altitude, cold and the going underfoot reminded him of the mountain ranges on the Afghanistan-Pakistan border. A recollection came of the Pashtun interpreter scoffing at the idea of a 'border', saying it was a Western invention.

Twenty years, trillions of dollars, and four presidents to replace the Taliban with the Taliban, he thought.

Through his earpiece came the communication that their quarry's location was approximately one hundred metres away.

They would be radio silent from here on in.

A couple of men in front slipped on the icy rocks, and Mike placed his footing more carefully.

His mind raced for a way out of this.

He found his hand dropping to touch his webbing pouches.

Connor frowned at the far-off noise that he thought to be a grunt of some kind.

He felt reticent to say anything, but then he noticed two of the dogs looking in the same direction he had.

Eric turned, and Connor gestured he approach him.

He whispered, "I heard what the dogs have heard. Sounded human."

The dogs grew more animated but without barking.

Eric looked at him and said, "That's not humans. It's wolves."

Connor looked into the darkness for a moment. "No harm in me checking."

He set his bergen down and began opening the top.

"I can go with you?"

"No," said Connor, taking out his body armour. "If there is an enemy there, I'll just be putting you in danger. If there isn't, then I'll have wasted your time."

Eric nodded. "Fair enough."

"Tell Arabella to put her body armour on, too."

39

Mike could sense the agitation in the group as the wolf howls got closer.

He knew wolves to be generally quite timid towards humans. And an average Canadian hunter could spend their entire life without seeing one.

Mike had only seen a wild wolf once but knew not to get too excited at their approach.

However, this sounded like a huge pack.

The patrol leader, a South African who Mike guessed to be used to dangerous wildlife, whispered over the net, "Stay calm, stay still. They'll pass us by."

Despite these words, Mike detected a twitchiness in one of the men in front of him.

The wolf wails got closer and closer. He surmised he could let one within four metres before considering firing.

Along with the howling, sounds of panting, snarls and growls carried on the night air.

Mike caught the murmurs of "Fuck, fuck, fuck."

"Stop panicking," Mike hissed.

"I ain't fucking panicking," came the reply, the voice full of fear.

As the snarling predators came closer, Mike felt his adrenaline spike.

Then he saw the enormous antlers of a caribou glinting in the moonlight.

An anxiety-ridden groan of "Fuck this" came out of the darkness.

Mike snapped onto it with, "No! They are hunting carib—"

The gunfire cut through his words.

Mike looked to his right at the rear man, who looked wide-eyed at the scene. Then Mike plunged his combat knife into his throat.

As per his Royal Marine training, Connor took a 'life-saving' step to his left and fired a few rounds before diving for the cover of a large tree.

It took him a few moments to ascertain the gunfire was not in his direction.

On hearing the death whimpering of the wolves and the shout of "Ceasefire!" his mind assessed the situation within a second; a patrol was tracking them, and some trigger-happy numpty had given them all away.

Seeing little point in warning the rest of the group, Connor decided to kill as many as possible.

He ripped open his grenade pouch.

He knew he wouldn't survive the return attack.

Any competent infantry unit knew to spread out to prevent mass casualties in the event of an area weapon attack, such as with grenades and mortar shells.

One of the advantages of using grenades would be that unless one of the patrols spotted their direction of travel in the darkness, they would not be able to ascertain his position immediately.

Once they did, they would simply run him over.

He grasped a grenade, asked the god he wasn't sure existed to watch over Grace and Jackson, and went to pull the pin.

Screams echoed out of the trees as grenades

exploded.

But he had not thrown them.

Immediately after the second detonation, Mike stepped out with his assault rifle on automatic and fired on the team *enfilade*.

He estimated he put down five before their scrambling for cover paid off.

The shout went up, "It's the fucking attachment. He's a traitor."

The weight of fire reverberated through the tree, threatening to cut it down.

He knew to step to fire would be suicide, but to stay would be the same.

Mike didn't fancy martyring himself. He had concluded back in Iraq that if the choice were between torture and suicide, he'd pick the former.

Just as he decided to step out, another ribbon of fire came through, followed by the scream of "Contact rear! It's an ambush."

He waited for their return fire, snapped out his barrel and head as far as minimal and fired into one of the operators.

The shout of, "Has anyone PIDed the second target?"

He heard answers shouted in the negative.

Mike felt a desperate urge to switch his position, at least, but couldn't risk it.

He clung to the knowledge that the second person or persons with an angle on the squad might prevent them from sweeping through his position.

The voice made him jump.

"Oi," he snapped around to see the Englishman from the bar.

The man continued, "How many did you—fuck me, you're the guy from the bar."

"Yeh, I—"

"We haven't got time. How many did you come with?"

"There were ten, including me, in this section of seven. A three-man surveillance team about half a click behind us with eyes on whoever you came in with."

"What's your name?"

"Mike."

"I am Connor," said the Englishman. "Let's roll through the rest."

Mike felt a spike in his already fever pitch adrenaline. He attempted to keep it off his face as he answered, "Roger that."

Attacking a numerically superior enemy was listed as a no-no in all infantry unit small arms tactics manuals. To do it with a man you had only just met would be seen as suicide.

The Englishman's voice surfed on a wave of confidence, halting any objection.

The Brit gestured he would skirt around to an angle.

The former American Special Forces soldier signalled back his acknowledgement and watched the Englishman disappear back.

A few moments later, he heard the fire and a South African shout of, "Contact left."

Mike sprinted to the next tree and began firing on the targets that had their heads turned to the Englishman's position.

The firing ceased.

The call came out, "Mike!"

"Yeah."

"What's your assessment?"

"Position clear."

"Hold on the position. I'll come to you."

Within moments, Connor appeared and whispered, "Let's do the dead-checks. If one is alive, let's try to keep him that way."

They swept through the position but only found one alive, who couldn't speak from having his jaw torn off.

Connor turned to him. "How many more?"

Mike ignored the question. "Why do you trust me?"

"I don't think you would have blown them up if you were on their side."

"Yes, but—"

"We haven't got time. If I feel rounds in the back as I turn, I'll know I was wrong to trust you," said Connor, the dirt flaking from his face. "How do you know if this second surveillance team doesn't have eyes on us now or has returned to base?"

"They'll be on their way here. The good news is I took out the radioman before he could get any communications back to the facility. The other team only had personal role radios."

"Do they have night vision?"

"Yes."

Connor looked around. "I have an idea."

40

Arjen, a tall, blond Dutchman and surveillance team patrol leader, fanned the other two soldiers out as they made their way through the forest.

He had lost communications with the Alpha team. Ordinarily, given his team merely consisted of three, he might have pulled back to base for reinforcements.

However, he wanted to assess the situation better; he suspected the ambush might have contacted some rear party earlier than expected. If that were the case, he'd look either cowardly or an idiot in abandoning the AO unnecessarily.

The team crept forward under hand signals. He scanned the treeline through the night-vision glare and failed to see any movement.

Arjen signalled for them to close in and move up, and they pushed deeper amongst the sentry-like trees.

He reckoned it to be another twenty metres to where he had seen the muzzle flashes.

His heartbeat began to rise upon realising the absence of the expected challenge. His core contracted on seeing the corpses through the green lens.

He halted his guys, and they took up their arcs.

His eyes snapped onto a slow movement, and he deciphered it to be a raising of a hand.

The team leader whispered into his mike. "Bravo Seven, hold on the area. Bravo Six, move up with me."

As he approached, the details came into focus. He breathed the smell of sweet charcoal smoke with a hint of sulphur.

The raised hand belonged to the ***FNG.***

"Bravo Seven. Can you see this? Over?"

"Yes."

"Close in, but keep a distance between us. If this is an ambush, they'll want us close."

"Roger that."

They prowled up, one at a time, one covering the other.

Reaching the hand-raising figure, the patrol leader whispered into his mike, "Bravo Six. Conducting the evaluation now."

When Bravo Six didn't respond, his head jerked towards his colleague's last known position. The raised hand snatched the barrel of his assault rifle.

A round punched through the base of Bravo Six's skull and came out of his mouth.

A bullet pierced Arjen through the crease where the underside of the jaw met the throat like an uppercut.

It severed his medulla along the way, just as a gunshot punched into the back of Bravo Seven's head.

Arabella's heart soared on seeing Connor unharmed and appearing from the treeline after answering the 'challenge'.

And for a moment, she didn't know whether or not her feelings were due to the protection he provided or solely for his well-being.

She watched him indicate to the group that

the man he had in tow was not a danger to them.

The two men began to climb down the glinting rocky outcrops.

Eric barked out a command in his native tongue, and his group reformed, so most of their weapons now pointed to their front.

The Elder approached Connor, Arabella followed.

Connor spoke, "They sent a reconnaissance team to check on the ranger. They decided to ambush us when they saw us."

"They know we are here. We should go."

"Not necessarily," said Connor. "This is Mike. He had an epiphany and attacked them. Took out the long-range radioman first."

Eric asked, "How can we trust him?"

"Because I saw him grenade and shoot the team that was about to ambush us."

Mike spoke. "We have about two hours before the base expects a report back."

"How many soldiers are there?"

"Three teams of seven left."

"Do you know the rotations?" asked Connor.

"Yes," answered Mike. "But I've identified only two blind spots in the compound, and even they are temporal."

"Weapons?" asked Eric.

"There are a slew of them around the corner," said Connor. "Unless you and your men are squeamish about using dead men's weapons."

"Not at all."

Connor must have noticed something she hadn't because he said, "I will give your men a quick tutorial."

"Thank you."

Connor said, "Now, we have to agree on what this will be—an infiltration that will likely end in gunfire or a surveillance mission."

Arabella watched Eric look at Connor and say, "You've already decided what you are doing, haven't you?"

"I decided when this all began," the Englishman admitted. "I need to kill this man."

"And you want us to help you?"

"I want you and your guys to provide overwatch. That's all."

"I will speak with my men. Is the woman…Arabella, staying with us during your…infiltration?"

Connor looked at her while speaking to Eric. "If I die, please take her back to the Italian Embassy."

Her heart lurched. "You're not planning on dying, are you?"

"I am a realist, Arabella; battle-hardened mercenaries outnumber us."

She looked at him. "Can I speak to you alone?"

He nodded. "You go on ahead. I am just going to speak with Eric for a moment."

After he had, he met her at the treeline.

She stopped and rounded on him. "Why are you doing this? Really?"

"I don't know."

"Yes, you do."

She watched him glare at her for a few moments.

"When I was young, I had to watch a woman close to me be subject to an… ordeal. I couldn't do anything to stop it. I was small. You might think I am trying to be honourable. The truth is, is that I don't have a choice. Psychologists specialising in trauma call it a coping adaptation."

"So you—"

"It's not about a promise to your brother. I had a lot of time for the guy, but I didn't know him very well. It's about you. This guy isn't going to stop until either you're dead or he's dead. Even from a prison cell, he'd put a price on your head. Do you understand?"

She straightened her back. "Yes, I understand."

"Good," he said. "Show me again how to use the watch I gave you."

"Hopefully, I won't need it."

"We're in the 'Be prepared' business, not the 'Hope' business."

41

Frank Johannes walked into the comms room and asked, "Check in OK?"

One of his men squinted. "Yeh, but it was garbled. Caught some of the code words. It's OK."

Johannes frowned. There wasn't a cloud in the sky. The clearer the sky, the less interference with the radio signal as it bounced off the ionosphere back to earth.

Given that they had pre-determined check-in times, he couldn't raise them again unless he considered it an emergency.

The next one would be in seventeen minutes. Johannes said, "If the next one is garbled, we go to an amber state."

"Roger that."

Mike watched the gap between the two antenna towers in the freezing silence of hope.

Mike had sent a text message twenty minutes before.

His heart sang as Kyle walked past the gap and opened and closed his hand twice—clear.

Mike slid down the gentle gradient. He couldn't help his tracks in the snow but hoped it would not matter.

Once through the gap, he signalled to the darkness behind him. Connor Reed glided from the shadows.

Once the Englishman converged on his position, Mike whispered, "I can guide us around the corner and down the straight for about twenty metres. After that, we'll have to hope whoever is manning the cameras can't watch them all at the same time and isn't a stickler for the timings."

"Acknowledged," said Connor.

They stalked forward as Kyle looked out from his position on the other side of the walkway.

He felt Connor grab the underside of his belt webbing in a reverse grip. This tactic allowed him to move with Mike while facing the opposite direction.

"Opening left," whispered Mike.

He felt the hand release him, and a second later, he felt the tap of a knee against his hamstring.

Mike blasted around the corner, ready to take on any targets, as Connor took a wider circle to face the same direction.

No one.

They stalked their way down in the cold quiet, with Kyle covering their six.

He opened his nostrils and slowed his breath as fear began to shake him.

Mike had switched his comms set back to the pre-set for the inner security net.

There hadn't been anything yet.

His heart leapt as the voice came on. "All call signs, all call signs, move to an amber state."

Connor spoke without looking at him. "What is it?"

"They've gone to an amber state."

"Surely it would be a red alert if they knew we were here?"

"Exactly."

"Could this help us?"

"It might."

The sounds of rapid boot steps chopped through the silence.

Mike said, "Follow me."

He led Kyle and Connor into a steel alcove and whispered. "This is the last blind spot I IDed. You'll follow me in a jog, but I don't think we should keep our weapons on aim. Hopefully, the camera guys will just think we are going to our designated positions. We have about ninety seconds, I reckon."

"An eternity," replied Connor. "Let's go."

Within seconds, Mike spotted a pair in the distance on the long boardwalk coming in the opposite direction.

He momentarily tensed; if they recognised him and that he should be in the reconnaissance patrol, they would be caught in a firefight they would lose.

They jerked away down a side gap without acknowledging them.

He raced down to a right-hand opening with metallic stairs on the left and a straight path to the right.

Kyle took a post on the stairs.

Mike led Connor part the way down, turned to him and said, "His residence isn't far beyond these doors. And it's definitely going to go live."

"Frag grenade?" suggested Connor.

"His son might be with him," said Mike. "I'll go first. Everyone knows you Brits can't shoot."

He felt Connor's hand on his forearm. "There're exceptions to every rule. Believe me, you'd have to be one of the best shots in the world to be better than me. Are you?"

"Probably not."

"Then I'll go first."

Though trained in differing TTPs, Mike knew where to put himself in relation to Connor and whatever structure they would be going into. And he knew the reverse to be true.

Connor and Mike whipped their heads towards a strange voice that challenged Kyle. "Why're you standing there? You were briefed to stand on the eastern point?"

"New orders."

"I didn't hear you receive new orders," said the voice accusingly.

"Then why else would I be standing here?"

"Who's covering the eastern point?"

"Fuck should I know?"

Mike watched Kyle whip his rifle to bear before firing.

Connor bolted up the stairs, seemingly to cover him, as Mike rapidly punched in the code.

ACCESS DENIED

Connor and Kyle manoeuvred back down.

Mike said, "The code didn't—"

Kyle brushed past him. "They changed it. I have the correct one. Mike, take the rear. You both ready?"

Mike, despite being taken aback by Kyle's new assertive demeanour, nodded, as did Connor.

He positioned himself at the rear, then heard the door open.

The firing drummed a percussion of five in his ears before Kyle shouted, "Clear! Follow me."

Even through the noise and chaos, Mike sensed a change in his partner. A confidence. A dominance.

"Take up my front," barked Kyle.

Connor slid into position as Kyle peeled back to the code unit and closed the door.

Now facing forward, the trio resembled a rifled phalanx.

"Where is he?"

"I am not sure," answered Kyle. "I just know he's down here."

Two sinister black-armoured figures appeared from the shadows.

"Don't shoot," screamed Connor, who launched himself at the pair.

Mike watched as Connor leapt at the pair like a feline predator, sweeping the feet out of one and forcing the barrel of the other's assault rifle away.

The outlaw bikers dived in after him, Kyle dealing with the grounded soldier and Mike aiding Connor to subdue the other.

Mike, in a frenzy, could see the operator beginning to press the trigger, but nothing happened. Connor had rammed a commando dagger beneath his jaw, freezing him instantly.

The gunfire assaulted Mike's ears.

Connor's bark of "Pin his legs" broke through his adrenal deafness.

Mike slung his weapon and dived for the legs of the firing enemy engaged in an upright grapple with Kyle. His fellow biker had his forearm knifing down into the crease of the armoured soldier's elbow. His other hand gripped the opposite wrist, forcing the firing rifle into the ceiling.

Mike's shoulder smashed into the enemy's knees, toppling him as the firing ceased.

Connor leapt on the thrashing beetle's chest

and punched the blade through the throat before sawing a geyser of blood everywhere.

When the being turned into a corpse, the Englishman stood. "Where are the cameras?"

Kyle answered, "There isn't any."

"How do you know that?" exclaimed Mike.

"I have no time to explain, but they purposely designed the subterranean area without cameras."

Connor said, "Let's split up. If they are all armoured like this, we're dead anyway."

"Don't suppose you have night vision?" asked Kyle of Connor.

"I do," said Connor.

Kyle rifled into his pack and pulled out two, handed one to Mike and said, "The electrics box isn't far. I'll cut it."

42

Connor felt a flicker of doubt at his decision to split their unit up.

He surmised if they came across those armoured juggernauts again at any range, they'd die as a trio rather than individuals.

The former Royal Marine remembered seeing another soldier get hit square in his helmet and the layers of Kevlar simply spinning the bullet around it and out the back.

The black operations agent hoped the facility going into an amber state had pushed most of the security outside.

He stalked down the corridor, hating how the lights bathed him.

Connor hadn't wanted to reveal his night vision in front of his two unlikely ***oppos***. He now suspected Kyle to be a government agent and didn't want the technology to be questioned.

He focused on his heightened senses, particularly his hearing.

CQB skills, such as knowing when to compress and extend his UMP, feinting, and hip alignment when approaching thresholds, had long been instinctual to him.

Connor thought he could hear the faint sounds of voices and began to follow—he barely made out a female's voice.

He latched the urge to speed up as he caught the 'civilian' tone in her voice.

And especially when he heard her scream.

He heard a boy shouting.

The voices seemed to calm and then fade away.

His Royal Marines training had drilled home the need not to get 'target fixated' at the expense of personal security.

Though he had trained extensively to shoot with an elevated heart rate, excessive adrenaline frayed the fine motor skills needed for accurate small arms fire. He slowed his exhalations and swilled saliva around his gums—a physiological ploy to trick the nervous system into thinking that the danger had receded.

The bark of "Freeze" trashed his efforts.

"Drop your weapon," said the stranger.

"It's me, you stupid fuck!" said Connor.

"Drop your weapon and turn around slowly."

Though Connor caught the hint of hesitancy in the voice, he'd have no hope of turning around and getting a shot off before he got himself unzipped.

If I go for it, I'll die. If I allow myself to get taken, I'll die eventually in excruciating pain, he thought.

The thought briefly crossed his mind to suicide himself 'by cop', but he knew to win some games, you just had to stay in them.

He allowed the barrel of the assault rifle to swing down by his thigh and began to turn around.

"Stop," barked the voice. "I said drop it, not lower it."

Connor knew the jig was up; he began to place his weapon on the floor.

Then the lights went out.

Huddled against a frosted rocky outcrop, Arabella shivered against her thermals and jacket.

It dawned on her that she felt more vulnerable being protected by the ten First Nations men than she had been with Connor on his own.

Arabella realised she could sense their nerves like electricity from a telephone line and remembered the Englishman's speech on the futility of displaying fear.

He never seemed to exhibit nerves. And now she knew his motivation to be cast-iron.

As she watched the soldiers pour out and take their positions on the perimeter, she felt certain Connor and the American had been discovered.

But despite the group's nerves, Eric commanded them to stay.

And now she prayed.

Connor plummeted as his hands snatched the UMP 45.

He felt the vacuum of the two rounds passing over his head as he let off a silenced burst.

His heartbeats went into its familiar supersonic cadence.

The grunt of bullets impacting human flesh sounded. He fired another burst.

Connor flipped down his night-vision glasses.

He pumped another burst into the writhing body.

Scrambling to his feet, he knew he had to clear the scene, as the gunfire would attract whatever security was down there.

He sprinted along the corridor, stopping short of the corner before 'slicing the pie' to peer around without unnecessarily exposing himself.

Clear.

Unlike inferior night vision, Connor's glasses almost turned the darkness into light apart from a tinge of green.

The sterile metallic of the entrance now began to morph into the individuality and comfort of a residence.

He began clearing the rooms; first, a kitchen that wouldn't look out of place in a top-tier restaurant.

It took him less than a minute to clear.

Back in the corridor, his heart rate gunned as he heard the voices again.

Ghost-walking along the corridor, he resisted the urge to speed to the voices.

Aware the vocal sounds might be a 'come-on', he forced himself to clear each room so as not to be ambushed from behind.

The next room appeared to be a storage room, almost hall-like in size.

Massive cylindrical containers with an assortment of hazardous stickers plastered over them.

Steel pillars stood like guards throughout the maze-like room, with roller-door standing cupboards looking on from the perimeter.

Connor took a breath and began to clear it, pissed off at his decision to split the trio.

The smell, like a more metallic version of bleach, lingered in the air.

He pushed deeper into the cavernous room.

A huge roller shutter door hung on the opposite end, and he heard voices beyond it.

Then he heard the patter of death; several feet had entered the warehouse—which discounted Mike and Kyle.

The quietness of the steps disturbed him the most.

Crouching rock-still behind a steel pillar, he wondered if they knew him to be there.

He considered his options; if they wore the black armour the first pair had, then he had no hope.

A black-glad figure appeared to his left, mercifully less armoured than the initial couple.

The Englishman's shot punched a red bolt through the medulla, stopping the enemy's trigger compression.

The shout, South African, went up. "Enemy. Twelve o'clock. Behind the—"

Connor had cut the man's target indication off by spinning around the pillar and firing.

The others—three—took cover.

He heard one snap, "No grenades in here."

Though thankful they wouldn't frag him, he knew one against three enemies who knew his exact position spelt death.

The quietness attacked his ears as he knew the team leader's orders were being given by hand signals.

He needed to switch his position without getting shot.

An idea flashed, and he ripped open his webbing pouch.

Pulling out a grenade, he launched it without pulling the pin.

On the scream of "Grenade!" Connor shot to his left five metres to take a firing position behind another pillar.

He caught the top of a head rising and blew it off like a freshly red-painted Frisbee.

Connor heard a hint of panic in the "Man

down, man down."

Then, "Backup needed down in Uniform Charlie. Over."

Fuck, Connor thought, but he kept his mental energy focused.

He slid out one of the spare night vision batteries from one of the pouches and began to sidestep around, sacrificing speed for silence.

Once he was almost perpendicular to their position, he under-armed the battery to the opposite side.

Connor's reptilian mind assessed that the team's anxiety would overcome their professionalism in maintaining their arcs.

He was only half correct.

The soldier had maintained his arcs, but the sound of the battery impacting the wall opposite had diverted his attention for a split second.

Connor's round billowed the soldier's goggled face into a geyser of glass, blood, plastic and bone fragments.

The return round hit Connor in his body-armoured chest.

Connor had been shot in the chest at close range before with body armour on.

However, unlike that time when the sledgehammer impact merely felled him, this time, he felt his senses shutting down. The hydrostatic shock wave briefly pounded out the regularity of his heartbeat.

He barely registered the return fire from the other pair, puncturing the steel cabinet over his head.

Time seemed to jump, and the pair stood over him with their rifles pointed at him.

He could barely make out their words but somehow knew it to be a debate on whether to kill him now.

His panic didn't have the strength to prevent his slide into unconsciousness.

43

Richèl watched Bianchi from across the soundproof room.

His previous evident agitation now seemed to border on outright fright.

He stood at the far end of the cavernous suite, shouting into the microphone as his men nervously palmed their submachine guns.

She remembered watching the Netherlands World Cup semi-final against Argentina a few days after her twenty-first birthday. This had been the first time her dad had taken her for a drink, despite the legal age in the Netherlands being eighteen.

Before the penalty shootout, her father told her how stress reveals a man's character.

At the time, he had been speaking specifically about football, but Richèl knew he meant it in general, too.

And now, watching Bianchi, she wondered why Larry MacKenzie had entrusted him with so much.

Larry had said, *'He stinks of an ambition for power he could never handle. It makes him easy to predict and manipulate.'*

She couldn't quite figure out what was causing the commotion but guessed it was serious.

Maybe there was a problem with the collection. Early tomorrow morning, the uplift of tens and tens of tonnes of narcotics would begin.

That had been the goal all along, she now knew. To cultivate the correct dealers, turn the areas into dens of fiends and then flood those zones with cheap, deadly narcotics.

And Larry would hammer the current Prime Minister in the subsequent political debates and take leadership of the cabinet.

And he'd hang it around the neck of organised crime; that would be his lead-in to 'clean up' the streets. The drugs would stop, and he'd be hailed as Canada's saviour.

Suddenly, Arturo's demeanour changed, and a broad grin appeared.

She made out the words, "They have him," and saw them all relax.

Connor came to and found his wrists secured by *plasticuffs*.

The pair had increased to five, who stood over him at professional angles.

He began assessing his chances.

At this moment, they stood at less than one percent.

Two of the men slung their weapons, gripped him by the underside of his body armour, where his arms poked out of it and hauled him upright.

One said, "Shouldn't we get him out of his vest, boss?"

"We'll move him to the secure room first and do it there," replied the man whose accent sounded Zimbabwean. He looked a grizzled forty with a grey beard.

The team slid into a formation around him like shape-shifting sand.

Grey Beard matter-of-factly stated to him, "If you make any sudden movements, the rifle behind you will fire into the back of your knees."

Connor replied, "None of us want that, do we?"

"Speak for yourself," came the flat reply.

They began to manoeuvre him towards the door.

Connor's mind zipped through possible courses of action to extract himself from the situation, but all ended in his knees being shot out.

He would comply and see if the winds of change would favour him.

In the corridor, he heard of the challenge of "Halt. What are you two doing down here?"

The formation froze around him.

Connor recognised Mike's voice. "There is an intruder down here."

"A bit late to the party. We have him."

The leader peeled off and entered the corridor, where Connor couldn't see.

"I thought you were tasked with the main party."

"There was an ambush at the site. Radio man down. I was sent back."

"There has been no communication telling us you had arrived," said the grey beard.

"Because I have been chasing the intruder from the ambush site. He came in through the north-western side near the ventilation systems. I don't know how he knew he could slide by surveillance from there, but I bet there is a mole here. Maybe you should ask him—hard."

Nice one, Mike, thought Connor.

After a few moments, the reply came back, "We are moving him to the secure room, and we can ask him hard in there. Mike, you take rear. Kyle, you take the twelve o'clock."

Connor heard both snap off their acknowledgements before the barrel of the rifle behind him prodded him forward.

He stepped out, not making eye contact with Mike.

He felt like a nut clamped by an adjustable spanner as they formed around him again.

The shots sounded off the steel walls like a giant hammering from the outside.

44

As the pair on either side of him turned to face the threat, Connor smashed his clasped hands into the base of the right one's skull.

The Englishman dropped to a crouch as the gunfire exploded like a wall of fire.

He now faced the opposite way and braced himself for a round to punch through his back.

The firing stopped.

Connor stood, stretched out his arms in front of him and power-rowed them back. The plastic cuffs snapped against his torso.

Mike and Kyle closed in.

Kyle said, "I've managed to disable the outer access. The problem is that Bianchi is inside the secure room. If I access it, then access from the outer perimeter becomes possible."

Mike exclaimed. "Who the fuck are you, Kyle?"

Connor watched Kyle straighten. "I am a CSIS agent, Mike."

The moment breezed past. "Holy fuck!"

"It's OK, Mike, you're helping now. Can't say much for the rest of the club."

"You're a rat?"

Connor spat, "A rat is an informer already within an organisation. This man infiltrated yours. There's a fuckin' difference. And you need to make a decision now."

Mike nodded. "Doesn't look like I have a choice."

"You have the choice to shoot him in the

back. That's what he's worried about."

"I wouldn't shoot any man in the back."

"That's settled," said Connor before turning to Kyle. "What's the significance about tonight?"

"We have intelligence they are about to uplift a weight of narcotics that will wipe out most of Canada's addicts."

Connor said, "And you haven't got comms to your people?"

"The only way is via the secure room. Once inside, it's a race against time between us relocking the door and the security team outside getting to us. I have to do it from the panic room's internal computer. Once the door closes, I can send the signal."

"Then what happens?"

"Then the cavalry arrives and saves the day."

"Let's get to it," said Connor.

Arturo Bianchi stepped back from the monitor in horror.

He screamed, "Tell Johnson to get his team down here, now!"

The technician announced, "Johnson can't get access unless we release the door."

"Then, fucking release it! What're you waiting for?"

"Because it'll open this door as well."

Arturo, his wild eyes zooming around the room, "Them. Grab her and him."

He fumed at their creased foreheads and non-action. "These people are not going to shoot a woman and child, so fucking grab them."

His men went into action. Bianchi ignored his

son's confused exclamations of "Dad?"

The black-haired bitch just looked at him with beacons of hate and disgust. As she came into range, he backhanded her.

"Don't be scared, you cunt. There are worse ways to go."

She spat back, "You better hope so."

He held back hitting her again before sneering, "They won't kill me unless I suicide myself. Because they need what I know."

He could see that his words had hit her harder than the slap did.

His men dragged them to the door, his son now screaming.

45

The faint screams briefly halted the trio at the entrance to the control room.

Kyle began. "Sounded like—"

"He's using his kid as a human shield," said Connor.

"Cunt."

"Steady on. He's just a kid."

"I meant—"

Connor's laugh cut him off before he righted himself and said seriously, "I am not letting that tactic get the better of me."

"Used to do that in Iraq," murmured Mike.

"Anyone else he could use as a shield?" asked Connor.

"A woman. Some type of outside advisor. Maybe he'd use her."

"Fantastic," said Connor. "Do you have smoke grenades?"

"One," said Kyle.

"Give it to me. You'll open the door, I'll sling it in, but we'll go in before the smoke properly builds up, agreed?"

The two men nodded.

"You can console yourselves with the fact that if we fail, it was impossible to succeed in the first place."

"That good?"

"It might be famous last words."

Richèl's heart pounded in her ears as she stared at the

door.

She couldn't believe he was about to sacrifice his son.

The thought spiked in her as to the rarity of meeting the number of genuinely evil men as she had.

Her heart flew to her mouth as the doors pistoned open.

She thought she heard a clanging over the gunfire.

A burst of compressed liquid fired from the torn fire extinguisher.

The smoke pissed from a canister on the floor before diving into her throat to choke it from the inside. Her eyes streamed.

The sound of firing intensified for a moment before dying back down.

Then she froze seeing him—the man who had rescued her from the island in the Adriatic.

Everything seemed slow—like a sudden old age had impeded her movements.

Richèl saw him shouting but couldn't hear anything.

Then everything came back as someone from behind python-wrapped a forearm around her throat, and a metallic circle pressed hard against her head.

Bianchi's breath hummed in her ear. "Drop your weapons, or else she gets splattered!"

Connor's brain took a second to process the scene. The surrealism had hit him—*the girl from the island.*

His brain zipped the information into a separate compartment.

A boy sat in the corner, his hands clamped over his ears and elbows clamped to his knees.

Then, he silently cursed.

Though confident of catching the Mafioso without hitting her, he didn't have a line on an entry point to the medulla—the messaging centre that would prevent a trigger twitch from killing the woman.

And the mercenaries would be now en route.

Connor decided that if she died, she died for the greater good.

But then she screamed, "Kill him. Even if it means killing me, do it!"

Her tiny hands shot back, and she clawed at his face.

Instead of shooting her, the Italian-Canadian switched his forearm for his hand to clamp her throat and lifted her.

He then took the pistol away from her head, twisting its trajectory towards the Englishman.

Connor's shot skimmed the flesh off Bianchi's cheek as the crime lord's went wide.

The Brit's second round smashed Bianchi's pistol-gripping hand, sending the pistol clattering to the floor along with his glasses as the woman escaped his clutches.

Connor ran up and smashed his boot into the larger man's chest, toppling him before stomping on his head.

Bianchi lay on his side, inert and with his eyes closed. Connor brought his weapon to aim at his face.

"Contact rear!" screamed the pair behind him.

He barely registered the son lying motionless over the pounding of many boots coming down the hall.

The former Royal Marine performed a

magazine change.

As Kyle furiously tapped away on his device, Connor and Mike took up positions either side of the yawning door.

Mike and Connor fired in unison, halting the swarm from appearing.

A barrel appeared like a vicious snakehead around the corner.

Connor spun back into cover as it spat death metal into the corner of the entrance.

There was a clang followed by Mike screaming, "Grenade!"

Connor turned to see the American dive on top of it.

46

Richèl watched as one of the men jumped onto the floor. The other crouched but kept firing.

The prostrate one's body bounced up once under a dull thud.

Figures resembling upright humanoid beetles approached the open teeth of the door as the man with the dirty blond hair reloaded.

The heavy fire spewed through, smashing the screens, desks and chairs all around her—and prevented him from re-engaging.

Her involuntary intake of breath coincided with the metallic teeth snapping shut.

Connor scrambled over to a barely writhing Mike, hoping his body armour had taken all the blast fragments.

On turning him over, this faith disintegrated, witnessing the shrapnel-torn throat.

Connor began to reach for his med pack, but Mike waved his palm. Kyle slid close on the other side.

Mike turned his hand in and rasped, "I am sorry, brother. I got lost along the way."

Connor knew he was speaking as a Special Forces operator and not as an outlaw biker.

Kyle nodded. "You found your way back. Just in time."

"You'll get them, won't you?"
"Yeh. We'll get them."

Connor saw Mike's grip loosen and his head sag to one side.

Arabella had felt her hope almost extinguish when she had seen the swarm of black figures follow Connor and the pair into the compound.

And she could tell by the Tlingit group's demeanour that each moment that passed eroded their faith.

Her thoughts drifted to the unfairness of life; this man had sacrificed his life for hers—a stranger—but probably for nought now.

He might as well have left her in that car park in Cheshire to be led to her death.

Then Eric began to talk into the radio. After which, he began to issue commands to the group.

They began to lift themselves into a crouch. Eric shuffled over to her. "One of my men will stay with you."

"Is he alive?"

"I do not know."

Her heart gained weight, and she asked, "Who will stay with me?"

"My nephew, Myeengun," he replied, gesturing to a bright and wide-eyed man who couldn't have been more than twenty.

She realised then Eric was protecting him as much as her.

The Elder's bergen slid off, and he eased it onto its side next to her.

He heaved out the C14 Timberwolf sniper rifle case.

"Our friend told me this would be more useful in your hands."

She looked at him. "From not allowing me to discuss 'Men's Business' to letting me shoot a big gun."

"He's a persuasive man."

"He's an insistent man."

Eric nodded. "He insists that if you shoot this, it is better to shoot-to-wound—ties up the enemy, he says."

When she didn't reply, Eric re-joined his men, and she watched them slide away into the night.

Connor stood and asked Kyle, "Have you called it in?"

"Yeh," he replied, tearing his eyes away from his fallen comrade. "Not that we can save ourselves. They have hydraulics and burners. It won't take long before they are in here."

"Why did they throw in a grenade knowing Bianchi is in here?"

The woman walked over. "They work for Larry MacKenzie, not Bianchi. And all he cares about is the election."

"Your name is Richèl Vergeer," said Connor. "It's too much of a coincidence you're here."

"That might be for Miss Robson to explain to you."

Connor let the surprise wash over him without answering.

"And what's the relevance of the security working for MacKenzie, not Bianchi?" asked Kyle.

"The Yukon Search and Rescue—funded by MacKenzie—will arrive in less than thirty minutes. They'll begin airlifting out the narcotics that have been killing people—now that they have been primed."

"And the witnesses have just trapped themselves in this box?"

She nodded. "In a building lying on tonnes of explosives that can only be set off from the control room on the opposite side of the compound."

"OK," said Connor. "Any other exits?"

"No," she answered before walking over to comfort the boy.

Connor felt a lurch in his stomach as he thought of a possibility and then thought of Arabella. He turned to Kyle. "There is a small group outside. I know their PRR frequencies. Can you raise them off the computer?"

"I might," he replied.

Bianchi kept his eyes closed despite regaining consciousness.

Once he ascertained the voices—not his men—were not talking about him, he risked opening one eye slightly.

The way he had fallen, he had tucked one arm just beneath his hip. Not far from his back pocket, which nestled a Beretta Jetfire—4.5" long and 3.3" tall. The 25 ACP might not have great stopping power, but it wouldn't matter at this distance.

Two of the bastards stood in urgent conversation over the third, who looked to be dead.

Good.

He began pressing his heels into the floor to raise his hips.

He'd shoot the one facing in his direction first; the other would not have time to turn around.

His fingers touched the bottom of the pistol

grip and began to edge it out.

The prostrate man seemed to be taking his last breaths, capturing the attention of the two others.

The Beretta slid out into his hand.

He began to raise it.

A heeled shoe slammed down on his wrist, flipping his aim away.

He fired into the steel wall opposite before turning to grab her ankle. However, his smashed hand made it impossible to grip, so he hooked it with his arm.

Her tiny fist began to repeatedly '*thack*' into his face as he scooped her leg and freed his firing hand.

A vice grip snapped onto his wrist, forcing him to release it.

Her body flew off him, and another fist landed like a jackhammer on his nose, the cracks bouncing off his eardrums as the pain rocketed around his head, further blurring his vision.

His fingers hovered around the impact site.

He heard laughing before a British voice said, "On the bright side, it'll help with that coke habit, Arturo."

"You're fuckin—" started Bianchi before the spluttering cut him off.

"That smell of iron is your blood choking you. Sit yourself up, you daft 'apeth."

Bianchi shuffled to a sitting position, scraping up and putting on his undamaged glasses. His eyesight began clearing as the blood tumbled down his throat.

The man with the dirty-blond hair had a pistol trained on him.

Bianchi said, "I'll fucking kill you."

The man's face morphed into a mask of fear. "Really. Please don't do that."

"We'll see if you're laughing when they come through the door."

"Seem to be taking a while, don't they?"

He had expected to hear them by now but said with injected confidence, "They'll be coming."

"They won't. They'll be making sure we can't get out. Then they'll blow this place to smithereens—you included."

"No, they..." Bianchi's reply withered in the truth of the statement.

The blond shook his head. "You daft cunt. You could have been MacKenzie's right-hand man—for as long as you were useful, at least. But now you're going to die in here."

Bianchi felt a surreal mix of fear and rage course through him.

"Unless you know of anything that can help us get to the control room."

Bianchi's mind clawed for a solution and finally nodded towards the computer. "You can blow up sections here. I don't know how to do it. I saw the access code once."

"Then you better access it."

"You'll just kill me afterwards."

"Certain people want to speak to you, Arturo. Can't break your omertà if you're dead. Why do you think I didn't shoot you in the head?"

The words cooled Bianchi's nerves—whoever these people were, they probably worked for people who would want to speak to him.

Maybe he could cut a deal.

"Fine. I'll help you access it."

As he began straightening, the Englishman said, "Just tell us the access code."

"No. And you're not watching me."

"Careful man, eh, Arturo. Off you go then."

Bianchi forced himself to stand, his left wrist throbbing almost as much as the pulpy stumps of his fingers.

He waddled over to the computer. He moved his left index finger painfully slowly over the keys.

The Englishman's laugh went through Bianchi as he said, "Bless your cotton socks. Do you want some help?"

Bianchi grimaced in reply and completed the taps.

"You're in," he said.

The Englishman gripped him under the armpit and lifted him out of the chair like a child.

Then he noticed the eyes of his son, who leaned back into the arms of Richèl. He walked towards him.

"Come here, son."

His son spun in her arms to face away from him.

His voice raised. "I said, come here."

As he stepped to stomp towards him, a boot between his shoulder blades pitched him forward.

The floor flew up and smacked him before he raised protective hands.

His cheekbone and jaw throbbed as the vice-grips snatched both his wrists, plastic cuffs zipping a cutting tightness on them.

He began to protest, only for a pad with stretch fabric strips attached to stuff itself into his mouth.

And then he caught a different look on his son's face that infuriated him more—contempt.

47

Connor watched the monitor over Kyle's shoulder.

The initial stage of the plan seemed to be working.

The security apparatus of the facility had been drawn to the east side of the complex, leaving a team of three to watch the door.

As he observed them, he was reminded of his time in Afghanistan defending their Forward Operating Base (FOB).

"They are nearly all within the kill zone," murmured Kyle.

"Fucksake!" said Connor. "My guys are encroaching on it, too."

"They are already in it," said Kyle.

"Give me the comm."

"Why?"

"Because I need them to dress back, you fuckin' div," said Connor.

Kyle looked up at him. "No, you don't."

Within a fraction of a second, the dark subtext dawned on Connor.

Ciara drove through the London traffic in her grey Audi RS3.

She remembered her initial outrage at vehicles, especially black taxis, pulling out on her at roundabouts. She quickly realised that one would get nowhere fast in London by being a timid driver.

Despite the operation in Canada, Bruce had taught her the art of being on hand while conducting her daily business.

Her display showed an incoming call. She answered, "Yes."

"We've received confirmation," her CSIS counterpart said, the line crystal clear.

"I haven't had any contact with my man."

"We have with ours."

Ciara leased her sense of indignation at him, only now telling her of an embedded CSIS agent.

Grow up, this is the business, she admonished herself. Instead, she replied, "Two options are better than one."

"Exactly. Don't worry, your man is with him."

"What's next?"

"We'll despatch a team."

She caught something in his voice and asked, "What's the ETA?"

"Be several hours."

"You said you'd despatch a QRF as soon as the nature of the facility was ascertained?"

"There are anti-aircraft weapons present. They can't risk a direct aerial assault."

"And in the meantime, our agents are left on their own?"

"They are within the facility's safe room."

Ciara didn't say anything for a moment. "Has your man found evidence of who is behind this?"

"Arturo Bianchi."

She watched Marr's micro-expressions and instantly could tell he knew who the backer was.

"Of course," she said. "I take it this matter will be dealt with 'in-house'."

She felt a surge of cold smoke in her solar plexus at his following words.

"I think that is a safe assumption."

She realised then just how expendable Connor was.

Connor smashed a scything forearm into Kyle's chest, shunting him back from the monitor.

The Canadian used the web of his left hand to uppercut the forearm off—his hand shooting for his sidearm.

Connor snatched the wrist and stiff-armed it to prevent the unholster. He rammed the blade of his forearm into the Special Forces soldier's throat, driving him back against the wall.

"Stop," he ordered.

Kyle remained tense against him but ceased to struggle.

Connor continued, "I know. It's a clean-up. The CSIS doesn't want this to get out—unless it's on their terms."

"Right. The Russians and Chinese are making a play for Canada. You've seen it yourself here—division is tearing the country apart. We need a Prime Minister who will listen."

"You mean that will be your puppet?"

"Yes. That we control before it's too late. The files are downloading. We will get something to bring him to heel because if Canada falls—if the first democratic western country falls to the radicalisation, then your country won't be far behind."

"I get it—to make an omelette, you have to break a few eggs for the greater good."

Connor felt him relax a little more.

"Exactly. We are both still soldiers doing our patriotic duty."

"But I guess I am expendable too—being a foreign deniable."

"I was expressly told that you remain alive. Seems your chief has some sway with my bosses," smiled Kyle. "Besides, we need one another to get out of this."

Connor mirrored his smile. "Well, you need me."

The Englishman's forehead rocketed into the CSIS agent's nose, shattering it.

He wrenched the pistol-gripping hand up and into Kyle's stomach.

The barrel, stuck between them, pointed out sideways, away from their stomachs.

A hand snatched his ear in a crushing fist. Connor caught the wrist, keeping the balled hand against him so as not to have his ear separated from his head.

Connor, holding his opponent's pistol-gripping hand with his left, and the ear-gripping hand with his right, resembled a ram, smashing a further three head butts into his antagonist's face.

The grip on his ear remained twistingly tight until Connor shot a tight *over-hook* on the offending arm, pulling him close and clamping a bite into his cheek.

The fist released.

As the scream filled his ears and the liquid iron filled his mouth, Connor dug his trapping elbow into his own ribs harder to prevent Kyle from reaching for his ear again.

He felt his grasp weaken under the vibrating force of Kyle's attempts to free the pistol.

Connor's last vestiges of grip strength ebbed

as he fought desperately to control it.

His mind scrambled to his next move once he inevitably lost his grip.

Kyle released the hold first. His clawing fingers flew to Connor's eyes.

Connor released both his jaws from the cheek and his overhook, violently shoving his antagonist.

The Brit then raised the pistol.

An impact between his shoulder blades shunted him, stumbling forward and sending the shot wide.

48

The Canadian's retractable baton whip-hammered a nerve-deadening blow to Connor's wrist.

The pistol clattered away.

Instead of going for the gun, the CSIS agent dived on him, snapping on a front headlock.

Connor blocked the knee, rushing to his face with his forearm. His wrestling training kicked in as he instantly performed a *turnout* by grasping the elbow of the arm, attempting to guillotine him, and throwing his opposite leg out the same side as his head.

The Englishman snaked onto the former Canadian Special Forces soldier's back, barely deflecting another kick from Bianchi.

Another Bianchi stamp coincided with Kyle bucking him like a bronco, frustrating his efforts to reach the pistol.

From his back, Connor kicked Kyle two-footed into a roll.

He snapped upright with a *technical stand-up*, firing a ferocious left hook, instantly collapsing the Mafioso.

Kyle slid towards him and chopped down with the baton.

Connor barely avoided it.

He knew if fully fit, he'd have made short work of the pair.

However, the arduous trek, the injuries he had sustained, and adrenaline fatigue had put him at the mercy of this baton-wielding soldier with murder as his mission.

Kyle feinted a jab to Connor's head but

switched to his thigh, which Connor blocked with his shin.

The metallic impact rocketed the agony through him as the Canadian rode the sting out of Connor's return punch.

The Brit attempted to adhere to the Spartan practice of *Kateria*—to show no emotion when hurt in battle—but squinted in failure.

He didn't want to risk the time needed to grab the chair, or computer, or search for the pistol.

The former marine took a step forward, aggressively feinted, ducking the baton swipe before smashing his forehead into Kyle's solar plexus.

Knifing his hands into the back of the knees, he drove forward, tipping his opponent onto the floor.

Connor blocked the next baton swing, mounted him and transitioned to an arm bar.

As he lay back to finish it, Bianchi once again stumbled towards him and raised a stamping foot.

The gunshots hammered his eardrums, jolting Bianchi in tandem before pitching him on top of them both.

The noirette stood over the three men and pointed her pistol at Kyle.

"Stop fighting him."

Kyle raised his hands in a calming gesture. "Steady, I am a government agent. This man is a criminal and—"

"Shut up," she snapped.

Connor said, "Can I get out from underneath this fucking tub of shit?"

"Yes."

He began to scramble out before heaving

himself upright. The effort seemed to exhaust him.

He extended his hand. "Could you give me that, please?"

She did without hesitation.

He pointed it at the CSIS agent. "Get out from beneath him and turn onto your front."

Kyle did so as Connor hid his fatigue and pain.

"Hands behind your back. Interlace your fingers."

Connor took out a couple of pre-looped plasticuffs.

Placing a knee firmly into Kyle's lower back, he secured the wrists before doing the same to the ankles.

He bolted to the monitor, commanding the woman to "Watch him. If he twitches, shout."

Connor set about the communications unit. He attempted to calm himself on hearing static.

He kept trying.

If he couldn't inform Eric to retreat further back, he'd have to decide whether to sacrifice his party.

It wasn't a difficult decision for Connor—he wouldn't martyr Eric and his men.

He tried them again.

His optimism spiked as he heard the garbled return—he willed Eric to find a better position.

He heard Kyle croak, "Use the enhancer. It's in the devices file."

"Why would I believe anything you say?"

"The consequences of lying wouldn't be pleasant for me in my current situation."

Connor acknowledged the point and accessed

the folder.

"It's asking for a code."

"Nineteen zero five nineteen eighty."

Connor shook his head—Bianchi had gone with his date of birth.

"Safe-key code."

"Reverse the last code."

"Fucksake," murmured Connor.

Now in, he selected the radio booster and attempted to raise Eric.

Nothing.

Fuck.

Then, his voice came through with clarity. "Yes, Connor?"

The former soldier ignored the complete lack of voice procedure and said, "Pull your men back at least fifty meters. And get them into cover."

"We can go around them."

"No, pull back now before they start flanking you. Do it now. If I leave it much longer, some of the enemy will escape what I am about to do."

A crackle, and then Eric said, "The woman is safe. If you choose between sparing my men and killing the enemy, you know which one to choose, my friend."

"Get a move on," said Connor, hoping it wouldn't come to that.

His nerves settled as he watched—it was in the hands of the gods now.

He walked over to the CSIS agent, knelt and said, "Either you can detonate just the explosive units required, or we can risk me fucking it up and blowing us all up?"

After a moment, Kyle said, "I'll do it."

Connor said to Richèl, "Where's the boy?"

"I sent him to the corner."

"OK, stand back," he said before cutting Kyle's restraints.

Keeping the pistol trained on the Canadian, he watched him sit at the console.

After a few moments, Kyle said, "You tell me when, chief."

Connor's eyes flicked to the satellite monitoring screen—they had a few moments.

"Just know, if you try anything, your brains will be splattered over the screen. Obviously, I'd be careful not to shoot the screen itself."

"I got it. Thanks for the imagery," said Kyle. "You do know that they will still be danger-close."

"I am aware," answered Connor, keeping any indecision out of his voice.

He watched the monitor. The position of Eric's people was not ideal, but now the blast radius encompassed all the mercenaries.

Remembering Eric's words, Connor commanded, "Now."

The fireballs popped in a square-shaped sequence like a Bonfire Night display. A second later, the sound shook the panic room.

Connor watched the mercenaries resemble static or frantically moving fireballs. His gaze switched to Eric's men.

He could see the insidious lick of the flames catching at least one.

"Pan out and check for any other movement within the compound."

Kyle did so—nothing.

Connor looked at him. "Which compound are

the drugs located?"

"We need to impound them for evidence."

"You sure?" said Connor, looking at him carefully.

"How else are we meant to bring him to justice?"

"So you have the evidence to link him to Bianchi?"

Kyle nodded to the monitor. "It'll be on the downloaded files."

The girl's voice cut off Connor's reply. "You won't find anything here."

Kyle turned to her and said, "We have you."

Connor watched her complexion pale. She said, "I won't talk. You can't protect me from him."

"You either talk, or you can spend the rest of your life in prison—in fact, we can float that as an out for MacKenzie. That you were the brains behind it all. That—"

The bullet from Connor's pistol vacuumed Kyle's face through the back of his head in a geyser of blood, bone, and brain matter.

He slowly turned to her. "If I hadn't killed him, you'd have never made it out of Canada alive?"

She nodded. "I have all the evidence you need to link MacKenzie with Bianchi."

"Good," he said. "Now I am going to have to work out how to blow up what needs to be blown up in this place. Mainly the drugs."

"I can do that," she said in a tone of confidence.

"Good. Then do it so we can get out of here before a swarm of Canadian GI Joes arrive."

49

The inability to move rushed Arturo Bianchi to the surface of consciousness just as he began to come around.

The ropes wrapped him against the tree like rough-skinned pythons.

Petrol fumes rose to assault his nasal passages as the wet wood crunched beneath his feet.

The men and two women stood in a semi-circle around him—their eyes made him feel like a deer in the dark being watched by wolves.

Richèl and the two he knew—Connor and Arabella—stood as the only whites; the rest looked like 'Canadian Indians', a term he used to refer to all the so-called natives.

Connor approached him.

Bianchi could see the excited amusement in his eyes.

"They don't see this as torture, Arturo. In their culture, they see it as giving an enemy the opportunity to die with honour. The less emotion you show, the more honour you die with. We had something similar in the marines—I say similar, we'd get our arses whacked with a flip-flop, and we'd have to take it 'non-emotionally', probably a bit different from being burnt alive."

Bianchi's bladder released as the Englishman laughed at his own joke.

"It's OK. It's OK," continued Connor after his eyes flicked to Bianchi's crotch. "The test is to show no emotion—not the absence thereof. Pissing yourself doesn't count, so don't worry."

The saliva-soaked gag caught his pleas and threats until Reed held up a matte black blade.

It slid against the side of his neck, and after a sharp tug, the gag fell away.

Bianchi began, "My people will kill you if you go through with this."

"You'll have to do better than that, Arturo."

Bianchi took a few deep breaths. "I can pay you."

"Oohh, tell me more."

The crime lord spewed the words. "I have millions in offshores. I have instant access. Name your price. I can—"

He stopped when the Englishman's face crumpled in apparent hilarity before gasping, "Sorry, sorry, sorry—go on with this offer of millions, Doctor Evil."

Arturo snarled. "You think you're a tough guy with me tied like this?"

"I do think of myself as a tough guy. But not because of this," smiled the Englishman. "Now you're risking failing this honour challenge. And remember, you're the one who revelled in being ruthless."

The Englishman stepped back a few paces. One of the Indians handed Connor a fire torch.

As the flickering flame approached, a memory of watching a war film with his dad appeared in his mind. His eight-year-old self had asked his dad what the German soldier had thrown.

A *Stielhandgranate*—Stick hand grenade.

His heart began to expand in his throat as he felt the warmth on his face.

Connor said, "All you have to do is to be

brave for a few moments of pain before your nerve endings go. From what I have read, you'll probably die from suffocation due to the hot gases burning your respiratory tract."

"Please. I'll do anything."

Connor widened his eyes and repeated, "Anything?" before pulling down the zip of his trousers.

Arturo felt a glimmer of hope dashed by his antagonist's laughter before the words, "I'll see you down there, Arturo. Tell Carlo and your brother I said hello."

The flames whooshed their evil onto his legs. The stench of burnt pork and fabric flew in to choke him.

His agonised roars drowned the crackling before the inside of his throat began to blister.

The more he gasped for precious oxygen, the more the hot gases seared and closed his trachea.

His body began to pump involuntarily against his restraints.

The simmering image of a smiling Connor Reed through the flames formed his final memory—though Bianchi thought he had already died.

Larry MacKenzie watched the Formula One rockets-on-wheels scream at impossible speeds around the Circuit de Monaco.

Later, he would attend the prodigious *Danse du cygne* Art Auction.

He knew what every wealthy person knew—that the art market is the least regulated in the world. The auction houses had no obligation to disclose who the buyers and sellers were.

Not that he would directly bid himself, anyway—he would use a call-in proxy under the guise of a shell company. From there, the bought pieces would find themselves in one of his favoured free ports and sit for years to inflate in value.

His high-rise private stand overlooked the back of the heads of the spectators below; as the breeze wafted the faint smell of burnt rubber, petrol fumes and sea, he vaguely felt like an emperor overlooking the Colosseum games.

Indeed, he had felt more like one before the destruction of his plan to flood the Canadian inner cities with deadly drugs.

Even amongst billionaires, there was a hierarchy; he read that ninety-four percent had ten billion or less, five had between ten to thirty, and one percent had thirty or more—he knew a few in the tech industry that might have this amount.

MacKenzie hadn't quite made it out of the lower tier yet.

Despite his failure to hang a catastrophic drug epidemic at the feet of the Prime Minister, his poll numbers had stayed high, and he remained on course to win.

This compounded his sense of self-loathing when he received the encrypted e-mail from the private detective agency. He had no qualms regarding opening it as this mode of communication had been pre-determined.

He had learnt a long time ago that difficulties mastered were opportunities won.

Almost a week had passed since the facility had been destroyed.

And no one had approached him regarding his involvement.

Richèl had disappeared, and he had contracted one of the world's best—and most expensive—private detective agencies to search for her.

In his experience of using them, they usually located the target within forty-eight hours.

Except this time.

And then he had been hit with stark evidence of his involvement with Arturo Bianchi.

The tremors from the memory still iced his insides.

He had the *Evap* app installed on his phone, allowing him to send messages without a number, immediately deleting them and blocking screenshots.

He used it to message his contact at the agency. He informed MacKenzie they had no knowledge of such an email.

The next time the agency contacted him had been to inform him that one of their investigative officers—a Cristina Rowan—would present herself to his protective detail during his visit to Monaco.

The agency said they would send a picture of her shortly before her arrival.

Despite his abhorrence of being dictated to, he relented in the face of their insistence.

His phone pinged. An image of the said detective came through. *Very nice*—he thought. She had short blonde hair and looked almost Nordic in her features. He chastised himself for being distracted by her looks; that was one of his mistakes in hiring Richèl.

MacKenzie beckoned his head of security

over and showed him the image.

"When she gets here, let her pass."

He saw the lines appear on the man's forehead, who said, "I'll have to search her."

MacKenzie held his chastisement—he couldn't afford to take any more risks.

"Of course."

His security boss nodded and returned to his position while speaking into his wrist communications unit.

Barely minutes later, the said Miss Rowan appeared—taller, broader and straighter-backed than he expected.

After passing security, she approached and shook his hand—a brutish grip.

MacKenzie opened with, "Would you like anything to drink, Miss Rowan?"

"I am fine, thank you."

He pretended not to be taken aback by the British accent.

"Why the cloak and dagger?"

"Mister MacKenzie, I am not an employee of Drinkwater Investigations. My organisation has temporarily hijacked their communications so we can arrange this meeting."

When his eyes involuntarily flickered to his security team, she said, "Relax, Mister MacKenzie, I am not here to kill you."

"Who in the hell are you, then?"

"That's dependent on you. I could either be a representative of a charitable organisation you help fund for nobility—AKA a tax write-off—or the point of impact where all this unravels for you."

MacKenzie opened his mouth to speak, but

no words came out. She continued, "As you know, even the army of hot-shot lawyers you can bring to bear would find it difficult to refute your being the driving force behind the attempted genocide of thousands of Canadians."

MacKenzie's will overriding his surprise said, "You know it would take years to get to court if it ever got that far."

Her smile hit him. "Now your popularity has remained high—helping solve a housing crisis would do that—which begs the question of why you attempted to do what you did. Maybe that's a question between you and God. But the election isn't years away. And the court of public opinion is near instantaneous."

He attempted to smile back. "Blackmail is also a crime."

"We commit a lot of crimes."

"I am not so silly as to hand you a cent. What's to say that you wouldn't release the so-called evidence after you've received the money?"

"It's not a lump sum. It's a steady stream for the rest of your life."

MacKenzie stared and took a breath. "How much?"

"Two point three million Canadian dollars every quarter."

He frowned. "Why such a specific amount?"

"It's the amount our analysts deem just beneath your comfort threshold. Any more, you might attempt to take action against us—which wouldn't end well for you, but we wouldn't receive the said monies. This will be the amount you'll pay without a fuss because there is no negotiation about this, not a dollar less."

It took him less than a few seconds to realise the truth of her words.

Cristina, if that was her real name, held out her hand again. He shook it despite himself.

She released it and said, "If you make any attempt to discover who we are, or who I am, then the evidence will be released. Your friends in Silicon Valley wouldn't be able to stop the release of evidence against you going viral. And you will call off your investigation into the whereabouts of Richèl Vergeer."

With that, she turned.

MacKenzie threw the next question at her back. "Where is this donation going to?"

His phone pinged—despite him being certain he had switched to vibrate—the secret app he used that didn't display the number and self-destructed the messages showed the account details.

He knew it would be a different one every quarter.

A sigh escaped; he knew as long as he paid, he'd be safe—no person or organisation would risk jeopardising a free nine point two million dollars per annum.

50

Connor read *Heat 2* by Meg Gardiner and Michael Mann in the private hospital bed.

The knife wounds, the bullet fired into his mercifully armoured chest, the blows he'd endured and the arduous hiking had compounded to leave him in as bad a state as he could ever remember being in.

Despite the IV, it had taken a couple of days for him to do anything more than use the bathroom and sleep, let alone read.

The 1995 film *Heat* has been a Ryder family favourite since he could remember, and the book had captured a similar enthralling world of lethal urban chess.

Still, the thought of exercise felt repellent to him.

Before the journey out began, the First Nations chief pulled him to one side. He told him that not only did Arabella continually fire on the mercenaries, thus saving the lives of his men, but he believed she killed more than one.

Eric had arranged for his men to take Richèl Vergeer and Louis, the most direct route back to civilisation where Ciara had arranged for them to be picked up.

Connor and Arabella couldn't be afforded the same luxury.

Despite working for The Chameleon Project for years, the organisation would still surprise him with its capabilities. Only trusting the main roads—especially the Mighty Dempster Highway—to be free of potential enemy, their hike to a small private airfield just outside Whitehorse a week ago had taken his strength's last vestiges.

He might not have made it if it hadn't been for Eric and his guys.

The only mental reprieve for him en route had been witnessing a grizzly bear in the far distance chasing down a caribou. The predator had looked shockingly athletic in Connor's eyes.

A Beechcraft Bonanza with a monosyllabic pilot flew him and Arabella to a private hospital in Alaska in which he now lay.

Ciara had told him it was for a thorough check-up.

The doctor and nurse did not ask how he sustained his injuries; they just got on with treating him.

Arabella had been placed in a room next to him against his initial protest—he wanted her in with him. In code, she pointed out that he had promised to protect her from Bianchi, not watch over her forever.

He felt a strong pining for home, which he couldn't remember being this strong before. His thoughts drifted to Grace and Jackson—to watch a film in bed with her and to play monster chase with him.

The nurse popped her head around the door, and his heart rate increased when she said, "You have a visitor."

It calmed, but only somewhat, when Bruce McQuillan appeared behind her.

The nurse excused herself.

Connor asked, "Alright?"

"Not too bad," replied Bruce, descending his tall, broad frame into the seat next to the bed. "These long flights aren't as charming as they used to be."

"I am honoured that you endured it just to see how I am."

The Scotsman smiled. "You'll have to stay for a day or two. I've arranged a safe passage back for both you and Miss Andaloro. She'll go first."

"What's going to happen to her?"

"I'll spare you the details, but Miss Andaloro was hiking in the Yukon without a phone signal when Claudia Lowndes was murdered. Miss Lowndes was a victim of the same Armenian armed gang that had hit various locations in the southeast over the past few months. They seemed to have decided to expand their area of operations."

"And?" Connor asked.

"The suspects were shot dead by **MO19** armed response officers attempting a lawful stop and search."

Connor didn't ask whether the Armenian gang's deaths came before or after the decision to pin Claudia Lowndes's murder on them.

"I'll need a secure line to phone certain people in London and Calabria before she's taken back. I need to make sure it's truly over."

"I understand."

"I was under the impression everything would be coming from Ciara from now on."

"I need your help."

"OK," Connor replied. "She knows about whatever operation this is?"

"She knows I need your help."

"Where am I going?"

"Ukraine."

"Why is it always these places that are fucking

cold? Are there no bad guys in the Caribbean?"

"Ukraine isn't particularly cold. What's wrong with you, you jessie?"

"It was the last time."

"It's either there or Gaza. I am unsure why a British criminal would want to go there."

Connor watched the Scot's eyes as he said, "You think the two conflict zones are linked?"

"I have my suspicions."

Connor didn't want to ask Bruce why he wasn't using his resources within **The Circus** or hadn't passed this on directly to Ciara. He was indebted to the older man, and if he needed a favour, then so be it.

"Take it, I need to go now?"

"You can take a few days to return to the UK; say bye to whoever you need to."

The way he emphasised 'whoever' stirred Connor, who looked at him. "How long have you known?"

"Not that long."

"Long enough to rescue her from an acid attack in Roundhay Park, though."

"How did you know?"

"Grace described the incident. Seemed strange she'd be distracted just as the lad keeled over. Kudos to your team."

"It wasn't my team, it was Ciara's."

When Connor didn't speak, Bruce said, "I reckon more of your family know than you think."

Connor stared at him for a moment, and it dawned on him that this was his way of telling him that it was his cousin, Curtis, who informed the FOC (Franklin Organised Crime) group of his son's existence.

And that he was behind Curtis's assassination.

Connor didn't speak for a moment before saying, "Thanks for protecting them."

"You're an asset."

Connor smiled at that and asked, "I wanted to ask you, off the record, but are there any conspiracies you know to be true that you can tell me about? I'll never tell my mates you told me."

Bruce frowned. "Like what?"

Connor shrugged. "Did MI6 murder Diana? Was 911 an inside job? Are there aliens? How can the makers of 'The Simpsons' predict major global events? Things like that."

Bruce looked at him before turning his eyes towards his own forehead. Finally, he said, "Ciara told me once you were interested in the possibility of big cats in the British countryside."

"Yeh, I did for a bit. Surmised that with everyone and their dog having a camera phone, not to mention all the drones, that one might have been properly photographed."

"Aye," replied Bruce. "But what I will tell you is that your lot shot 'The Beast of Bodmin' back in nineteen eighty-three."

By 'your lot', Connor knew he was referring to the Royal Marines.

"Holy fuck! What was it?"

"A black panther that had once been someone's exotic pet. It ripped the throats out of nearly a hundred sheep before a Royal Marine sniper team managed to shoot it dead."

"Thanks for sharing," Connor smiled, genuinely chuffed at receiving the information.

The Scotsman said, "This tasking will just be you, me, and Jaime, providing logistics and tech."

"How are you going to be allowed out on the ground? I thought you had taken a polished shoes role now?"

"There seems to be a gap period from leaving my current position to beginning a new one."

Connor knew that meant if he got caught, The Circus could claim he went rogue. And Connor couldn't discount the possibility that might be the case.

"You know, you didn't have to come out here to send me to wherever you want."

"If you order a man to do something for you, you can do it by any means. If you're asking a favour, you should ask him personally."

"Alright. Can you tell me anything at all about the mission?"

"Nothing specific here," answered the black operations veteran. "But imagine an enemy who not only profits from conflict but funds, plans and initiates wars anywhere in the world, without committing any personnel of their own."

Ciara stood with her back to the Basilique du Sacré-Cœur, admiring the skyline of Paris.

She had rehearsed all the reasonably probable speeches and retorts for the meeting she was about to engage in.

Anything more might prove counter-productive, so she enjoyed the view.

Watching the various lights, she briefly wondered what a romantic relationship would look like.

She knew she'd have to decide between this profession and children. The Russian proverb, *'If you chase two rabbits, you won't catch either'* rang true to her.

Being highly sexed, she knew she needed a casual relationship with a man who knew how to keep it so.

She smiled at Connor's assertion that, *'If you fuck a woman enough times, she is evolutionarily programmed to get attached.'*

Ciara had found men just as needy; she had a few seemingly talking to themselves in her WhatsApp box. One—a heart surgeon, no less—had gone from merely sulking, which was bad enough, to viciously insulting her, much to her amusement. She would have called him the week after if he had stayed cool.

She caught the CSIS officer alighting from a black Mercedes approximately eighty metres away.

The owner of the bull-neck, straining against the dark tie-holding white collar, stood about six feet one inch with broad shoulders, thus resembling a bodyguard.

He ascended the stairs and stopped a couple of feet away from her.

"I want your man handed over immediately," Philip Marr announced.

"You know that won't happen."

"Your man killed one of my agents, and you were going to have a working relationship after this? This is what happens when they recruit for diversity instead of competency."

Ciara smiled at the last statement. "My agent prevented tonnes of the deadliest drug from flooding your major cities. You're welcome, by the way."

"We wanted to control him. We can't—"

"And that's why you wanted those drugs to hit the streets. You wanted this current administration out—you see their laxness towards the Russian and Chinese threats to be on par with their militancy towards dissenters within their own population."

"That's a dangerous accusation to make."

Ciara said, "Not only did your agent bear arms inside Canada, in direct violation of the law, but—to be less churlish—he confessed to the said accusation."

"So says your agent," said Marr. "However, we exist to protect Canadian interests against all threats."

"I know that," she answered sincerely. "And MacKenzie still looks like a lock for the premiership, and as you say, you want to control him."

Ciara reached into her pocket and pulled out a lighter.

She clicked a side slider, shook out the top and showed him the inside.

"There are two Micro SD cards within this that have all the evidence you'll ever need—not just for the operation he conducted with our Mafioso friend, but all his nefarious deals worldwide."

"OK," he said with a tone of caution.

"Seems you were right to keep your cards to your chest. Seems that a judge you may or may not commune with in a secret court is in the pocket of MacKenzie. Seems he was one of a number who helped leverage the secret installation of the compound, Lubor Lenses and foreign workers' permits."

That some CSIS senior officials would go to a bunker in Ottawa to file and discuss warrant applications with judges designated by the Federal Court, was an open secret amongst the intelligence community.

When Marr didn't reply, she held out the lighter. "Anyway, this is your control."

After a few moments, he raised his hand and took the lighter. "Miss Vergeer was one of yours all along."

"I can't answer that. But I would appreciate it if you'd stop using any resources to obtain her whereabouts. It's a waste of your time and a headache for us."

"Why did your guy kill my guy?"

"I didn't sanction that if that's what you're asking. Might have had a personality clash."

"He was one of our better agents."

"He can't have been that good."

She saw a ghost of a smirk appear on his face, and she continued, "Unlike your organisation, ours is not entirely funded by the government. We are taxing MacKenzie, and we'd like to continue that."

Philip tilted his head back to laugh. "You think I am going to allow you to extort a Canadian national after I was the one who permitted you to help us with the operation in the first place?"

"Yes, because it'll be seven-hundred and fifty thousand dollars clean into whatever account you want every quarter."

He stared at her for a moment. "And how much are you getting?"

"Slightly more. It's my deal."

He snorted, "OK."

"OK," she replied. "Are we done?"

He looked at her and asked, "Would you like

to join me for dinner?"

She took a moment to reply. "OK. When and where?"

"Ten O'Clock. Créatures. It's a rooftop res—"

"I know where it is. I'll see you there," she said, brushing past him.

She got a few steps before he called after her, "You said you're not entirely funded by your government, which begs the question of who are you people?"

She stopped, turned and asked, "The unofficial-official answer or the poetic version?"

Marr shrugged, "The poetic."

"We are the Devil's Nemesis."

AUTHOR'S REQUEST

Please leave a review of The Devil's Nemesis

As a self-published author, Amazon reviews are vital for me getting my work out to as many readers as possible.

By reviewing, I can continue to write these books for you.

Thank you so much

Quentin Black

The Devil's Nemesis Review

GLOSSARY

Ali Babas— American and Canadian slang for Iraqi and/or ISIS bad guys.

Bubble—Cockney rhyming slang for having 'a laugh' as in 'bubble bath'.

Cazzo— Italian for 'Fuck'.

Cazzuto— Italian slang for a very smart and tough person, badass.

(The) Circus— A nickname for MI6, which originated from John Le Carré's fictional novels.

Clearance Patrol— A patrol around a defensive position to ensure its security.

Consigliere per la Sicurezza— A Mafia colloquialism for a captain who can be sent anywhere in the world to conduct or organise assassinations, kidnaps, and other paramilitary operations. Literally translated as 'Security Advisor".

Bagging off out of watch— Royal Marine term for cheating on your spouse.

Enfilade— A volley of gunfire directed along a line from end to end.

Fica (or Figa) — Italian derisive term meaning 'Pussy'.

Figlio di puttana — Son of a bitch.

FNG— Parlance used by some Western military units meaning 'Fucking New Guy'.

Ganners— British serviceman slang for Afghanistan.

Gitanes— A French brand of cigarette.

Giving out— Irish phrase to scold or complain.

Hooped— (Canadian slang) If something is hooped, it means it is screwed up and cannot be fixed.

Hoser— An uncouth, beer-drinking man.

Jackets— American military terminology for the cartridge case of a round. British military generally refer to them as 'casings'.

Kimura (Lock)— A double wristlock that primarily attacks the shoulder joint. Named after Japanese judoka Masahiko Kimura, who used it to defeat Helio Gracie in 1951.

Loonie and Toonie— Canadian slang for $1, because the coin has a picture of a bird, a common Loon. So a two-dollar coin is now known as a Toonie.

LRR— Long-range radio.

Mangiapatate— A derogatory Italian slur translated to potato-eater.

MARSOC— United States Marine Forces Special Operations Command is the US Marines' contribution to the United States Special Operations Command (SOCOM).

MO19— Specialist Firearms Command that provides the fircarms response for the Metropolitan Police.

Muling— A person who personally transports illegal drugs.

Omertà— The Mafia code of silence

regarding criminal activities.

Oppo— Royal Marine term for a friend, or battle partner within the service. Derives from the term 'opposite number'.

Out for a rip— Going on a drive, usually something a little extreme like off-roading or snowmobiling. Or to relax and have fun with friends.

Over-hook— A clinch hold performed by wrapping your arm over the opponent's arm.

Paras— Colloquialism for the Parachute Regiment, the airborne and infantry regiment of the British Army.

Plasticuffs— 'Plastic handcuffs' made up of a pair of wide cable ties. Americans typically refer to them as 'flexicuffs'.

PCSO— Police Community Support Officers are recruited to support frontline police.

Pogey— Canadian unemployment or welfare benefit.

Reg (the)— slang for the Parachute

Regiment.

Rocker—Curved cloth strip worn on biker patches. Top Rocker contains the club's name. The bottom contains the location of the chapter.

ROE— Rules of engagement

Technical stand-up— A method of returning to the feet from one's back, which minimises the exposure to strangles.

(The) Sand— US and Canadian military slang for Iraq and/or Afghanistan.

Sass bloke— Member of the SAS

Sea Hat(s)— moniker members of the Parachute Regiment use for Royal Marines.

SOPS— Standard Operating Procedures.

Sprog— Inexperienced soldier.

Tyche— Greek mythological goddess of success, fortune, luck and prosperity.

Uke— In Judo and other Martial Arts, the

word for a person executing a practice or demonstration technique is *Tori*, the person 'receiving' the techniques is the *Uke*.

Vadge— Derisory term for a person meaning vagina.

Vale Tudo— Derives from a Portuguese phrase roughly translating to 'Anything goes'. It's a combat sport with relatively few rules.

NEXT BOOK

The following is the first chapter of Quentin Black's follow up novel—*Armageddon Games*

Eighteen months ago

Bruce McQuillan entered the room to the faint smell of tobacco despite the absence of a smoking apparatus.

The long, angular table reflected swirls of African blackwood-like clouds whorled by von Kármán vortices.

The Star of David shone from its centre.

A glass cabinet housing books and drinks ran along the left edge.

Bruce kept the surprise off his face on being confronted with the presence of a man he had not expected.

To his left stood Ann Zurer, clasping her hands and smiling like a hotel maître d'.

Zurer, a handful of years younger than his

fifty-six, headed *Tevel*, the *Mossad* branch tasked with fostering relations with foreign intelligence.

A mulberry ribbon held back the ***noirette's*** hair, accentuating eyes Bruce thought hinted oriental.

She stepped towards him and extended her hand, which he shook.

Bruce noticed Zurer did not cover his hand with her free one—a power play of body language he had seen her doing to other *SIS* officers at the Vauxhall Cross meeting months back.

"I am glad to see you again. Thank you for coming to Tel Aviv," she said.

"Thank you for the welcome. It isn't often a British intelligence officer is treated to the luxury of a top-floor room at Sheraton Grand. James Bond was independently wealthy, I am afraid."

"I cannot take the credit for that," said Ann, stepping back and spreading her fingers across the collar of her seventies-style blue suit. "The boss here insisted."

She gestured to the man most of the world's media would label the most dangerous in Israel—Naftali Avidan, the head of Mossad.

The tall sixty-two-year-old stood barely an inch off Bruce, with a full head of grey and white spikes tipping him over.

A natural ectomorph, Avidan cut a more slender figure than the broader McQuillan.

His hand felt softer than Bruce had expected, and his pallor had an unexpected greyish hue.

His voice, noticeably lower than his 'television' manner, said, "I am sure money is not scarce in your life, Mister McQuillan. After all, the Tanakh says that 'In all work, there is profit—'"

Bruce completed the quote for him, "'—but mere talk produces only poverty.'"

Avidan's dark blue suit with a cream shirt appeared unfinished without the lighter blue tie worn in public.

"Precisely," said Avidan, still grasping his hand. "We know you have been a man of action long before a man of words."

He released Bruce's hand, and the Scotsman understood the underlying duality of the statement—*I am complimenting you but also letting you know that I know more about you than you wish.*

Avidan swept his hand to present the third member of the trio—the man *Bruce* considered the most dangerous man in Israel and perhaps the Middle East.

The Mossad chief said, "This is Raz Sharir. He is the head of one of our foreign infiltration units."

The former SAS soldier did not wish to reveal that Avidan's vagueness was unnecessary. McQuillan knew Sharir to be the head of **Caesarea**, the rough equivalent of the CIA's Special Activities Division, which dealt with covert operations.

It also housed the **Kidon**, an estimated forty elite assassins, many of whom held dual nationalities and were fluent in foreign languages.

Though a couple of inches shorter than the Scotsman, Bruce reckoned Sharir's farmer-esque frame to hold at least a stone more.

The receding and cropped grey head of hair matched the shade of his moustache, giving way to a trimmed white beard.

He wore a dark grey wool shirt over jeans,

with seemingly no attempt at style.

Bruce stepped and reached over the corner of the table, as Sharir did not move.

The two men clasped calloused hands, shook twice and released.

Bruce noticed the prominent nose and black eyebrows stood as chief supports to the dark eyes.

Avidan said, "Please, let us take a seat. Can we get you anything, Mister McQuillan?"

Bruce didn't like that his seat presented his back to the door.

The Mossad chief leant back a touch when Bruce said, "A black coffee, please," before pressing the underside of the table.

Within moments, a gentle knock at the door preceded a young female voice. "Yes, sir?"

"A black coffee for our guest, Michaela."

"Yes, sir," she answered before disappearing.

The Scotsman had long ago learnt to accept offers of coffee—they came in handy as props to allow himself to consider his answers.

Avidan afforded him a tight smile and said, "Ann told me she was very impressed with some of the observations you had made during her visit. So I reached out to Miles Parker, a man I have known for many years, and he tells me you are perhaps the best he has seen within our particular area of expertise."

Avidan referred to the chief of SIS. For the last few years, Bruce worked as an interservice liaison officer between SIS, MI5 and Scotland Yard.

However, regarding expertise, Avidan was referring to covert black operations.

The Glasgow native lamented how his profile had risen from mystery to his talents being advertised to a foreign intelligence head in just a few short years.

That said, if there was one spy agency that might have known about him prior, it may have been Mossad.

With another gentle knock, the door opened, and a white ceramic cup with blue Hebrew writing appeared on the table before him.

Neither fluent in the language in its spoken nor written form, Bruce recognised the text as Mossad's former motto of *'By way of deception, you shall engage in war'*—a phrase from Proverbs 24:6.

"Thank you," Bruce said to the young woman, whose cacao skin contrasted with her darker curly hair.

She left him with a curt nod.

"Can I call you Bruce?" asked Avidan.

"Yes."

"So, Bruce, why do you think we have engaged you for… consultancy?"

Bruce took a sip of coffee and replied, "Israel and Saudi Arabia are on the precipice of a historic agreement with huge trade and security implications. Naturally, Iran does not like the thought of their main Middle Eastern antagonists completing the **normalisation** process. You're anticipating an Iranian spanner to be thrown into the works through its proxies. And you're leaving no stone unturned to prevent it."

The trio looked at him, and with a nod, Avidan observed, "An accurate assessment."

"What would you like to ask me, sir?"

"Please, call me Naftali," said Mossad's chief. "From an outsider's perspective, what do you think the Iranians' play might be?"

"A coordinated attack through HAMAS. Large enough to ensure the government orders a severe response from the **IDF**. The resultant media fallout displaying dead Gazan children might pressure the Saudis to put the brakes on."

Parker had warned Bruce off from using the word 'Palestinians', as many within the Israeli intelligence services agreed with the statement made by the nation's current minister of defence that *'There is no such thing as Palestinians, they are Arabs.'*

Avidan looked at Ann, who said, "The general feeling in the government is that their mandating the increase of work visas to Gazans has mellowed HAMAS's stance against us. Indeed, reports indicate that the previous two sustained rocket bombardments from the strip have been the responsibility of Islamic Jihad and not HAMAS. Tapped phone conversations of the HAMAS leadership have corroborated this."

Bruce stated, "**Shin Bet** phone taps, not by yourselves."

Ann shifted. "Why do you say that?"

"Because you said 'the government', not 'we'."

Sharir's head retracted a few millimetres at that.

Avidan said, "It is true that the maintenance of security in the West Bank and Gaza is more within the realm of our **Shabak** cousins."

"You want my thoughts on Hezbollah?"

"Yes."

"They are more organised, better trained and greater in number than their HAMAS counterparts. Their tunnel system is more intricate and extensive. But crucially, the security of their lower rung members is more disciplined—to be specific, your technological advantage is being negated by their refusal to use phones."

Bruce heard one of the doors outside in the corridor shut.

The Mossad chief smiled. "It is good to know that Miles Parker isn't one for hyperbole."

Sharir curtly spoke for the first time, "Any suggestions regarding solutions?"

"I assume the common method of communication between middle and lower management involves a summons to a meeting point via a pager, where orders are given in person."

Sharir answered without taking his gaze off Bruce, "Correct. That and portable, handheld, two-way radios."

"Walkie-talkies."

"Yes. Walkie-talkies."

Bruce, only looking at Sharir, said, "Form a dummy company to provide Hezbollah with the pagers. I believe you have assets embedded in the mid to upper levels of Hezbollah's organisational structure who might alert the logistics decision-makers to potential mass-bulk purchases."

"To what end? The information gleaned from pager taps is insignificant in relation to the work and risk."

Bruce lifted his case onto the desk, opened it using a complex rotary code, and handed the chief of assassins a twenty-page document.

The British black operations master said, "In there is the information you need to rig the pagers with explosives and have them detonated upon receiving a transmission of your choosing. Have the guys at the Glilot junction look at this. I am sure the information could be adapted to walkie-talkies, too."

Bruce had used 'the guys at the Glilot junction' as a synonym for **Unit 8200**, responsible, among other things, for collecting signal intelligence, code decryption, cyber warfare, and surveillance.

Inside Unit 8200 lay a section specialising in developing surveillance tools and weapons.

And though subordinate to **Aman**—Israeli military intelligence—they often worked with Mossad.

Avidan said, "Enough explosive to kill?"

"In the document is an outline of how to delay the denotation after the message is received—gives them enough time to bring the pager to their face to read or else explode whilst still in their pocket. Besides, survivors of the attack will be identified as Hezbollah by the fact half their stomachs or faces are missing."

Bruce thought he caught a glimmer of a smile on Sharir before his expression straightened, and he said, "I will take your recommendation under advisement. Is there anything we can do for you?"

The Scotsman would have thought the last statement to be bordering on disrespectful towards Avidan had it not been for Mossad chief's complete lack of reaction.

"I don't believe so."

They all rose from their seats.

Avidan shook Bruce's hand first. "We thank you for your time. I understand foreign relations is not necessarily in your job description."

"No one wants to experience World War III in this nuclear age."

Avidan released his hand. "Ann will see you

out, Bruce."

This time, Sharir stepped to close their distance, gripping Bruce's hand. "An individual, organisation and nation are not rich through their fiscal wealth—but through the quality of their relationships."

Bruce replied with a nod of acknowledgement before their clasped hands released.

ABOUT THE AUTHOR

FOLLOW ME

Follow me on Amazon to be informed of new releases and my latest updates.

Quentin Black is a former Royal Marine corporal with a decade of service in the Corps. This includes an operational tour of Afghanistan and an advisory mission in Iraq.

AUTHOR'S NOTE

Join my exclusive readers clubs for information on new books, deals and free content in addition my sporadic reviews on certain books, films and TV series I might have enjoyed.

Plus, you'll be immediately sent a **FREE** copy of the novella *An Outlaw's Reprieve*.

Remember, before you groan, 'Why do I always have to give my email with these things?!' you can always unsubscribe, and you'll still have a free book. So, just click below on the following link.

Free Book

Any written reviews would be greatly appreciated. If you have spotted a mistake, I would like you to let me know so I can improve reader experience. Either way, contact me on my email below.

Email me

Or you can follow me on social media here:

IN THE CONNOR REED SERIES

The Bootneck

How far would you go for a man who gave you a second chance in life?

Bruce McQuillan leads a black operations unit only known to a handful of men.

A sinister plot involving the Russian Bratva and one of the most powerful men within the British security services threatens to engulf the Isles.

Could a criminal with an impulse for sadism be the only man McQuillan can trust?

Lessons In Blood

When the ruling class commoditise the organs of the desperate, who will stop them?

When Darren O'Reilly's daughter is found murdered with her kidney extracted, he refuses to believe the police's explanation. His quest for the truth reaches the ears of Bruce McQuillan, the leader of the shadowy Chameleon Project.

As a conspiracy of seismic proportions begins to reveal itself, Bruce realises he needs a man of exceptional skill and ruthlessness.

He needs Connor Reed.

Ares' Thirst

Can one man stop World War Three?

When a British aid worker disappears in the Crimea, the UK Government wants her back—quickly and quietly.

And Machiavellian figures are fuelling the flames of Islamic hatred towards Russia. With 'the dark edge of the world' controlled by some of the most cunning, ruthless and powerful criminals on earth, McQuillan knows he needs to send a wolf amongst the wolves before the match of global war is struck across the rough land of Ukraine.

Northern Wars

The Ryder crime family is now at war... on three fronts.

After ruthlessly dethroning his uncle, Connor Reed must now defend the family against the circling sharks of rival criminal enterprises.

Meanwhile, Bruce McQuillan, leader of a black operations unit, The Chameleon Project, has learnt one of the world's most brutal and influential Mafias is targeting the UK pre-BREXIT.

Counterpart

Can Connor Reed survive his deadliest mission yet?

Bruce McQuillan's plan to light the torch of war between two of the world's most powerful and ruthless Mafias has been ignited.

Can his favoured agent, Connor Reed, fan the flames without being engulfed by them?

Especially as a man, every bit his equal, stands on the other side.

An Outlaw's Reprieve

"When there is no enemy within, the enemies outside cannot hurt you."

Reed, a leader within his own outlaw family, delights in an opportunity to punish a thug preying on the vulnerable.

However, with his target high within a rival criminal organisation, can Reed exact retribution without dragging his relatives into a bloody war?

The Puppet Master

For the first time in history, humanity has the capacity to destroy the world.

When a British scientist leads a highly proficient Japanese engineering team in unlocking the secrets to the biosphere's survival, some will stop at nothing to see the fledging technology disappear.

In the Land of the Rising Sun, can Bruce McQuillan protect the new scientific applications from the most powerful entities on earth?

And can his favoured agent, Connor Reed, defeat the deadliest adversary he has ever faced?

A King's Gambit

Can the Ryder clan defeat a more ruthless organisation that dwarfs them in size and finance?

When the **dark hands of a blood feud** between Irish criminal organisations begin to choke civilians and strategies to halt the evil fail, fear grips law enforcement in the United Kingdom, the Republic of Ireland and continental Europe.

When this war ensnares the Ryder clan, Connor wrestles with the choice between trusting the skill and mental fortitude of untested family members, along with the motives of his enemy's enemy.

Or the complete **annihilation of his family.**

Printed in Great Britain
by Amazon